Narky's father had almost drowned once, as a boy. It had haunted his nightmares his entire life, that feeling of breathing thick heavy water instead of air. He had moved away from the sea, surrounded himself with pasture lands, and now here he was, drowning in the village square. But this was impossible, it was ridiculous! *You're dreaming again,* his mind scolded him. *Wake up.*

The flames of Karassa's sacrifice died on the altar, while all about it the bodies of the villagers were strewn here and there, all gaping in horror at this impossible thing that was happening to them.

Wake up! If you don't wake up, you may die in real life!

Why wouldn't he wake? It usually didn't last this long, not to the point where his bowels and bladder gave up, where his head began to cloud and he forgot who he was. It never lasted this long.

Wake up! his mind screamed.

N S DOLKART

Silent Hall

GODSERFS BOOK I

ANGRY ROBOT
An imprint of Watkins Media Ltd

Lace Market House,
54-56 High Pavement,
Nottingham,
NG1 1HW
UK

www.angryrobotbooks.com
twitter.com/angryrobotbooks
The gods must be angry

An Angry Robot paperback original 2016

Cover by Andreas Rocha
Set in Meridien by Epub Services

Distributed in the United States by
Penguin Random House, Inc., New York.

ISBN 978 0 85766 567 6
Ebook ISBN 978 0 85766 568 3

Printed in the United States of America

9 8 7 6 5 4 3 2 1

To Nathan, Miriam, David, Becky, and Kate,
in order of appearance.

Book I

Introductions

1
Narky

Narky came from a long, distinguished line of cowards. As far as six generations back, neither his father nor any of his forefathers had ever been to war, at least as far as anyone knew. The Parakese crossbow that was kept ready by the door had never been used in battle. It had been purchased by Narky's father before he moved from Tarphae's seaside capital farther into the island. He had bought it in case of wolves, many of which did make themselves known out near the forest, but he kept his sheep in such fortress-like conditions that the wolves never bothered with them. Other people's livestock were much easier to poach.

There weren't even so many sheep to begin with. Narky's Pa was not a rich man, only a conscientious one. His farm stood on the edge of the forest that covered much of the island of Tarphae, a three-day walk from the port capital of Karsanye. He claimed the sea air was not good for his health, but it was widely suspected that Narky's father was simply afraid of the sea and its potential for storms, flooding, and other everyday problems that normal people took as a matter of course.

So Pa had sought high ground, and built himself a safe haven from all his little terrors. The sheep, at least, benefited from his protective zealotry. The fence in which they were enclosed was a veritable palisade, whose posts extended several feet below ground to keep out burrowers. The neighbors were rather contemptuous of the farmer and son whose livestock were kept behind such high fences. Narky's mother had been equally contemptuous, and so she had run off with a traveling ironmonger when Narky was eight, leaving him and his father bitter and alone. People joked that Narky was an only child because his Pa had only had the courage to approach his wife for sexual relations once over the course of their nine years together.

Narky's least favorite part of the week was when Pa sent him on the three-mile trip into town to sell wool or milk, and to pick up supplies. Walking along the little cow path with his barrow was no trouble, but his interactions with the townsfolk were always strained. At the age of sixteen, Narky had had much longer conversations with his father's sheep than he had ever had with another human being. Which is why he was especially dumbfounded when one day, out of nowhere, Eramia the baker's daughter spoke to him.

He was in town buying nails when the young woman walked confidently up to him and began a conversation. "Hi," she said. "You're the coward's son, right? What's it like, living in that house?"

Narky did not know what to say. Frankly, he had no idea why she had decided to speak to him. "What do you mean, what's it like? I haven't got much to compare it to."

Eramia laughed a fetching laugh and folded her arms across her chest. She was an attractive girl, narrow of waist and wide of hip, with big dimples in her cheeks and a subtle one in her chin. She was named after a minor continental love goddess, and though Narky did not know much of theology, he was suddenly certain that Eramia the baker's daughter was an excellent representative for her namesake.

"You don't spend much time in town, do you?"

"Do you?" It was a stupid question. Of *course* she spent

time in town – she was a baker's daughter, for Karassa's sake! Stupid, stupid, stupid. He had no idea how to talk to women.

Eramia laughed again, for some reason not put off by his foolishness. "Yes, I live here. Maybe I'll see you next time you're in town?"

"I guess so."

That night, he replayed the exchange over and over in his head, trying to divine its meaning. 'Maybe' was such an uncertain word, but he knew he wanted to see her again, the sooner the better. He imagined her kissing him – he knew he would never have the courage to initiate something like that on his own – and he vowed to himself that he would see her again soon, and that this time he would make a better impression.

He had an opportunity a few days later, when his father sent him back to town for the week's bread. Narky was so nervous that he mumbled his order and had to repeat himself twice to Eramia's father, to the latter's growing impatience. As Narky was putting the loaves into a burlap sack, someone touched his shoulder and he startled, letting the sack fall and trying desperately to catch the two loaves that seemed to be conspiring to outflank his hands. He caught one; Eramia caught the other.

"You're back in town already!" she exclaimed, chuckling, "And on my doorstep, no less."

Narky did not know what to make of this, so he just nodded his head. Eramia lifted the sack off the ground and helped him put the rest of the bread in.

"Better put your loaf away fast, before the rats take a nibble."

She smiled as if this was some sort of joke, but Narky was not sure he understood it. He muttered a thank you and slouched away, his cheeks burning.

"See you later!" the girl called after him.

Embarrassed, Narky kept his head down and had not

walked three paces before he collided with someone. The young man into whom he had bumped caught him by the shoulders.

"Where are you going, coward's son?"

Narky looked up and recognized the young man as the blacksmith's apprentice, Tank. Tank's full name was Tankarass, but even his father called him Tank. His father was a cowherd whose lands abutted those of Narky's father, and who was well known and well liked as the best talker in town. The son had arms as thick as Narky's head, but he was no more violent than his sire, though just as talkative.

Narky had not yet managed to find an answer, but Tank didn't wait for it. "She's not for you," he said in a soft voice, pulling Narky closer.

"I'm sorry?" Narky said, dumbfounded.

"Eramia, she's not for you. She's Ketch's girl." Tank put an arm around Narky's shoulder. The half-smile on his face was supposed to be kind, Narky thought.

"She's not really his though," Narky said. "I mean, they're not married."

Tank squeezed him a little, probably a little harder than he meant to. "No, but they will be just as soon as Ketch plants a kid in her. Might have done it already, you never know." He winked, hideously.

Narky fled home and did not go to town any more that week, or for much of the next. He thought about what Tank had said, and his stomach churned. How could Eramia soil herself with a lout like Ketch? Tank must be mistaken. Rumors were dangerous things, Father always said. If she was really... Ketch's girl, as Tank put it, then why did she talk to Narky or smile at him so, and make his heart pound the way it did? Did she realize how he loved her?

Eventually, Narky's father grew frustrated with his son's evasiveness when asked to run chores in town. He was a good man, but he was not sensitive enough to realize that Narky's reluctance was not due to laziness on his part, but to the natural moping tendencies of lovesick youth. As it was, after ten days of tolerating his son's excuses, Narky's Pa finally caught the poor boy by the arm and threw him out of the house with a wheelbarrow full of wool and sheep's milk, and instructions on what to buy after he had sold them. It was the heat of the day, when most of the villagers took their afternoon nap, and the waves of hot air rippled off the ground. Narky walked as slowly as he dared down the cow path to town, stopping frequently to shake imaginary rocks from his sandals, or to admire the placidity of Tank's father's cows. Did those cows know of love and its heartaches? Surely not. Happy, happy cows.

Narky was only on the very outskirts of town when he spotted a large group of village youths, lying about in the sparse shade of a few tukka trees. The dry season had parched the grass, and the bent, gnarly trees looked like a congregation of skeletal crones having a meeting out in the fields. Narky gulped when he saw that Eramia was among those spread out under the trees, and that both Tank and Ketch were there with her. Ketch looked up as Narky approached, grinned, and got to his feet.

"Narky Coward's Son!" he called out, extending a hand. "We have a lot to discuss."

Narky stared down at Ketch's hand, but made no move to take it. "What do you want to talk about, Ketch?"

"Well, for one thing, I hear you've been eyeing Eramia, making her uncomfortable. And that makes *me* uncomfortable."

Narky snorted. "I guess you take great care of her."

He had thought even a dumb lout like Ketch couldn't have missed the sarcasm in his voice, but Ketch just smiled.

"I do, Coward's Son, I do. Look, I know you're just a rude little guy, but you should really shake my hand when I offer it. You think you're impressing someone by being disrespectful?"

Narky looked down at Eramia, following Ketch's gesture.

What would she think if he refused to shake Ketch's hand? He reluctantly reached out his own hand, much though it pained him to do so. Immediately, Ketch caught Narky's hand and twisted it painfully behind his back. Narky cried out as Ketch bent him over and spanked him mercilessly. Tears sprang into his eyes as he struggled and could not break free from the larger boy's hold, and his pride hurt far more than his buttocks as Ketch kept relentlessly at it, to the laughter of the group.

"You have eyes on my girl?" Ketch spat in his ear. "You rude little turd. You have eyes on my girl? Answer me, coward."

"No."

"What's that, Coward's Son? I can't hear you."

"No! No, I don't! I never did."

Ketch laid off the spanking and bore Narky further into the ground. "Why not, Coward's Son? Don't you think she's pretty?"

"Hey!" Tank's voice cut through Narky's sobs. "Ketch, that's enough."

Ketch let go as the ironworker's apprentice pulled him away.

"The kid didn't do anything," Tank said. "Besides, we *all* like Eramia. You're a lucky man."

Ketch laughed. "Damn right I am!"

Narky rose to his feet, wiping his eyes as best he could. Eramia held a hand over her mouth – was she shocked, or trying to hide a smile? Either way, he did not wait to hear what she had to say. Instead, Narky ran home as fast as he could. His father was asleep when he arrived, still holding back sobs and rubbing his eyes furiously on his sleeve. He wanted to hide under his bed and never come out, but Pa would be angry when he found that Narky had left a barrow full of wares out on the road, unsold and unguarded.

There was only one way Narky would be able to face Ketch, or Tank, or any of those horrible people without breaking into tears of utter worthlessness. He took his father's crossbow and quiver of bolts from their place by the door and stepped back out into the sun. Maybe if he came armed for war, no one would dare bother him.

The barrow was still there when he got back, though half the sheep's milk had been drunk or spilt by the louts who had laughed at his humiliation. The teens themselves were absent by now, so Narky put the crossbow in his barrow and went about his business. He sold his wool to the carder, and did his best to consolidate the milk into a few presentable skins, which he sold at a slight discount. Then he stopped by the well to wash out the remaining skins and have a drink. He filled the skins while he was at it, hoping that his prudence would save him from having to make a trip to town tomorrow, with a bucket. Then he sighed and headed homeward.

Past the tukka trees, Ketch was waiting for him. He was leaning against a fencepost with a languid expression, and roused himself with a studied nonchalance as Narky approached.

"Hey, Coward's Son," he said. "Hope I didn't hurt you too much. Just don't disrespect me like that in front of my friends again, all right?"

Narky pulled the crossbow from his wheelbarrow. "Don't come any closer, Ketch. You're a bastard, and you don't deserve her."

Ketch laughed. "Put that bow away. You want another spanking?"

Narky just stood there, shaking. With anger, he told himself.

"Hey, did you hear me?" Ketch jerked forward as if to charge, but then stopped with a smile. He'd been faking it.

Narky shot him. The threat was clearly over by the time Narky released the catch, but somehow the signal did not reach his fingers in time. Narky watched, horrified, as the bolt sprung from the bow and buried itself deep in Ketch's chest. Ketch reeled back, his smile remaining on his face as if he did not really believe what had just happened. Then he fell.

Narky stood there for a moment, just staring. Ketch did not move. *O Karassa, what have I done?* Narky wanted to drop the crossbow, but for some reason his fingers would not open. *I'm going to be stoned,* he thought. *They're going to come for me, and they're going to stone me.* He could just imagine the rage on the townspeople's faces as they tore him from his father's house, each trying to take a piece out of him on the way. No. No. There had to be another way.

They would know it was him. They knew what Ketch had done to him, and they knew his father owned a crossbow. Nobody would listen to his side of the story, besides which, what *was* his side of the story?

Narky took up the quiver and slung it onto his back. Then he took the water skins and tied them around himself with a piece of extra rope he found at the bottom of the wheelbarrow. He hung the pocket that held his money around his neck, and began to walk away. After a few steps, he broke into a run. He was glad that nobody seemed to be around to notice him as he tore down the road that led to Karsanye and the sea. Justice would follow him soon. If he wanted to survive, he had to get off the island.

2
Lord Tavener

"Perhaps it's my fault," Lord Tavener explained. "After all, it was my idea to name the boy Hunter. But he doesn't enjoy life. He doesn't *live* his life, you understand?"

The Oracle of Ravennis inclined her head. "What keeps him from his life, to your mind?"

The Tarphaean lord looked down at his hands, and at his sword hilt. "War," he said, looking up. "The boy does nothing but train for war."

The Oracle smiled. Her teeth were even whiter than her pale continental skin. "You are a high lord of Tarphae, your king's right-hand man. You were his champion in many battles. Is it not right that your son should follow in your path?"

Lord Tavener sighed and shook his head. "At his age, I was kissing girls and drinking my father's wine. I only trained for war in order to impress the girls. But Hunter, he trains for the sake of the training. Never mind that it's my older son, Kataras, who will be the king's champion if we go to war again. Kataras is like me; he *enjoys* life. Hunter spends his days tiring out the swordsmaster, and his nights sitting alone, sharpening his weapon and concocting new ways to best the master tomorrow. If the swordsmaster were not such a loyal friend, I swear he would have left us long ago. Hunter doesn't pull his cuts. Even Kataras doesn't spar with him anymore – he's tired of getting bruised and battered, and I don't blame him!"

The Oracle nodded. "So you have come here to learn how you might soften your second son's warrior spirit."

Lord Tavener sighed again. "Well no, not exactly. I wouldn't want him to lose his spirit; I just want him to get more out of life. The boy never *smiles*. You know what they say about those who live by the sword. I want Hunter's life to be long and meaningful."

"So your request is that I ask the God how you might make your son Hunter's life a long and meaningful one?"

The lord smiled, relieved. "Yes. Yes, exactly."

The Oracle stood. "Very well," she said. "I shall put your question to Ravennis, the Keeper of Fates, and perhaps He shall answer."

"Perhaps? Doesn't my payment earn me more than a 'perhaps'?"

The black-haired woman shook her head. "The God of Laarna does not always answer, and when He does, it is not always an answer people like to hear. Sometimes a thing is impossible, and it falls to His messengers to deliver the bad news. And sometimes the answers leave much larger questions in their wake. It is good to be precise when we ask Him, but the fates are complicated, mystifying things. Great Ravennis does not always unravel them for us, even if He does give us a glimpse of them."

"Well, please just ask Him for me."

The Oracle nodded her head again, the dark locks spilling around her pretty young face. They were very attractive, these Laarnan women, with their skin even lighter than the Atunaeans' and their hair black as obsidian. The Tarphaean islanders had black hair too, of course, that went more naturally with their dark skin. But where the islanders' hair rose in jubilant curls, continental hair was straight and solemn. Which was attractive too, in a funerary sort of way. Lord Tavener had married twice, both times to Tarphaean beauties, but if he took another wife, he thought he might try a continental girl. The color contrast on this young Oracle was quite compelling.

Tavener had expected a much older woman when he came to seek out the famed Oracle of Ravennis, but what did he know? On Tarphae, only two Gods mattered: Mayar of the Sea, and His daughter Karassa, who had raised the island and made it habitable so that Her people might live and praise Her.

The famous Oracle of Ravennis had turned out to be three women in the three ages of life, and for reasons unexplained, Tavener had been given the young one to tell his troubles to. When he had asked her how long she had been doing this, the young Oracle had smiled.

"Five years, my lord. Ravennis usually gives His Young Servant the questions that are more easily asked. When we look upon our supplicants, we feel, all three of us, who is best suited to ask each supplicant's question. The Venerable Servant usually gets those whose questions require the most unraveling and the most tact, and the Graceful Servant often gets those questions that are of a sensitive nature, those that one might not feel comfortable discussing with me. I was called to you, so however complicated the answer to your question might be, the *question* must be relatively direct."

That made its own kind of sense, Lord Tavener supposed, but it did disconcert him to be speaking to an oracle easily half his own age. The Oracle now rose and retreated to the sanctum. After some minutes, the Tarphaean nobleman felt wingbeats on his heart, as if one of Ravennis' sacred crows had just alit from his soul. It was a strange, light feeling, but it soon passed, and his heart returned to its earlier feeling of foreboding. Oh, Hunter. What was a father to do?

The king had laughed to hear that Tavener wanted to take his problems to an oracle. "Now, Tav," he had said.

"Isn't there an easier, more traditional way to get your boy's mind onto girls? Why go see some old woman when you can bring him a young one?"

Lord Tavener had not told him that he had tried, and that Hunter had glared at him as if the old lord had threatened to take his sword away. At first Tav had wondered whether his son might not be attracted to women at all, but Hunter had seemed mostly put off by the *dishonor* of his father's suggestion. Honor. The only other thing Hunter seemed to care about, besides swordsmanship.

Long minutes passed, and still the Oracle did not return. Was the God giving her a long answer? he wondered. Or was He simply taking His sweet time getting back to her? What did the Oracles really do in that sanctum of theirs? Gossip with each other, perhaps? Drink wine and laugh about their supplicants' foolish questions?

He should not think thoughts like these. The Oracle of Ravennis was well respected, and Ravennis was, after all, the only God he knew of who claimed a concern with fate. One would have thought that Elkinar, being the God of both Life and Death, might have some interest in fate, but apparently not. Tav did not understand these continental Gods.

For one thing, there were simply too many of them. Back on Tarphae, sacrifices were made to Karassa or to Mayar. But here on the mainland, there were so many Gods to keep track of that Tav wondered how people kept them straight. Other than Mayar, who was also worshipped along the coastline, there was Mayar's divine brother, Magor of the Wild, and a second pair of brothers, Atun the Sun God and Atel the Messenger. There was Eramia the Love Goddess, who was supposed to be the sister of one of the others… Elkinar, maybe? Elkinar was God of the Life Cycle, and then there was Pelthas, who had something to do with scales – was he the God of Justice, or of merchants? There was Ravennis, of course, and some mountain God whose name began with a C, and countless smaller ones. Tomorrow evening began Karassa's summer festival on the island of Tarphae, but how the people of the continent managed to keep track of all *their* holidays and festivals, Tav would never know.

Next week would be Hunter's seventeenth birthday. Advice from an Oracle had seemed like a good present yesterday. Anyway, it could not possibly be as counterproductive as his previous gifts. At fifteen, Hunter had received his sword, and at sixteen his armor and shield. He had obviously appreciated both presents, and trained with them as much as he was allowed to, but Tav distinctly felt that they had only contributed to his son's strange malaise. What could a loving father give to a son whose passion was eating him from the inside?

At length the door to the sanctum opened, but it was the gray-haired Venerable Servant who stepped forth to meet him. "My Young sister will be with you shortly," she told him. "Please keep your question to Ravennis in the forefront of your mind until she emerges."

Oh, very well, Tav thought. *How can I make Hunter's life long and meaningful? How can I make Hunter's life long and meaningful? How long am I going to have to wait here? All right, how can I make Hunter's life long and meaningful?*

Finally, the younger Oracle came out to meet him. "Do you remember what your question was?"

"Yes," Tav said impatiently. "How can I make Hunter's life long and meaningful?"

The Young Servant raised her two hands, her thumbs and middle fingers pointed toward each other in the symbol of Ravennis. "Return to the island of Tarphae, to your home, as quickly as you can. Do not stop anywhere along the way, except to ensure your passage. When you arrive, find your son Hunter and make sure that he leaves the island that very day, on the first available vessel. Do not rest for an instant until you have seen him off the island."

"What?" Bile rose in Lord Tavener's stomach when he thought of sending his son off into the unknown, without so much as an explanation. "That day? Even if I can make it home by tomorrow afternoon, I'll be lucky to get him to the docks before evening and the start of Karassa's festival! Chances are, there won't be any ships leaving port by then. Can't it wait until the day after?"

The Oracle glared at him. "The God of Laarna has spoken. Do not hesitate, and do not tarry. Your son's long life and happiness depend upon it."

3
Galanea

Galanea hid her curse well. She had come to the island as a maiden, driven to find a place where no one knew of her family and its… peculiarities. It had turned out to be a good choice too, for but a year later her home city of Ardis rose up under the High Priest of Magor and put both its king and his deformed advisors to the stake. All their magic had not helped them then, against the priest's righteous zealotry. From what Galanea had heard, Ardis was now ruled by a council of generals headed by High Priest Bestillos himself.

But where her family had been proud of their monstrosity, and wielded their fearsome appearance against their adversaries with the same gusto that they wielded their magic, Galanea was made of softer stuff. With her powers she had changed her eye color from its brilliant gold to brown, the scaled webbing of her neck vanished into silky skin, and her sharp, clawed feet now held a gentler, more common shape. With her monstrosity in check, she had found herself a husband among Tarphae's young noblemen, a man of pride and pedigree.

For three years, Galanea lived a life of beautiful normality, until her body betrayed her in a way that she should have long anticipated. It became pregnant. She suffered then, as her husband became ever more loving and attentive, knowing that her peaceful life was about to end forever. She prayed that her baby would be normal, that it would have its father's natural brown eyes and curly hair, and his big, kind hands. She prayed that her child's inevitable scales would drop off in the womb, leaving only its father's black skin underneath. She prayed to her parents' God and to every God she knew, knowing that none would answer her.

Her son was born with four-fingered claws for hands, with golden scales that stretched back as far as his forearms and eyes like the four o'clock sun. The baby did have curly hair, at least. She named it Criton, after her father, because her husband wanted nothing to do with it. He beat her then, he who had been so loving, and shut her in his house with her infant, telling her never to so much as set foot outside or he would have her and her demon child drowned. Galanea did not blame him, though perhaps she should have. She had known that it would end this way. Her three years of childless marriage would remain the happiest of her life.

When baby Criton burped, little jets of flame licked out from his mouth and singed her clothes. But he was not a fussy child, though his claws scratched her terribly when she fed him. Perhaps in another world, his father might have thought his golden scales beautiful to look at. But in town, it was known that the infant had died, and that Galanea herself was terribly sick. How kind of her husband, they all said, to bring her all the food and medicine she needed, right to her bed. How devoted, the women said, and how they wished that their own husbands were so kind and understanding of them. To be Galanea, they imagined, was to be a pampered invalid.

And Galanea *was* grateful to her husband. She was grateful that he had let her keep the child, even in miserable secrecy. Perhaps, she thought, when he grew older, Criton would learn to disguise his deformities as she had hers, and then he would be able to venture out into the world without fear of a crowd's retribution.

As the boy grew, her husband seemed to hate him even more. Criton was a sweet, sensitive boy, but his father couldn't see that. The child was disciplined harshly for scratching the furniture – which he could not help, sharp as his claws were – and when he became sick and ran a fever, Galanea's husband would hold his head in a bucket of cold water until he was nearly drowned. It was prudence, her husband would insist, because Criton tended to breathe small gouts of flame when he was feeling unwell.

Criton grew and grew, and Galanea taught him all she could about the world, and his unique place in it. He asked her all about her family and its origins, but Galanea did not like to speak of such things. She told him stories instead, stories of the life she imagined for him. Still he persisted, until Galanea finally told him that her family had called the curse 'being dragon-touched,' and that there were no more dragons in the world. The Gods had punished them, though she did not know why. Still he asked her, over and over, as if she could somehow have acquired more knowledge on the subject without ever leaving the house.

The boy would not believe the truth. He did not believe that the dragons were gone, and he would not believe that the man who held his head under water was truly his father. His favorite game was to play dragon finder, to look under the bed and in the closets for his imaginary dragon father. His real father found the game grotesque, and beat the child whenever he saw the boy playing it.

Galanea was afraid to train her son in magic in his father's presence, and for some time Criton's magic developed uncontrolled. Eleven proved to be a very destructive age, but when the child turned thirteen, he began to express more control over the outbursts. His voice also dropped, from its high squeal to a low growl, transforming almost overnight, it seemed to her. And he grew bigger, eventually even surpassing his father's height. By this time, Galanea had forgotten whether her husband was a tall man or a short one. There was nobody but her son to compare him to. She hadn't seen any other men in over a decade.

To Galanea's great joy, Criton learned how to assume a more pleasing shape when he was about fourteen or fifteen years old. But unlike his mother, Criton did not keep this shape all the time. He adopted it when his father came home, and went happily back to his hereditary deformities the minute his father left the house. This Galanea did not understand, but then the boy was dragon-crazy, and though he still did his best to avoid his father's beatings, he did not want any part of his father's shape or culture.

By this time, Galanea was plotting a way to get her son out of the house before any more disasters could befall her miserable little family. Her husband was a broken, bitter man, but he still had a temper, and boys of Criton's age could be known to get very aggressive. She was not sure what she feared more: her husband beating Criton to death, or her son tearing his father's throat out with his claws. One way or another, she had to get him out.

Her son did not agree. As a boy of his age, he relished the idea of tearing out his father's throat. The revenge fantasy consumed his every thought, and Galanea had to fight very hard to restrain him. Then one day, when he was fifteen or so – who even knew anymore? – Galanea finally found a way to persuade him.

"Criton," she said to her son, "tonight is Karassa's summer festival. Your father will be out late at the fires. Take his money from the bedside table, and find a ship to take you away from here."

The moment had finally come for her son to leave his mother behind, to go on the adventures that his young mind had always craved – yet there he stood, suddenly filled with fear.

"But, Ma," he said, "what will I do out there, among your husband's people?"

"You will play dragon-finder," she choked, tears welling in her eyes. The boy had not played the game in years.

For a moment, Criton's eyes lit up. Then he said, "And leave you here with him? I can't do that to you."

Galanea wiped away her tears, which only came faster. "Criton," she said, "the years before I had you – before he realized what we were – those were the happiest years of my life. Your father and I loved each other once, and though we will never love each other again, I still care too much about him to let you two argue and fight until one of you kills the other. If you wish to have your revenge on him, take his money. But you have to go now."

Galanea's husband never locked his money away. He had the only key to the house, and he knew that Galanea and her son were too afraid of his anger to risk being seen at the window. But now the festival was about to begin at Karassa's temple, and the streets were mostly empty. Nobody saw Criton climb out the window. When his feet were safely on the ground, he took the form that his mother liked best, clenched his newly fleshy hands and walked out toward the late afternoon sun, its golden color reflected in his eyes. Galanea craned her neck out the window to watch Criton go, but he had soon walked around the corner of the house and disappeared.

It had been fifteen years since Galanea had prayed. She knelt now on the floor and bowed her head, still wiping tears from her eyes. *May the Gods protect you, my sweet son. Go safely, and find your dragons!*

4
Two-foot

Two-foot scrambled up the guardian tree, swinging from pointed branch to pointed branch, the sap sticking to the pads of her hands. Near the top, she found her goal – a nest of twigs and the occasional stray bit of sheep's wool, with five eggs inside, one larger than the others. She gathered up all five and put them in her makeshift pouch, then climbed back down to where Four-foot awaited her.

"See, Four-foot? Eggs, just like I told you! You can have these four, but I want this one. It's a cuckoo, just like me. It doesn't belong."

Four-foot devoured his eggs in the manner of his kind, and whined a little when he saw that Two-foot had not yet finished hers. She preferred to delicately poke a hole in one side with a twig or a guardian tree spine, and then suck out its contents. She preferred this way because then none of the egg spilled, and because if she did it right, it left her with a beautiful hollow egg that she could carry around in her pouch until it broke. Her kind were more sentimental than Four-foot's.

Actually, Two-foot did not know very much about her kind. She knew that they lived in the little wooden hills outside the forest, the ones that made gray clouds in the evening. But though her memories of her childhood with her own kind were vague, she knew that she had not liked it. There was some menace, some danger in her kind that kept her away from those cloud-producing hills, except when Four-foot could not find any food and she had to climb over their thin spiky tree-things to catch a lamb or a shoat.

She thought that she had once been in a sort of giant leaf on the water, but she did not remember much about it. And though she spoke to Four-foot after the manner of her kind and not of his, the only words she could ever remember hearing were, 'wicked child.' She thought that meant that someone hadn't liked her, but she could not say why. It had been before she met Four-foot, she was sure of that. And there had been so much water under that leaf, far more than in any of the forest streams that she and Four-foot drank from. She didn't entirely know what to make of that image.

If she was called 'wicked child,' she wondered what they would have called Four-foot, had they known him. Wicked something else, maybe? But Four-foot was not wicked. There were so many of his kind, who hunted together and sang at night, but only Four-foot was her friend. She usually slept in trees in case his kind came looking for him and were mad at her for being there. He was big and strong and would protect her, but some of them were almost as big, and there were more of them. He had got in a fight for her once, and lost one of his ears. She didn't want to make him do that again.

She admired Four-foot, who was stronger and faster than she was. But he didn't know how to climb trees, and most of the spiky tree-things that her kind put up around their animals were too tall for him to jump over. And he couldn't prick his eggs and suck them out, not that he seemed interested in doing so. In the heat of the day, when Four-foot lay down to pant in peace, Two-foot's favorite thing was to lie down with her head on his chest, listening to the ban-doo ban-doo of his heart and the heha-heha of his breath. She wondered if he heard the same ban-doo when he put his head on her chest, but of course he couldn't tell her.

Four-foot stood for a moment wagging his tail at her, and then loped off. He was much faster than Two-foot, but she knew he was just going to get a drink from the brook. She followed him, and drank this time in his manner. It was much more practical for her to kneel and raise the water to her mouth with her hands, but she liked to honor him sometimes by lapping it directly from the stream as he did. Her ragged covering got even muddier and tore a little further, but that was no trouble. Her kind buried their dead in stone gardens still covered with their skins and furs, so it was really no trouble to find more coverings if she needed them. As long as she and Four-foot reburied the bodies, her kind never seemed to notice.

They must be scared of the dark, she thought, because when she and Four-foot stole out of the forest at night, her kind never seemed willing to venture past the openings of their wooden hills. They would stand there with the light behind them, staring out into the dark and calling, "Who's there?" while she and Four-foot snuck right by on the way to the stone gardens, or to stealing a lamb from behind the spiky tree-things. Two-foot was afraid of the dark too, a little, but not like the others were. As long as she didn't fall out of the tree she slept in – which did happen sometimes – she would be all right.

When the sun went down today, though, Two-foot did feel a little fearful. Most nights, the warm wind whispered comforting things to her until she fell asleep. Tonight it whispered urgently to her in a language she did not recognize. She lay silent for some time, propped between the branches of a tukka tree, listening to Four-foot's reassuring breaths below. When she did finally drift to sleep, she dreamt that the wind was trying to warn her about something. She saw her forest as a mere clump of trees within a small garden surrounded by water. A leaf like the one from her childhood bobbed up and down as the waters rose higher and higher. At last the malevolent tide covered the whole land in water, and her lungs filled with its sloshing heaviness. All were drowned, and only the bobbing leaf remained.

When she awoke with a gasp, the wind was still whispering about death. Two-foot climbed down from her perch, still gasping for breath. Four-foot was awake by the time her feet touched the ground, and she held his comforting head against her chest. Did he hear the ban-doo ban-doo there, or was there only the terrible sloshing of her lungs?

"We have to go," she sobbed, holding him tight. Four-foot whined a little.

When the sun rose some time later, they were already on the edge of the forest. *We have to find that leaf,* Two-foot kept thinking, *before the waters cover everything.* But when they reached the treeline, Four-foot stopped. It was not safe to walk through the gardens of Two-foot's kind during the day. If they saw Four-foot, they would chase him away with sticks, or worse.

"I'm frightened too," she told him, "but we have to go. Maybe they'll listen to me if I say you're my friend."

She did not really think they would, but she wanted to reassure him. The words 'wicked child' came back to her, gloating and nasty. Who had said them to her? A part of her feared that whoever had said those words would be out there, waiting for her among her kind to punish her for crimes unknown. But only her kind had those big leaves, so if she wanted to get onto one, she had to risk it. How could she bring Four-foot with her, though? Her kind did not get on with his, and they would hurt him if they saw him. She would have to hide him somehow.

A sudden noise made her throw herself down in the

tall grasses next to her friend. A big wooden thing with a man on top was rolling along the road ahead, pulled by a donkey. Neither the man nor the donkey noticed them, the man because he was preoccupied and inattentive, and the donkey because he was blinkered. Two-foot crawled forward until she was almost at the road, and the man, donkey, and contraption had passed by. At night, she knew, in the rainy season, her kind would drape coverings over their horses and donkeys to keep them warm. A covering like that would be big enough to conceal Four-foot, if he would hold still for it.

A few minutes later, she had spotted the dwelling she wanted. It was one of the larger wooden hills, the ones with bigger entrances that never produced any clouds. The animals slept there. When nobody seemed to be looking, she sprinted across the road and slipped in through the doors. It was coming back to her, in bits and pieces. She had once had one of these wooden dens, she thought. Why had she left?

It was musty in this den, where her kind kept animals imprisoned behind shoulder-high wooden walls. She heard hogs snorting about, but did not see them. The big square animal covers were folded neatly to one side of the door, on one of those wooden platforms that her kind put things on. She thought she had eaten from one once, or was the problem that she had *not* eaten?

Most of these covers were too heavy – it was so hard to lift one that she could not imagine also carrying Four-foot hidden underneath. Two-foot sorted through the covers, dropping them haphazardly on the ground until she found one that was lighter. With that one tucked under her arm, she walked out the door only to find a big man standing there in front of her.

"Hey!" the man said. "What do you think you're doing?"

She considered running, but that would have meant dropping the cover, and then she would have had to go through with this whole thing again somewhere else. That didn't seem worth the effort.

"I need…" she began, haltingly.

The man caught her arm and pulled it, painfully. The cover fell to the ground.

"You need to have your fingers off as a thief, that's what you need."

Two-foot did not bother reasoning with him. Her speech was out of practice anyway. Instead, she whistled. The man shook her, thinking that she was only being insolent. He realized too late that Four-foot was bearing down on him from behind, and he had only just let go of Two-foot and turned around when Four-foot knocked him to the ground, his jaws savaging the man's arm and shoulder. Two-foot had never heard one of her kind scream like that before. It frightened her, because it might attract others, with sticks. So she told Four-foot to leave off and stood surveying the damage to this screaming man's body.

She was not sure whether he would die. Another animal might last a few hours or a day like this, but her kind could be ingenious. With help, this one might even last a week, or longer if his arm didn't swell and turn colors. The man stopped screaming and looked up at her, terror in his eyes. Four-foot sat at her side, cleaning the blood off his jaws and fur.

"Keep it off," the man whimpered. "Oh, please keep your wolf off. Don't let it kill me! You want money? Here, take my money." He made an impotent gesture toward a pouch at his side, and then started to sob.

Two-foot took the pouch, which clinked a little. Then she picked up the cover again, and walked away with Four-foot at her heels. A woman with a baby rushed past her toward the man, screaming and crying. Two-foot could still hear their sobs when she got back to the road and stopped to see what was inside the pouch. There were all these round shiny things in there, of varied metallic colors. She was not sure what they were for, or why the man had offered them to her. But they were pretty, so she kept them in the pouch, which she tied around her wrist. Then she lifted the cover over the other arm, whistled to Four-foot, and went on her way. Somewhere at the end of this road she would find one of those big wooden leaves. And in that leaf, her salvation.

5
Phaedra

Everyone said Phaedra danced through life. She was tall and lithe and surrounded by friends, and joyous and graceful and all the things that a girl from a good family ought to be. Absolutely glamorous, the whole city agreed. She was the most beautiful girl Karsanye had ever seen, and Gods, she could dance.

Her father was a former merchant who had succeeded well enough to give up his wandering days and become a financier. He had married above his birth, to the daughter of a master weaver, and the two of them had hurried to ready a home for their inevitable brood. Their first and only product was Phaedra.

No matter – the girl was flawless. Her father did what he was good at and adapted his plans. Phaedra would marry a nobleman one day, so long as she was well prepared. Her parents prepared her as best they could. They hired a nursemaid to feed her and watch her every move. She had to stay healthy and safe so that she could conquer the world.

When she was older, they taught her their most cherished skills. She took naturally enough to dressmaking, but her father dreaded teaching her the skill that had sent him so far in life. He had taught himself to read, and it was the hardest thing he had ever done. He was sure that his active little girl would struggle to sit still for her lessons.

He was wrong. Within weeks, her eyes were dancing across the page. His little library, which he had accumulated mostly as a show of wealth, became her favorite part of the house. Even after a long day of chores and playing with friends, she could always be found with one of his books in her hands, reading and rereading. Her father didn't even know what half the books were about – he hadn't really bought them for their contents. When her mother asked, Phaedra said that they were religious philosophies. Then her parents began to worry that she was *too* well-educated. No man wanted a wife who could outthink him.

By then, it was out of their hands. When her father had to travel for business, Phaedra would ask him to bring home a book. She loved to talk about what she had read, but her parents couldn't listen. Every erudite sentence was a reminder of their grave mistake. What if she frightened all her suitors away?

When her ramblings turned to Atel, they didn't even notice at first. Today she might speak of the Traveler God; surely tomorrow it would be the God of clay ovens or something. All their attention was turned toward finding a match for her before she developed an unhealthy reputation. But it caught their attention when she said she had to go on a pilgrimage.

In truth, Phaedra's recent fascination with Atel had a single cause: Atel's followers were expected to travel on pilgrimages. She knew about her parents' plans, and before she was married off to some respectable fellow, she wanted a chance to see the world she had read about. Her parents meant to refuse, but their daughter was well practiced in getting her way. She promised that upon her return, she would curb her intellectual spirit and marry whomever they chose for her, without scaring him off. To Phaedra, it seemed an easy enough promise to make. The obsessive fear of her scaring boys off seemed entirely ridiculous.

If dances were anything to go by, it wasn't even possible.

On a clear day, Atuna would have been visible from the docks of Karsanye. Today a mist rose from the water, concealing the far shore. Phaedra stood on the dock with her nursemaid, smiling and breathing in the sea air. Her parents had managed to stall and delay her journey right up to the eve of Karassa's festival, but at long last she was on her way. There was only one boat leaving the island before the summer festival, and it was just a fishing boat. She didn't care. It was perfect.

There was a narrow bench on the port side and a bin of fishing gear to starboard; the boat's center was taken up by a square-sailed mast and a low-rimmed vat, half full of fish. Kelina wrinkled her nose and suggested they wait to leave on a more appropriate vessel.

"Atel's followers do not fear rough travel," Phaedra said.

"And what do you know of travel, young mistress?" Kelina asked her. "You have never been off Tarphae, any more than I have. My old bones wouldn't do well on a fishing boat."

Phaedra nodded, and her smile turned sly. "If you like, you can stay here this evening and follow me when the festival is over. I will wait for you in Atuna at a nice inn, until your old bones have the chance to catch up with me."

"Now don't be cruel, miss. You know I would never let you out of my sight."

Phaedra took her hand. "We are going on the Traveler God's pilgrimage, Kelina. With all the power of His divinity, Atel still walks barefoot in all the pictures. Our pilgrimage would not be off to a very good start if we delayed our journey just because a fishing boat doesn't suit our high tastes."

Kelina narrowed her eyes suspiciously. She knew

Phaedra better than the girl's own parents did. She knew why Atel had become her latest obsession.

Before Kelina could say anything, Phaedra turned back to the boat's owner. "We will come with you to Atuna, if you will accept my offer."

The fisherman smiled at her. He was an aging continental man from one of Atuna's tributary villages. "The price of a day's catch, just to take you to Atuna? Can I accept it twice?"

Phaedra laughed excitedly as he helped her on board. The two younger men – the fisherman's nephews, apparently – lifted Kelina and placed her safely beside her young charge. Then they got the women's luggage, which they somehow managed to wedge between the bin of fishing gear and the mast.

"Get moving, boys," the owner said to them. "Let's make haste for our pilgrims."

The lads had just carried in the last of their newly repaired nets when a young man came jogging along, stopping at their boat. He was an attractive boy, slender and tall, with a strong jawline. His skin was too light for Tarphae, but too dark for the continent. When he had the fisherman's attention, he asked if there was room for him on board.

The fisher struggled visibly with himself, not wishing to make Phaedra feel overcharged, but afraid to frighten away a paying passenger. In the end he told the boy that he could join them for half Phaedra's price, so long as he was going to the same place. The boy agreed and paid without even asking where they were headed. Kelina, protective as always, stretched out as far as she could to prevent him from joining them on the bench, so he sat down on the box of tackle opposite them. Phaedra had to lean forward and yell over the fishermen's calls in order to introduce herself.

The young man's name turned out to be Criton. She told him about the holy site she meant to visit, an ancient abbey called the Crossroads that was sacred to the Atellan friars.

He listened politely, while Kelina fixed Phaedra with that wry look of hers.

Criton knew nothing of the continental Gods, so she told him about Atel the Traveler and about His brother Atun, the Sun God, who sailed across the heavens in a ship of gold. She told him about the friars of Atel who never stayed in any one place for long, and had surely seen the whole world. The fishermen gave the two of them dirty looks for talking so loudly, but Phaedra was too excited to care. Here she was, about to see the world herself for the first time! She was glad to talk to someone her own age about it. Her parents hadn't wanted her to tell her friends, for fear that it would start rumors of her being a fanatic for a foreign God. They'd just admonished her to come home as soon as she could.

Phaedra was still chattering happily to Criton when a young man with a crossbow appeared on the dock. "Hey there," he called out to them, "are you coming or going?"

"We're going," one of the fisherman's lads called back, "but there's no room for you."

"Can't you make room? I can pay good money." The fisherman seemed interested at first, but soon the boy was joined on the dock by a ragged girl carrying a heavy bundle.

"I might have room for one more," the fisherman said, "but not two. Sorry."

"What?" the crossbow-wielder asked. "Oh no, we're not together. I just want to get on myself."

The ragged girl passed him, walked right up to the boat, and without hesitation, tried to climb on.

"Hey!" the boat's captain said, getting belligerent. "This isn't a passenger ship! Unless you want to sit at our feet among the catch, there's no room."

The girl looked a little confused. "Sit," she said, awkwardly pointing to the boat around her enormous bundle. The bundle was nearly as large as the girl, a big pile of who-knew-what wrapped up in a blanket. It was obviously heavy, but the girl's thin arms must have had more muscle than met the eye. Whatever objects were inside, they occasionally shifted, making it hard for her to hold onto the bundle properly.

"Well, I suppose you could," the fisherman said, "if you had any money. But you don't look like–"

"Is this good?" the girl asked. She carefully put down her package and untied a pouch from her wrist.

The fisherman looked inside the pouch and turned red. "Welcome aboard," he said.

The girl sat down with her bundle at Kelina's feet, which Kelina moved back as far as she could. The girl looked filthy. Her hair was a gigantic tangled lump filled with sticks and mud and, Phaedra suspected, a sizable colony of lice. A whole civilization of them, as Father would say.

"Hey!" said the nervous young fellow with the crossbow. "You can't just let her on and leave me behind! I can pay at least as well as she can!"

"What is going *on* today?" Phaedra heard the fisherman mumble under his breath. "I doubt you can, lad," he said aloud, "but I'd love to see you try."

When the young man climbed aboard, he had no money left and no room to sit down. He wedged himself awkwardly between the bench and the little mast, trying not to step on the ragged girl or the reeking pile of fish among which she sat. With the fisherman standing at the tiller in the stern of the boat, his nephews would have to precariously share the prow in order to have room.

"Hurry now," the fisherman said, looking up at the sun.

On a good day, Atuna was two hours away. They would be lucky if they could make it there before dark. No fisherman in his right mind would sail in the dark, but the financial gain of this particular voyage was enough to make the boat's owner highly optimistic about his timing.

"Unmoor us," he said, "and get us out of here before some other lunatic tries to get on."

They were almost fast enough. The second of the youths was about to jump aboard with the end of the loose rope when a man's voice commanded them to halt. The fisherman's nephew swore and turned around, clearly disbelieving what he saw. A lord and his son, riding their horses right onto the dock. As they approached, Phaedra recognized the older gentleman as Lord Tavener, who was friends with her father. She had met Lord Tavener's son Kataras quite a few times, and she liked him a great deal, but she had only ever seen this younger one from afar. Hunter had a reputation for being no fun.

Just now, Hunter looked as confused and dismayed as the fishermen were. He wasn't bad looking, Phaedra decided, or wouldn't be, if he ever stopped scowling. He was shorter than his brother – or than Criton, for that matter – and he lacked the big showy muscles of which Kataras was so proud. But he was fit, and had surprisingly delicate features under that grim demeanor.

Lord Tavener dismounted and addressed the fisherman. "I wish to book my son's passage on your vessel. Drop him off in Atuna, or wherever you like, really. I'm sure he can get wherever he's going once he's on dry land again."

The fisherman shook his head, taking his cap off and gesturing with it. "Can't you see my boat's all full up? Wait till tomorrow, can't you?"

Lord Tavener brought out a large purse, inserted a gloved hand, and deposited a handful of gold in the incredulous fisherman's cap. "Kick one of these people off if you must," he said.

The fisherman stared at the money in his cap, but he held firm. "These people paid their fares honestly," he said, "and there's no more room. My boys can barely fit on themselves!"

The lord was apparently in no mood to haggle. He reached twice more into his purse and filled the man's cap nearly to overflowing.

"I am buying your boat," he said firmly. "You can leave your boys here with me until you come back. I will see to it that they are well cared for in your absence. When you return, I will give you twice as much again. Hunter, give this man any help he needs."

Hunter dismounted, looking extremely embarrassed. He was dressed not for travel, Phaedra noted, but for war: a shield slung onto his back and a sword at his side, with a shirt of polished scales glinting beneath his cloak. Phaedra imagined it must be stifling under all those layers, but Hunter was not even sweating.

"Father," he said, "you know I've never been on the water before. What help could I give?"

Hunter's father looked oddly terrified. "Don't question me," he said. "The Oracle of Ravennis told me to send you away on the first boat off the island, and by all the Gods of the isles and the continent, that's what I'm going to do."

Hunter opened his mouth again, but his father put up a hand. "Take these," he said, pulling a smaller purse from within his clothing. "Sell them as you need to. I will meet you in Atuna for your birthday, and we can discuss it all then."

He looked up at the fisherman, who stood frustrated and bewildered as Hunter took his place on the overloaded boat's prow. "Don't let me keep you," Lord Tavener said. "Take my son and go."

The fisherman glanced apologetically at his nephews. "I'll come back for you tomorrow, lads. Don't give this gentleman any trouble, now."

As the boat pulled away, leaving the boys behind, the passengers breathed a collective sigh of relief. Or perhaps it only seemed that way to Phaedra, who had felt as if the Gods themselves were hindering her progress for some mysterious reason. She looked over the side of the boat and saw a jellyfish drifting past. "Look!" she cried excitedly to Kelina. "We must have Karassa's blessing; She is bidding us farewell!"

Kelina looked down at the jellyfish, that sacred symbol of Karassa, and shrugged. "I say they're headed to the island for their mistress' festival. See, they're all drifting shorewards."

Kelina could have been right. Now that Phaedra looked, the jelly she had spotted was truly only one among many, all drifting in toward the island with the tide. But she still wanted to believe that the Goddess had blessed her journey.

The fellow with the crossbow shared her relief, anyway. Once the dock had fallen out of sight, his posture relaxed and his expression grew less tense.

The ragged girl had the opposite reaction. Now that the fishing boat was on the open water, the girl doubled over her bundle, shuddering and mumbling to herself. Poor girl, thought Phaedra. By the looks of her she had never had a decent meal in her life, let alone a bath. That bundle of hers probably held all of her worldly possessions. At least so Phaedra thought, until she noticed it moving.

As if in reaction to the boat's motion, the bundle had begun to wriggle agitatedly. Great Gods, what did the girl have in there? She had not been mumbling to herself, Phaedra realized now: she had been whispering to whoever was under that blanket, trying to calm him or her down! Phaedra looked around, afraid to say anything but desperate to see if others had noticed what she had. Hunter was still gazing out to sea, but Criton had definitely noticed. He eyed the bundle curiously, saying nothing. The fellow with the crossbow hadn't seen it yet, but then whatever was hidden under the blanket lurched against his leg, and he cried out in surprise.

At the noise, the thing under the blanket finally freed itself with a bark and a growl that startled even Hunter out of his reverie. The ragged girl tried to pull the blanket back over the animal, but it was too late: her dog was free. Oh Gods no, not a dog! A wolf!

Kelina screamed, and the boy with the crossbow fell against her in his attempt to get away from the beast. The wolf looked at them and snarled. Hunter came around the mast, trying to draw his sword, but his arm collided with the mast and stopped in mid-gesture. The wolf leapt at him and the two fell against the side of the little boat, with Criton clinging desperately to his box to avoid falling overboard as the boat listed from side to side.

The boy with the crossbow tried to rise to his feet to load his weapon, but the boat's movement threw him back down into Kelina. With a cry and a splash, the old woman tumbled backward into the water. Phaedra screamed and reached for her hand, but now the boat listed the other way, lifting her away from her nursemaid even as Kelina began to sputter and sink. Gods, she could not swim!

By the time the boat rebalanced, Kelina was well out of reach. Phaedra cried and shrieked for the fisherman to turn them around, but he must have been too distracted by the wolf to hear her. The wind grew stronger, stinging Phaedra's eyes and pulling the boat swiftly away. Soon Kelina had disappeared entirely from view.

Phaedra collapsed against the side of the boat, sobbing. One moment Kelina had been sitting beside her, and the next moment she was gone. How could it be so simple, so easy to lose someone? Kelina had been everything to her: her wet nurse, her teacher, her constant companion. And she wouldn't even have been on this godsforsaken boat if it hadn't been for Phaedra.

What would she say to her parents? No, she knew they wouldn't blame her. She wasn't even sure how much they would care, and that only made the grief grow heavier within her. Kelina's sons had left to make their fortunes back before Phaedra even knew how to speak – Phaedra was the only person in the world who would miss her.

If Phaedra did not make it safely to Atuna, nobody would care that Kelina hadn't made it either. She had to survive this, for her nursemaid's sake if not her own. She pushed her sadness down deep inside her, saving it for later. For now, she had to be strong.

She opened her eyes. It took her a moment to register what she saw. The ragged girl had somehow managed to pull the wolf off Hunter, who had since risen to his feet and drawn his sword. The fisherman must have gotten involved at some point, because he was sitting back against the tiller and bleeding from his left leg. His hand was clutching a bloody knife. The boy with the crossbow had loaded his weapon and was aiming it uncertainly in the wolf's direction, but the ragged girl was in his way. She and the wolf were pressed up against the box of tackle, which Criton had vacated. The girl was spreading her arms wide to protect the animal from harm.

"No," she was crying. "Leave him alone!"

Hunter made to advance on the wolf, but the girl shrieked again and he stopped. The animal was crouching behind her, alternating between whimpers and growls. It had been injured, Phaedra realized. Then she noticed Criton.

He was crouching on the prow, clinging to the mast with his claws. Claws? Yes. Razor sharp, four-fingered claws sprouting from flesh covered in shining golden scales all the way up his forearms, fading back into skin past the elbow. Phaedra suppressed a scream. When would the horror of this voyage end?

The boat rocked. The fisherman dropped his knife to steady the tiller, still swearing and clutching his bleeding leg with the other hand. The easterly wind that had risen up when Kelina was lost blew mercilessly against the sail, driving them ever onward.

"Wicked man," the ragged girl cursed at the fisherman. "Wicked man!"

None of the men knew how to talk to this girl; they would only make the situation more dangerous. Phaedra rose unsteadily to her feet.

"What's your name?" she asked the girl.

The ragged girl looked suspicious, but Phaedra spread

her arms and repeated her question. The girl seemed to take some time to think about it, as if she had not considered the subject before. "Ban-doo," she said finally, with authority.

Phaedra had never heard of such a name, but she thought it best to go along. "Bandu," she repeated soothingly. "I'm Phaedra. And this is Criton, and Hunter, and... do you have a name?"

The youth with the crossbow looked startled. "Narky," he said.

"Yes," Phaedra continued, "Bandu, this is Narky. Does your wolf have a name?"

The girl nodded vigorously. "He is Four-foot, and he is good. Not wicked. Good."

"Like hell he is!" the fisherman spat.

"Four-foot is good!" the girl shouted at him. "You are wicked! It's not his fault he doesn't like being on your leaf. Everybody wants to hit him!"

Bandu's grasp of language was tentative, Phaedra realized. Where had this girl been living?

"Bandu," she said. "Nobody wants to hit Four-foot. They're just afraid of him, because he's big and has sharp teeth, and he jumped on Hunter. Can you control him? Can you prevent – can you make him not bite them?"

"Four-foot only bites wicked people," Bandu asserted, pretty outrageously. "I talk to him only if you throw sharp things away."

Behind Phaedra, Hunter snorted. "Not likely."

"You don't need to throw your sword away," Phaedra snapped at him. "Just sheath it, for Karassa's sake!"

Kelina had always said that it didn't do for a girl to be so forceful, but at least in this case, she had been wrong. Hunter blinked at her and slid his sword into its sheath.

"That God-cursed thing bit me!" the fisherman protested.

Phaedra turned to glare at him. "Well, it looks like you stabbed it, so I think you're even. Just sail your boat and shut up!"

The man stared at her, but he didn't argue. "Give me a hand," he said to the boy called Narky. "No, just help me bind my leg. Obviously none of you know a damn thing about sailing, or you'd stop rocking the damn boat every which way."

Criton at least seemed to grasp what Phaedra was doing. "I have never seen a wolf before," he said to Bandu, trying to placate her. His hands were an ordinary shape again, which for a moment made Phaedra doubt what she had seen. But the mast still had claw marks on it.

"I'm sorry if we frightened it," Phaedra said. "It frightened us."

The ragged girl put an arm around her wolf. "Nobody frightens Four-foot," she said. "He just doesn't like water. When my kind try to hit him, he gets angry."

Phaedra nodded. "Of course. I didn't mean to insult him by saying he was afraid. I hope he's not offended."

Bandu seemed to take this at face value, and turned to whisper to her wolf. After a few moments of listening to the animal's incoherent growling, she announced that Four-foot was not insulted. Poor girl. What kind of life must she have had?

"When we reach Atuna," Hunter said, mostly to Bandu, "I would be happy to buy lodging for us all. Atuna is famous for its inns. If you'd be willing to leave your wolf outside the city, you could have a proper bed with silk sheets and pillows."

"Pillows?" Bandu repeated uncertainly. She did not seem to recognize the word.

Phaedra let out a breath and looked to the growing shoreline ahead. The danger seemed to have passed. She fell back onto the bench and put her head in her hands.

Behind them, Tarphae sank into the distance.

6
Tarphae

Once the fisherman's boys were settled in the otherwise empty kitchens, Lord Tavener set out at a run for the festival of Karassa. He hated being late, but what could he have done? The Oracle had been very clear, and everyone knew it was unwise to ignore a prophecy.

The fires had already been lit by the time Tav made it to the square. Commonfolk made room for him as he pressed forward toward the altar – as the king's champion, he was to make the second sacrifice. King Kestan was relieved to see him: the bulls were already being brought forward. Any later, and it would have been a bad omen.

There was tension in the air as the High Priest of Karassa said the preliminary prayers before sacrifice and handed the knife to Kestan. Tav tried not to breathe so heavily. He always felt nervous on holidays, and today was worse than usual. It came from being so close to the Goddess, from knowing that Her attention was on the island and its people, and it was worse because he was unable to focus on his duties. He had just sent his beloved son off into the world.

The king's bull stared at him through its right eye. Tav coughed nervously. The king approached and put one hand on its head, then turned to face the heavens. "O Karassa," he began, "watch over us as we…"

The bull collapsed. The knife hadn't even touched it, but it fell lifeless to the ground between Tav and the king. There were gasps in the crowd, and Tav's chest constricted as he stared down at the lifeless bull. What was happening?

There was a gurgle behind him, and he turned to see his son Kataras vomiting onto the ground. It was seawater – there were even bits of seaweed in it. Tav tried to breathe, but couldn't. His chest was too heavy, too full of saltwater and sand and kelp, and as he tried to scream, water poured out of his mouth and soaked his clothes. He fell to his knees and the crowd around him did the same, all drowning together in the warm summer air. He couldn't breathe, he couldn't breathe! His lungs were burning with the salt and the strain of trying to expel water that would never run out, never leave his chest clear. O Gods, why? What had gone wrong?

The water kept coming, kept bursting out of his mouth, and he felt himself slipping away into blackness. In his final, delirious moment, he saw Hunter on his boat, sailing away to safety. He died with Hunter's name on his lips.

Galanea spent the hour after Criton's departure trying to compose her thoughts and decide what she would say when her husband came home. But her mind was blank, and she knew it didn't especially matter what she said – he wouldn't be listening to her anyway. What would he do to her when he found out?

She knew she should have left here with Criton years ago. If she had only been strong enough, she could have left this prison of a house, this prison of an island, and started over again. It would have been better for Criton. It probably would have been better for her.

Tears came flooding into her eyes again. Letting Criton

go meant admitting that she had been living all these years in a prison of her own creation, that she could have walked out the door any time she wanted to and never come back. Whatever her husband did to her, she thought she might deserve it. How many times had she let him beat their son, let him torture their beautiful boy with the golden scales? She could have protected him, but she hadn't, and she had failed to act out of the worst kind of selfishness – the kind that made your life worse instead of better.

She had stayed out of fear, prioritized that fear over her son's safety and her own. There was no excuse for what her husband had done, but she had excused him in her mind because it was easier than admitting she could have done something about it.

She could have changed her appearance again, to something completely different and new. She could have left years ago, walked right past him on the street with Criton swaddled tight, and he would never have known. But she had been too afraid of change, and too afraid of her own magic. And she had foolishly thought she deserved to suffer for what she was, and for escaping her family's fate and surviving when the rest of her people had died.

Her lungs filled with cold water so suddenly that she fell straight to the floor, coughing and convulsing. As she struggled to breathe, her body rebelled against years of control and went back to its hereditary deformities. Yet where was the fire that had always terrified her? The fire that had caused her so much pain and suffering when Criton was still in the house, and that she had thought for years would doom her? It was dead, extinguished. After years of wishing she could put it out, now she coughed up water and wished that it still burned inside her, anything rather than this terrible sloshing portal to the sea.

Her claws scraped against the floor where she lay drowning, but her breath had been stolen by the water that poured from her mouth. In her final moments she thought back to the way her husband had held Criton's head in that bucket, punishing him just for being himself and being sick.

Was this her punishment?

Narky's father had almost drowned once, as a boy. It had haunted his nightmares his entire life, that feeling of breathing thick heavy water instead of air. He had moved away from the sea, surrounded himself with pasture lands, and now here he was, drowning in the village square. But this was impossible, it was ridiculous! *You're dreaming again,* his mind scolded him. *Wake up.*

The flames of Karassa's sacrifice died on the altar, while all about it the bodies of the villagers were strewn here and there, all gaping in horror at this impossible thing that was happening to them. *Wake up! If you don't wake up, you may die in real life!*

Why wouldn't he wake? It usually didn't last this long, not to the point where his bowels and bladder gave up, where his head began to cloud and he forgot who he was. It never lasted this long.

Wake up! his mind screamed.

7
Narky

Narky was grateful for the inn stay, but he still didn't think he liked this fellow Hunter. He was a tough guy, which reminded Narky of Ketch. Hunter had paid for two rooms: one for the two girls and one for Narky, Criton, and himself. There were two beds in this room, and a straw mattress had been laid out on the floor. Naturally, this ended up being Narky's bed. Now Hunter was downstairs, no doubt buying drinks for Criton and asserting his dominance. Narky despised such people. If only he had some money of his own, he would be able to buy his own room next time, with a proper bed.

And why shouldn't he find some money somewhere? This inn was full of wealthy merchants, the kind that Pa had always admired, who came to Atuna in order to buy stakes in the success of its many cargo ships without ever risking their own lives or even setting their dainty feet on a boat's planks. Atuna was the greatest seaport in the known world, and it attracted these sorts of people. Oh sure, Hunter could shower Criton and the others with his wealth. Narky would find money his own way.

The room next door was locked, but it was a warm night and the windows were all open. The rooms were not far apart, and, by clinging to the shutter of his own window, Narky managed to plant his foot on the next room's windowsill. Then he had only to transfer his hands to the next window's shutter, and he was soon inside. But Narky's heart nearly leapt out of his chest when he realized that the room was occupied.

A mustachioed man was sleeping in the bed, snoring softly. One of those financiers, judging by the fancy clothes piled at the foot of the bed. On a little stand beside him stood a candle burnt almost all the way down, next to a thin chain necklace and a large coin purse. Narky tiptoed over and lifted the necklace, giving himself some time to think about how to remove money from the purse without making too much noise. He definitely had no intention of taking the whole purse, firstly because this merchant might recognize it if he saw it on Narky, and secondly because Hunter and the others knew that he didn't have *that* much money.

The necklace was silver, its centerpiece a rather ornate bird design. Very distinctive. He would have to sell it in some other town, far from here. Narky carefully slipped it into his shoe. The fellow in the bed stirred a little, and rolled over to face away from the candle. Narky breathed. He wondered how much this man had had to drink. He hoped it was enough.

As carefully as he could, taking only one coin at a time, Narky transferred some of the man's considerable wealth into his own empty pocket. When he thought he had taken enough to strain credulity, he climbed back out the window and returned to his room. That had gone remarkably well, he thought.

The next day, Hunter led them to Atuna's temple square, where travelers from all over the known world could buy wine, goats, doves and even the occasional bull for sacrifice on one of four public altars. Little shrines to various Gods dotted the square, dwarfed by the grand buildings and tall spires of the established local churches. Travelers yammered to each other in all different languages, their foreign tongues mixing in with the bleating of goats and the cooing of birds. The Atunaean workers who cleaned the altars in between patrons chatted with the visitors of the larger temples, swinging their buckets idly. The city's patron God, Atun, had the greatest church here, but other popular choices such as Elkinar the life God and Atel the Traveler God also came well represented.

Narky was grateful enough to have escaped Tarphae and justice that he followed the pretty girl's lead and bought a dove to sacrifice to Atel. The girl thanked the Traveler God in beautifully chosen formal words, which Narky tried unsuccessfully to repeat. When that was done, she sacrificed a second dove to Atun, with a prayer for His hospitality, and then a third, tearfully, to Elkinar, who was apparently a God of death as well as life. Go figure. The ragged girl called Bandu just stared at the proceedings, and Narky didn't blame her. The rituals didn't make much sense to him either, and he hadn't spent his whole life in a ditch.

The pretty girl was very forceful. She had bought a pair of shears and a razor upon their arrival in Atuna, and had forced Bandu to sit while she sheared off all her tangled hair and burned it. She burned Bandu's clothes too, after dressing her in the drowned nursemaid's spare garments. When the bundle of clothes and hair was aflame, the number of agonized bugs that hopped about in the fire was truly astounding. Not that the radical change in appearance did Bandu much good. Without her hair and in clothes meant for someone twice her weight, she managed to look a good deal more pathetic than she had to begin with.

She approached him now, standing uncomfortably close. "Do you know about hits?"

Narky wondered if pretending not to hear her would make her go away. He doubted it. "I don't know what you're talking about," he said.

The girl looked frustrated with his lack of understanding. "When you hit with sharp things, and it gets red and bad."

"That's called bleeding."

More frustration. "No! No, not bleeding. After. When it gets red *after*, and hot."

Narky scratched his arm. "Like an infection?"

"In fiction?"

"Yeah, an infection. When the skin changes color all around the cut, you mean, even after the cut's not bleeding anymore. They're very dangerous."

Bandu looked excited. "Dangerous, yes! In fiction. Do you know how to make in fiction go away?"

"Well, you can cauterize it before it gets infected. Burn the wound shut. It usually works, I think."

Bandu nodded and took him by the hand. "Show me. Show me to help Four-foot."

Oh Gods, what did I just agree to do? Narky wanted to shake loose, but the girl wouldn't let go of his hand. He could probably yank it away from her if he really tried, but he honestly didn't know how she'd react if he did. The girl lived with a wolf; who knew what would happen if he angered her? He let her drag him most of the way out of town before he even thought to stop for supplies, and then it took some convincing to get her to wait while he bought a tinderbox and a knife, and a skin of strong spirits. He didn't know if the wolf would drink spirits, but it seemed worth a try to him. If he was going to go poking a wild animal with a piece of heated metal, that animal had better be slobbering drunk.

They cleared the city wall and crunched their way into a small dry wood, Narky getting progressively angrier at himself. Bandu couldn't be more than fourteen years old, yet here she was, bullying him. A coward's son indeed.

With a growl, Bandu's wolf slunk toward them out of the trees.

"You know," Narky said. "I think you should do this, not me."

Bandu glared at him. "You help," she commanded.

Narky withered. "All right," he said. "I'll help. But you do the burning. You have this, this, *relationship* with the wolf, and I don't. Burning out a wound *hurts.* If *I* do it, the damn thing's gonna bite me."

"You don't talk that way," Bandu said darkly. "Four-foot is not damn thing, Four-foot is my friend. I don't call your friend damn thing."

"I don't have a friend," Narky said. "Anyway, since Four-foot is your friend and not mine, I think you should do the burning."

Thankfully, Bandu accepted his logic. She whispered in the wolf's ear and it lay on its right side, staring at Narky as if daring him to comment on its wound. The wound was long and shallow, stretching down from the wolf's shoulder toward its belly. The fisherman had slashed at it wildly as it turned toward him, and whether his blows or its teeth had made their marks first, neither had been well aimed for a kill. Yet the length of the wound would make the burning a good deal harder, which made Narky doubly glad that he had convinced Bandu to cauterize it herself. It was hard to see, through the clotted blood and fur, whether an infection had taken hold, but Narky helped Bandu to build a small fire, and he gave her the skin of spirits so that she could clean the wound while he heated the knife.

Narky often wondered, afterward, how they had ever managed to hold the wolf still while its flesh burned, or how Bandu had been able to talk it down from biting them. She was like a girl out of one of the fairy stories that Narky used to bring home from town, those that terrified his father so. They were full of witches and monsters, cruel elves and cannibals, and everybody in them seemed to meet a bad end. Narky even asked Bandu if she was using some kind of magic on the wolf, but she didn't seem to understand the question.

Bandu refused to leave her wolf when they were done,

so Narky walked back to the inn alone. Why had she asked him for help? he wondered. Why not any of the others?

When he arrived, he found the common room so crammed with people that he had to shove his way through to find the other islanders. People gave him stares and shushed him – someone was giving a speech.

It only took a second for Narky to recognize the voice: it was the fisherman who had brought them to Atuna, and he wasn't giving a speech, he was telling a story.

"They'd fallen out of their chairs, poor lads. Dead and drowned on dry land. My brother's eldest boy had seaweed coming out of his mouth! If you'll pardon me, boy, I thought at first maybe the lord of the house had killed them himself. My nephews were the only people in the house, so I went out.

"The city was just as empty as the docks, until I found them all in the square outside Karassa's temple. The whole city was there, dead just the same as my lads. Lungs filled with seawater, and wet all over. The bulls for sacrifice were dead too, just the same way. But the king wasn't there. I don't know if Mayar spared him, but he wasn't with the other dead ones where he should have been.

"Well, I didn't stay long after that. I didn't even go looking for the money the lord still owed me, I just ran for the docks. It felt haunted, like there might be ghosts about. I was coughing all the way home like I'd caught the plague too, I was scared to death. But it stopped when I got home, thank Atun.

"It's an island of the dead now, Tarphae. I wouldn't go back for all the world."

Narky had only just made his way through the crowd to the others, but now Hunter stormed past him toward the door, shoving people out of his way. Criton broke down in tears, and the pretty girl too.

"How do you know they're all gone?" Narky asked the fisherman. "How do you know it's not just the capital?"

The fisherman stared at him. "You think the Gods would put a plague on Karsanye and leave the rest of the island alone? Fish heads. There weren't no other people picking around that city, looking for survivors. *Everyone* was dead."

Narky nodded solemnly and turned away from his sobbing companions. He was not *really* glad – not really. He was sorry that all those people had died. It was obviously devastating news. But all he could think about was that he was the luckiest damn murderer the world had ever known.

8
Criton

It felt as if the world had ended. The only person who had ever loved him was gone. Criton had always thought he would come back one day to rescue Ma from her husband. They would live in a cave like the dragons were supposed to do, and if anyone came to bother them, Criton would chase them away. Now that would never happen.

Hunter did not reappear until the evening, and when he did, he paid for another night's stay for them all and then went straight to bed. He was grieving in his own way, perhaps, but neither he nor the others could possibly feel the pain Criton did. Narky hardly reacted at all. It would have made Criton angry, if he had been able to think of anything but his poor mother.

The next morning was dreadful. All of Atuna seemed intent on talking to them about what had happened, crowding into the inn's taproom to argue about which God had punished Tarphae and why. Some claimed that Karassa was being punished by Her father Mayar for some reason. They said that the king had only survived by treacherously rededicating his sacrifice to the angry Sea God. Others insisted that it was Karassa who was punishing Her people for not obeying their king. Each story seemed somehow darker and truer than the last, as human minds struggled to conceive of an answer terrible enough to justify the calamity that had befallen the island. And behind each story was the same assertion, spoken with the same brittle confidence: such a thing could never happen here. Atun would protect His city.

"I'm leaving today," Narky told Criton over a late lunch. "It's not safe here. Plagues jump from person to person – what if that fisherman brought it back with him? It could be in Atuna already, looking for us."

Criton gulped. Could the plague really be seeking them out?

"Where will you go?" he asked.

"I don't know. Away from here."

Criton looked down at his food. It was his second lunch. Eating was better than thinking, and besides, he never seemed to stop being hungry these days. Ma would have said he was hungry because he was growing, but he was already taller than most everyone in Atuna. How much taller could he possibly grow?

A man at the next table raised his voice, angrily repeating his own disgusting theory of Tarphae's demise. Narky was right. It was time to go.

"Phaedra is on a pilgrimage for the Traveler God," Criton told him. "We could go with her."

Narky shrugged. "There's safety in numbers, I guess. When's she leaving?"

"I'll ask her. Have you seen Bandu?"

"Yes," Narky answered reluctantly. "She's out in the woods, looking after her wolf. She wouldn't leave it after we burned its wound."

"You burned out her wolf's wound?" Criton asked incredulously. "Together?" He was surprised that Bandu would ask Narky, of all people.

Narky lifted his hands in acknowledgment of the absurdity. "Don't ask me why she chose me. It's not like I'd done it before."

Criton nodded. As little as he and Narky understood her, Bandu probably understood them even less. She seemed to have the same grasp of language that Criton had possessed at the age of three or four. How long had she lived alone in the woods, with only that wolf to talk to? It struck him how hard it must be for her now, out among society.

"See if she'll come with us," Criton said. "Phaedra's pilgrimage was going to be to an abbey of Atellan friars. They could be good healers."

"All right," Narky said with resignation. "You talk to Phaedra, I'll talk to Bandu."

Criton watched him leave, unable to focus his thoughts. What would he say to Phaedra? Ever since he had met her, she had filled him with – well, something. He had certainly never felt anything like it when he was living with his mother. He loved the shape of her face, loved the way her hair had been woven into hundreds of tight braids and piled elegantly on her head in such fascinating patterns. Her voice was clear and sweet, and she seemed to know something about everything. All this made it hard to imagine what he would say to her.

He found her upstairs, going through her luggage. She was sitting on the floor of the room she shared with Bandu, surrounded by piles of clothing, various beauty items such as hairpins, combs and tiny vials of perfume, and a number of mysterious cylindrical tubes. The shears were in her hand, and she was hacking at her beautiful hair.

"What are you doing?" he asked in dismay.

Phaedra looked at him through puffy wet eyes. "You've never seen someone in mourning before? I need to shave my head, and that means these braids have to go."

Criton blinked. Yes, mourning. How had he not thought of that? His mind wasn't functioning the way it ought to.

"Well, don't just stand there," Phaedra sobbed. "Help me." She dropped the shears.

Criton picked them up. "What were you doing in here? Before you started cutting your hair, I mean?"

"Going through all my things and seeing which ones I still need."

"To travel?" Criton asked.

"I don't need much to travel," she said curtly, wiping tears away with her hand, "but the plan was to come home after my pilgrimage, wasn't it? My parents wanted me to marry well. Well, now the island is cursed, and having a rich father is meaningless. All I have now is what I brought with me in these trunks. I have to sell what I don't need, and start from the beginning."

Criton snipped. One by one, her braids fell to the floor. "What will you do?"

"My mother was a weaver. I'll buy a loom. If she could work for her living, so can I."

Criton did not know what to say. Phaedra had lost everything – in some ways, a good deal more than Criton had – and she was already planning a completely different life for herself. Her mental fortitude was outright intimidating.

When he had finished with the shears, he handed them back to her and she started on his hair. He picked up one of the metal cylinders and turned it over in his hands.

"What are these things?" he asked.

"Scroll cases," Phaedra told him. "They're very expensive, but I'm not sure I can part with them. Those scrolls are important to me. They're writings on the nature of Gods. That one you're holding is Katinaras."

Curly locks fell around him. "Are you familiar with Katinaras?" she asked.

"No," Criton admitted. "I don't know much about religion, except that my mother's people were killed by a priest of Magor."

"Really?" Phaedra stopped what she was doing and moved to look straight at him, her eyes wide. "Were they all – like you?"

She lowered her eyes. Had she been about to say "monsters?"

"Yes," he said.

She went back to cutting. "What happened to them?"

"They lived in Ardis, and a priest of Magor killed them. That's all I know."

Phaedra nodded. "I've read about Magor; I'm not surprised His priests are warlike. He's supposed to be the Sea God's brother, Karassa's uncle. The God of the Wild. His followers believe in the virtue of strength above all else, and they don't consider killing to be a sin. In their teachings, no one has any inherent rights, they just have whatever respect they can gain from others through their strength of arms or magical power or what have you. They say that the women of Ardis –" she paused, embarrassed.

"Yes? What about them?"

She finished with the shears and sat down. There was something enchanting about the way she looked down at her lap. "Well," she said, fiddling with the shears in her hand. "They say that the women of Ardis lie with more than one man in a night, and let the seed do battle in their wombs. Later, whichever man the child resembles is honored at their spring festival. A great man is supposed to be able to have his children carry him from his home to the temple of Magor without his feet ever touching the ground."

"Huh," Criton said. They were both silent for a time.

In the stories Ma had told him, the hero usually met a beautiful woman and swept her off her feet. Was that really what men did? He imagined lifting Phaedra off the floor and, and – he couldn't do that, could he? Was it as simple as that? He had no experience at all, and something told him that any mistake would be catastrophic.

Phaedra broke the silence first. "I've read a lot about the Gods. Katinaras is my favorite. He disputes the notion of Godly kinship, which is interesting, but his finger-in-the-mesh analogy is pure genius. I can explain it to you some time."

Criton said nothing. He was still wondering about Ma's stories.

Phaedra handed him a razor and a bowl of water. "I'm ready. Were you here to talk to me about something else?"

"Oh, uh, yes." What was he here for again? "Narky and I were talking about leaving Atuna, and I remembered you were telling me about this place – the Crossroads – and I thought, um, do you want to go there? Narky thinks the plague might follow us here. If you're still planning on finishing your pilgrimage…"

Phaedra nodded, and he drew the blade away from her scalp. "I am. My career as a weaver can wait a couple of weeks, and I think traveling will clear my head. Narky could be right about the plague, too."

She sighed. "I don't know where Hunter is right now, but if we're all going together, we should make him come with us. He was supposed to meet his father here. He'll just waste away in this city unless someone pulls him out of it."

They would all go together. The thought raised Criton's spirits.

"I'll find Hunter," he said, standing up. "The rest of my hair can wait."

It took quite some time to find him. The lord's son was in none of the expected places. Criton finally found him harborside, standing near the customs house and staring silently out to sea as the ships came and went. He had shaved his head since Criton last saw him, but his appearance was otherwise the same. He was dressed for war still, with his meticulously polished armor glinting in the late afternoon sun. With his shield on his back and his hand resting on his sword hilt, he looked almost as if he was anticipating an invasion.

"Hunter?" Criton began, tentatively.

"Yes." Hunter didn't even turn his head.

"What are you doing out here?"

"Thinking."

Criton took a deep breath. "About your father meeting you here?" he ventured.

Finally, Hunter's eyes met his. "About my life. If everyone's really gone, then I have nothing. I wanted to be Tarphae's champion one day. I thought I would stand before an army, challenging the enemy's best warriors, and I would slay them for the glory of my people. Now I have no nation to fight for. The king I would have championed stands alone on an island of the dead. I can't even go back, because the plague might be waiting for me there. My life is pointless."

Criton had no idea what to say in response, so he awkwardly changed the subject instead. "Isn't it hot for you in all that armor?"

Hunter's mouth twitched in what could have become a smile, but didn't. "It used to be, when my father first gave it to me. Now I'm used to it."

"Oh." There was nothing for it but to charge ahead, blind. "The rest of us are going to leave Atuna," Criton said. "Do you want to come?"

Hunter looked back at the sea and paused in thought. "You're the only countrymen I have left to fight for," he said finally.

"I don't think there'll be any fighting," Criton told him. "We're going to an abbey."

They set out late the next morning, traveling southwest along a well-worn dirt road. Phaedra sold much of her luggage before they left, and now traveled with a pack slung over her shoulders. Even so, she was a very fast walker. Criton had never walked so far before, and he soon began envying the others for their shoes. Bandu didn't have any either, but her feet were hard and callused, and she didn't limp when the pebbles dug into them. He considered letting his feet revert to the scaly claws he had been born with, but then everyone would see. It was bad enough that Phaedra knew – he was lucky she hadn't denounced him.

Four-foot limped along beside, occasionally baring his teeth at Narky. Apparently, Narky was not yet forgiven for teaching Bandu how to burn a wound.

"A wolf shouldn't travel on the roads," Narky told Bandu. "What if we run into some other travelers? Remember what happened on the boat?"

A short argument ensued, and they were all quietly relieved when Bandu agreed to take Four-foot and follow some distance behind them, staying off the road.

"You walk, we hunt," she said darkly, and when Phaedra asked if she would get lost without them, replied, "Four-foot can smell you."

Whatever he had hoped, traveling only made his thoughts darker. This was what Ma had wanted for him: a life outside her house, going wherever he must to find the dragon kin that he longed for. In Ma's stories, the hero usually had a long and arduous journey on the way to fulfill his final goal. Criton's journey was only just beginning, but he felt it couldn't get much worse than it already was. His mother was dead – wasn't that arduous enough?

He walked in a haze, even as the scenery should have fascinated him. The birds, the trees, the sounds and smells of the country – all were unfamiliar to him. He felt he ought to learn about these places, even though he didn't terribly care. Ma would have expected it.

They entered a forest whose scent was pleasant, if a little overpowering, and he decided to ask his companions about the trees. Thus he learned from Hunter that they were called guardian trees, and that the finest warships were made of their wood; he learned from Narky that they poisoned the ground for fruit trees and tukka trees, which were harvested for gum; and Phaedra told him a story about a soldier long ago who had transformed himself into a tree so that he could forever guard his love. His head filled with new information, Criton refrained from asking any more questions.

Another mile, and the road ran beside a brook, with a fen on one side and the woods on the other. It was a charming spot, really, with all the mystery and romance that lack of visibility can bring. It reminded him of how Ma used to let him look out the window on foggy days, so that he could imagine that the mist concealed his real father coming to reclaim his son.

A man stepped out of the woods in front of them, raising a hand to halt their approach. He was a tall man in his twenties – about Criton's height, in fact – with a long sword at his side and a grim expression on his face. Half of his upraised arm was covered with a tattoo of a boar.

"Right, then," he said, very matter-of-factly. "Let's have your weapons on the ground first, then your valuables. Nobody makes any trouble, nobody dies, yes?"

There were some other men visible now as well, two in the fen and three in the woods, standing with bows ready. Narky swore and put down his crossbow, but Hunter hesitated. He was clearly considering fighting his way out of this. Criton shook his head.

When he was still a boy playing at dragon-finding, Ma had used to laugh and warn about bandits on the road. Something about the way she had said it made him imagine the bandits as grinning buffoons who could never really stop a boy with dragon's blood and a dream. But these men were not buffoons, and they were not grinning. This was their livelihood. Criton's haze of mind was gone, and every muscle in his body longed for this fight, but his mind prevailed. How could a few boys whose beards were not yet full grown even consider resisting them?

There was a sudden bark from behind, and Phaedra screamed. The bandits turned their heads, which was enough of an opening for Hunter to attack. In an instant he was charging the woods, sword and shield in hand. It was too late for caution then. The thought made Criton's heart leap with a vicious joy. He looked to the fen and found the men there backing away from Four-foot's onslaught, their arrows already loosed ineffectually and their faces showing panic.

There were several more screams.

The leader of the bandits ran toward Criton, Narky and Phaedra, sword raised. It wasn't clear whether he meant to kill them or take them hostage, but Criton did not wait to find out. He drew in a deep breath and imagined that the man was his Ma's husband. Flames leapt from his mouth. The highwayman threw up his arm to shield his eyes, and when he dropped his arm again, blinking and trying to find his assailant, Criton tore his face off.

The man's screams were horrifying. Narky stared, and Phaedra was sick.

"What in the Gods' own...?" was all Narky seemed able to say.

Criton didn't answer. He was trying not to be sick himself.

Soon Hunter returned, his sword still clean. "They ran," he said, and then stopped short when he saw what Criton had done to the bandit leader.

They were all staring at him now, demanding an explanation. Criton suddenly felt that he had so much to answer for, he didn't even know where to start. He had killed someone, someone who had been alive just a moment ago. And it had come far too naturally to him.

His claws dripped blood. "My family is descended from dragons," he said.

Ma had always told him to hide his true nature from others, so that he wouldn't be persecuted in the outside world. What would they do to him, now that they knew what he was?

He could see Hunter trying to decide whether he still counted as a countryman to defend, or whether he was a dangerous monster to be slain. He had apparently not decided yet when Bandu arrived, surveying the bodies and looking pleased with herself.

"Now you are glad Four-foot is with us," she said.

"Yes," Hunter said, and turned his head toward the wolf. The hero of the morning was busy feasting on one of the fallen men. Criton's hands might be covered in blood, but for the moment he was forgotten.

Thank the Gods for that.

9
Bandu

After that, nobody objected to Four-foot's company. He and Bandu were welcomed into the pack, and they all traveled together toward the abbey, which was apparently just another word for a big den made out of stone. Bandu did not think she would ever understand why people needed all these different words for the same few things. Four-foot's kind never wasted their time finding new ways to say the same things.

Poor Four-foot. His cut was swelling, and she didn't like its color. Was it supposed to do that, after they burned it? She didn't know, but she hoped the abbey people would. What would she do, if Four-foot died? Her memories from before she met him were vague and disturbing. Just thinking about losing him made her feel more sympathetic toward Phaedra, who had already lost her own Four-foot.

The others had been awfully surprised about Criton's scales and sharp hands, and now they seemed to have decided to pretend nothing had happened. Bandu wondered how they had failed to notice it all to begin with. They weren't very perceptive people.

They were being just as blind now, ignoring that angry crow. It had been following them for some time already, ranting about some slight it had received. Bandu did not think the crow's anger was directed at her, but she couldn't be sure. She left it a piece of the dried meat that the others had bought for their journey. Even if it wasn't mad at her personally, she could at least be courteous.

The abbey, when they reached it, was a very large den with one of her kind's stone gardens to one side. A man came out of it to greet them as they arrived, blessing them in the name of his God. Bandu did not know much of the Gods, though she remembered a big man who had once prayed for guidance. Was it her father? He had been crying, but the next day his expression was hard as stone. Bandu did not like the Gods.

Phaedra spoke to the abbey man, and Narky told him about Four-foot. The man looked concerned. He came closer, reaching out his hand for the wolf to smell. Four-foot seemed to like him. Bandu relaxed.

"I am Brother Gedrel," the man said. "May I look at his wound?"

Four-foot licked Brother Gedrel's hand, and Bandu nodded. While he inspected Four-foot's side, Narky spoke. "You're not dressed like any priest I've ever seen."

Brother Gedrel only smiled and said, "I am not a priest. Priests are leaders, those who can pray and give sacrifices on behalf of others. A friar is but a man who has renounced worldly pleasures and dedicated his own life to the service of his God. I pray and sacrifice as any other man would, and command no greater authority."

"What good is that, then?" Narky asked.

Gedrel laughed. "I do not know. What more can a man hope to gain, besides the favor of his God?"

"I don't know, how about a wife and children, and power and respect, and some money to wash it down?"

The friar did not reply to this. Phaedra looked as if she could have punched Narky.

"He means no harm," Hunter said, putting a warning

hand on Narky's shoulder.

Narky shrugged the hand off. "Don't tell me what I mean." But he was quiet after that.

Brother Gedrel finished inspecting Four-foot's side and stood up. "We can do our best, but I'm afraid it doesn't look good. To burn a wound is not enough: one must keep it clean after cautery. Perhaps even more than before it."

Bandu looked at Four-foot and began to cry. "He will die?"

"I can't know for sure," Brother Gedrel said, "but, like I said, it doesn't look good. We'll do our best."

Phaedra put her arms around Bandu, and Criton came too, more timidly. Bandu knelt and cried into Four-foot's fur, while the new members of her pack closed around her.

"Please live," she whispered to him, and he whined at her distress. "My kind are not enough."

They stayed with the friars for many days, while the weather grew hotter and Four-foot grew weaker. His cut turned black, and its bad color grew outward. He was in pain, she knew, but she could not end his life, much though the others urged her to. The friars had a drink that they made from flowers to take the pain away, and when Four-foot could no longer lap it up on his own, Bandu sat with his head in her lap and gently poured it down his throat.

He died with his eyes open. Bandu's pack mourned with her, even though they had been afraid of him at first. She was grateful for their company. The friars offered to bury Four-foot in their stone garden, but that was not the way of his kind. Instead, Bandu left him out for the angry crows and the other animals to feast on. The others in her pack were shocked, but they let her have her way. Narky said it was too hot to dig holes anyway.

Phaedra asked how she had met Four-foot, but she could not remember. That made her cry again. It felt as if, with Four-foot gone, Two-foot's memories were slipping away too. She did like the name Bandu though, and she was glad she had chosen it. It meant that she would carry Four-foot's heartbeat with her forever, which was what Phaedra would have called 'appropriate.' Nobody else knew why she was called Bandu, and that was also appropriate. Four-foot's heartbeat had been a secret that only she knew about, and she wanted it to stay that way.

The day after Four-foot died, Brother Gedrel left them. He said only that he had stayed too long, but Phaedra understood what he meant. She explained to them that the Brothers of Gedrel's order never stayed in one place for more than a year or two, but went from holy place to holy place in between larger voyages. Gedrel had been in charge at the Crossroads not because he was smarter or stronger or older or better than the others, but because he had been there longest and would soon be leaving. After he was gone, Brother Tanatos was the head of the friars. Bandu did not like him as much. He spoke more, and listened less.

Criton talked to Brother Tanatos a lot. He asked very many questions about some kind of things called dragons, and Brother Tanatos always gave him long answers. Those answers clearly bothered Criton. He seemed especially sad when the friar said the word, 'Extinct.'

Phaedra seemed to understand everything, and she didn't mind explaining. Bandu was glad to have her. Phaedra used a needle and thread to make Bandu's new coverings fit better, and Bandu agreed to practice her speech with her. If she couldn't live in the forest with Four-foot anymore, she would have to learn how to speak better.

Phaedra did not really like it here, Bandu realized. Not anymore, anyway. She *wanted* to like it, but she didn't. The trouble was that Phaedra loved to learn new things, and she knew too much about this place already. She took to pacing around the little building, restless and bored. Bandu thought that people who loved to learn should not be so good at it. It would last them longer that way.

Bandu did not know what she would do without Four-foot, but she knew that staying here would not bring him back. If Phaedra was done here, that meant it was time to go.

But before they all managed to leave, Brother Tanatos found a way to pull Bandu aside and talk to her.

"You are about to become something that you never were before," he said. "It will be frightening, and you will think you are losing yourself. Don't be afraid, and don't blame it on your friends. Your sadness is the sadness of leaving childhood behind, which is something we all must do. You understand?"

Bandu's knowledge of words was getting better. It made her feel much more confident in her answer.

"No," she said.

10
Hunter

They would travel together for safety until they found reason to part ways. Hunter doubted it would take long: Criton wanted to go looking for dragons, Narky didn't, Bandu was most comfortable in the woods, and Phaedra had only ever slept in a bed. Soon Hunter would have to make a decision. Where would he go? With whom would he stay? There was no obvious answer, but that was not really the problem. The problem was that he didn't care.

He had had plans before, for a whole life. Now those plans were useless, and he could not think of a new one. It seemed that he was not as resourceful as Phaedra.

When they left the abbey, the crows were waiting for them. There must have been at least fifty of the birds watching them from outside the grounds, and they greeted the survivors of Tarphae with a chorus of raucous voices.

"I wish those damned birds would quiet down and go away," Narky said.

"Quiet," said Phaedra. "The crow is sacred to Ravennis."

"They must be here for me," Hunter said.

Narky stared at him. "Why would they be here for you?"

Hunter let his breath out through his teeth, and tried to explain. "Father went to see the Oracle of Ravennis, the

Day Before. That's why he made me go."

He thought they should understand, but they clearly didn't. Oh, well. Hunter had never been very good at explaining himself. Father and Kataras were outgoing, talkative people, but Hunter and his mother were quiet by nature. When he was having a bad day, Hunter used to go and sit with Mother in her room. They never spoke, but he would sit beside her and polish his shield while she did needlework. An hour of their focused silence always made him feel better.

"The day before what?" said Narky, and Phaedra asked, "What did the Oracle say?" Bandu said nothing, but she was looking at him in that unsettling way of hers.

"Father asked how to give me a long life," Hunter said, feeling their eyes on him. "The Oracle told him to send me away from Tarphae on the first ship he could find."

"Makes sense," said Narky. "But I don't see why that would make Ravennis send a bunch of crows after you now."

Neither did Hunter, but it was the only connection he could think of. "Maybe we should ask," he said.

"Oh, sure," Narky said, and stepped toward the crowd of birds. "O holy birds, what are you here for?"

A crow flew at his head, cawing furiously, and Narky had to duck and beat it off with a cry of surprise. Criton laughed, but the others were solemn.

"Don't insult the Gods," Phaedra scolded. "Have you learned nothing? Our people were killed by a God, possibly because someone was foolish enough to insult one. The Gods take these slights seriously."

"Why should they?" Narky asked, looking rueful.

"Now is not the time," she said sternly. "I suggest you apologize to Ravennis as soon as you get the chance. Through sacrifice," she added, when it looked as though Narky might make a sarcastic apology to the murder of crows.

Hunter sighed. "What I meant was, we should go see the Oracle and ask what we've done to anger Ravennis."

"The Oracle is at Laarna," Phaedra said. "North of Atuna."

"Where do you learn these things?" Narky asked.

As they turned northward, the crows took flight. It gave Hunter an ominous feeling. He did not think the birds would leave them alone for long.

After some time, Bandu asked, "What is oracle?"

Phaedra explained it to her, as best she could. It seemed that Phaedra had studied continental religions extensively. When she had finished explaining about oracles, she expounded upon the nature of Gods, Their servants, and Their need for humans to do Their work.

"The Gods are infinitely greater and more powerful than people," she said at one point, "but that doesn't mean They don't need us, because Their power is remote. I like the way Katinaras puts it best. He likens the heavens to a wire mesh, with the Gods on one side and our world on the other. The Gods are huge and powerful, but that makes Them too big to fit through the gaps in the mesh. Only Their fingers are small enough to fit through, so as powerful as They are, Their power does have limits in this world. Especially when They're opposed by another God.

"They're not really fingers, of course, Bandu, that's only a metaphor. A metaphor is – well, no, let's not get into that. But that's why the Gods pay so much attention to what we people do. When we worship Them and give Them sacrifices, we strengthen the fingers, and when we oppose Them or slay Their followers, it weakens Them and makes Them angry. Because even though we see only a tiny part of Them in this world, we play a big part in Their relations with each other."

"How?" asked Criton.

"Well," Phaedra said, "the Gods are frequently in conflict. Since our actions can strengthen or weaken a God's fingers, we can have a real effect on these conflicts. If your fingers are completely cut off, you can't really stand up to your enemies on your own side of the mesh. Obviously it's a lot more complicated than that, but that's why I love Katinaras' analogy. It makes so much sense, even if it is a little simplistic."

Hunter scratched at his scalp, where the hair was just beginning to grow back. "My father once said that when the men of Ardis conquered the plainsfolk to their north, they killed their Gods. Are you saying those Gods were actually killed on Their own side of the mesh by the Ardismen's God?"

"Yes, exactly."

Hunter considered this. He thought he was beginning to understand the analogy, but he suspected that his understanding would dissipate as soon as Phaedra stopped explaining it all. He also couldn't help but notice that now everyone *but* Bandu seemed interested in the conversation. The girl's eyes had glazed over and she was tromping along silently, her gaze fixed on the road ahead.

"But if someone insults the Gods," asked Criton, "that can't possibly weaken the fingers all on its own, can it? What harm can it do?"

"I guess it humiliates Them in front of everyone They know," Narky said suddenly.

"Yes," said Phaedra, surprised. "Yes, I guess it must."

They were traveling due north, not quite the same way they had come, but their journey still took them through the same thick forest of guardian trees and tall milk-rimmed shrubs. The road here became a narrow path through the undergrowth, at times barely discernable. Their progress was slow and loud, until Bandu tapped Hunter on the shoulder and whispered, "Stop."

Hunter looked about, trying to find whatever was distressing her, but he could see and hear nothing out of the ordinary. Then Bandu pointed and he saw, in the branches high above the path, two creatures silently watching them.

They were tall as men, with bald heads and teeth filed down to points, and their hands and feet were great birdlike talons. Their bodies were pale, and at first he thought that they were wearing black cloaks, but then he realized that those were actually huge black wings, folded at rest.

Hunter unslung his shield from his back as quickly as he could, and tightened the straps around his arm. "What are those things?" he whispered.

Bandu shook her head, and Narky said, "What things?" followed by, "Oh hell!"

At this, the pale monsters spread their wings and leapt from their boughs, screeching like birds of prey. Hunter drew his sword, and in an instant the things were upon them. His sword caught one in the chest as it flew at him, and the force of it knocked him off his feet and wrenched the sword from his hand.

Criton had not ducked as quickly as the others, and the second monster caught him by the shoulders with its lower talons. Its wings beat the air, and its upper claws made to tear at his face. Yet before they could, the pale thing had suddenly let go and flipped backward onto the ground, ducking under a burst of flame from the young man's mouth.

Hunter had never seen Criton's fire before, though Narky had told him about the bandit leader. For a moment he just stared. But the monster had dodged the flames unharmed, and it now leapt at Criton again, knocking him onto his back and tearing at his flesh. Hunter rose to his feet and charged the creature, throwing his weight against his shield. At the impact, the thing let go of Criton and fell against the ground next to Hunter, who rolled to his feet and was ready once more. The monster shrieked and its claws reached out, but Hunter knocked them aside with his shield and caught the monster's face with it on his backswing. While it reeled, his hand found the knife that he kept in a sheath at the small of his back. After another bash of his shield against its head, he ran the blade across the monster's throat.

Blood spattered and the thing collapsed on the ground, shrinking away from him. Then the strangest thing happened. The monster went right on shrinking, shrinking under its feathers until it became a simple raven with its throat cut open. Hunter looked with surprise back at where the other had fallen, and found another raven impaled upon his sword. The sword looked so strange, yards from where he had lost it, now several times the size of the creature that had borne it away.

Criton staggered to his feet, his face and shirt covered in blood. "What were those things?" he asked.

"I don't know," said Hunter, at the same time as Phaedra said, "Angels."

Criton wiped his face on his sleeve, revealing a fairly deep scratch above his eye and a bloody nose, but no more. His chest and shoulders were bloodied too, though he still seemed to have full use of his arms. That was a good sign.

"Angels?" Narky said disbelievingly. "Those things?"

"An angel is a messenger from a God," Phaedra told him, in an irritated voice. "There is no other meaning to the word."

"Then we're in real trouble," said Hunter, retrieving his sword and trying to shake the dead raven off it. "Ravennis might have been warning us earlier, but now it looks like He's just trying to kill us."

"But why?" Phaedra asked. "What was He warning us about? He can't possibly be the one who sent the plague to Tarphae – why would He have told your father to save you before, if He meant to kill us now? We must have recently offended Him, but I can't think how. The Gods sometimes forgive those who repent their sins, but you can't repent for a sin you don't know you've committed!"

"Well, we don't have time to ask the Oracle," Narky said. "If we're going to pray for forgiveness, we'd better do it now."

"Yes," Criton said, "now would be the time." The forest had grown suddenly dark, and he was pointing up at the skyline.

Hunter looked up, and his heart sank. It was only just before noon, but the sun was nowhere to be seen. The sky was black with birds.

11
Narky

When the sky turned dark, Narky could not help himself. He ran, ran from the others, ran into the forest as if it could shield him. He did not even know why he ran, pointless as it was, but his unreasoning reasons were good enough for him. The sky blackened further, and he tripped and fell to his knees. Maybe the birds would content themselves with the others. Maybe they would forget him here.

He rose to his feet again, and ran some more. Where was the sun? Shouldn't some angry Sun God be coming to his rescue right about now? Why should Ravennis go after *him* like this? He knew no oracles, and had done nothing more to harm the God than to talk sarcastically to a bird. Still, he repented for that as he ran. If what the Gods wanted was repentance, They would have it. Gods, They would have it.

He tripped over roots and tore his way through brambles, but deep as he got into the forest, the darkness was always behind him. Behind and above. Behind and above, and coming closer. He repented for his callousness and his sarcasm. He repented for his rudeness to others. He repented for the murder, though he didn't see why Ravennis should particularly care about that. No, that was no good! He repented for the murder again, harder.

For a boy who had thought that getting killed by a mob was the worst thing that could happen to him, he was certainly having his eyes opened. The fear of that was nothing next to the primal, unreasoning fear of being torn to pieces by the Gods themselves. Or by Their messengers. Or by an Aspect of a God, or whatever they wanted to call it; it was beastly and horrifying. He ran, ran and wished that he could shed his skin, if it would let him run any faster.

"I'm sorry if I humiliated You," he gasped as he ran. Or maybe he only thought it, but thought it so loudly that he could hear it in his skull.

I should have known what it was like. When they humiliated me, they laughed and stared and made me want to die. But when someone humiliates You in front of the other Gods, You actually do die, don't You? They sense Your weakness, and they kill You, sooner or later, unless You can prove Your strength. I'm so sorry. I'm so small and weak, and please, you don't need to kill me to prove Your strength. I'm so afraid, can that be enough? Please forgive me, I didn't mean any of it. I will never laugh at a friar again, or be sarcastic to a bird, or do anything to make You angry. Oh Ravennis, forgive me!

The air grew darker, darker than he knew it could be, and heavier. His chest burned and his limbs ached, but still he ran.

I'm sorry, he thought, *sorry about the murder. I hated Ketch, but he didn't hate me. He thought I was nothing, just a rude nothing, and he was right. I didn't kill him on purpose, but I wanted to. I meant to. So what if it was a mistake? It was a mistake I wanted to make, or otherwise I wouldn't have taken the crossbow with me. Why did I need a crossbow? It's not like I thought Ketch would try to kill me, I just didn't want him to hit me again. To spank me, and make me feel like a stupid, weak child. I'm sorry. He didn't deserve to die, but I do.*

Please, I repent! I know I deserve it, but I really, really don't want to die this way! Why can't I die an old fool in a bed, surrounded by foolish children? Oh, please let me die like that. What are another fifty years to you? Oh no, no, I'm sorry! I can't help thinking this way, I'm sorry I'm sorry I'm sorry I'm sorry don't kill me please.

Could Ravennis hear him? Did the Gods only listen to prayers that were spoken over a sacrificial altar, with a bull's blood running down its sides? What wouldn't he have done to have an altar like that here in the forest! He would slaughter seven bulls and seven rams, and however many doves it took to feed a sky's worth of ravens. Bandu was so smart to have given her wolf to these ravens. Surely Ravennis would forgive *her*.

The darkness was closing in, he could feel it. The sound of millions of feathers, thousands of wings beating all at once. Every moment they were growing louder. Usually a flock of birds beat its wings in unison, but there was no unison in this, no pulse, just a chaotic roar of so many wings flapping as hard as they could. What was Ravennis a God of, other than ravens? Narky wished he could remember. Ravennis had a famous oracle, and crows were sacred to Him, and that was all the attention Narky had paid to the subject. Was He a God of mercy? No, Narky remembered now, He was the God of Fate. Cold and impersonal. Unavoidable, like the beaks and talons of so many birds. How long would it take them to tear all the flesh off his bones? It would happen much faster than Narky could repent for all his sins, that was for sure.

He was sorry for the disrespect he had shown his father, and for the dryness with which he had taken the news of his death. Of everyone's death, really. Eramia, and Tank, and the farmers and shepherds, the blacksmith and the fisherman's lads; even Mother and her ironmonger, who must also be hidden somewhere on the island with seawater in their lungs. Why had he not mourned them? Death was such a horrible thing; people needed to be pitied and mourned and forgiven, yes, forgiven! He forgave his mother, as well as he could. What had she ever done to him? Only left. She had not killed him, had not humiliated him on purpose, had never murdered anyone. She had only run off and tried to be happy. Surely she did not deserve to die for that! Why had he condemned her so quickly in his mind?

Any second now, any second. They were so close – they must be! But he was too afraid to turn his head and look.

Would he meet Mother again, in the afterlife? Would he have the chance to apologize for hating her so? Would he be able to apologize to Ketch? For the first time, he hoped so. He hoped he could apologize to his pa, for disrespecting him just like everyone else did, and to Eramia for misunderstanding her. She had never loved him, but she had never meant to lead him on. She was only being friendly, friendly! He had never had a friend before, and had not understood.

He should have been able to call the other refugees his friends by now, but he had never really been *their* friend. He thought they could become his friends, if he could stop being so rude to them all the time. Now it was too late though, wasn't it? People did not make friends in the afterlife, he was sure of that. They were too busy being dead.

What a wasted life! He wished he had more time to sort himself out. He could have been a really worthwhile person, he thought. He would learn from Criton and Hunter, who had killed others only to protect themselves and their friends, not out of anger or pride. He would learn from Phaedra, who was so interested in the Gods that surely *she* would know how to repent properly. Hell, he would even learn from Bandu, whose love for her wolf had been so much stronger than anything Narky had ever felt. For all her savagery, Bandu was far more human than he was.

How could he repent for all the harm he had done, for all the potential he had wasted so completely? Yet there was even more to repent for – there *must* be more to repent for! He repented for the dove that he had sacrificed without any meaning, and for being so useless both times that the others had fought for him. He repented for his inability to heal Four-foot, and for his suggestion of burning a wound that would never heal. He repented for his greed, and for his theft back in Atuna, and for... oh Gods! The necklace in his shoe! Narky fell to the ground and pulled his shoe off, and there it was: the silver bird symbol, upon which he had been stepping for some three weeks, all the way from Atuna. Stepping on it! It was not just any bird. It was a raven.

O Ravennis, he thought, as the crows engulfed him. *I'm sorry!*

12
Phaedra

After the ravens swept over them, Phaedra and her companions looked around in confusion. They were all unharmed, except for the one that was missing.

"Where's Narky?" Hunter asked.

The ravens had done such damage to the undergrowth as they flew through the forest that any trail Narky might have left by catching on brambles or pressing down on the moss was completely covered over.

"Birds," said Bandu. "Everything smells like birds."

When they finally found Narky, he was lying unconscious in a pool of clotted blood, breathing very faintly. His face was bruised, and his skin lacerated. By the looks of it, he had nearly bled out. Clutched in his hand was a silver necklace, adorned with a symbol of Ravennis. Phaedra took her spare traveling clothes out of her new pack, and she and Bandu did their best to bind Narky's wounds with them. In the meantime, Criton monitored Narky's breathing, and Hunter just stood and watched.

"How foolish," Hunter said, out loud but clearly to himself. "I trained so hard for war and never thought to learn how to care for wounds."

"Narky knows this better," Bandu said sadly. "He helped

the leaf man, on the water."

Phaedra gave her a pat on her shoulder. "Nonsense, Bandu, you're a natural."

They had to cut him out of his shirt to get at his chest lacerations, and there they found something very strange indeed. Amid the clotted blood and loose skin, a symbol had been burned onto Narky's chest, identical to the one on the necklace.

As they did their best to wrap one of Phaedra's longer skirts around his body, Narky moaned. He did not open his eyes.

"I think we'd better stay here tonight," Phaedra said, "and let him wake up on his own. He's lost so much blood."

"It's a good thing it's still dry," Hunter reflected. "We have no tents and no shelter."

"He needs to drink," Bandu stated. "He needs more for blood."

They coaxed some water down Narky's throat and then settled down around his body, as if by sitting on all sides of him they could protect him from further harm.

"What do you think happened?" Criton asked.

"I guess it was Narky Ravennis was after," Phaedra said. "He must have repented for whatever it was he did. Ravennis wouldn't have let him live otherwise."

Hunter looked down at Narky curiously. "Where did he get that necklace, I wonder?"

Narky woke up once during the night, while Phaedra was taking watch. He was mumbling deliriously, and seemed to be under the impression that he had died. He whispered that he wished he could have been their friend, and apologized repeatedly for something that he could not quite explain. If his eyes had not been open, she would have thought him to be dreaming.

The next day, they decided that it would be safe to move him. With Hunter on one side and Criton on the other, Narky staggered along until they came out of the forest at a small village on the edge of a plain. There were only some forty villagers in total, but they were kind and hospitable, and they let the islanders stay with them a whole two weeks while Narky recovered.

Phaedra was beginning to question whether she would ever become a weaver in Atuna. They had all been on the verge of parting ways when the ravens had changed their plans – could the timing really be a coincidence? She had the uneasy feeling that the Gods were watching all five of them a little more closely than They ought to be. Ravennis had clearly taken an interest in Narky for some reason, and His oracle was responsible for saving Hunter. When the fishing boat had been delayed over and over again, Phaedra had felt as if the Gods were conspiring to make her wait. Now she wondered if they really had been.

The Gods must still have been watching over Narky, because he recovered quite nicely, without any trace of infection. When he could once more walk independently, he recruited the others' help in building an altar.

Phaedra was going to offer to buy a goat from the villagers, but rather than sacrificing an animal, Narky placed his crossbow and his quiver of bolts upon the altar and set them ablaze. "Let my cowardice burn," he said, and placed the silver symbol of Ravennis around his neck.

Toward the end of Narky's recovery, the villagers became noticeably nervous. The few elders seemed to be sadly shaking their heads every time Phaedra looked at them, and the

younger villagers whispered urgently to each other and looked often at their children. Phaedra asked one of the grandmothers about it, as the woman came to inspect Narky's final set of bindings. She was in her forties, her hair just starting to gray. Like the others of her generation, she shook her head sadly.

"The young ones want us to leave the village, before the Gallant Ones come back."

"The Gallant Ones?"

The woman nodded. "You can ask old Garan about them, she knows all 'bout history and them things."

Garan was the oldest woman in the village, a crone of seventy-some years who walked with a stick. When Phaedra found her, she was rendering a small pot of chicken fat.

"The Gallant Ones?" she repeated. "Eh, I can tell you 'bout them."

She stirred her pot contemplatively. "Started in Atuna, some forty years ago. They had a king there once, just like the Ardismen did before they rose up and gave themselves a war council instead. Well, in Atuna the king was no good, the way kings is, and their people up and killed him and put a council in his place, like they have now. But there was a princeling got away with some half the king's hearthmen, and they been waging war ever since. They've got no chance against Atuna, of course, it being a walled city and all, and them being only thirty strong or so, but so long as the Atunaeans don't send out an army to find 'em, they keep riding round and making trouble."

Phaedra had found a stool next to Garan's, and she now sat with her knees by her chin, her hands clasped around her ankles. "And these people have been here?" she asked.

"Well, the princeling was only fifteen at the time, but he's a reglar old bandit now, some forty years on. They come here 'bout a year ago, took our money and ate our lambs and said they'd be back next year. The young ones say we oughta leave and take up with that wizard fellow, but we older folks don't like the thought of saying goodbye to our village."

Phaedra was not sure she had heard her right. "Did you say a wizard?"

"You heard me right. Psander, he calls himself, come here some two or three months ago, said he was settling in the area and wanted to offer us permanent shelter in his fortress. Said we could live in his walls and feed our livestock on the plains, and all he wanted was to share our food and maybe get some help 'round the house now and then."

The old woman looked at her sharply, noting her excitement. "Oh sure, the others love that idea when there's Gallant Ones about, but it sounds far too good to be true to us as has brains."

Phaedra did her best to look as though she agreed. She didn't mean to be rude, but an actual wizard! Living nearby! It was fair to worry about moving to live with him permanently, but for the curious traveler, it *was* almost too good to be true. Wizards were supposed to have knowledge and power beyond the realms of men – they were also supposed to be secretive and aloof. Here was one who actually invited visitors!

"I'm sure you're right," Phaedra said soothingly. "I've heard that wizards are dangerous. But can you afford to feed the Gallant Ones next time they come?"

Garan shook her head. "We're lucky it's been a good year; no one starved this time. If they'd stayed longer..."

"If this Psander is offering protection –"

"I didn't say I liked going hungry, but won't no good come of trusting a wizard."

When Phaedra told the others about her conversation with Garan, Criton became just as excited as she was. Narky did not. "Wizards are supposed to be evil."

"You're just basing that on stories," Phaedra said. "Doesn't finding out the truth interest you at all?"

"Not really."

"If all the townspeople leave," Hunter pointed out, "we won't be able to stay here anyway. Did she say when they were planning to make up their minds?"

"They're deciding what to do tomorrow. Hopefully they'll go, and we'll be able to tag along with them."

The islanders were not invited to the next day's town meeting, but the final decision was hardly kept a secret:

the younger townsfolk had won the day. The next few days were spent packing up everything but the houses themselves, preparing for the journey. Narky put up some resistance, but after his experience in the woods, he was too afraid of being left alone. Phaedra told him that they were all going, and that was that.

Nobody knew exactly where Psander's fortress was, but it was supposed to be somewhere upon the plain, and the wizard had apparently told the townspeople that those who sought him in peace could not fail to find it. At last they set off, driving animals in front of them and lugging their pots and pans, pushing barrows and pulling little children along beside them. Laden as they were, they had barely gone ten miles before the sun dipped below the horizon.

But as the sky grew dark, a path lit up before them. There was a new moon that night, and the stars were hidden behind clouds, yet ahead of them stood a moonlit path. The younger townspeople proclaimed it a miracle, but even through her excitement, Phaedra had to admit that the magic gave her an ominous feeling. It felt like a challenge to the Gods and a rebellion against nature.

They traveled another hour down the eerie path, while the young villagers slowly succumbed to their elders' anxiety. Their initial cheers were soon forgotten, and they plodded onward in silence. After a time, the clouds drifted on, and the stars could be seen above. Then the path abruptly ended.

Everyone stopped and looked around, but in the dark, this field was indistinguishable from the rest of the landscape. Each traveler looked to the others, weary and frightened, for answers. Criton was peering ahead into the darkness, as if staring intently enough could make a fortress appear. Narky shuddered, and put a hand on his chest where the burn was hiding underneath his shirt. Bandu only sniffed the air and kept walking, past the villagers and past the end of the path.

"Bandu!" cried Phaedra, chasing after the girl, afraid of losing her. She heard the clank of Hunter's armor as the rest of the islanders joined her, following Bandu into the darkness. Bandu hadn't gone far, but she did not stop walking until Phaedra caught hold of her arm. "What in the Gods' names do you think you're doing?"

Bandu looked at her silently and made a gesture with her other hand, palm upward. Phaedra followed her motion and stopped, gaping. A huge fortress stood in front of them where there had been none before, rising to the sky, blocking out the stars.

Book II

Silent Hall

13
Criton

For a moment, they all just looked at each other. Hunter, one hand on his sword hilt, stepped forward and knocked on the gate. His first raps were quiet and timid, his next few loud and aggressive, as if he was trying to quickly compensate for a weak first impression. At length, a voice called down to them from above.

"Who are you, and what business do you have with me?"

It was Phaedra who answered the voice. "We're here with the people of a village, who heard that there were safe lodgings to be had with you here."

"I see. And who are you? Where do you come from and what Gods do you worship?"

"We five are from Tarphae, where Karassa is worshipped."

There was a brief pause. "Tarphae?" the voice repeated. "Fascinating. You'd better come in. But first tell the others that they may not bring their mules here. Other livestock may enter, but they must set their mules free."

A strange request, Criton thought, but Phaedra passed the message back, as the first villagers caught up with them. This set off a brief debate, as the owners of the mules naturally objected to the wizard's conditions. But they had come this far and had little choice but to comply in the end.

As soon as they did, the gates opened of their own accord.

Hunter was slow to move, so Criton led the way. As he stepped over the threshold, a fire sprang up ahead. They walked between long walls of stone in order to reach it, and soon after found themselves in a huge courtyard.

Behind a blazing fire pit stood a middle-aged woman in what appeared to be a nightgown. She did not speak, but waited until the villagers joined them. The geese, sheep and goats came first, plodding wearily through the gates and then, once their drivers were no longer concerned with them, standing in everybody's way. Yet for all that, they made very little noise. Something about this place was cowing them into silence.

At last, the woman spoke. "I am Psander," she said. "Welcome to my home."

Criton looked around incredulously, but he found the crowd in awe. In awe of a woman in a night robe! Were they seeing what he was seeing?

"O Great Wizard," one of the villagers said. "We have heard that you accept guests, or tenants, if you will. For those who would serve you."

The woman smiled. "You are all welcome here, though you will have to obey my rules so long as you live within my walls. I will not impose many of them."

The villagers all nodded nervously. A baby cried.

"Settle yourselves," the woman said. "It is late, and you have traveled far."

The villagers accepted this without audible complaint, and several more fires sprang up around them, lighting the courtyard and revealing a number of large tents all clustered around a single well. It seemed that Psander was well prepared for their arrival.

The woman beckoned to the islanders and walked past them to one side of the gate, villagers bowing out of her way. The height of the fortress was in the tower above the gate, which rose imposingly for several stories before vanishing into the night sky. A door in one side, through which Psander led them, opened on an austere entry hall.

"Survivors from Tarphae," she said, shaking her head in some wonder. "Remarkable."

"You know about the plague?" Narky asked suspiciously. "How?"

The woman shrugged. She had mousy brown hair above a narrow face, with light-colored skin even paler than the villagers. But her eyes were lively, and despite her age, she did not look as if she had ever known physical hardship.

"These things are known," she said. "Let us leave that for later. Stay for a few days, and there will be plenty of time to talk. But first, I must know about *you*." She pointed at Bandu. "I haven't seen your kind of magic in a long time."

Bandu shook her head. "I don't know magic."

Psander made a bemused expression and turned to Narky. "What do you see, when you look at me?"

Narky looked as if he was being asked a trick question. "A wizard," he said. "I've never seen one before, but you look like one. Tall, long beard, coat of sigils and all that. Regular wizard, I suppose. I'm sorry, I'm not a very polite person. You should ask someone else…"

"No," said Psander. "I think that will do just fine. The reason I ask is that what your two companions see is this."

She did nothing, made no motion, and yet suddenly Phaedra snorted – Phaedra, of all people! – Narky took a step back, and Hunter just stood in place, blinking.

"You're not a wizard," Phaedra said, "you're a–"

"I *am* a wizard," the woman said sternly. "I believe you have never met one before?"

Phaedra had nothing to say to that, but she still looked at Psander incredulously.

"Pardon me for not dressing better," Psander said drily, "but those without the Wizard's Sight can't see what I'm wearing anyway. I wasn't expecting to find two sighted people traveling with a town's worth of goatherds. Why don't you introduce yourselves?"

They all did so, a little stiffly. But before they could ask her any questions, Psander said, "Let us adjourn until tomorrow morning. I'm sure your stories will be fascinating, and I hope you do not plan on leaving very soon. The townspeople will make their beds in the courtyard, but I do have spare rooms indoors, if you like."

After their night of traveling, everybody but Bandu seemed happy with this idea. In the end even she consented to stay in, perhaps because none of the others were willing to sleep outside with her. Psander led them up a staircase by the light of a ghostly candle that appeared and hovered above her palm. She showed them to a set of rooms on the second floor. The boys each chose a room, but Phaedra and Bandu stayed together. They had grown close since Fourfoot's death.

Criton dreamt that Psander was asking him all about his childhood, and that he was telling her about dragon hunting instead. At first it was sort of a funny dream, because she seemed to grow comically frustrated at each answer, but then she began to ask him more about dragons, and when he did not know the answers to her questions, he found himself telling her about his childhood after all. It was a pleasant dream, and until he awoke, it did not trouble him at all.

In the morning, Phaedra seemed sleepy, Bandu angry, and Hunter quiet and a little sad, which was really just the same as always. Narky, though, looked terrified in a way that Criton had never seen before. Had he also dreamt that Psander was interrogating him? If so, then what about?

Thanks to the villagers, breakfast was goose eggs with bread and pickled capers, a meal that even Psander could not help but join them for. She was dressed more appropriately today, in a long brown robe with flowing sleeves, but it soon became clear that the others still saw a man with a beard. Hunter looked at her suspiciously, and Narky squinted as if he could will himself to see the woman again. Bandu ate in brooding silence.

"How long have you lived here?" Phaedra asked.

"Not long," Psander said, a corner of her mouth twisting wryly. "Fortresses need not take so long to build, if you know what you're doing."

After breakfast, Psander told Criton she would speak with him alone. "Concerning dragons," she said.

Before he could follow her, Bandu caught his hand. "Be careful," she warned him.

"I'll be fine," he said, though he was hardly sure of it. He knew he was letting his childhood passion for dragons override his good sense, but it was a risk worth taking. When would he get another chance?

Psander had a library like nothing Criton had ever imagined, even when Phaedra spoke of her father's library. Shelves upon shelves of scrolls rose twenty feet into the air in all directions. There were no ladders. When Psander called a name, a scroll rose off a distant shelf and fluttered down to her outstretched hand.

"I'm afraid that dragons are not my expertise," she said, "though they were a hobby of my mentor. He had many more writings about them in his own tower, before it was destroyed. He was trying to compile a codex about them, I believe. A codex is a wonderful thing, you know. It's marvelous not having to find your place in a long scroll, but being able to save your spot with just a piece of straw, or a chicken bone, or what have you. My mentor was altogether enamored of them.

"Where was I? Oh yes, dragons. I know something of them, and of your people. In fact, I have here a short piece of writing by Gardanon, about the regime of the Dragon Touched in Ardis. The original text is over two hundred years old, though mine is but a copy. It was written very shortly after the dragons' war ended. I believe it's the sort of book you're looking for."

"How do you know what I'm looking for?" Criton said. "Was that really you, in my dream?"

She smiled that dangerous smile of hers, and kept the scroll pressed against her chest. "Of course. It is always best to know everything you can about subjects before you have to deal with them. It's just the same with people. But I didn't have to walk your dreams to know that you were Dragon Touched. Just as you saw my true form the moment you gazed upon me, I also saw yours.

"Mind you, I'm not all that surprised that there were some Dragon Touched who survived the purge of Ardis. What really astonishes me is your companion, Bandu. She has all the markings of fairy magic, but I could swear she was a pureblood human. I'd love to know how she does it."

She was keeping that scroll from him, after making such a big show of it, and now she was changing the subject. "Can I have that scroll?" Criton asked. "Do you want something for it?"

Psander nodded and spoke on, still meandering. "I traveled extensively after my mentor died, but when I say that I have settled here, I mean that quite permanently. Circumstances have changed, and I would rather not go out and draw attention to myself. But there are things I still need from the outside world, things that I would pay quite well in order to acquire. The Boar of Hagardis, for example. Have you heard of it?"

Criton shook his head. "It is a monster," Psander went on. "A boar the size of a horse, they say, or a bull. It terrorizes the whole region of Hagardis, but the warriors of Ardis do nothing to stop it because boars are sacred to Magor. Yes, that same Magor whose followers killed the last of the Dragon Touched. Or, you'll pardon me, what were *thought* to be the last of the Dragon Touched. If someone were to bring me the boar's carcass, I would pay dearly for it. I would happily give you this scroll, and perhaps another one or two of the little I have on dragons."

She waved her hand at the shelves behind her, as if to suggest that what little she had on dragons could fill more than a few of them.

"The size of a bull?" Criton asked in dismay. "I don't know much about animals, but couldn't such a boar tear us all to pieces?"

"Well yes, I don't doubt it could. But you would have help. That's what the Gallant Ones are for."

That gave him pause. "The Gallant Ones? You have dealings with them?"

Psander laughed. "Oh, yes. I have much that they want, not that they will ever retake Atuna even with my help. The Sun God has taken up with the people's council there. Unless He could be made to abandon them, or they Him, all my magic in the Gallant Ones' hands would only serve to make Atun angry."

Criton looked at Psander suspiciously. She invaded people's dreams, and she had dealings with the Gallant Ones. Was there anything she wouldn't do?

A horrible thought came to him. "Are you the one who sent the Gallant Ones to the village, to extort them and scare them into coming here?"

Psander lifted an eyebrow. "How brilliantly unscrupulous that would be of me. No, I'm sure I didn't." She was not very convincing.

Criton thought about Bandu's warning. What would he be getting into, if he started dealing with this wizard?

"I'll think about it," he said.

When he turned to go, she called after him, "Do send for your friend Hunter. I think I'll speak to him next."

14
Bandu

Bandu did not like this place. The wind did not speak here, and when birds flew above, their voices could not be heard. The villagers knew it. They called their new home Silent Hall, and spoke in whispers even when Psander was not around. The animals lowered their voices too, even the goats. Kids and lambs cried out in desperation, afraid of their own shrill bleating. Despite ample room and good water, Silent Hall was not really a place for sheep. It was the den of a predator, and the animals knew it.

Narky felt something too. "I feel weird in this place," he said, scratching at his chest. "Unwatched, somehow."

"I don't think I know what you mean," Phaedra said. They were sitting in Bandu and Phaedra's room, waiting for Hunter to come back from his talk with the wizard.

"I feel watched here all the time," Phaedra continued, "even when I'm dreaming. It's frightening, feeling like that wizard knows all about us, and yet we don't know anything about him. Her. Her, I meant. It's so odd seeing that bearded man and knowing that it's really a woman!"

"It's not Psander I was talking about," Narky objected. "I mean, you're right, Psander's watching us all the time. But it's something else."

"What is?" Hunter had come back, and was standing in the doorway. "She wants you next, Phaedra."

Phaedra hopped to her feet, motioning for Hunter to take her spot on the bed. She wasn't one to sit still for very long anyway. It had not taken Bandu long to realize that Phaedra liked to be in constant motion, in her body no less than in her mind.

Criton looked up at Hunter curiously. "Boar of Hagardis, right? What did she promise you?"

"Nothing specific. She just talked about what a menace that boar is, and said she'd be grateful if we'd deal with it. I don't need anything from her. If the rest of you want to go, I'll come with you anyway."

Narky raised his eyebrows. "Do you think it's really possible for us to hunt the boar without getting killed?"

Hunter shrugged. "Psander seems to think so. She's probably right. With thirty Gallant Ones, it should be fine. I don't know if they'll even need us."

"You should have asked her for something then," Narky said. "If she's willing to reward you for doing what you would have done anyway, take her up on it! I mean, if she'll give you a sword that always stays sharp or something, then why not?"

"I *like* sharpening my sword," Hunter told him, and even Bandu could tell that he was missing the point. What she didn't know was whether he was missing it deliberately.

"I think she is a wicked woman," she said. Her mind was still full of the dreams that Psander had forced upon her. Bandu hated those dreams. She did not believe them.

The others went on talking, but Bandu did not listen. She was saving her head for her own talk with the wicked woman. She knew there would be a talk. The wizard was meeting with all of them, one by one. Soon Phaedra came back holding a metal tube and sending Narky off in her place.

"I don't know what good I'll be at boar hunting," she

said, "but Psander offered me access to her library if I come along and make sure you get back safely. I'm trusting you, Hunter, that this is doable. I told her I'd only go if she gave me one scroll now, in advance. You should have seen how quickly she agreed! I should have asked for more."

"What did you get?" Criton asked her.

Phaedra presented the tube triumphantly. "This is a treatise on Ravennis, written by a priest who was an attendant for the Laarna Oracle in his acolyte days. I don't know much about the God of Laarna, and obviously I should. I've been thinking about the mark on Narky's chest. I don't think it's just a sign of his punishment. I think it's more of a brand, to signal Ravennis' ownership. It might come with expectations that Narky ought to know about."

Phaedra pulled a dry curled-up sheepskin out of the tube, uncurled it, and spent the next half hour staring intently at one side of it. Bandu went over to see what she was looking at, and found that Phaedra's side of the skin was covered in black marks. Now and then, Phaedra opened her mouth and spoke as if she was the priest of Ravennis herself, which made Bandu think that perhaps the priest's spirit was trapped in the skin, and trying to possess Phaedra's body.

"Phaedra!" she cried, and Phaedra immediately turned to her and said, "What's the matter?" It must be all right then. Phaedra's spirit was younger and stronger than the one in the skin, and she could come back if she needed to.

After another ten minutes or so, Narky returned to them. He was trying to look more angry than frightened, but it was the other way around. He didn't tell anyone what the woman had said to him, or what he had said to her. But he insisted that they had to bring her the animal she wanted.

Then it was Bandu's turn. She met Psander in a big dusty room full of dried skins, all curled up on shelves. "Bandu," Psander said quietly. "I've been looking forward to speaking with you."

"You are a wicked woman," Bandu spat back at her.

"Your dreams are lies, and the birds do not sing in your den."

"You're right about the birds," said Psander. "I do miss the birdsong, but it was a necessary casualty of my solitude. You're wrong about your dreams, though. They are *your* dreams, Bandu, and *your* memories. I only called them up and probed them a little, until you expelled me."

"You lie!" Bandu leapt forward and scratched at Psander's face, and the older woman fell back in surprise, a spot of blood welling on one cheek. Bandu burst into tears. "You wicked woman, dreams you give are not real!"

Psander had sat down heavily on a stack of marked skins and dried leather, but she now stood up again. "I'm sorry," she said, wiping her cheek and looking ruefully at the red spot on her sleeve. "I only wanted to know more about you. I thought perhaps, if I looked into your past, I might discover how you came to learn fairy magic. I didn't find what I was looking for, if it makes you feel any better."

The apology seemed sincere enough, but Bandu still hated her. "You are selfish," she said.

"Yes," Psander said, "I'll admit that. But I think I can help you, if you'll help me."

"You don't help me."

Psander picked up one of her little stacks of dried skins and began idly flipping through it. It was bound on one side, Bandu saw.

"There was once a great warrior mage, whose wife died while she was still young," Psander said. "By magic, he tore his way into the underworld and retrieved her, and she lived with him another fifty years."

Bandu picked up a curled skin and smelled it. It had been goat once, definitely goat.

"You say I have magic, just like Narky says before. Magic is a way of tearing things?"

This surprised Psander. "You don't even know...?" The wizard shook her head in disbelief. "Where do I start? There are rules that everyone knows about the world, right? Simple rules. People cannot fly. Animals cannot talk. Magic is really a word for anything that seems to be breaking those simple rules. Now it gets very complicated, because there are different kinds of magic: God magic and dragon magic and fairy magic, which is what you do without knowing it. And those magics aren't *really* breaking rules, they're just obeying rules that most people don't understand."

"I don't understand your words," Bandu said, even though she thought she might, "and I don't care."

Psander's eyes flashed, but she said nothing for a time. Bandu could tell that she had hurt her, and it made her glad. After the dreams, Psander deserved to be hurt.

"Either way," Psander said, gritting her teeth, "this wizard I was telling you about went and rescued his wife from the underworld. Now personally, I would never attempt such a foolish expedition. It is more than dangerous. It imperils your body, your mind, your very soul. But research on the underworld is substantial, and comes from sources both clerical and academic, from priests and blasphemers alike. There is even some guidance as to how such expeditions might be attempted again. *Now* do you understand what I am offering you, Bandu?"

Bandu shook her head. She was not just trying to hurt her this time: Psander's words were big and unfamiliar. They made Bandu feel stupid – stupid because she did not understand, and stupid because she could not ask Psander to repeat herself.

"You want to give me something?" Bandu ventured. She knew the word *offer* well enough.

Psander's mouth tightened. "I do not *want* to give you anything. What I would *like* is to spend some time studying you, to see if I could ever replicate your form of magic. But what I am *offering* you, in return for your help, is the opportunity to use my research to your benefit. I'm offering to give you Four-foot back."

When Bandu got back to the others, they were all looking expectantly toward her, waiting to hear what she would say.

"If Psander wants a dead pig," she said, "we give her a dead pig."

15
Narky

The Gallant Ones arrived at noon the next day. The pair of brothers who had taken the village sheep out to pasture came running back to Silent Hall, throwing themselves frantically against the gate until Psander let them in.

"They've found us!" they gasped, their eyes wild. "They're here! The Gallant Ones have come!"

The tall, manly image of Psander only nodded. "Tell everyone to stay inside," she commanded, in her mask's powerful baritone. "I'll deal with the Gallant Ones."

She turned to the islanders. "Come with me."

They followed the wizard into her tower and up a long flight of steps to the high window that overlooked the gate. The Gallant Ones had nearly reached that gate by now, and the sight of them was almost blinding. Thirty breastplates of polished bronze made for an eye-watering glare, as did the swords and spears and polished shields that the men were carrying. Though their hair was gray, the Gallant Ones bristled with weaponry. Their leader raised his fist and the company stopped, their heads tilting up toward the window.

"Psander!" the leader cried. Narky couldn't tell if he was upset or amused. "I see you've taken in some guests!"

"I have," Psander answered. "But forgive me, Your

Highness, I have no time for chatter. I hope your horses are well rested. I need something from you."

There was a rumble of anger from the company, but the prince of the Gallant Ones silenced it with a gesture.

"You always do," he said. "I think it's about time you held up your end, Psander. When will Atuna be mine?"

The wizard laughed a chilly, calculated laugh that ended almost as abruptly as it had begun. "You've hardly done anything for me. Certainly nothing to warrant my giving you the greatest city in the world. What have you done, Tana? An errand here and there? For this you want Atuna? That hardly sounds like a fair exchange."

"What sounds fair to you, wizard?" the prince spat.

Psander's tall form folded its arms. "The Boar of Hagardis."

There was another angry ripple from the company below. "The great boar sacred to Magor?" someone said. "The beast has razed whole villages!"

"It has," Psander replied, "as have the armies of Atuna. If you want my help retaking Atun's city, bring me Magor's sacred beast."

"We may as well storm the city ourselves," grumbled one of Tana's men, loud enough that Narky had no trouble hearing him over the snorting horses. "Magor is a vengeful God."

The grizzled old prince turned on him. "And am I not vengeful?" he asked, his voice dangerous. "Am I not a son of kings, a son of Atun? Let Magor fear us as He fears the burning sun."

He turned back toward the window. "How can I know that you will keep your faith with us, wizard?"

Psander smiled and shrugged.

"I am sending these youngsters to help you," the wizard said. "Perhaps you have heard of the calamity that befell Tarphae? These are the island's sole survivors. As you ought to know, survivors interest me. These ones are young, but also very talented. They may prove useful to you. Either way, I will be glad to see them returned unharmed."

Prince Tana frowned, but then he gestured for the islanders to join him. It dawned on Narky that Hunter had been right: the Gallant Ones needed no help in hunting the boar. But of course, Psander had not recruited the islanders because she needed more huntsmen. She was giving them away as hostages.

The journey was extremely unpleasant. The Gallant Ones did not take well to having tagalongs. Even during the hour of rest, when they reined in their horses and found a shady spot to lie down in, still they made a show of being burdened by their new company. They sneered at the very suggestion that the islanders could be of use to them, and laughed openly when they realized that only Hunter was armed. The contempt with which they looked at Narky and the others was unmistakable. He thought they might look at him differently if he told them he had killed a man, but he stayed silent. Maybe the Gallant Ones would be impressed by that sort of thing, but the other islanders would not. And, as Bandu would have put it, the islanders were his pack now.

Narky had never been part of a pack before, and it felt surprisingly good. The others did not always seem to like Narky, but they had dragged his near-lifeless body out of the forest and stayed with him during his recovery. They had helped him build his altar, and Phaedra was even trying to help him learn what Ravennis wanted from him. And they did not call him the Coward's Son.

It was funny: Narky had always assumed that Hunter would assert his dominance at some point. He had misjudged Hunter, he could see it now. Hunter was not a leader, any more than he was a boisterous drink-buyer. It was the others – the girls especially, but even Criton and Narky – who pulled Hunter along with them and decided where to go and what to do. His only purpose, apparently, was to protect them from danger. Narky was glad enough of that. Gods knew, they could use his protection.

The islanders each rode behind a Gallant One during their journey, despite the several riderless packhorses that trailed along behind them. Apparently, the Gallant Ones did not want to risk letting their hostages ride their own horses. This suited the islanders just fine, though. Among them, only Hunter and Phaedra knew how to ride.

Narky spent the first day riding behind Hearthman Charos, who was curt and scornful throughout. Most of these men were in their sixties, but they carried their arms with the confidence of those whose destiny was to conquer. Exiled from their homes for the last forty years, they dreamed not of reconciliation but of power. They called Tana their King Betrayed, and frequently began sentences with, "When we retake Atuna..."

After the first few days, Narky rode with Hearthman Tachil, who was friendlier. He asked about the circumstances of Narky's flight from Tarphae, and despite Narky's evasions, seemed to understand all too well.

"You're not so different from the way I was, when I was young," he said. "Not so different at all."

Narky shrugged. "I guess your skin has changed colors since then."

The Atunaean chuckled. "You're funny," he said.

When they stopped to let their horses rest, Hearthman Tachil showed Narky how to plant a spear in the ground so that the weapon would not be wrenched out of his hands when the boar ran into it. The spear was very long.

"If the Boar of Hagardis is as big as they say it is," Tachil warned him, "you'll need every inch."

"We don't have enough of those to go round," Hearthman Charos interrupted. "He'll have to make do with a halfspear or a crossbow."

When the Gallant Ones raised their tents at night, they left only one for the islanders to share. Narky expected Phaedra, at least, to object to this arrangement, but she did not. Apparently she did not feel safe here without Hunter and Criton's constant protection.

Neither the boys nor Phaedra undressed much at night, despite the warm southern wind. Hunter took off his armor, at least, but he also cautiously unsheathed his sword and slept with his hand resting on its pommel. It was Bandu who embarrassed them all by stripping completely naked and stretching out comfortably in the night heat.

Hunter escaped the situation by turning his head the other way and dropping off almost immediately, but Narky and Criton had a harder time of it. Even in the dark, with only the dim reddish glow of the Gallant Ones' bonfire flickering through the tent walls, enough could be seen to keep them lying rigidly in their places, awake and miserable. What made it even more maddening was that Phaedra took it upon herself to guard Bandu's nonexistent modesty by staring at Narky and Criton, ready to pounce if she saw them looking Bandu's way. When it came down to it, all Narky really saw was a blurred skinny figure blending into the dark ground. But his imagination supplied the rest.

Narky did not awaken early enough to see any more. When he woke up, drenched in sweat from sleeping in his clothes, only Criton was still inside the tent. Criton certainly looked tired, but Narky noticed enviously that he was also perfectly dry. The night's heat probably hadn't bothered him at all, the reptilian bastard.

To Phaedra's consternation – but to nobody's surprise – the process repeated itself every night for the rest of the week. Even during the daylight hours, it was hard not to think of Bandu's casual nakedness every time Narky looked at her. It was as if she was imbued with some new, special power, and she wouldn't even acknowledge it. Hunter politely didn't acknowledge it either, but at least Criton felt it, to judge from the enlightened and respectful look on his face. Narky didn't feel the same way about it at all. It felt like Bandu had something over him now, and he hated her for it. Between the lack of sleep, the miserable climate, and the depressing feeling that he was somehow missing an enormous opportunity, he thought it was only a matter of time before he went insane.

After a week of quiet resentment, the Boar of Hagardis finally gave him something else to think about. They came upon a ransacked hamlet, its few houses destroyed and the residents lying gored and feasted upon, partially by the boar and partially by the crows and vultures that had come by later. There were many of these still about, and the sight of them filled Narky with dread. They were watching him as they fed on their ghoulish meal. Not just looking, *watching*.

The Gallant Ones shooed the birds off – heavens forgive them – and went about trying to make sense of the tracks. Bandu studied the bodies instead.

"Four days maybe," Narky heard her say to Hunter. "Not safe."

Not safe for what? he wondered moodily. *Cannibalism?*

The boar's tracks were hardly fresh, but they were still easy enough to spot. Deep cloven hoofmarks the size of Hunter's boots could be seen everywhere, from the ground on either side of a broken wall to the stomped-in ribcages of the dead villagers. Prince Tana and the Gallant Ones looked at each other warily, and even Hunter seemed unsure of himself after seeing those marks. Criton, however, looked furious.

"This boar is sacred to Magor," he spat, speaking to no one in particular. His voice carried his condemnation.

"We can't do this," Narky whispered to Phaedra. "Even if we killed the thing – which we can't, by the way – Magor would carve us to pieces. A God who holds this monster sacred is not as merciful as Ravennis."

Phaedra shook her head. "We were never on Magor's good side," she said. "He might even hate us personally. The robbers on the way to the Crossroads were worshippers of His. You're right that killing the Boar of Hagardis is going to get His attention, but I don't see what choice we have. The Gallant Ones won't let us go until the boar is dead, and besides, Criton wouldn't turn back even if he could. Magor's high priest killed his family."

"But you saw what happened to me!" Narky pointed to his chest, where the burn mark lay concealed beneath his clothing. "I insulted Ravennis – not on purpose, mind you – and I got this, even *after* he spared me! And *I* didn't go killing any sacred animals!"

Phaedra looked worried, yes, but not nearly worried enough. She could not understand; nobody could understand without feeling that divine anger pointed at them, focused and deadly.

"The Boar of Hagardis is one of Magor's fingers," she said, definitely less sure of herself than she pretended to be. "Yes, it has Magor's attention, but if we cut off the finger, He should also be weakened for a time. Another God could take advantage of that weakness, and a God who was in conflict with Magor might protect us just to spite Him. They must be able fend each other off, because some Gods have been in conflict for generations without ever smiting each other's followers personally."

Narky wanted to object again, but before he could, Tana made a gesture and the Gallant Ones closed around them all. "We ride on from here," the princeling said. "If you hunt the boar with us, you take weapons and stand alongside us. Then if the boar kills you, you do not die as cowards and children."

Despite the 'ifs,' there was no 'if' in his tone of voice. Tana expected them to die, and Narky couldn't really disagree. But at least the Gallant Ones respected them enough to give them weapons.

Bandu moved first, holding her hand palm up. Tana nodded, and one of his hearthmen placed a long knife there. Criton accepted a bow, though Narky doubted he would ever use it. Would he be able to keep up the pretense of normality if and when the boar came at him? His savage claws seemed like a much more likely weapon, considering the look on his face. Hearthman Tachil offered a bow to Narky too, but Narky shook his head.

"I will not take a coward's weapon."

They gave him a spear instead.

Just as Hearthman Charos had suggested, Narky did not get a spear the same length as the others. He was given a halfspear. A boar the size of a bull would find it no impediment, but what could he do? Maybe there would be an opportunity to flee from the Gallant Ones when they met the boar. If they chased him down afterwards, a halfspear might come in handy.

He hoped an opportunity for escape would arise. If they all faced the boar, only two things could happen: either they would die, or the Gallant Ones would bring them back to Psander. And once they were in Psander's power again, Narky suspected that he would never be free.

Gods damn that Psander! Narky had been on a course of redemption, ready to leave his old life behind and become a real, worthwhile person. He was planning to stay out of trouble, at long last. Then Psander had read his past, and she had seen everything. He wished they didn't have to go back to her. He wished she would die. There was nothing like blackmail to turn you ugly again.

It was not just this boar; that was what worried Narky most. If it had just been that, Psander would have focused her attention on the combatants. The Tarphaean boys might at least be useful during the hunt, besides making for good hostages. But if that were all she needed, then why bribe Phaedra? The Gallant Ones certainly wouldn't have cared if they had been given only three or four hostages instead of five. Narky suspected that the real reason Psander had sent them all together was that she wanted to get all five of the islanders accustomed to serving her.

They followed the boar's trail for three more days on

horseback, bringing them to the foothills of the mountains that had seemed so distant when they left Silent Hall. On the third day, Narky awoke to find himself alone in the tent. As he was preparing to leave, a dark brown patch on the ground made him look twice. Those were definitely blood stains, on the ground where the girls had slept! Panic struck him as he imagined what must have befallen Phaedra and Bandu while he lay blissfully unconscious. How could he have slept through a fight?

Criton ducked his head inside the tent, and Narky looked to him in alarm. "What happened last night? Are they still alive?"

"Huh?" Criton scratched his head. "Yes, everybody's fine. Why, what's the matter?"

Narky pointed to the patch of blood, and Criton shrugged. Shrugged! "It must be one of the girls," he said. "They bleed sometimes, you know."

"What do you mean, they bleed sometimes?"

Criton rubbed his elbows and looked uncomfortable. "Well, Ma used to bleed sometimes, and the first time I noticed blood on her sheets, she told me that all women did that. She said it was normal."

Narky eyed him skeptically. Could this really be true? From what he had told them at the Crossroads, Criton's mother had been a freak like him. How could she know what normal women were like? It sounded decidedly monstrous, and not at all normal.

"Really," Criton said, sensing his skepticism. "It just happens now and then."

"You're sure they're all right?" Narky asked doubtfully. It was certainly hard to imagine someone getting injured without the sound waking him up. Criton's theory did explain *that* mystery pretty well.

He shuddered a little, and got up. Did Eramia bleed like this? It annoyed him that Criton might know something about women that he didn't. For Karassa's sake, the man hadn't even been out of his house until the day Narky met him!

The girls were indeed both healthy. Narky couldn't even tell where they had bled from. But he couldn't stay quiet forever – he had to ask Phaedra.

"Is it true that you bleed sometimes?" he demanded.

"Excuse me?"

"Criton says that women bleed now and then. Is that true?"

Phaedra glanced at Criton, a little angrily. "Yes," she said, "not that it's any of your business. You didn't know that already? I thought Bandu was the one raised by wolves."

"Are you bleeding now?"

"No!"

"Is Bandu?"

Phaedra stuck her finger in his face. "You stay away from her, Narky. Don't humiliate her with your stupid questions."

How can I humiliate someone who has no shame? Narky thought, moodily. But he didn't say anything to Bandu. Instead, he asked Hunter if he had known anything about this whole bleeding thing. Hunter just stared at him, silently, until Narky became uncomfortable and walked away.

Shortly after noon, Bandu cried, "Stop!" and the company came to a halt. She dismounted and the others followed suit, taking their spears with them. "Pig is close," Narky heard her say.

They dismounted, and the Gallant Ones took some minutes to don their armor and prepare themselves. When they were done, Tana turned to Phaedra. "Stay with the horses," he commanded. "If they all run off while we're hunting the boar, it will be a long walk back."

Phaedra nodded and looked relieved. At least her presence was of some use. The others continued on foot, following the boar's trail. "How do you know it's close?" Narky asked Bandu, but she put her finger on her lips and clutched that long knife as if she was afraid it would try to fly away. That was when he realized that the low thundering he heard was not coming from the horses behind them.

The Gallant Ones spread out, their spears at the ready. The horses had been left at a low point between hills, and, as the hunting party neared the top of one of these, a huge boar appeared over the crest.

'Large as a bull' did not do the Boar of Hagardis justice. It was *tall* as a bull, but twice as massive, its long body supported by thick, stocky legs. The boar's tusks jutted upwards from its jaw like curved swords, several feet in length. And its eyes – Narky did not even want to think about those eyes. The whole eyeball was like one giant pupil, pitch black and filled with malice.

With a cry, the Gallant Ones knelt and planted their spears in the ground against the boar's charge. It mowed through them like they were scattered mice. There was the snapping of spear ends and of bones as the boar broke through the assembled hunters and turned to rush down their whole line, trampling everyone in its path. The Gallant Ones leapt every which way to avoid the onrushing animal, and when it reached the end of their line, it wheeled about and began coming the other way, toward Narky. Narky forgot about his spear and ran farther up the hill, trying to get out of its path. When he turned, Criton was standing alone facing the boar.

He had abandoned his bow and was in his natural form, his golden scales shining against his dark skin. The boar charged him and he breathed fire at it, a long burst of flame like Narky had never seen before. The boar ignored the flames even as its bristles singed and burnt away, filling the air with foul smoke. Criton just stood there, unwilling to admit defeat. The monster bore down on him. At the last second, Hunter appeared out of seemingly nowhere and tackled Criton, and the two of them went rolling out of the boar's path.

The animal swerved to chase them, but Bandu shouted,

"Here!" and it turned to face her instead. How it heard her amid all the clamor, and why it responded to her voice among all the others, Narky did not know. Its manner registered confusion for a moment, or so it seemed to him. Bandu was not far from Narky, but now she ran at the boar while it came uphill toward her. Narky watched in horrified fascination as the two of them neared each other, girl and monster. There could be no question of what would happen when they collided.

But they did not collide. The boar must have misjudged her trajectory just as Narky had, because Bandu leapt straight past it, her knife flashing out even while its singed bristles grazed her skin. There was a horrible ear-splitting screech, and the boar spun about wildly, one of its eyes slashed.

Prince Tana blew his horn, and the Gallant Ones re-formed their line. At the sound, the monster wheeled back toward them, its one good eye bleeding hate just as surely as the bad one bled fluid. The Gallant Ones were better prepared for its charge this time, though it did them little good. The boar crashed through their wall of spears once more, fearless despite the many spearheads that impaled its flesh and snapped off when it spun round.

It was getting bogged down, though. One of the hearthmen's spears was lodged in its knee joint, and the boar stumbled this way and that, unable to find its footing. Tana drew his sword and approached to deliver the death blow, only to be flung broken into the air when the animal suddenly bowed its head and then jerked it up again. Only when the Atunaean prince's body came crashing down to earth did Narky finally realize that the Gallant Ones would not be able to do this all on their own. They were old and they were strong, but Magor was stronger.

He never knew what possessed him, but suddenly Narky was running toward the boar – toward danger! He changed his course often, trying always to keep on the animal's blind side as it struggled and flailed. Then he was upon it, and he lifted his spear and thrust it with all his weight and all his might into the boar's bad eye. The shaft went halfway in before the monster shuddered and went still.

There was no celebration. Instead, everyone gathered around Tana as the gray prince looked up at his friends and companions and softly breathed his final words. His back was broken, and his arms and legs fell at odd angles. "There is no pain," he said.

One of the prince's grizzled hearthmen knelt before him, tears welling at the wrinkled corners of his eyes. "We will retake Atuna for you, my lord."

Tana smiled. "Atuna," he said. "Atuna is mine."

His breathing stopped. A moment later, his eyes began to widen of their own accord. The kneeling hearthman reached out a hand and closed them.

"Put him on his horse," Hearthman Charos ordered the others. "There is not enough wood here for a pyre."

They lifted him onto their shoulders along with seven other broken men, Tachil among them. The islanders followed solemnly as they walked down to the horses. The Gallant Ones tied the dead men to their horses, and then set their six packhorses to drag the boar. They seemed to grow old before Narky's eyes, as the soul of the man who had kept them young fled the world. There was no more talk of Atuna.

Narky's fellow islanders clapped him on the back, hugged him and congratulated him. Somehow, inexplicably, he had become a hero. Then Hearthman Charos turned on them.

"This is all Psander's fault," he said, hefting his spear. "Take up your arms again, boys, and let's teach that wizard a lesson."

16
Phaedra

"Wait," Narky said. "Wait a minute! We just *helped* you!"

"Psander said you were precious to him," Charos replied. The rest of the Gallant Ones were following his lead, brandishing weapons and moving to surround the islanders. "He asked Tana to keep you safe even as he sent our king to his death. To his death! This won't go unanswered."

"But it's not our fault!" Phaedra cried. If the Gallant Ones chose to punish them for Tana's ill fortune, there was nothing the islanders could do to stop them.

"No," Charos conceded. "It's not your fault. But you are the wizard's creatures."

"No more than you are," Narky retorted. "We're all just tools to Psander. You think the wizard cares what happens to us, really? If you kill us, it'll just be a convenient excuse not to reward you for the boar."

The Gallant Ones considered this point, even as they held their spears and short swords ready for slaughter. "This is how you islanders plead for mercy, is it?" Charos asked. "By calling Atuna's finest warriors mere tools?"

"We are not Psander," Hunter insisted. "If you want to punish Psander personally, you should leave us unharmed. She may let us all into the fortress together, if there's no reason to suspect foul play."

"Did you just say, 'she'?" one of the Gallant Ones asked from behind them.

Charos dismissed the question before Hunter could sputter a response. "Psander owes us," he said. "We *will* collect our reward, after which we will take the wizard's head."

"Fine by me," Narky said. "I hope to see it happen."

Phaedra held her tongue. She did not share Narky's animosity for Psander, and she found his tone chilling, but she had to admit that it put the Gallant Ones at ease. They turned their spears from the islanders and slapped their horses, and the group moved on toward the forest.

When a pyre had been built, loaded, and set aflame, the Gallant Ones decided to roast the boar's carcass and eat it. It was a defiant choice, but also a practical one: the animal was far too heavy to drag all the way back to Psander's hall.

There was more than enough meat to go around, but Phaedra was nervous about eating Magor's sacred beast.

"Isn't there some place where they eat their enemies' sacred animals?" Hunter asked. "Or was that just a story I heard?"

"The Tigra of Mur's Island did that," she told him. "They believed that eating the sacred animals of an enemy's God gave them that God's strength."

"Did it work?" Narky asked.

Phaedra sighed. "Most of them died in a famine," she said, "and the rest were slaughtered or enslaved by Atuna in the sea raids of '42. Some blamed the famine on their blasphemy, but the Atunaeans probably would have defeated them anyway, because the tribes of Mur's Island didn't work metal."

"So you don't know if eating this will help us or get us all killed," Narky said irritably. "Great. Thanks, Phaedra."

"Magor is God of wild things?" Bandu asked. "Wild things eat wild things. Dead pig is food for them. Magor is more angry if we *don't* eat pig."

"She might be right," said Narky, his eyes transfixed on the halfspear that was still buried in the boar's head. "It's a little too late to worry about offending Magor now, isn't it? I'd be more worried about the meat poisoning us."

"Meat now is good," Bandu insisted. "Only bad if we wait."

Phaedra nodded, but she still didn't eat. It didn't feel right. "What we need," she thought aloud, "is divine protection. Karassa can't save us from Magor all the way out here. I want to dedicate the Boar of Hagardis to the local Gods so that maybe They'll protect us from Magor's wrath. But I'm afraid to ask."

"Maybe we can sacrifice the parts that aren't getting eaten," Hunter suggested. "They can't possibly mind that."

The Gallant Ones had already burnt the boar's heart as an offering to their Sun God, Atun, but they had discarded most of the other organs as offal. So in the end, the islanders were able to dedicate the boar's one remaining eye to Ravennis, God of Fate; they gave its trotters to Atel the Messenger; its nether parts to Elkinar, God of the Life Cycle; and its lungs and kidneys to Pelthas, God of Justice. When all that was done, the islanders finally took up their knives.

When the grim feast had ended, the Gallant Ones began bundling up the boar's bones and lashing them to their packhorses. It took a long time, during which the islanders sat back and watched, feeling a little sick. Phaedra held her stomach, wondering if perhaps the boar had defeated them after all.

"Ravennis would have had us eat the boar too," Narky said suddenly. "Crows eat whatever they can find. They wouldn't avoid a sacred animal."

"That's true," Phaedra admitted.

"And we did dedicate part of the boar to Ravennis. If He's still watching me, He might keep Magor off our backs."

Hunter turned to them curiously. "What made you

choose the eye for Ravennis, Phaedra?"

"The scroll that Psander gave me," Phaedra told him. "I haven't finished reading it, but it's very good. It describes the God from His worshippers' perspective, which is incredibly helpful. Ravennis' followers hold that eyes belong to Him, as a seer of fates."

"I suppose that's why ravens always go for the eyes first," Narky said. "They're collecting His share."

"Yes," Phaedra agreed.

"What else did it say in there?"

"It's very encouraging, actually. I can lend it to you."

She fished the scroll out of her travel pack, but Narky did not take it from her. "I don't read," he said.

"Oh," she said awkwardly, and then added, "I can read it to you, if you like."

How foolish she was! Of *course* Narky would not know how to read! She had assumed he would just because he was quick witted, but she should have known better. He was a peasant, a farmer's son. And she had accidentally pulled rank on him.

She wanted to apologize, but she doubted he would accept any apology with grace. So instead she unrolled the scroll and began to read it to him. Narky listened with rapt attention until the Gallant Ones finished packing, and when they stopped for the night, he asked her to stay by the fire and finish reading to him. One by one, the others around the fire retired, leaving just Phaedra and Narky with their scroll. Narky did not often interrupt her. When she had finished reading, he sat back in wonderment, gazing up at the stars.

"So that's what it means to be a servant of Ravennis. It's not as bad as I thought it would be, I guess. I thought His watching me meant He expected me to do something, and that He'd be angry if I didn't do whatever it was fast enough. But maybe it's not like that. He could be watching *over* me. His mark is a sign that He's taken ownership of me."

"Yes, it seems like it could be a sign of good favor," Phaedra agreed. "You're lucky."

Narky made a sound halfway between a chuckle and a snort. "I've been nothing *but* lucky for a while now," he said. "Not that I've done anything to deserve it."

"Maybe you will someday," she suggested. "Ravennis is the God of Fate. He could be rewarding you in advance."

Narky nodded thoughtfully. Then he yawned.

"We'd better join the others," Phaedra said.

They covered the fire with dirt and stumbled into the islanders' tent. The Gallant Ones easily had a second tent to spare for them now, but they had decided that it was still unsafe to separate. Perhaps more so, considering how close the Gallant Ones had already come to murdering them.

Though watching Narky trip over a naked Bandu *did* make her start to reconsider.

Phaedra had tried over and over to make Bandu understand why it was inappropriate to strip naked in front of the others, but the girl simply had no conception of social conventions. The next morning, Phaedra tried telling her that the others would like her more if she kept her clothes on. The truth behind that statement was doubtful, but at least Bandu accepted it. She also accepted Phaedra's wool and linen menstrual pads, much to Phaedra's relief: she wanted no more conversations with boys on the topic of bleeding.

Perhaps it was the discomfort of sleeping in clothes, but Bandu was in a bad mood the following morning. Phaedra asked if everything was all right, but didn't quite understand Bandu's answer. All she said was, "Psander is wicked. She gives bad thoughts."

Maddeningly, she refused to elaborate. Ah, well. Phaedra had to admit that Psander had a sinister side to her, and she had not failed to note that the wizard had forbidden the villagers from bringing mules within her gates – mules, the animal sacred to Atel. Even so, Phaedra looked up to her.

There was something wonderful about the casual ease with which Psander wielded her power. She answered to none but herself.

Psander had put all sorts of strange thoughts in the others' heads. When they stopped at midday to take shelter from the heat, Criton asked Phaedra, "Do you know anything about fairies?"

Phaedra could not help but raise her eyebrows at him. "Fairies? No. I like stories about things that really exist. Fairy stories never really interested me."

Criton did not seem satisfied with that. "They must exist. What she said doesn't make any sense otherwise."

Phaedra looked at him incredulously. "They 'must' exist? Elves and pixies that kidnap people and drag them to another world, and then sometimes bring them back for no reason? You must have misunderstood something. The only people I ever knew who actually *believed* in fairies were children or drunks."

Well, that wasn't entirely true. Kelina had always insisted that she believed in fairies, but Phaedra had never been quite sure whether Kelina really did believe, or whether she just wanted Phaedra to. There had been a part of Kelina that wanted Phaedra to remain a child forever.

Criton looked irritated. "Psander said that Bandu uses fairy magic. She said she wished she could study Bandu to see how she does it. So they have to exist. Could you tell me any of the stories?"

"Hold on, really? She really said that?" It all sounded so silly, but there was nothing childish about Psander.

"Yes," Criton said. "I don't know how she could tell about Bandu's magic, though. I've thought Bandu might have some ever since I saw the way she spoke with Four-foot, but Psander recognized Bandu's magic the minute she saw her."

It took Phaedra some time to digest this. It was hard enough to accept the possibility of fairies, but Bandu a wizard? The contrast between her and Psander was downright comical.

"So," said Criton, "what do you know about fairies?"

"Tell me about Bandu first. She's a wizard?"

"No," Criton said. "At least, her magic's nothing like Psander's. But I think animals understand her, even when she's talking normally. It's like there's something about her that *makes* them understand. She distracted the boar just by yelling at it, when it might have trampled me and Hunter to death."

"I knew it," said Narky, and Phaedra jumped. She had had no idea he was listening behind her. "I knew she had some kind of magic."

"But about the fairies!" Criton insisted.

"They're supposed to kidnap children," Phaedra said. "Don't ask me why."

"They use them as slaves," said Narky. "They steal children right out of their beds and force them to serve in their fairy castles, where they starve and beat them. You're not supposed to call them what they are, though, in case they're listening. So people call them the Kindly Folk. They creep out of tree trunks when there's a new moon, and go looking for children to be their slaves. They like the bad ones best, because Karassa doesn't watch over those."

Phaedra turned back to Criton. "You see why I never believed these stories?"

Criton nodded reluctantly. "Hey!" Narky protested, "I didn't say *I* believed in them! You're the one who asked about the damned fairies, anyway."

There was no more talk of fairies that day, but Phaedra resolved to ask Psander about them. Perhaps Psander had a useful scroll on them, though somehow Phaedra doubted it. Nothing Phaedra had ever read had given any reason to take the tales of elves seriously. She suspected that any writings on the Kindly Folk would be mere compilations of absurd stories.

And yet... Psander not only believed in their existence, she actually recognized their form of magic! A strange mix of feelings bubbled up in Phaedra – irritation at the fairies' intrusion into a world she had thought she understood, and excitement at the thought that there might be so much more to the world than even the greatest theologians could dream about. Did the Kindly Folk live in the Gods' world, and somehow slip through the mesh to run among humans? Did they dwell in hills in this world, as Kelina had claimed? Were they creatures of the underworld, stealing people away before their time? Why did the Gods tolerate their existence?

These were yet more questions for Psander to answer, so long as the Gallant Ones didn't kill her first. Phaedra's trepidation grew overwhelming when they finally came near enough to Silent Hall to see shepherds from the village out in the fields. The hall was nowhere to be seen, but the poor frightened villagers led them straight to it by running for its shelter. The Gallant Ones simply followed until they reached the spot where the shepherds had disappeared. The heat rose off the baked ground, shimmering and blurring their vision. Phaedra closed her eyes for a moment, and when she reopened them, Silent Hall stood before her.

Psander stood in the window above the gate, her disguise wearing a robe of dancing fire. The robe was beautiful, and knowing that the real wizard was wearing no such thing did not diminish its beauty. It amazed Phaedra to think that Psander had probably designed the robe this morning.

Psander was clearly pleased to see them. "Come in, all of you," she said, in her mask's powerful male voice. "Your reward awaits."

The gate opened of its own accord, swinging back with a creak. *No!* Phaedra thought, horrified, as they rode through to the courtyard. The Gallant Ones meant to kill her – how could Psander fail to see that? With the gate open, what was there to stop them from ransacking everything inside?

Phaedra heard cries from up ahead. The villagers knew they were coming.

When they rode into the courtyard, the townsfolk were cowering in the entrances of their new tents, staring up at the riders with fear and hatred. Their eyes were no kinder to the islanders. *They think we're monsters,* Phaedra thought wretchedly. *They think we joined the Gallant Ones on purpose.*

Phaedra heard the tower door swing open behind them. "Dismount, all of you," Psander's voice boomed. "Dismount when you are in my hall."

There was a loud clicking noise, and the Gallant Ones wheeled around. Above Psander's head, the walls of the tower were covered in crossbows, held by stone arms that aimed them perfectly at each rider, three to a man.

"Dismount," Psander repeated. "I would highly recommend it."

The riders alit from their horses. Phaedra could barely contain her relief, for all that it wasn't over yet.

"Tana does not ride with you," Psander noted. "Charos, leave your weapons and come speak with me."

Charos' eyes burned with fury, but he obeyed. The two spoke quietly for a time, while the others watched in silence. Were those crossbows real? Phaedra couldn't be sure. Surely Psander must have *some* defenses besides a simple gate. But how many of her defenses were psychological?

In the end, Hearthman Charos nodded and withdrew. Psander disappeared into the tower and returned with a sack of gold. She paid the old men and they remounted their horses. Phaedra let out her breath. They would leave in peace.

Narky, emboldened by the Gallant Ones' apparent defeat, took the opportunity to pester the riders about their extra horses and equipment, hoping to buy some of it cheap. Hearthman Charos did not bother to keep the disgust from his face while Narky suggested a price, but neither did he bother to hold up his side of the haggling. He still had his eyes on the crossbows. He signaled to his compatriots, and they unloaded the boar's bones and Narky's purchases of a clean halfspear, a packhorse and a pair of tents. Then they spurred their horses and galloped out toward the gate.

Criton eyed Narky curiously. "Where did you get the money to buy all that? I thought you gave all of yours to the fisherman."

Phaedra did not hear his reply because Psander was already beckoning them, and Phaedra hurried to join her. Psander's male figure was still wearing that robe of fire, but when Phaedra concentrated and tried to look beyond the vision before her, she thought she could see the real, female Psander underneath, wearing a sensible grey dress with a low hemline.

"Congratulations," Psander said. "I understand you lot made yourselves useful after all. I thought you might, though I must say I'm surprised to hear it was Narky who dealt the death blow."

Narky stiffened. "If you didn't think I'd be any help, why did you bother sending me?"

Psander opened the door to the tower and ushered them in. "In battle," she said, "it's better to have too much than not enough. Never use force unless you can use overwhelming force. Now come in. We have much to discuss."

"We do," agreed Phaedra, entering first and turning back to face the wizard. "Why did you want that boar so badly? You were willing to trade us and the Gallant Ones in for it – it has to be important."

"Oh, it is," Psander agreed. "But magic theory is too complicated to explain in an afternoon. Suffice it to say that the boar has some of Magor's power in it, power that I shall use to protect myself from Him."

"I hope you plan on protecting us too," Narky said. "If Magor didn't hate us before, He sure does now."

"You will be safe with me," Psander said magnanimously. "Is anything else troubling you?"

"Do you have time to tell us about the fairies?" Criton asked. "You told me Bandu used fairy magic, so you must know something about them."

Both Psanders nodded. "I do, though less than I might. I never studied elf magic thoroughly, and a good deal less is known about it than about dragon magic, for instance. Even in the heyday of academic wizardry, we knew very little about the Kindly Folk."

"Tell us what you do know," Phaedra demanded, and then hurriedly added, "please."

Psander smiled. "When I was young, there was a group of wizards who had built a tower upon an old fairy gateway in order to study the strange energies it emitted. I apprenticed there for some months, though my tasks were mostly mundane. The tower is gone now, as are the wizards who lived in it. So I hope you understand that I am no expert on the subject. In fact, there are no experts left alive in this world.

"You are familiar with the writings of the Tarphaean sage Katinaras, yes? His mesh analogy was very popular within the academic community. The accepted theory back when I studied at Gateway was that there is a second mesh between our world and that of the Kindly Folk, much like the one between us and the Gods, except tighter. It was thought that this mesh was so tight that the Kindly Folk and their prisoners could only travel through at very particular times, when the mesh is weaker due to various factors only some of which were well understood. Those who built Gateway were hoping that one day the gate would open and a fairy would step through to be captured and studied. Given enough time, it probably would have happened that way. But Gateway is no more.

"It's a terrible shame, because there is so much we don't know about the world of elves that we might have known had we been able to ask one."

"The world of elves?" Criton asked. "Is there a difference

between elves and fairies?"

"No," Psander answered. "As far as I can recall, the Kindly Folk call themselves elves, whereas 'fairy' is a human word. But my studies at Gateway were a long time ago. I can't even remember the source of that theory, let alone what evidence we have to support it.

"In any case, the fairy magic that came through at Gateway had a very distinct flavor, if you will, from the magic of this world. When I saw Bandu, it was like tasting a food you haven't had since childhood. I immediately thought back to my time there, and knew that this was something special."

"So if Bandu uses fairy magic," Criton asked, "does that mean she has fairy blood? Is she Elf Touched?"

"No."

"How is that possible?" Phaedra asked.

Psander shrugged. "Humans are remarkable creatures. Dragons breathed magic. It grew on them like hair, without thought or effort. It is believed that fairies are the same. The Gods may actually *be* magic, without anything resembling bodies on Their side of the mesh. But we humans are different. We produce only the weakest of magical fields, and that field is remarkably generic. No particular form of magic is innate to us, yet through careful study, we can use them all. In truth, there is no such thing as wizard magic. We wizards are simply humans who use our knowledge of magic theory to harness and imitate God magic or dragon magic or, in some rare cases, fairy magic."

She shook her head and let out an exasperated chuckle. "I say 'we'. The fools who run around nowadays calling themselves wizards are not students of magic theory, only idiots who have learned some limited number of tricks and go about trying to impress people with them. Between the Gods, their servants, and our rivalries with each other, the community of academic wizards has been entirely obliterated. I am the last of the academics."

Criton frowned. "I didn't learn magic by studying. My mother said I was born with fire in my lungs."

"Yes," Psander said, "the Dragon Touched are different. Even the little bit of dragon's blood that was passed down to you is enough to let you live and breathe your lesser magic almost like a dragon would. You can develop it, of course, with practice, and the rest of puberty should help you with that too. I say it's like hair, but in some ways a muscle is a more apt analogy.

"But," she added, turning to Bandu, "what's really remarkable is you. You seem to have somehow hit upon an aspect of fairy magic without any study or even a drop of elf blood. Gods know how you did it, I ought to say, though somehow I doubt They do."

Narky gasped. "You can't insult Them *all* like that!" he whispered urgently. "They're always watching us."

"They are not," said Psander, with eerie certainty. "Not here, anyway."

17
CRITON

Psander regarded their shocked faces with obvious pleasure. "As I said," she continued, "dragons and fairies have never been my specialty. My research as a wizard was focused on the Gods, which is how I have been able to evade Their gaze for so long. The Gods we know and fear are not entirely omniscient. They are fairly localized, for one thing, and They rely to a surprising degree on Their followers and sacred animals to notice things for Them. They also rarely cooperate with each other, except against a shared enemy. Once, the dragons were that enemy. But some twenty-five years ago, the Gods turned Their gaze on the academic wizards.

"At first, when priests and zealots began to pick fights with us, we assumed that they were driven by ignorance, and fear, and mortal ambition. We were wrong. The Gods were behind every attack and every wizard hunt. The more secrets of the universe we unlocked, the more They turned against us. They destroyed our towers of learning and hunted us down one by one. It did not take long. What had once been a peaceful academic rivalry between wizards and priests became an all-out war, and it was not a war we could win.

"I did my best to stay out of sight during this time. I traveled for a long time, keeping one step ahead of the fanatics and one failed ward away from a divine smiting. In my travels, I gathered what I needed to build a place like this. Sometimes I had to pick through the ruins of my colleagues' homes, but in the end you can see the results of my labors.

"We are standing in a fortress designed to act as a blind spot for the Gods, a place that stands not against Them, but outside Their field of vision. We are near no cities, no great rivers or mountains, and yet this is not so wild a plain as to be considered Magor's territory. We are not on the sea, nor on any of Atel's roads. The wards I have placed on my walls are wards of invisibility to Gods, and to Their priests and zealots and sacred animals. That is why the birds do not sing here, and why mules and other sacred beasts may not enter my gates alive. If there were a God of sheep, you can be sure that the villagers would be living outside my doors rather than within them. It is only pure luck that I warded so heavily against Ravennis, for He has marked Narky and could otherwise have seen my hall through his eyes."

"So you're hiding here," Criton said. "And you can't ever leave?"

Psander nodded. "They would smite me the moment I stepped outside, and then all would be for nought."

Narky frowned. "What do you mean, 'all would be for nought?' This isn't just about your survival, then?"

To Criton's surprise, Psander looked completely shocked. "Of course not!" she said. "I didn't build this place to keep *me* safe! I built it to house the books I rescued. The Gods and Their servants wish to blot the academics and our findings from memory, and I cannot let that happen. If that means imprisoning myself, then so be it.

"I know that you do not all like me. You think I am manipulative and callous. You're not wrong. But my work has a purpose. When I ask you to bring me something like the boar, it is to strengthen my wards so that I may preserve some part of the knowledge we acquired before the towers of learning fell. I am not some petty hedge wizard who jealously guards her knowledge from the rest of the world. Everything I know and everything I have I will share with you, if you continue to help me."

They all stood in shocked silence for a time. "I didn't mean to tell you all this so soon," Psander said, "but my need is great. If you need some time to discuss this…"

"Yes," said Phaedra, "that would probably be best."

"Of course." The wizard bowed her head, rose and withdrew.

"We *have* to help her!" Phaedra said, once the door was closed.

"Phaedra," said Narky, "she's on *all* the Gods' bad side. If we help her and she fails, nothing in the world can protect us."

"But she *shouldn't* fail!" Phaedra insisted. "The Gods are wrong to persecute her."

"The Gods are wrong?" Narky repeated. "What's the matter with you? Since when do you say that sort of thing? You're always telling us what the Gods want, and how to keep Them happy with us – you're practically a priestess!"

"I'm not a priestess," Phaedra corrected him, nearly in tears. "I just want to understand the way the world works. That's what theology is about. But that's also what academic wizardry was about! They were trying to see how it all fits together. We can't let all their knowledge disappear."

"Phaedra's right," Criton said. Psander was the only person he had met so far who knew anything about dragons. If she and her library were destroyed, he might be empty forever.

"Really?" Narky asked. "You're sure this is worth dying over?"

"Yes," he and Phaedra said in unison.

"You're suicidal!"

"I don't know," said Hunter. "Psander says They can't see this place, and we have two Gods that want us dead already: Magor, and whoever sent the plague. Unless that changes somehow, this might be the safest place in the world."

For Narky, those were magic words. "I guess you could be right," he said reluctantly.

Bandu shook her head. "Psander is bad. Gods are bad, but Psander is bad too."

"Yeah," said Narky, "but Psander doesn't want to kill us."

That settled it. Bandu shrugged sullenly, but she did not object any further.

Criton was grateful to Hunter, and impressed too. It was easy to assume, with a man so quiet and so focused on combat, that he would have nothing particularly useful to say, but apparently the opposite was true. He certainly knew how to motivate Narky.

Phaedra took a deep breath. "So I can tell Psander we'll help her?"

"You tell her," Bandu said. "I'm tired now."

She left them there, closing the door none too quietly behind her.

"I'll talk to her," Criton said. He had wanted to speak to Bandu alone anyway. There were questions he had to ask her.

He found Bandu sitting on the windowsill in the girls' room, looking out past the courtyard to the fields and mountains beyond. She had one of Phaedra's scrolls – a genealogy, Criton thought – and she had unrolled it partway and was fanning herself with it. She barely glanced at him when he entered the room.

"Bandu." The girl went on fanning herself. "Um, can I talk with you?"

No head turn. "You can talk."

Criton cleared his throat nervously, but she would not look at him. He soldiered on. "You remember what Psander said, about the Wizard's Sight?"

"No."

"Oh. Well, she said that you and I could see through her disguise because we had the Wizard's Sight. Do you remember that now?"

Bandu nodded absently. He wasn't sure she was listening.

"Bandu," he said again, and she finally turned to him, looking annoyed. "Bandu, did you see my claws the first time you saw me, when you got on the boat?"

"What are claws?"

Criton lifted his arms, letting them shift back to their natural form. "These. And these, the scales. Did you always see them?"

She nodded again.

"And you weren't frightened?"

She shook her head this time.

"Why not?"

Bandu shrugged. "Why are others frightened?" she asked him.

"Well, because..." Criton broke off. It seemed so obvious, after Ma and her husband and everything. But somehow, no explanation came to him.

Bandu answered her own question. "Others are frightened," she said, "because you don't look like one of our kind. Why do I care? Our kind hate Four-foot, and they kill their young. They kill their young! You don't need to be like them to be good."

She was crying now. What was all this about? Criton sat down next to her on the windowsill and asked, as gently as he could, "What do you mean, they kill their young?"

She said nothing – only put her head in her hands. They killed their young. He thought of his own head, being held under water by Ma's husband. He had breathed some water in, and it was the most horrible feeling he had ever had.

Bandu's mood must have something to do with the dreams. She had been angry at Psander ever since their first night here, when the wizard had invaded their sleeping minds.

"Bandu," he asked. "When Psander was in your dreams, what happened?"

She shook her head and would not look at him. "Bandu," he said again, "what did you see?"

She said something then, but he could not hear her through the sobs. "What?" he asked, leaning closer.

Her words came back in a whisper. "My father," she said.

He felt the water in his lungs again, cold and heavy and awful. "Father?" The word had to fight its way out of his mouth.

Bandu looked up at him, her eyes filled with tears. "I kill her when I come out," she said, "and he hate me. He not have your, your... ah!" She screamed in frustration, unable to express herself as she wished to.

"It's all right," he prodded her, "go on."

She took a few slow breaths. "For food," she said, "not enough for food. He not want me, he wants another one like her. He says I am bad because I kill her, and not clean, and he wants another one, but nobody wants him with me. And not enough food, but he still has to give me some. So he pray for me, because he doesn't... doesn't?"

"Didn't," Criton said gently.

Bandu nodded. "He didn't know what to do, so he pray. Then he takes me to trees and leaves me there."

"Your own father?"

She nodded again, and new tears burst from her eyes. "He thinks I die. He want me to die, but afraid himself to. So he leave me."

Criton did not want to hear anymore. It made him sick. A real father, leaving his daughter to die in the forest. Not a stepfather, not an imposter. Bandu's father. He felt nauseous. He wished he hadn't heard this, hadn't asked her about her dreams. It could not be. If Bandu's real father could abandon her in the woods, then maybe the man who had held Criton's head under the water really was... no. No. Criton had no father.

A little smile crept onto Bandu's face, even through her tears. "I not die," she said. "I find Four-foot, and he takes care of me. We are friends, is better than father."

The smile vanished, and her face contorted again. "Then I kill him too!"

She buried her face in her hands, and her whole body shook with her sobs. Criton put an awkward claw on her back. "You didn't kill him," he said.

Her body curled so that her forehead touched her knees. "I kill him," she said. "I take him on leaf – on boat – because I am scared of the water. And man hits him, and cut turns bad, and he die. Because I take him with me! I think water will cover island, will kill everything. But no water, only sickness. Kills people! Only *my* kind. His kind happy, they live, and only he dies because of me."

She fell against him, sobbing even harder. "I kill Four-foot," she cried. "I love Four-foot and I kill him."

"No, Bandu," he said. "It's not your fault. You thought you were saving him too. You weren't being selfish, you just didn't know. None of us did."

She nodded a little, into his chest. He wanted to comfort her further, but his mind was distracted. How had she known that the people of Tarphae would drown? Nobody had known that. Nobody *could* have known that.

He tightened his arm around her, a little guilty to be so preoccupied with her magic instead of her emotions. But what knowledge had her fairy magic given her? This girl had seen what nobody else could see, and knew all sorts of things that she shouldn't have known. Somehow, she had known the island was going to drown. And she thought that made her a murderer.

"You didn't kill Four-foot," Criton said, carefully bringing up his other claw to pat her head and stroke her short, fuzzy hair. "The fisherman, the man who gave him that cut. He killed him. The Gods who let the infection spread, They killed him. You did nothing wrong, Bandu. Really. You only did what you thought was right, what you thought would save him. It's not your fault at all."

Bandu looked up into his eyes. Then she kissed him. She kissed him and would not let him go, kissed him until his shock subsided and he stopped wanting her to let him go. She kissed him until Phaedra walked into the room and gave a little squeal.

"I'll come back later," Phaedra said in a hurry, and dove out of the room again. It didn't matter at all. Bandu kissed him, and she didn't stop.

18
Hunter

When Phaedra walked into Hunter's room, he and Narky were both there. The room had a view out to the forest and did not overlook the courtyard. Thanks to the villagers' animals, Hunter's room had the most tolerable smell.

Hunter looked up and saw Phaedra's expression. "What's wrong?"

"Nothing," Phaedra said. "Nothing's wrong. You don't mind if I stay here for a little while, do you?"

"We don't mind at all," Hunter said. "You haven't seen Criton, have you? He's not in his room."

"No, I haven't seen him," she said, trying and failing to control her face. She was definitely lying. Oh. Now he understood that expression.

"You know," Narky said thoughtfully, "I wonder if Bandu can turn into an animal."

"Excuse me?" Phaedra looked shocked, horrified, guilty.

"Fairies are supposed to be able to turn into animals," Narky said. "They can sneak into your bedroom as a mouse, and snatch you away even if your door is locked. And if you make them angry, they can turn into lions or bears and tear you to pieces. I wonder if Bandu can do any of that."

"She's never done anything of the sort," said Phaedra.

"I don't think she's ever tried," Hunter said. "If it's anything like swordsmanship, you have to practice all the time if you want to improve."

He sighed. He wished he still had someone to practice with. He wished… no, this was life now. He was a warrior. He would survive.

"That's a good idea," said Narky. "Magic practice! Bandu and Criton can work on their magic together. Maybe they'll figure something out."

Phaedra looked like she might explode. "I think Criton may have considered that," Hunter said, and Phaedra squirmed until he threw her a lifeline. "What's that scroll Psander wanted us to give him?"

"Oh!" She looked immensely relieved as she fished it out. "A History of the Dragon-Touched," she read, "by someone called Gardanon. Wow, this scroll is old. Look at how dark the vellum is! I think it's deerskin."

They let her inspect the scroll for a time in silence. Hunter wondered how long it would be before Criton joined them and Phaedra could return to her room. The waiting seemed hard on her.

Hunter pulled his sword from its sheath and took the whetstone from his pack. Sharpening his sword always calmed him and helped him focus. The repetitive motion had a meditative aspect to it, and the sound soothed his ears. Narky did not feel the same way about it, as Hunter had already discovered; he grimaced at the sound of the metal scraping against the stone, and tried to drown it out by talking more.

"You said that Magor killed Criton's family," he said to Phaedra. "Do you know anything about them? When we were staying at the Crossroads, he told me he'd never been outside his house 'til the day we met him."

Phaedra put down her scroll. "Really? He said he lived indoors all his life?"

"Yes. I guess his father didn't want anyone to know his

son was a freak."

Phaedra regarded Narky sternly, but she didn't say anything for a while. She was hard to read sometimes. At first, Hunter had thought that she liked Criton very much, but he supposed Criton's draconic lineage had put her off. She certainly related to him better when his claws were hidden.

"So Criton was living in Karsanye all this time?" she asked. "Or was he somewhere else on the island?"

Narky shrugged. "I think he was in Karsanye. Nobody can keep any secrets in a smaller town."

"But who could have hidden someone for that long?" Phaedra asked. "His parents would have to bring him food, and never let anybody visit, and keep him away from all the windows. His father must have had a large house for his voice not to be heard or noticed."

Hunter stopped sharpening his sword for a moment. "Lord Tenedros' son," he said. "The one with the sick wife."

Phaedra gasped. "Oh Gods, you're right. She had some terrible illness, so no one could visit, and he brought her all her food... people said her sickness took so much out of him, and the whole time he was keeping Criton and his mother locked away like prisoners."

Narky clearly had no idea who they were talking about. Phaedra tried to enlighten him while Hunter went back to sharpening his sword. Until Phaedra had come in, Hunter would never have imagined that Criton and Bandu could connect romantically. Frankly, he had never considered Bandu capable of love for anything with less than four legs. But whatever was happening in the girls' room as they spoke, it made much more sense to him now. Criton and Bandu had more in common than he had imagined, raised away from society as outcasts and freaks, loving, each of them, only one other creature in the whole world. And now both Four-foot and Criton's mother were gone.

Would Hunter ever have someone like that, who

understood his joys and pains so completely? He had never even looked for someone like that. His brother Kataras had had many women, and Hunter had always considered them to be somehow his brother's domain. Father would eventually find some match for Hunter, unless he died valiantly in battle first. Now, for the first time, Hunter thought he might like to find a wife one day. Not yet; he had no house to bring her home to, no lands to support them, no security to offer her father. Besides, death could still take him quite soon if Psander's tasks were as dangerous as he imagined, or if Silent Hall fell and the Gods blamed them for helping Psander. But if Hunter lived, he hoped he would one day love as well.

Narky and Phaedra were still talking about Criton when he walked into the room, glowing with unrepressed bliss. "I'm sorry, Phaedra," he said, not looking sorry at all.

"Sorry about what?" Narky asked, but Phaedra was already leaving.

Criton responded instead, though to Hunter's mind he shouldn't have. "Me and Bandu were just sitting in her room, um, talking about sad things."

"Like what?" Narky wasn't getting it. Criton looked to Hunter for help, but Hunter stayed silent, pretending to focus on his work with the whetstone.

Narky turned on him. "Will you stop that? You can already shave with the damn thing – how sharp has it got to be?"

As always, Hunter said nothing. Narky soon backed off. "Anyway," he said to Criton, "I thought Phaedra said she hadn't seen you."

"Oh," said Criton.

"We brought you the scroll you wanted from Psander," Hunter told him, changing the subject. He hated these uncomfortable conversations, and he hated stating the obvious. Criton was clearly relieved to have something new to focus on, and he took the scroll from the bed where

Phaedra had been sitting.

"Thanks," he said. "I'll read it soon. I think I'll lie down first."

And so he did.

He lay on his back for some time, smiling up at the ceiling, while Hunter put away the whetstone and Narky sat on the windowsill, looking glumly out over the forest.

Silent Hall really was a very apt name, Hunter thought. The townsfolk and their animals were always making some sort of ruckus out in the courtyard, but on this side of the tower he could barely hear them. He wondered if Psander knew what people called her home, and if so, whether she cared. She had certainly made no effort to supply them with any other name.

"I think I'll read this now," Criton said suddenly, sitting up. "You don't mind, do you?"

Narky looked over from his spot at the window. "Is there a reason I should?"

"Well," said Criton. "I don't read quietly like Phaedra. I need to sound all the words out."

Narky opened his mouth again, but Hunter spoke first. "I don't mind," he said. "Read."

"Thanks." Criton unrolled the scroll, and began to read aloud.

"Blessed is Atel, protector of His servants. Blessed is the one who walks His road.

"I came to Ardis from the east, wishing to lay eyes upon the famed Dragon Touched. The people of Ardis welcomed me in the name of God Most High, who was once worshipped by the dragons and is now the God of their descendants. The commonfolk of Ardis mostly worship Elkinar, the inland God of the Life Cycle, and Magor of the Wild, but they do not keep images of these Gods for fear that they will be discovered by their draconic tyrants. God Most High is a vile, jealous God, and in Ardis the penalty for worshipping other Gods is death. The mere possession of sacred images is enough to doom an entire family. Even images of God Most High are forbidden, so that He may conceal His evil appearance.

"Though their God's jealousy is a point of pride for the Dragon Touched, they nonetheless claim that He is peace-loving and just. Truly, most of the principles they claim for God Most High are unobjectionable; but He must be judged also by the secret rituals that take place when watchful eyes are absent. Let it be known that any God worshipped by the dragons or their descendants is no friend to humanity.

"I asked the commonfolk, in the privacy of their homes, whether my status as a friar of Atel would endanger me. The answers were varied. A few said that as an outsider I might be safe. The Dragon Touched are an inherently greedy race, and so great is their thirst for gold that they would welcome their worst enemies into Ardis so long as those enemies were poorer when they left the city than when they arrived. Yet although the Touched do not wish to frighten away any foreign merchants, others warned me that their greed is no protection from trickery and false charges. I was told tales of priests being burned in dragon's fire for the supposed crime of subversion. I therefore resolved to keep my identity hidden, and go about my work in secret.

"Posing as a recent convert to God Most High, I gained admittance to the Hall of Records. The Dragon Touched are exceedingly proud of their heritage, though their race may be little more than two centuries old. Even young as they are, their origins appear to be entirely unknown, at least according to the manuscripts I was permitted to read. One theory expounded upon by the human locals is that the Dragon Touched emerged into this world when a pair of sisters copulated with a dragon and gave birth each to a pair of Dragon Touched twins, boy and girl. These cousins married each other in order to perpetuate the race, but one of the boys took a second wife, a human, whose offspring developed the same draconic features and magical abilities as their half brethren. Thus it was discovered that all who breed with the Dragon Touched pass their monstrosity onto their young.

"The commonfolk of Ardis tell many frightening tales about the secret rituals of God Most High. Some even claim to have seen the elder Dragon Touched feasting upon human children. I hoped, while in Ardis, to enter in upon these rituals of God Most High and verify some of the commonfolk's claims for myself. I was, however, unable to do so. I do not know whether the Dragon Touched saw through my disguise or whether they are especially cautious around their human recruits, but I was never invited to attend these rituals.

"According to the cityfolk, it takes years of careful indoctrination before converts are trusted enough to be allowed to bear witness to the true worship of God Most High. Those who are not trusted are sometimes seduced into believing in their acceptance, and after a year of being carefully watched, are finally invited to an occult service, only to be set upon and devoured by the priests and acolytes of the Dragons' God. Not wanting this fate to be mine, I abandoned my attempts to infiltrate the Dragon God's cult.

"Instead, I focused once more on the Hall of Records. I was unable to discover, during my investigations, which dragon copulated with the sisters – sometimes referred to as the Foremothers. There is consensus that both Foremothers bred with the same dragon, but aside from the dragon's golden coloring, little is known about who he was. It was remarkable to me that the Gods would allow their creations to be sullied by dragon's blood, but the Ardisian sages note that at the time of the Foremothers' impregnation, Gods and dragons still coexisted peacefully.

"It appears that, for a time, the practice among the Dragon Touched was to take human wives, knowing that their draconic blood would overpower our own. Their race could undoubtedly be larger in number and greater in influence if they had continued in this way. Yet, luckily for all of humanity, the Dragon Touched are so vain a people that they prefer to couple exclusively with their own kind."

Here, Criton paused. His breathing had long grown heavy, and he seemed to be struggling to focus on the words. Hunter and Narky waited for him to continue, and at last he took a deep breath and resumed his reading.

"I should note that there are no Dragon Touched within the royal family, but the king of Ardis has nonetheless committed himself completely to their reign of terror. The clan of Dragon Touched served as his father's advisors and enforcers, and now seems destined to maintain its position as long as the king's line remains intact. Their stranglehold on power is total and unyielding.

"During my time in Ardis, I witnessed the selfishness and cruelty of the Dragon Touched in innumerable ways, large and small. They are a venal, greedy, and power hungry people, and their leaders are the cruelest among them. Brothers murder brothers in the pursuit of power, and sisters, sisters. The current Matriarch is said to have poisoned her eldest son in order to maintain control over her clan.

"Yet perhaps even more than their vile leaders, the most dangerous Dragon Touched are those who conceal their draconic features and become spies among the people, sniffing out the worshippers of true Gods so that they may be executed in the service of God Most High. One must watch for these everywhere, even outside of their stronghold. Those who are discovered in human territory should be slain without hesitation.

"Before I left Ardis, the people of that city gave me one final warning. Some of the Dragon Touched may appear to have abandoned their cruel ways. However, their words of peace should never be trusted. They are tricksters, seducers, and rapists, and though they may at first appear to pose no threat, one must never doubt their evil nature.

"Although the Dragon Touched deal harshly with those few of their own kind who have abandoned their God, even these dissenters are to be regarded with the utmost suspicion. Having betrayed their God and their people, they are the lowest and meanest of the world's creatures. Do not trust them, but slay them immediately.

"The words of Gardanon, Friar of Atel, in the year 7393. Be warned."

By the time he finished reading, Criton looked truly sick. His face had turned yellowish and Hunter thought he might vomit, but somehow he contained himself.

"It's all lies," he said at last, his voice shaking.

"It's probably exaggerated," Narky said, "but how do you know they're *all* lies? Your mother was one of the ones who left. Maybe she left home for a reason. I mean, how much do you really know about your relatives?"

In a flash, Criton seized Narky by the neck, his claws leaving marks in the flesh of the young man's throat.

"Criton, stop!" Hunter shouted, his hand falling automatically to his sword.

Criton turned his head to face him, a hunted look in his eyes. "None of it is true," he choked.

"I know," Hunter said, though he knew nothing of the sort. "But let Narky go."

Criton did as he was told and then collapsed on the bed, sobbing. Narky breathed heavily and rubbed his throat, but he abstained from speaking.

Hunter wasn't sure what to think. It was hard to deny that Criton had trouble controlling his feelings, especially anger. Could this be a symptom of his draconic nature? Hunter liked Criton, and that made him want to make excuses for him. Was he being naïve?

Being Dragon Touched definitely made Criton more dangerous. There were plenty of full-blood humans who could not control their anger, but they also could not breathe fire. Hunter's instincts told him that Criton was not a danger to him or to the other islanders. Either Gardanon had been exaggerating, or Criton was different from his ancestors.

"None of it is true," Criton was repeating to himself.

"Of course it's not true," Hunter said, trying to reassure him. "The writer never gives you a chance. He says to kill the Dragon Touched no matter what, without even talking to them. But if he never talked to them, how does he know what they're like?"

"Right," Narky said. "All I was saying is that it's hard to tell what's true from what isn't. The Dragon Touched must have oppressed the people of Ardis, at least, or the people wouldn't have had any reason to hate them."

Criton's eyes flashed, but he contained himself this time. Any angry or aggressive move he made, he seemed to realize, could be seen as confirmation of Gardanon's words against his people.

None of them said anything for a time. Hunter would have to think about this. Was he right to discount Gardanon's warning, or was he letting his loyalty to his only countrymen cloud his judgment? He would have to be twice as vigilant going forward. If Gardanon was right about the Dragon Touched, then Criton could not be trusted. Even if Gardanon was wrong, the islanders were still in greater danger than they had known: Criton had enemies in the world, enemies who had never even met him. He would need more protection than Hunter had realized.

19
Bandu

Bandu did not understand why Phaedra was giving her so much trouble. She had too many rules. Don't take your coverings off. Don't let bugs live in your hair. On and on.

Now Phaedra was angry because she hadn't stayed in the room when Bandu and Criton were kissing, and for some reason this was Bandu's fault. It made no sense. When Four-foot's kind were in heat, they mated in front of each other without any trouble. It seemed that Bandu's kind were not even supposed to kiss in front of others, which struck her as more than a little ridiculous.

"I don't want to see it, I don't want to know about it," Phaedra said, which was very strange because Phaedra obviously wanted to know everything. She asked Bandu about the kissing, and about what else had happened, and insisted the whole time that she did not want Bandu to tell her. It was very confusing, so Bandu decided to trust Phaedra's words and didn't tell her anything. This seemed to annoy Phaedra even more, but there was nothing Bandu could do about that. She thought Phaedra should decide what she wanted already, and not say anything until after she had made up her mind.

Bandu would not have been able to explain herself

anyway. Phaedra asked Bandu questions using words Bandu had never heard before. When Phaedra finally became frustrated and went to sleep, Bandu sighed in relief.

She stayed awake some time on her own, thinking about Criton. He understood her. They were both wild things, and they fit so well together. She wanted to mate with him, but he did not seem ready for that yet. That was all right; he would be ready soon. She knew it.

Bandu woke up happy and excited, but Criton was different that day. He could barely look at her, and she felt his fear. Why wouldn't he look at her? It had something to do with the dried animal skin, the one he gave to Phaedra to look at. The spirit inside was a bad one. Phaedra looked at the skin and became angry.

"This is pure poison," she said at last. "It's so full of hatred, you can't even tell which parts are skewed by his perspective and which are completely made up!"

Criton did not look any happier, and Phaedra said, "You didn't take it as the plain truth, did you?"

He shook his head, but then said, "It doesn't matter if it's true. It's what Gardanon said. It's what people think. That my mother's people were greedy and selfish and ate children. It's what they see when they look at me. It's what *he* saw when he looked at me."

They were bad, they were wicked, these dry animal skins. They made Criton sad and angry, and they made him not hers. She wanted to take the sharp thing the horse riders had given her and tear that animal skin to pieces. Then Criton would be free to love her again.

Instead, Criton took the skin back to Psander so that he could yell at her. "You said this was a history!" he said. "You gave me a scroll of evil, vicious, *awful* lies about my people and this is my *reward* for helping you?"

Psander raised her hands to stop his shouting. "I gave you what I promised. If it was not what you wanted, you may blame yourself."

Little licks of flame came from Criton's mouth. "It's not a history! It's a pack of lies!"

"That *is* a history," Psander said. She did not yell, but her voice was hard. "If you want something else, then don't ask me for any more histories. History is not truth. A history is just a piece of writing about the past, and a good history will teach you about the present too. The truth of Gardanon's writing is this: Gardanon existed, and he wrote about a visit to Ardis. He told us what he believed, or what others believed, or what he wanted us to think he believed. Either way, the scroll tells us what he, living at his time, thought that we should know. His history is the truth he wanted, and it was preserved because it was the truth that others wanted too. So don't bring your anger to me because you wanted someone to tell you your people were loved and respected. I offered you a history, and that's exactly what I gave you."

Her voice grew calmer as she spoke, but Criton was not calm. "You wanted me to know that I'm hated."

Psander answered him sharply. "You don't think that's something you should know? You would prefer to walk into Ardis one day, asking about dragons?"

Criton had nothing to say to that. Bandu hated this, she hated all of it. Why couldn't he have smiled today, and been angry another day? She had thought today would be happy and special.

Phaedra said, "This history is poison."

"Many histories are poison," Psander told her. "They are so poisonous and so insidious that you often don't even recognize them. You didn't believe that a woman could be a wizard, because nobody ever told you that it was possible. Why? Do you think I am the only woman who has ever become one? I am not. You love to read, girl, but you obviously do not read carefully enough. The authors of all your scrolls, and all of mine, wrote what they wanted people to know, and no more. Some knew more than they said, and some said more than they knew. Some lied intentionally. It is not our job, as seekers of wisdom, to take what we read for the whole truth.

"Take, for example, the sage Katinaras of Tarphae. Yes, Katinaras, your favorite. There was once a man named Phalendron who claimed to have interviewed the sage's parents. According to Phalendron, your beloved author of religious philosophies disappeared from his bed at the age of six and reappeared just as mysteriously three years later. His parents thought he had been kidnapped by elves. And yet Katinaras never once wrote about his disappearance. Apparently, he did not want anyone to know – yet you consider him a trustworthy source."

For a time, Phaedra's control of her language was worse than Bandu's. "That's not pos – you can't be – I mean, there's, that's – you can't say–"

Psander cut her off, turning back to Criton. "Perhaps I should have warned you what you would be reading about beforehand. I apologize if you were expecting something else. If you want something unendingly positive about dragons, read something by the Dragon Knight. I offered you a history and you accepted my terms, so that is what I gave you."

Phaedra bowed her head and didn't say any more. Bandu was glad. She didn't want to talk to Psander anymore. It was a good thing the talking was over.

"Well," said Narky, when they were all back in the room where Bandu and Phaedra slept. "She really sent us off with our tails between our legs."

Bandu had never heard this saying before, but it was one that she instantly understood. Tails between our legs! She would remember that.

"I wonder who this Dragon Knight was," Criton said. He was less angry now, but Bandu could see that there was still something wrong. She wished she really had torn that dried skin. Maybe it would have helped.

"I'm sure Psander will tell us all about it," Narky said, "once we've nearly killed ourselves bringing her some God-forsaken thing from her list."

"When I get the chance," Phaedra offered, "I'll see if I can find anything about him in Psander's library."

Bandu did not want any more of this conversation. "I walk outside," she said, and left them there to talk.

She met Psander on the stairs, nearly walking right into her. "You," she said. "You are wicked. You make promises to me, and to Criton, and you don't give. Why we help you?"

"You're wrong," Psander answered her. "I *have* helped Criton, even if he doesn't know it yet. I admit that I have had little time so far to research expeditions to the underworld for you, but I do have a scroll or two I could lend you..."

"No!" Bandu shouted at her. "I don't want animal skin – I want Four-foot!"

She stormed past the wizard and left the tower.

She had only just reached the gates when Criton came out of the tower door and called for her to wait. She did not wait. With a heave, she swung back one side of the heavy gate and walked out into the morning sun. Criton could run to catch up.

Her stomach growled, which made her angry. They were weakening her with their regular meals. When she had lived in the forest with Four-foot, she had never been this hungry so soon after eating.

Outside of Silent Hall, the world came to life. There were sheep and goats in the fields, and Bandu watched a hawk dive out of the sky to catch something small and furry and delicious. Then Criton caught up with her. He was a little out of breath, and annoyed for having had to run.

"Why didn't you wait for me?" he demanded.

Bandu shrugged. "I don't like it there. Everyone is talking, talking, talking. Like Psander. Psander loves to talk."

"Well, you could have invited me to come with you instead of just running off."

Bandu studied his face. He was hurt. *He* was hurt. "You don't want me today," she said. "You are angry because of animal skin. Why you need wicked animal skin? Everything Psander has is bad. You can take one from Phaedra. They only take her away a short time, and she is not angry when she comes back."

Criton looked confused. "That doesn't make any sense, Bandu. Phaedra doesn't have any scrolls about dragons. What would I need her scrolls for?"

"I don't know!" Bandu screamed at him in frustration. "I don't know why you need any! Why *she* needs them? They are wicked and you shouldn't take them! They take people away, and give them back sad or angry or just the same! They're no good. You should, you should *burn* them."

She did not think Criton listened to her, because he laughed. She pounded his chest with her fist. "Not funny! No laughing!"

To her surprise, Criton hugged her. "Thank you," he said.

"You don't listen," she said into his chest.

"I do," he told her. "I'm sorry. I should have realized that you don't know about reading."

He let her go. "Bandu, the scrolls don't take people away. People write on them. They make these symbols, these, um, these little pictures that people can read. The pictures are all words, just like you would say, but instead of saying them out loud, you can write them – draw them – on a parchment or a piece of bark or anything really, and then anyone can pick it up and read it and they can know what you said. I can show you when we go back inside."

Bandu turned away. "I don't want to."

"But Bandu – well, all right, it's not important right now." They walked quietly together for some time, feeling the hot sun and the warm breeze, and the grass against their ankles.

Criton was not happy; she could feel it when she walked beside him. He wasn't angry anymore, but he was tense from top to bottom. Finally, he stopped walking. "Bandu?

Did I – did I seduce you?"

The question made him very uncomfortable, which was frustrating because Bandu had no idea what it meant. "What is seduce?" she asked him.

"Never mind," he said, and started walking again.

She could not take any more of this. "Why are you sad? Criton?"

He shook his head, and for a moment Bandu was worried that he wouldn't tell her what was wrong. "You're right," he said at last. "That was a wicked scroll. Really, truly evil. The thing is, I don't know how much of it is true! I know I said it was all lies, but the fact is, I barely know anything about my family. Maybe they were as bad as the scroll says. Maybe I inherited some of it from them. Ma was afraid I would kill her husband. That can't be normal, can it? I mean, maybe we *are* all cruel and violent and lustful, just like the scroll says."

She wished he would speak in smaller words. Inherited, violent, lustful – what was he trying to say? All Bandu could tell was that he thought he was bad because of the skin, the scroll.

"You are not wicked," she said.

Criton wasn't satisfied. "But what if I *had* killed him? I wanted to. I was almost ready to. What if we are all like that?"

Bandu looked him dead in the eye. "Your mother is like that? She kill people?"

"No!"

"Then why you think you are like that? You get sharp hands from her and scales from her and eyes from her. You think you are wicked too, because of her? If she is good, how she makes you wicked?"

Criton looked so relieved, it was beautiful. Bandu tasted victory. She was chasing Psander's wickedness out of his soul. At least here, with him, she was stronger than Psander and her animal skins.

"My Ma was never angry," Criton said. There was a tear in his eye. "She was always very sad, all my life, but she was never angry. I was angry all the time. Her husband beat us, and he threatened to kill us, and I just wanted to, I just wanted to..."

"He give you angry part," Bandu said. "Sharp hands come from her, angry come from him."

He looked at her with surprise. He would think about himself differently now, because of her. Psander's wickedness was gone, and maybe his father's wickedness was starting to die too.

"You know, you're wonderful," Criton said.

"I know," Bandu told him.

They walked on. "I think some of what that scroll said must be true," Criton said, but he was not angry or frightened anymore. "My family really did control Ardis for a long time; maybe some of them were as bad as the people thought. And I don't know anything about their God. My mother didn't even tell me about Him."

He went on talking about the scroll and his family, but Bandu was no longer worried, so she did not listen very closely. He was hers again, that was what mattered. She could protect him and he could protect her, just as it had been with Four-foot – except that Criton would also be her mate. What could be better?

She liked his eyes and his golden scales. The way they shone against his dark skin was so beautiful, she thought. His sharp hands felt a little strange when he touched her, but she knew that they could tear her enemies to pieces, and that was important. Her enemies were the ones who put bad thoughts on animal skins, the ones who wanted Criton to hate himself. Bandu wanted to tear them limb from limb. And one of these days, she would.

20
Hunter

Phaedra and Criton spent the next two weeks trying to read their way through Psander's library while Narky and Bandu grew increasingly impatient. Hunter was sympathetic to both parties. It wasn't exactly pleasant here since they'd returned with the Gallant Ones. The villagers no longer trusted them. As for the library, Psander had collected more books than could be read in a decade – an incomparable treasure for Phaedra, but Bandu and Narky were illiterate.

He supposed he'd prefer to leave, but his personal feelings on the matter were not strong. What did it matter whether they stayed or not? It all struck him as meaningless.

They seemed to be stuck in stasis, at least as far as Hunter could tell, but after two weeks, Bandu and Narky prevailed. Neither Psander nor her books apparently held any clue as to which God had cursed Tarphae, and the readers had yet to uncover any new information about dragons. Criton's enthusiasm had begun to flag.

"We've got to get out of here," Narky insisted. "If we stay any longer, I'm going to go insane. The villagers hate us. Psander doesn't care where we go, so long as we're useful. Isn't there any other place that interests you?"

Phaedra sighed. "We could go to Anardis," she suggested.

"What's in Anardis?" Criton asked.

"The central temple of Elkinar. The priests of Elkinar are supposed to be the best healers in the world. Psander said they might still have some academic texts on healing magic from before the purge."

Criton frowned. "Is Anardis close to Ardis?"

"Yes," Hunter told him. "The region is called Hagardis, and the two cities used to be rivals for supremacy there. Then there was a war, and Anardis lost, so now its king has to pay a tribute to Ardis every year."

Criton didn't say anything to that, but he didn't have to. "Psander gave us a whole list of other things she needed," Narky pointed out. "If you insist on helping her, we can look for some of those."

"I don't know how we'd find half of those things," Phaedra said. "Tangletwine leaves? Blueglow mushrooms? And I think calardium ore comes from up in the mountains somewhere."

"We *could* go to the mountains," Criton said. "Ma always said the dragons lived in the mountains."

Bandu nodded her agreement. "Mountains are good. If we go to city, we are always in rooms. Outside is better."

Phaedra turned to Hunter. "Well, what do you think?"

"I say we stay away from Magor's territory as much as we can," Narky said.

"I was asking Hunter," Phaedra scolded.

Hunter hated having everyone look at him like that, expecting him to say something intelligent. "I guess three of us already want to go to the mountains," he said.

Phaedra looked disappointed. Maybe she had expected him to say something else, but what could he do? He didn't really want to go anywhere right now. He just wanted to sharpen his sword and think.

"We can go to Elkinar's temple afterwards," he said hurriedly, but the damage was done.

They found Psander in her library, switching her gaze

back and forth between a codex and two scrolls, like a child watching her parents fight.

"Did you say you needed calardium ore from the mountains?" Criton asked her.

Psander did not even look up. "I did," she said. "This mountain range near us is called the Calardian Range, you know. There are pockets of the ore throughout it. The mountain men use calardium in their fire pits and take it with them on journeys. It radiates heat, which is why some call it dragonstone. If you find a way to obtain some calardium, I will gladly pay you for your troubles. And, of course, you are welcome to anything you need for your journey."

So they left Silent Hall, just like that. The journey went smoothly for a time, which cheered up everyone but Hunter. Nothing much *could* cheer him up, he supposed. The others had their share of wanderlust, but traveling only reminded Hunter that he was homeless. What good were a people without a homeland? They were no better than the Gallant Ones.

Criton and Bandu spent much of their time walking together now. They seemed to be finally taking Narky's advice about practicing their magic, because they spent some hours walking beside the packhorse while Bandu carried on a conversation with it. Narky joined them for this, looking fascinated. Criton did not look happy about Narky's presence, but Bandu didn't seem to mind him at all.

Phaedra was the one who really liked to travel. She had quickly recovered from the disappointment of not seeing Anardis and was now walking ahead of the others, tromping along with her eyes raised to the mountains. Hunter joined her at the front of the pack, mostly so that he could give Criton and Bandu their privacy. The only trouble with that was that Phaedra expected far more conversation than Hunter was used to providing.

"I'm glad we're moving again," she said at one point.

"Bandu has a point about the outdoors. It can be stifling in Silent Hall."

Hunter nodded. "Must be hell for Psander," he said.

"Definitely," said Phaedra. "Although," she added, "if you had to be imprisoned somewhere, Psander's library wouldn't be a bad choice."

"You'd need a ladder though," Hunter said, and Phaedra laughed.

It took them two weeks on foot to reach the edge of the mountains, traveling due west. There were many small villages across the plain, and, no matter which way the wind blew, the air was thick with the smell of cow manure.

"We're going to want to buy furs before we go up," Narky pointed out. "People freeze to death in the mountains, at least according to my pa."

By the time they had bought warm clothes for everyone, Hunter's funds were beginning to run low. They should have asked Psander for money, he realized. The precious stones that Father had given him would fetch a much better price in a city, and nobody disputed Narky's contention that they should hold out for the best price.

"Don't worry," Phaedra said. "I have plenty of money too. You just wouldn't know it because Hunter's always paying for everything."

Hunter shrugged. "I don't mind paying."

The fur traders had suggested a path that led to a few mountain villages, and, following the traders' directions, they soon found the path and began their climb. It was not too treacherous, at least at first. The wind blew more strongly up here, but that was tolerable for now. They passed a carob tree, much to Bandu's excitement, and she spent the rest of the climb chewing on the sweet brown pods and spitting out the seeds. The path continued steadily upwards for about a mile before leveling off and beginning to wind its way onward, sloping sometimes up and sometimes down. The trees obscured their view most of the time, until suddenly they would come upon a place where the vegetation was sparse and the glory of the Calardian range opened up before them. These were the places where they would rest, gazing down in wonder.

Huge was the only way Hunter could describe it. Until he saw it from a mountain, he had had no concept of just how very big the world really was. Atuna, the greatest city in the known world, could have disappeared into the vastness of the Calardian range without their even being able to spot it. Its bustling streets would have appeared as tiny cracks in the earth. Hunter took in the views while the others ate. The cliffs were so sheer, and the ground so far below. Some perverse part of him wanted to jump.

They continued their climb, worried that they might fail to find shelter before nightfall. Phaedra was getting further and further ahead, and Hunter hurried to catch up. He felt a little dizzy. It was probably from staring downwards for too long. He could not catch up to Phaedra like this, and he called out to her. Then he fell.

The earth was moving, shaking, spinning. It was horrible. There were voices – the others asking him what was wrong, and whether he was all right. He was not all right. The mountain was trying to throw him off!

"Hunter," Phaedra's voice was saying. "Hunter, what happened?"

He was extremely light-headed, and his eyes wouldn't focus. "I want to go home," he told her.

Narky was rummaging through Hunter's supplies. "All his food is still here," he said. "His water skin's almost full!"

"Oh, Hunter!" Phaedra exclaimed.

"Drink this," Narky said.

He drank. The mountain was slowing down.

"Hunter," Phaedra said, "why haven't you been eating anything?"

Why were they bothering him? "Not hungry," he mumbled. "I don't want to be here, I want to go home."

"There is no home," Narky said. "You can't go back."

Hunter shook his head. It felt too heavy for his neck. "I should have stayed. I never wanted to go anywhere to begin with."

"Too much talking," Bandu said. "Drink more water."

After they had forced some more water down his throat, they helped him to sit up and feed himself.

"I don't understand," Phaedra said. "Why didn't you eat when we were all eating?"

Hunter closed his eyes. "I wasn't hungry. I didn't think it was important."

Phaedra wouldn't let it go. "Why? Did you think you could just starve yourself?"

"It's not important!" Hunter said, his voice rising, then giving way to a groan as the world threatened to spin again. He closed his eyes once more. "What are we even doing here? Why are we still alive? It's pointless."

"That's not true," Phaedra said. "We're here for a reason, Hunter. The Gods sent your father to that oracle. They sent me on my pilgrimage. They've even marked Narky, for Karassa's sake! We're part of something. Psander knows it too; that's why she wants us working for her."

Hunter opened his eyes. "You think the Gods have plans for us?"

Narky looked skeptical. "I don't see it, Phaedra. Anyone can go visit an oracle, and Ravennis' interest in me... is accounted for. Besides, if the Gods have plans for us, how come They're not giving us any guidance? It seems to me like we're wandering aimlessly, doing jobs for Psander until we find something better to do."

"But that's how it is for heroes!" Criton objected. "The hero in a story never leaves home on a quest. He finds the quest after he's already left. In my ma's stories–"

"This isn't one of your ma's stories, though," Narky interrupted.

"The Gods probably *do* have plans for us," Criton insisted.

"Phaedra's right. It's just that They haven't revealed what they are yet. When we find our destiny, we'll probably look back at these moments and think, 'of *course* we had to go there.' When the Gods have plans for you, They don't just tell you about them."

Phaedra took up Hunter's pack and handed it to him. "They wouldn't let us separate when we left Crossroads, and then They brought us to Psander. Have faith, Hunter."

Hunter sat up straight, and took the pack from her hands. He felt suddenly ravenous.

When he had finished eating and was feeling better, they took his armor off and added it to the packhorse's load. He felt clear-headed now, but still walked the rest of the way with the others crowded around in case he fainted again. It was extremely embarrassing. To make matters worse, his collapse and recovery had taken up precious climbing time. Sunset was likely no more than an hour or two away, and there was still no village to be seen anywhere.

"Come on," Narky said. "Hurry! If we don't get there soon, and the sun goes down–"

"We're almost there," Phaedra said, pointing to a sawed-off tree trunk a little further up the path. If someone nearby was chopping trees, a town couldn't be far.

Sure enough, they reached a village just as the sun was setting, its last yellow rays stinging their eyes before retreating behind a lofty peak. The village was just a tiny hamlet really, some eight or nine houses crowded together in a shallow dip between peaks. Still, it would do nicely. All they needed was a place to shelter from the bitter wind.

A group of villagers, or perhaps the whole village, was gathered around a fire pit in the center of their little town. They looked up as the islanders approached, and Hunter noticed that the men all wore hatchets on their belts. They gripped these, staring at the approaching party. Hunter suspected that, living so far from the sea, these folk had never seen dark skin before. Did they even know that the archipelago existed?

Hunter spread his arms, leaving his sword at his side. He wouldn't be able to fight them all off anyway, certainly not after his fainting spell. "We are only travelers," he said, trying to seem friendly and disarming. His brother Kataras would have done this better.

The mountain folk said nothing, but their children crowded around them in fear. They all looked remarkably alike, with light hair and strong cheekbones. All one family, Hunter thought. Finally, an elder spoke. His beard might have been fully gray, though it was hard to tell by only the firelight and the pink glow of the western sky.

"Come where we can see you," he said.

The Tarphaeans approached cautiously. When the villagers saw that there were only five of them, two of them girls, they relaxed somewhat. The elder, who must have been the village patriarch, said, "Where do you come from?"

"Tarphae," Hunter said, while Phaedra said, "The sea."

"And what are you wanting?"

Phaedra took command. "Shelter," she said. "Our island is warm, and the wind does not blow so hard there."

There was a ripple of laughter among the villagers. "The wind is low today," one of them said.

At least the mountain folk's laughter drained some of the tension from the meeting. "Come sit with us," their patriarch said. His voice was welcoming, but Hunter sensed danger behind his eyes. "May Caladoris bless you. What brings seafolk to the mountains?"

"We heard that dragons used to live in these mountains," Criton answered him. "We were interested in seeing their caves."

"We were also wondering if we could buy some calardium ore," Phaedra added, "if that is permitted."

The old man scratched at his beard. "Cursed caves and sacred stones," he said. Then he smiled. "We are a gift-giving people. Calardium and guidance are most precious gifts indeed. We are happy to provide them to our exulted guests."

His smile was very wide. Though he spoke of gifts, there was no doubt that he expected something very substantial in return.

"May all the Gods bless you," said Phaedra. "We are grateful for your hospitality and your generosity. I wish we had such precious gifts to give you. I'm sure you have no use for gemstones..."

The man's eyes lit up. "The very exchange of gifts is sacred," he said. "We give what we can. The offerings need not always be of equal value."

His manner spoke otherwise. Now that they had been mentioned, only gemstones would do.

Hunter looked warningly at Phaedra. They could not afford to spend his whole fortune on directions and a pile of rocks!

"For our people," Phaedra said, "three is a sacred number."

"I am curious to hear more about your people," the patriarch answered her. "We are not so very different, though for us, the number six is sacred."

"On the island of Tarphae," Phaedra continued cautiously, "white quartz is considered a rare and precious jewel."

"I find that extremely interesting," the old man said, "since in these parts, it is the purple amethyst that is revered above other gemstones."

Hunter could see where this was going, and he didn't like it. For one thing, his father had not given him six amethysts. Three or four might be more like it, with some additional uncut sapphires and semiprecious white quartz. He had to prevent Phaedra from giving away more than they actually had! Yet all he could think to do was to nudge her with his foot.

"A shame that we have no amethysts," Phaedra said, "or

we would most surely give you every last one. But failing that, I think it would be a beautiful thing to receive a gift symbolic of both our cultures. Six pieces of white quartz, the stone we value above others, in the number most sacred to your people."

The elder nodded. "Yes, that would indeed be a most suitable marriage of our different ways."

And just like that, it was all over. In exchange for a bag of warm rocks, Hunter gave over six pieces of quartz, relieved that Phaedra had spared him the amethysts, and yet privately cursing her for having ever mentioned gems to begin with.

"Tomorrow morning," the patriarch said, "Thasa will take you to Hession's cavern, the dragon cave in Mount Galadron."

He pointed to the mountain behind which the sun had disappeared. "You would do well to leave your horse with us, as the climb can be very treacherous. We will take good care of it during your absence, and expect to see you again the following evening. It's a hard climb, but not such a long one."

Hunter was not sure he liked the smile on the old man's face. He was keeping something from them, Hunter was sure of it. But what could he do? At least the mountain men would provide them shelter.

They led Hunter and his companions to the largest building in the village, which turned out to be a barn. No matter. It was warm, and it kept the wind out. Even so, for once Hunter did not fall asleep first. As the others dropped off one by one, Hunter tossed and turned and remained anxiously awake. In his mind, the old man was still grinning.

21
Phaedra

They set out the following day with a townsman named Thasa as their guide. Thasa was about Phaedra's age, with wiry arms and a scraggly beard that grew in ugly little patches all over his jawline. He was not especially friendly and not especially bright, and the only redeeming quality that Phaedra could find in him was that his teeth were straight. When Criton asked him about the dragon whose cave they would be exploring, Thasa shrugged and said he didn't know anything about it, and that the dragons weren't around anymore, so who cared? After that, nobody bothered asking him questions.

Phaedra was excited to explore the dragon cave, but her excitement was overshadowed by her concern for Hunter. She had known that he was the brooding type, but until he had collapsed yesterday, she had thought he was adjusting fairly well to their new life. That was the danger with him: he was strong and quiet, and didn't make any trouble. It seemed obvious now that he had been neglecting his own needs for some time, but his presence was so solid and so stable that nobody had noticed.

Why had she stopped paying attention? It had been clear to her in Atuna that Hunter was trying unsuccessfully to stifle his emotions. He had put on a mask of stoicism, yet all along he had been the one most in need of mourning. Alone among the islanders, Hunter had had no desire to leave Tarphae. He had had no thirst for exploration, no alienation from his home. Phaedra loved her parents and her friends, but she had left them of her own accord. Hunter had been forced to leave without warning because of an oracle he had never met, and because his father cared for him. And even then he had wanted to stay. Even standing on the docks, with Lord Tavener booking his passage, he had wanted to stay. Phaedra's heart went out to him.

Today's climb was much harder than yesterday's. In some places, they had to scale fifteen feet of cliff face in order to reach any semblance of a trail. It didn't help that Thasa kept looking around nervously, as if expecting some sort of danger to be creeping up on them at any moment. Narky asked him what he was looking for, but Thasa just kept repeating, "Nothing," in a way that made Phaedra more suspicious than ever.

"What's he so worried about?" Narky asked when Thasa was out of earshot.

"I think," Criton said, "that the mountain clan has enemies in this area. I heard their elder tell Thasa to watch out for the farmers."

"The farmers?" Phaedra could not imagine anything resembling a farm up here in the mountains.

Criton shrugged. "It doesn't make much sense, but I'm sure that's what he said."

They found the cave late in the afternoon. They had reached a lower summit, and the peak of Mount Galadron stood far across from them. In between, Hession's cavern sank deep and dark, like a hole into black oblivion.

Thasa refused to go any closer. "I'll wait here," he said. "Set up the camp, and I can watch over it for you while you go down."

They left him there to put up their tent as best he could,

considering how rocky and uneven the ground was. They had only brought one, since they had to carry it themselves. They did not leave any of their other belongings with Thasa – they weren't fools.

Before they began their descent, Narky stopped them for a moment in order to say a prayer to Ravennis. "Let fate be kind to us," he implored, "and spare us from danger. Um, yes, I guess that's all. Amen."

The way to the cave began with a steep decline, but the ground leveled out for a time as they approached the cave mouth. Then at last they crossed the threshold into darkness and stood for a moment, waiting for their eyes to adjust. Ahead, their path ended in a yawning chasm.

"We should have brought rope," Criton said. "I don't know why, but I always imagined dragon caves would be more... horizontal."

He was right. Their only rope was being used right now to put up the tent, and this black pit probably went a long way down. It was impossible to know for sure without more light. Bandu was carrying a few torches that the villagers had given them, but they would have to stay in her pack for now. It would hardly be practical to climb down there with a burning torch in one hand.

"I go first," Bandu suggested. "My eyes are better."

"Are you sure?" Criton asked. "The climb would be easier for me with my claws, and I could always light my way by – hey! Bandu, wait!"

The girl had already dropped down and swung her legs over the edge, feeling for a foothold. Soon her hands were gone too. Criton swore, said, "wait here," and began to follow.

Phaedra stood nervously with Hunter and Narky, listening and waiting. Criton breathed a small burst of flame once, shedding some light on his progress, but he did not do it again. "Damn it, Bandu," they heard him say, panting a little as he climbed after her. "You're not invincible."

Phaedra was just beginning to regret coming here when Bandu's voice called out, "Over here! Is good over here."

They stared down into the blackness. After what seemed like ages, an ambient glow became visible from somewhere down below.

"There's a shelf here," Criton called up to them. "It's not that far down, but there's a bit of an overhang between us and you. Can you see well enough to climb?"

"I think so," Hunter called back. "It looks like there are plenty of handholds."

Phaedra looked down toward the light, and had to quickly look away again. The light from Bandu's torch only revealed more blackness below. How far down did this cavern go?

"You're kidding, right?" Narky asked. "This is a death trap. Besides, I can't climb down there holding this spear."

"Leave it behind then," Hunter suggested. "I doubt you'll need it down there. Here, wish me luck."

Phaedra watched him go. His progress was fairly smooth, and he soon disappeared under the rock that Criton had called the overhang.

"That last bit is a little tricky," he called up, "but we can help you with it when you get here."

Phaedra and Narky looked silently at each other. Narky clearly hoped that Phaedra would volunteer to climb down before him, but she didn't feel ready for that.

"Do you want to go next?" she asked. "Then you won't be left up here alone, to go last."

Narky shook his head. "No, you go. I need time to, uh, think."

Phaedra shrugged, and looked back toward the edge. She did not like to admit it, but she was terrified. The thought of climbing down to the others in the semi-dark made her want to curl up in a ball and hide. Standing there quietly with Narky, she was even beginning to hear things: a sort of constant tip-tap-tap that came from somewhere far below.

"Do you hear that?" she asked Narky.

"You know," Narky said, "I think I'll just stay up here. I don't really need to see any more of this dragon's cave in order to satisfy my curiosity. It's really you and Criton who wanted to explore down there – I'd be happy to just wait for you up here."

"Phaedra?" Criton called out to them. "Narky? Are you coming?"

Phaedra took a deep breath. "Yes. I'm coming down now."

It was foolish to stand here like a frightened child. Three of her friends had made this climb already, and no harm had come to them. This was only a test of her will. She smiled, despite Narky looking at her as though she was mad. Willpower had always been a strength of hers. She was her parents' daughter.

She knelt at the edge of the rocks, turned to face Narky, and lowered one foot until she found a solid foothold. She lowered her other foot, her hands still clinging to the ground above. She found that she was making a noise, a little high-pitched squeal at the back of her throat. She made herself stop. She looked down to see how far she had to go, and the distance seemed to stretch out below her. *Keep going,* she told herself.

The rocks were surprisingly warm – perhaps there were calardium deposits down here? Phaedra's foot slipped, and she cried out, but her hands held tight until her foot found purchase again. She breathed, and went on.

She was at the overhang now, what Hunter had called the tricky part. When she extended her leg, it simply hung out over nothingness. Her chest tightened. Gods, what was she doing?

She could not do this. She would climb back up to Narky. There was a foothold up by her knee that she could push off in order to reach that handhold up there and then… and then her foot slipped.

Phaedra had already been reaching for the handhold, and her chest lurched as her hand also missed its destination. She screamed as she fell, past the light where Criton, Hunter and Bandu were standing aghast, past the shelf of rock that they were standing on. Her knee scraped against a jutting rock, and her right hand, wildly grabbing at the air, tore itself upon another. Then she hit bottom on a second shelf, and her legs buckled.

She lay there for some time, unable to move. The light was dim here, only a faint glimmer from above. The others were calling her name, but she could not answer. She hurt all over. Oh Gods, she hurt all over. Her lungs were burning, and she was sure every limb was broken.

"Phaedra, are you there?"

"Yes," she said, finally finding her voice.

"Are you all right?"

"No."

She had images of Tana, the princeling of the Gallant Ones, lying with his limbs splayed. "There is no pain," he had said. She tried moving her right leg. It hurt all right. Her left? Agony. At least they both moved, though. She tried to sit up. Gods above! All right, maybe it was too soon for that.

Was it just her, or was that tapping growing louder? Tip-tap-tap, tip-tap-tap. What sort of creature made that noise? Phaedra had never heard anything quite like it, but she did know one thing: it was definitely coming closer. She struggled to her feet, fighting through the pain. Her knees were wobbly and her right hand had been badly scraped, but she found that she could stand.

"Help me!" she shouted up at her friends. "Oh Hunter, Criton, help me!"

"What's the matter?" Hunter answered her. "What's going on down there?"

"Something's coming," Phaedra said.

"Hold on," said Hunter. "Don't move. We'll be right there. Just don't go anywhere."

It was too late for that. Whatever was making that tapping noise, it was almost upon her. It was coming from somewhere to her left. What was that, looming toward her in the dark? She took a step back, stumbled, and screamed. She had stepped onto empty air and was falling again, or sliding, really, down some kind of rough chute. Even as she fell, the ticking was growing louder. It was coming from all sides now. She tried to slow her fall by spreading her limbs to press against the side of the chute, with moderate – if painful – success. The tunnel into which she had fallen was met by others at different points, and now and then her arm or leg would meet empty space, only to get smashed or jolted when a wall reappeared.

Phaedra's battered body finally came to a stop on something soft and moist that made a vague squishing sound when she landed on it. The smell down here was overpowering, like hundreds of dead animals rotting. She nearly vomited. What agony! It felt as if her ankle had been shattered, and she was sure she had broken at least one rib as well. There was a stabbing pain in her chest every time she breathed in. It even hurt to sit still. When she looked down, she could dimly see her ankle in the bluish light, swelling before her eyes.

Phaedra blinked. How was there light down here, so deep below the surface? It was coming from the ground, or rather, from large patches of phosphorescent mushrooms that grew on the lumpy cavern floor. Perhaps these were the blueglows that Psander had asked for. Were they the ones producing that horrible smell? Groaning, she plucked one of them from beside her and brought it to her nose. It was hard to say. The reek didn't seem to get any *worse* when she sniffed at the mushroom.

Phaedra eased her pack off her shoulders and put the mushroom inside. That was when she discovered that her pack had torn during her fall. She sighed – Gods, how that hurt! – and stuffed a few mushrooms in her shirt instead.

She hoped these were the ones Psander wanted.

She looked up at the shaft that had brought her here, and saw nothing but blackness above her. The thought of climbing back up filled her with despair. She tried not to think about it. Somehow, she would survive this. She would survive and return to the surface, and in time she would surely laugh about her ineptness at climbing. They might even come to consider her fall a lucky accident. If she survived.

Phaedra began to cry, just thinking about having to climb back up to her friends. They were too far up for her to drag herself to them on her broken bones. But she had to try – what else could she do? She put her hands on the ground, so that she could push onto her good foot.

The ground squelched, and the stench got worse. Phaedra raised her hands, and found that they were covered in blood, sticky and mostly congealed. O Gods in heaven, she was sitting on a corpse! Or rather, in one. The corpse's ribs were right there beside her. The skull had mushrooms in its eye sockets.

Phaedra really did vomit this time, and it felt as though she was being stabbed in the chest each time she heaved. She wiped her mouth on her shoulder as best she could – the thought of bringing her bloody hands anywhere near her mouth was sickening. Then she froze. There was that tapping sound again! It was getting closer. Something was coming.

Phaedra sat as still as she could, hoping that she would be mistaken for another corpse. The sound was coming from one side, where another dark shaft opened horizontally. There it was! A dark, shiny something, faintly glinting in the light of the mushrooms. Was that a suit of armor?

It was an ant. An ant the size of Four-foot. Its six legs tapped against the rock and dirt of the cave floor, and squelched when it reached the bodies. O Gods, don't let it notice her! Its mandibles would be able to tear through her flesh and bones without any trouble – they could cut off her legs or drag her away by her flailing limbs, to be eaten by the nest. Phaedra dared not breathe. The ant climbed about the corpses, its meandering path coming ever nearer to Phaedra. It was eating the mushrooms, she realized with relief. These ants did not eat people! Or at least, they seemed to prefer the mushrooms. Not that this was all that reassuring, on second thought: the mushrooms were all growing out of human corpses.

The ant was only two feet away from her when it veered off. Phaedra did not even let out a sigh of relief until she was sure it was gone. There would be others. Lots of others. She had never thought much about ants, but she knew that each nest contained hundreds, perhaps thousands of them. If there were nests like this so near the village, why hadn't the clansmen said anything about them? These bodies had to have come from somewhere.

She thought about Thasa, glancing about so nervously. If the mushrooms only grew on corpses, then the ants that gathered those mushrooms were almost like…

Farmers. The mountain men knew them, feared them, and had deliberately not told Phaedra and her friends about them. Why? Maybe they hated the islanders for worshipping different Gods. Maybe they hated them because their accents were different, or because their skin was black. Maybe they just wanted the packhorse.

The giant farmer ants would be back to gather more mushrooms, and if they found Phaedra there, she would become just another corpse. She took as deep a breath as her ribs would allow, and rose to her feet. The pain in her ankle brought tears to her eyes, but giving up would mean death. Gruesome death, in an ant's jaws. The ceilings in this chamber were low; the shaft above her was within reach. It was confiningly narrow in places, but that meant that Phaedra would be able to hold herself up by pressing against the walls. Even here, where the tunnel was wider, there were plenty of handholds.

Phaedra could not believe she was even going to try this. Her hands were torn and bloody, her ankle shattered, her ribs broken, and probably her tailbone too. She was going to fall, or worse yet, climb right into the waiting jaws of another ant. But what could she do? Nothing. This was her only option, her only hope. *I am my parents' daughter,* she thought grimly. *I can do anything I set my mind to.* She wiped her eyes on what she hoped was the cleanest part of her sleeve, whispered a prayer to Atel, and began to climb.

22
NARKY

Narky did not just take the rope, he took the canvas too. He left Thasa standing confused beside a poorly erected tent frame, its few contents completely exposed. As soon as Narky was back at the cave, he called down to let the others know that he had returned.

"Where the hell were you?" Criton shouted up at him.

"I brought the rope," Narky yelled back. "Is Phaedra still there?"

"No." That was Hunter's voice. "There are all these shafts down here. She must have fallen or been dragged down one of them."

Narky crept to the edge of the cavern and looked down. Hunter and Criton were visible far below, carrying torches. Bandu was on the ground, sniffing at one of the large holes in the cavern floor.

"Very bad," she said. "Very dead things, and other bad things. Phaedra! Can you hear?"

"Do you want me to throw the rope down to you?" Narky asked.

"How much do we have? Not much, right?"

"No," Narky admitted. "Not much."

"The climb is hardest near the top," Hunter said. "Can you

find a place to tie the rope so it reaches past the overhang?"

Narky doubted it. "I'll try," he said.

It took some time for him to secure the rope. His hands kept fumbling. When he had successfully tied it to an outcropping stone and thrown the other side over the edge, he found that the rope did not stretch nearly far enough. Oh, well. He hadn't really expected it to. He took out a knife and began to work on the canvas from the tent. He tore it into strips, twisting them together and tying the ends until he had several additional yards of makeshift rope. When he tied these new lengths together, they were long enough to disappear past the overhang.

Narky was just testing his knots' strength when he heard shouts from below, and the familiar sound of Hunter's sword being drawn. Clutching the rope, Narky cautiously eased himself over the rocky edge until he could see what was happening.

Below, his friends were facing what looked remarkably like a large black ant with its forelegs cut off. It was a little hard to believe that the creature really was an ant, because from this distance, his friends too appeared rather ant-like. An actual ant shouldn't have been visible at all. Yet the creature's jerky movements were unmistakable. How large was that thing?

As Narky watched, Hunter raised his sword with both hands and brought it down on the ant's head. The ant collapsed, and dark bluish liquid sprayed from its broken head. Hunter jerked out his sword and looked around warily, expecting another.

Bandu knelt and put both her hands on the ground. "More coming," she said. "Over there! Criton, behind you!"

She was pointing in two separate directions, but Hunter at least was ready. He leapt toward one of the holes in the ground that Bandu had indicated, and plunged his sword downward just as another ant was crawling out. His blade slipped between the insect's mandibles and stuck for a moment before he pulled it back.

Criton was less ready. The ants moved so quickly! By the time he had turned around, another pair was mere feet away. Criton was still holding both torches, but he did not bother to drop them. Instead he breathed a steady stream of flame, and Narky watched in relief as the ants writhed for a moment and fell onto their sides, their legs curling.

Narky stepped away from the edge and took up his spear. Did he dare climb down with it to join his friends? Would he be of any use down there? What if more ants were outside the cave, foraging? If the others survived and tried to climb back up, any ants here at the top could make short work of them as they climbed. It was best to stand guard, he thought.

Poor Phaedra! She had fallen right into the ants' nest. It was unlikely she had survived. Even if she had, how could she ever make it back up alive? The tunnels would be simply crawling with the gigantic insects, and if any of these chanced upon Phaedra during her climb, that would be the end. It would take a miracle for Phaedra to come back to them. A miracle.

Narky knelt and prayed. Ravennis had taken an interest in him once; maybe He was still watching.

Please, he thought, *let Phaedra come back to us. If I have ever deserved Your mercy, she definitely deserves it more. What's she done to deserve this death and burial in a nest of ants? She's far more devoted to wisdom than I am, and she's kinder and more caring, and much more worthy than I ever was. O Ravennis, let Phaedra come back to us!*

Narky finished his prayer and opened his eyes. If he was going to be a rearguard, he had best do some actual guarding. He went to the mouth of the cave and looked out to see if he could spot any more ants. He did not see any just now, but something else caught his eye: Thasa had gone. The filthy clansman had fled back homewards, useless runt that he was. He probably knew about the ants, and had led the islanders here anyway. Had this cave even belonged to a dragon? Or was it simply a trap?

A sudden noise made Narky look up. One of the giant ants had just entered the cave from above, and was crawling upside-down on the ceiling. For a moment, Narky hesitated. Would poking at this thing just make it angry?

Don't be ridiculous, he told himself, *they're fighting a whole nest down there. The least you can do is to make it safe for them to come up.*

Narky took a quick breath and lifted his spear high – and found to his dismay that it still didn't reach far enough. He knelt for a stone and threw it, but it only bounced off the ant's thick carapace and skittered to the ground. This was enough to irritate the ant, though. It searched left and right for its attacker, and not finding one on the ceiling, stopped there for a moment with antennae waving. Narky threw another stone. The ant craned its body toward the source of the projectiles, and fell suddenly to the ground. It bounced once and turned over, completely unharmed. Then it charged him.

Narky knelt and planted his spear on the ground the way Hearthman Tachil of the Gallant Ones had taught him. The ant was so *fast.* His spear's point was too low, and the ant ran over it toward him. Narky panicked and leapt back, though he knew the ant was faster than him. He nearly tripped over a knee-high rock, but managed not to fall as he backed around it. Oh, he was going to die. The ant was about to reach him, and then…

With a sudden spark of genius Narky leapt forward, kicking off the rock to sail over the ant's head. He landed on the other side and scrambled to retrieve his spear. The ant's vision was poor, but it had felt the tremors in the ground as he fell. It wheeled around almost immediately. Its mandibles clicked in irritation as it rushed him a second time, but this time Narky's aim was true. His spear's point found the mouth between the mandibles and the charging ant impaled itself, pushing farther and farther up the spear until Narky had to let go and leap back again for fear of losing his hands. The ant convulsed for a moment and then lay still.

Oh, Ravennis above! Narky thought. *Do I really want that spear back?* Yet he needed his weapon. What if more came? He took hold of the spear's end with both hands and pulled. Nothing much happened. He put his foot on the ant's head and tried again. No, the angle wasn't right. The ant's body was too heavy to lift, and the spear would have to come out the same way it went in. There was nothing for it. Narky lay down on the ground, braced both legs against the ant's head, and pulled with all his might. The spear came out then, faster than expected so that the butt hit him in the upper chest. Oh, that would leave a bruise all right.

The whole spear was sticky with the ant's blue-gray blood, but Narky held it firmly anyway. Cleanliness could wait for a time when he was no longer in mortal danger. He went to stand once more in the mouth of the cave, gazing up and down the mountainside in search of more ants. Having survived his encounter with one of them, he felt vindicated in his decision not to join the others. He had not been cowardly at all, really, only prudent.

Some shouts from down below called him back into the cave. "She's down there!" Bandu was shouting. "She's alive! Oh, Phaedra!"

Narky rushed to the edge of the chasm and looked down to see Hunter pulling Phaedra out of one of the ant tunnels. Even from up here, Narky could tell that she was terribly battered. Hunter lifted her broken body and slung it over his shoulder. "Let's get out of here," he said.

"I'll be right there," Criton said, turning back toward the tunnels. He got down on his hands and knees with his head over one of the holes. The great burst of flame that followed turned the tunnel into a halo of light around his head. Even in the midst of Narky's worries about Phaedra, it was a beautiful sight to behold.

The jutting rock that Hunter called the 'overhang' obscured most of the climb from Narky's vision. Now and then a flash of light from Criton illuminated the cavern walls, but the climbers remained hidden. Narky was forced to wait nervously at the top, watching the mouth of the cave for any more ants and listening for signs of trouble from down below. It was an agonizing wait, and Hunter's loud grunts were hardly reassuring. But then he felt a tug on the rope, and knew that the ordeal was almost over.

There was some discussion about how to get Phaedra safely over the last hurdle. The girl had apparently lost consciousness during their climb up, and now Hunter, Criton and Bandu set about devising a safe way to tie her to the rope without injuring her. When they were satisfied, Bandu came up to help Narky. Her face was worried. They pulled on the rope silently while Criton climbed beside Phaedra, ready to make adjustments to her fastenings if need be. His help was especially needed when Phaedra reached the overhang and Criton was able to partially lift her on his own to avoid scraping her against the rocks. Finally, they reached the top.

Phaedra looked dead. There was no better way to put it. Her whole body was broken and bloody, her hands torn, her ankle grotesquely swollen. But more than anything, it was her stench that made him sure they would lose her. Her smell sickened him.

He leaned closer to her anyway, to see if she was breathing. Yes, he could feel it, weak though it was. His heart nearly ceased its beating when Phaedra took a shuddering breath and then went still. One second, two, three, four, and Phaedra's breathing started again. Narky found that he had been holding his own breath, and he let it out slowly. They untied her as delicately as they could, and threw the end of the rope back down for Hunter.

When they were all together once more, they carefully

transported Phaedra out of the cave. The sun had already gone down outside, and they lit new torches to guide their way through the twilight. How far would they have to go before they were no longer in danger from the ants' nest? Further than they could carry Phaedra, no doubt. They found a level spot to lay her down, and kept watches through the night.

During the second watch, Criton woke them up with a gout of flame that roasted an approaching ant. Narky sat terrified during his own turn, clutching his spear in one hand and a torch in the other, but luckily the rest of the night was uneventful.

He awoke the next morning to find Bandu eating the dead ant. She had somehow dismembered it and was cracking its legs with a knife and scooping the meat out with her fingers. Hunter and Criton looked sickened, but neither was brave enough to say anything about it. Narky had no such reservations.

"That's disgusting," he said.

She regarded him disdainfully. "I eat, you starve."

Phaedra did wake up once that day, with some coaxing. She did not speak, but did drink some water, and moaned whenever she moved.

"She can't walk like this," Hunter said, "but we need to get out of the mountains. I'm going to go get the packhorse for her to ride."

"Don't go yet," said Narky. "It's still too steep up here for a horse to climb. We'll have to get Phaedra at least halfway down before a packhorse will do any good."

It was a wonder they were able to move Phaedra at all, in her condition. Yet somehow with the help of the rope, their ingenuity, and a double portion of luck, they managed to get her most of the way down the mountain before the sun set that night, to a place the horse would be able to reach. As well as they managed it though, the climb still took a toll on Phaedra. She moaned often, but the worst was when they accidentally dropped her against a rock and she didn't react at all.

Narky hardly slept that night, for fear that he would wake up to find Phaedra dead. His dreams were full of wriggling ants, and of black birds circling in the sky.

Phaedra did not die that night, though neither did her situation improve. At dawn, they said goodbye to Hunter. The young warrior looked grimmer than ever in his soiled armor, and the heavy scales seemed for the first time like a burden to him rather than a second skin. When Bandu pressed the majority of the remaining food and water on him, he stood in hesitation.

"I can't take all this," he said.

"Take it," Bandu said. "You need strong."

"But you'll need food too, while I'm away."

"We eat," she reassured him. "I can feed them. They eat with me."

"Not ants, I hope," Narky said.

But it was ants that Bandu had in mind, ants and crushed acorns and the furry little melon-like creatures that clambered about the rocks on their comically short legs. Narky had never even noticed them until Bandu brought back a pair of dead ones, but after that he began to see them everywhere. Their bodies were a dull gray color that blended in perfectly with the rocky mountainside, and they had a tendency to lie perfectly still for minutes at a time, with only their occasionally blinking eyes to show that they were alive. Narky had no complaint with this behavior. His complaint was with their taste.

Two days passed slowly while they waited for Hunter to return. Bandu spent much of that time foraging, while Narky and Criton spent it watching over Phaedra and arguing over whether they should do anything to help her heal. Criton insisted that they had to do something besides praying, but Narky was afraid of causing her more pain, especially if she ended up dying anyway. His experience with Four-foot still haunted him. In the end all they could agree to do was to clean her open wounds and keep giving her water. That could do her no harm, at least, though Narky knew it wasn't enough. Her skin was alarmingly hot to the touch.

Washing her proved to be its own struggle, since Narky had to carefully peel her clothes from her skin to see how badly she was injured. The motion woke Phaedra a few times, but she only babbled and stared unknowingly at him before lapsing back into unconsciousness. Criton was clearly uncomfortable with Narky's examination, and to be honest, so was Narky. He just had to keep reminding himself that she needed his help, and hoping that she would not be angry with him when she recovered.

To Narky's great relief, the open wounds on her hands and legs turned out to be the only ones she had, though her entire body was covered in dark bruises. Oddly enough, he found that she had hidden a number of mushrooms in her shirt. He handed them to Criton to pack carefully away. When her cuts had been washed and dressed to the best of his ability, and he had successfully poured some water down her throat, they were forced to simply sit back and wait.

The waiting was hard on Narky. It seemed he had nothing to do besides worry. Criton, too, spent most of his time brooding. He experimented with his magic, turning his claws to hands and back to claws again. He changed his scales to skin, and then went the other way and turned it all to scales. His hair seemed to melt back into his head, from chin to scalp. It was a frightful look and Narky was glad when Criton went back to his normal hybrid state.

"Is that all you can do?" Narky asked. "That and the fire, I mean?"

Criton sighed. "I can't heal her, if that's what you mean. I'd probably kill her, trying."

"Oh," Narky said. "I guess that makes sense. It just seems like there has to be more to magic than lighting fires and changing shape."

"There is," Criton said, looking annoyed. "But this is what I know how to do."

"Try doing something else."

Criton looked down at his hands, and Narky's eyes followed. "Stop looking at me," Criton said. "I'm trying to figure something out."

Narky snorted and looked the other way for a moment, but he did not keep his eyes off Criton for long. The other boy was staring intently into his open claw now, concentrating. It was hard to tell in the daylight, but Narky thought there might be a bright something in Criton's palm. A little bead of light, like a dewdrop suspended just above the scales. Narky might not even have noticed it, if not for the way it fluoresced in the sunlight. It skittered around in Criton's palm, blinked a bright pink, and then disappeared. Criton furrowed his brow.

"Practice," he mumbled. "It'll get better with practice."

Hunter returned that night, leading their packhorse. Bandu was roasting another of her melon-creatures, and the flickering light made Hunter's face appear gaunt and hollowed out.

"What took you so long?" Narky asked.

"It went badly," Hunter said. "I killed two men."

"They were hoping the ants would take care of us," Narky said, and Hunter nodded in confirmation.

"How is Phaedra?"

Criton shook his head. "Bad. She's been asleep for hours now."

Hunter knelt by Phaedra's body and felt her forehead. "Gods above," he murmured. "She's burning up."

Phaedra's eyes shot open. "He's watching," she said, catching hold of Hunter's arm. He tried to pull gently away, but her grip was clearly too strong.

"Magor's watching," she said, "and He wants us dead."

23
Bandu

Phaedra spent much of the night babbling incoherently, and shivering no matter how they piled their furs on top of her. She looked so frail and cold that Bandu joined her under the furs even though Narky thought it was wrong to touch sick people.

"Fevers can jump from one person to another," he said, and Criton looked worried.

Phaedra sweated a lot that night, and Bandu woke up almost slippery with it. Phaedra looked a little better than before, but she was definitely not ready to travel. Bandu didn't know if she would ever be ready. It was not much of a recovery, and it could just as easily get worse again.

"I'm going to die," Phaedra mumbled, when Criton asked her how she felt.

Narky said that was fever-babble, but Bandu knew it wasn't. Phaedra's eyes could see them now.

"You're not going to die," Hunter more or less commanded. "You're going to break this fever, and then we're going to carry you out of these mountains."

Phaedra looked dismayed. "I can't," she moaned. "I can't go any farther than this. Moving hurts too much. I'm dying, Hunter."

"You were strong enough to climb out of there," he told her. "You can do this too."

Phaedra sighed, but she did not object again.

"We go today," Bandu suggested. "Too cold here for you."

They carried Phaedra down the mountain on Grayleg's back. Grayleg was slow and careful, but Phaedra still cried out faintly whenever the horse's movements jostled her too hard. Nobody could blame Grayleg: she was doing her best, but going down the mountain would have been hard enough, even without Phaedra on her back. Anyway, that was not the worst part of their journey. The worst part was when the crows began to follow them again.

"Go away," Bandu told them. She saw how they looked at Phaedra.

"There is no meal for you here," she said. "Go, or I will eat you."

She tried to say it quietly, but Narky heard her. He gave her a very angry look, and apologized to his God. Still, the birds stayed farther off after she threatened them. They knew that she wasn't joking. Crows were no fools.

They had only one tent now, since Narky had used the other one as a rope. Narky insisted that crowding Phaedra was unhealthy, so tonight Bandu and Criton agreed to sleep outside. At least Bandu was used to it.

Criton had never slept out in the open before. He turned over and over and could not get comfortable, and the whispering wind was not a comfort to him. Bandu pulled him near and laid his head on her chest.

"Do you hear it?" she whispered to him.

"You mean your heart?"

"Yes," she said. "What it says?"

Criton looked up at her. "It says, 'I love you.'"

She laughed, her worries momentarily forgotten. "What it *really* says?"

"That's all it says!" He was smiling too.

"No," she told him. "I listen to Four-foot's heart. You

know what it says?"

"No," he said, half sitting up. "What did it say?"

She took a deep breath. "It says ban-doo. It always says ban-doo."

She saw his eyes widen with his understanding. "Did you used to have another name?" he asked.

"Maybe. I call myself Two-foot before."

Criton nodded. "Do you want to listen to my heart?"

When she put her head on Criton's chest, his heart was beating much faster than Four-foot's heart ever had. It was pounding in excitement. And it was saying her name.

They took the long way out of the mountains, so that they would not have to climb as much and Phaedra would not get bumped as badly. The travel was hard on her anyway, and she kept begging them to stop and rest a little while longer. Still, she was getting a little better, Bandu thought. She was awake for longer, anyway.

One afternoon, when they had stopped beside a mountain stream, Phaedra motioned Bandu to come over to her. "Where are the mushrooms?" she whispered.

"Mushrooms?" Bandu asked, confused.

"The ones I found in the farmer ants' nest," Phaedra said, her voice fading away almost to nothing. "They were blueglow mushrooms, Bandu! I saved a few for Psander. Are they safe? Did you pack them already?"

Bandu shrugged and checked the saddlebags. Sure enough, someone had stuffed some mushrooms in there. The sight of them enraged her. She even considered throwing them away. She had almost lost Phaedra in that cave – almost lost her! Her injuries might yet kill her. How could Psander still have a hold over her? Bandu wanted to destroy those mushrooms.

But she didn't. Instead, she packed them back where she had found them and tried to forget that they were there.

That night, Phaedra's fever finally broke. When they rose

in the morning they found her sleeping peacefully under her furs, a smile creeping onto her face despite the beads of sweat that glistened all over her skin. When she awoke, her eyes had lost their glassy look.

It had taken them only two days to reach the mountain called Galadron, but it took two weeks to reach the plains again. Phaedra's health steadily improved as the days went by. Bandu still watched her carefully, worrying that her cuts would turn colors the way that Four-foot's had, but Phaedra was lucky. The only thing she still complained about was that she had lost her scrolls when her bag tore. Bandu was secretly glad, though of course she said nothing. Criton had told her that scrolls were just skins covered in old words, but Bandu still did not like them. Dead people should not be able to talk.

When they came out of the mountains, Hunter turned them northward.

"Hold on," Narky said. "Shouldn't we go back to Silent Hall?"

"Later," said Hunter. "First we're going to Anardis. She said the priests there were healers, and I think a temple library would be a good place for Phaedra to rest right now. Besides," he added, "I said we could go there after the mountains."

"Aww," said Phaedra, a weak smile playing across her lips. "Thanks, Hunter!"

Bandu sighed in relief. The less time they spent in Silent Hall, the better. It was a wicked place.

"I'm glad Phaedra's doing better," Criton said that night, when the two of them were alone outside the tent. "I really thought we were going to lose her."

Bandu nodded. "I know. Don't talk now."

"When she came out of there," he went on, "smelling like death..."

"I don't want to hear!" she scolded him. "I remember."

"I'm sorry," he said, "but I have to talk about it. It's eating me up. I can't get it off my mind. I thought she was going to–"

She stopped his mouth with a kiss, and when he tried to say something, gave him another. He soon forgot to talk, which was good. There was too much talk. Talking all the time made her feel weak and stupid, when she knew that she was really strong. In silence, they were equals.

She did not expect it to hurt when they mated, but it did. He did not fit as easily as she had thought he would, but he tried anyway, far too hard. She cried for him to stop, and saw his face change: anger and frustration beat down upon her from his eyes. He didn't understand.

"What's the matter?" he asked. He was trying to control himself, but his voice was not as gentle as it should have been.

Bandu glared at him. "It hurts! Why you are angry with me? I don't hurt you!"

"I'm not angry," Criton lied. "I'm just – I'm not angry."

He covered himself and moved away. Bandu said nothing, just watched him while he glared off into the distance.

"I'm sorry it hurts," he said finally. "I didn't know it would hurt. Did I – did I do it wrong?"

Relief rushed through her. He was worrying about her now, and not himself. "It is better later," she said, putting an arm around him. She hoped it would be.

"So what now?" he asked.

She pushed him gently down and laid her head on his chest. "I listen to your ban-doo."

"My Bandu," he repeated. "My Bandu." He began stroking her hair.

She awoke to find herself bleeding. It had been about a month since the last time, so that much was normal, but Phaedra gave her a funny look when she asked for one of those pads that were so useful. Bandu wondered if something was wrong.

"Next time we're in town," Phaedra said, sounding

normal enough, "we can buy more wool and linen and I'll show you how to make your own."

That evening, Phaedra finally revealed what was going on in her head. While Hunter was busy putting up their tent and the others were out looking for firewood, she leaned over and asked Bandu, "So, what is it like?"

Bandu looked at her curiously. What was 'it?'

"I heard you two sneaking off," Phaedra explained. "How does it feel?"

"What feels?" asked Bandu. "What is sneaking? I am sneaking off what?"

"Oh, you know," Phaedra nearly whispered. "Off to make love. With Criton."

Oh. Bandu shook her head. "It hurts."

Phaedra nodded, as if this was normal. "They say it's supposed to hurt the first time. I guess it doesn't later. But congratulations! The first time is special."

"Why?"

"Well, because it's a big change. You were a virgin, and now you're not."

"What is virgin?" Bandu asked.

"Someone who hasn't done it before. A maid, like... well, like me."

There was a sinking feeling in Bandu's stomach. "I not like you now? Why changed?"

"Just because," Phaedra said uncomfortably. "Because it's different. You can never be a virgin again. Making love shouldn't hurt as much now, and it won't make you bleed again even if you want it to."

That was the most ridiculous thing Bandu had ever heard. "Why," she asked slowly, "do I want to bleed *more*?"

"Oh, you won't have to," Phaedra said hurriedly. "Criton won't leave you, so you're safe. It won't come up."

That made even less sense. What was Phaedra trying to say? Bandu didn't think her bleeding had anything to do with Criton, but apparently Phaedra thought otherwise.

Could she be right? If Criton left, would it make Bandu bleed more? Or did she mean that mating would hurt her all over again if she did it with someone else? What if she didn't want to mate with anyone else, or to 'make love,' as Phaedra called it? And if she did, how would her body know that it wasn't still with Criton? Bandu wasn't even sure what to ask first. In the end, she just said, "What?"

Phaedra might have been *trying* to confuse her, because she tried to make up for the nonsense of her words by saying them faster.

"Well, you know," she said, "some men take women's virginity and leave, which is terrible because then you've been disgraced and you can't marry anyone else. If you did, they'd find out you weren't a virgin because you didn't bleed. A lot of women in Karsanye ended up that way, and their fathers disowned them, and they had to become whores or starve. A whore makes love to men for money, Bandu. Everyone said those girls wished they could be virgins again, but it was too late. But don't worry, you'll be fine because Criton is a good man and he'll marry you."

Bandu scratched at a scab on her knee, and tried to make sense of all that. "What is 'marry?'" she asked. "Why it needs virgins?"

Phaedra looked a little shocked. "You don't know what it means to – um, all right. When a man marries you, it means you... you belong to him. And he belongs to you, sort of. You don't make love with anyone else. It's a lifelong bond."

"Why?"

Phaedra just stared for a moment. Bandu thought she had heard, but she repeated herself anyway just in case.

Phaedra wrinkled her brow. "Why is it lifelong, you mean, or why don't you make love with other people?"

Bandu nodded. "Yes," she said.

Phaedra looked a little horrified. "Because... because you've shed your blood with him! It's sacred!"

Sacred? Oh! "The Gods are angry?" she asked.

"Yes," Phaedra said, sighing. "Yes, it makes Them very angry."

"Why?"

"It just does. It insults Them."

It seemed to Bandu that the Gods were getting worse and worse. What business did they have deciding how people mated?

Hunter was listening to them, she noticed, though he was pretending not to. He was done with the tent, but he was still walking slowly around it and looking it up and down, as if he thought he might have made a mistake somewhere.

Phaedra was too frustrated and confused to notice. She saw Bandu looking elsewhere and asked, "What part don't you understand?"

Bandu blinked, and looked back at her. "I marry because I hurt every time I make love with a new man? Or because Gods want me only with Criton?"

Phaedra shook her head. "No, no, you're not listening hard enough. I thought I said, you can only lose your maidenhood once. After that, lovemaking won't make you bleed. But when you've lost your maidenhood, your virginity, you can't marry anyone except for the man who took it."

"Because then Gods kill me?"

Phaedra looked a little angry. "No, Bandu, because no man will want to marry you then. They only want to marry you if you're a virgin."

"Oh," said Bandu. She continued slowly, carefully. "So men only marry if virgin, but Gods only kill if I marry wrong person. If I don't marry, then is safe."

She was sure she had understood it this time, so why was Phaedra getting angrier?

"No, Bandu," she said. "You have to marry. If you make love to a man but don't marry him, you're no better than a prostitute!"

Bandu scratched her head. "Do Gods kill them?"

"No!" Phaedra nearly screamed. Then she turned and saw Hunter nearby, and lowered her voice. "Bandu, it's not about the Gods this time, all right? The Gods don't kill prostitutes. Oh, hold on, I should have said – 'prostitute' is another word for whore. Sorry if I confused you. The important thing is that men don't take care of prostitutes, they only pay them. Men take care of their wives, the women they marry."

This was why Bandu did not like talking. It made people angry sometimes, and she *still* couldn't make sense of what they were saying.

"I think I know now," she said to Phaedra, to calm her down.

It worked. Phaedra heaved a big sigh of relief, and calmed down almost immediately. "You understand, then?"

The trouble was that Bandu *wanted* to understand. "I try," she said. "I don't know why men marry only virgin. Can you say?"

Phaedra nodded warily, but she did not say anything for a long time. Bandu wondered if she had forgotten the reason. Finally Phaedra began to speak, slowly, as if she wanted to give Bandu time to hear everything. But Bandu suspected her real reason was that she needed time to invent an explanation.

"Men want to be the first," Phaedra said. "If you bleed, they know they were first. If you don't, they know someone else was first."

"Oh. Why they need to be first?"

Phaedra nodded at the question, but paused again before she answered. "They only want to marry someone who will be faithful to them. If they weren't the first, then they know you were already unfaithful to someone else."

Bandu snorted. She couldn't help it. "They don't know," she said. "Maybe someone else dead! Maybe someone else leaves, like you say about Karsanye. They know if they ask!"

"Well, that's true," Phaedra said. She tried again. "But

it's not really just that they want to be first, Bandu. It's that they want to be the only one. If they weren't first, then they couldn't have been the only one."

"Only one is important?"

"Yes," Phaedra said. "It's very important to them."

"Why?"

"Because it's more special that way."

Maybe they were finally getting somewhere. "Why more special?" Bandu asked. "And how you know if you are only one for them?"

Phaedra shook her head. "You don't. But you don't really need to be. Men are more experienced, and that's all right."

Now Bandu was getting annoyed. "Why all right? Man needs to hurt and make bleed so he feels good that he is only one, but he never bleed and doesn't need you to be only one for him? You say men are wicked!"

"No," Phaedra said. "Well, that is, not all of them. Anyway, if they marry you, they promise in front of the Gods that they'll stay with you as long as you both live."

So that's how the Gods were involved! Finally, an explanation!

"I understand," Bandu said. It was all starting to make sense. "They do not break promise, because then they make Gods angry and they die."

Phaedra looked extremely uncomfortable. "Well," she said, "it doesn't always work that way. It can take the Gods a long time to notice, and if They favor a man for some other reason, They'll often overlook things like infidelity."

Bandu's eyes widened of their own accord. "So you say men are wicked because they think Gods won't care?"

"Well, yes," Phaedra said. "I suppose that's true. But keep in mind, also, that men can't always control themselves."

It was Bandu's turn to be shocked. "But you say they need to be only ones for us! They want to hurt us, so they know they are only ones, and then they marry and break promise to Gods because they can't control? So you say men are wicked and stupid, and want to hurt us."

Phaedra shook her head, but she said nothing. Bandu understood. If Phaedra had nothing to say, that meant that Phaedra did not want Bandu to be right, but that she was right anyway.

"You are wrong," Bandu said gently, trying to reassure her. "Criton is not stupid, and he doesn't want to hurt me. And I don't bleed last night, only today. If he doesn't know about blood, and doesn't ask, then he doesn't care."

Phaedra looked surprised, even a little confused. "He's a good man," she said weakly.

"But you say first time is good and special," said Bandu, "and that is also wrong. If first time is special, then I hope only because first time is bad. I say if other people want to be virgin again, they are stupid. I am not stupid, and men are not all stupid."

"I hope not," Phaedra said.

"If some men want first time to hurt and bleed," Bandu said, "then those men are wicked. They are very wicked, and you should not want them."

Phaedra nodded noncommittally. "I'll have to think about that," she said.

Bandu hoped she would.

24
CRITON

They traveled northward for some time, hoping to encounter the same hospitality they had found for Narky not so long ago. But though the lands here were fertile and the villages robust and prosperous, the pale residents all shut their doors to the islanders.

"Black skin, black hearts," one old lady said, as she slammed her door in their faces.

Phaedra's health continued to improve, but she still could not walk. They rested under almond trees, passed through fields of wheat and rows of fig trees, and sampled the fruits when Hunter and Phaedra weren't looking. Phaedra claimed that they should be welcomed at any temple, but the first one they came to was closed to them as well. It was a temple of Pelthas, who Phaedra reminded them was the God of Justice.

"Get away, accursed wanderers!" the priest there shouted.

"Some justice," Narky spat. They moved on.

Criton wondered about the religion of his people. Was God Most High really a cruel God, as the scroll had said? Were His priests more hospitable than those of Pelthas?

"Phaedra," he asked, "do you know anything about God Most High?"

Phaedra shook her head. "I think He must be dead," she said gently. "After all, the dragons and your ancestors were all destroyed."

Criton nodded sadly. He had half expected her to say that. If the Gods really were in constant conflict, it stood to reason that a God no longer worshipped was a God no longer living.

"Do you know what killed the dragons?" he asked her.

Phaedra looked apologetic. "They say the Gods did, but they always say the Gods when they don't know the real answer. Sorry. Until I met you, I thought the dragons might have been just a legend."

"The same way you thought about fairies," Narky pointed out.

"You know," said Phaedra, frowning at him, "if you had said that with a smile and a joking tone of voice, it might not have come off as so rude."

"But it's not a joke," Narky said. "It's true. You thought that fairies were a myth."

"She realizes that," said Hunter.

"I don't see why people would smile or act like they're joking if they're really criticizing each other," Narky went on.

"It's only criticism if you don't smile," Phaedra told him. "If you smile, it's friendly teasing. If you're going to insist on pointing out people's faults, you may as well do it politely."

Narky shrugged. "All right, I guess I'll try that next time."

Phaedra arched her eyebrows. "You're welcome."

They continued northward along the mountains, leaving the tent to Phaedra, Narky and Hunter while Criton and Bandu slept outside. Criton wanted to try making love again, but he was afraid of the way Bandu might look at him if he suggested it. He sighed to himself and said nothing.

After perhaps a week, Bandu finally tugged at his arm. "Go with me," she said.

He started up immediately. "Really? You're ready now?"

She only tugged harder. "Phaedra hears us here," she said. "She always say she doesn't want to know things, and then she wants anyway. We go away then is good."

She was right. Then *was* good. At first he was afraid that he would hurt her again, or that she would make him stop because she didn't like it. He was afraid he would do it all wrong. So he followed her lead this time, and she guided him until her quickening breaths were the only guide he needed. After that, he stopped thinking.

They lay shuddering together for some time, even after it was over. When they finally separated, Bandu nestled into the crook of Criton's arm and laid her head on his chest. It was marvelously comfortable, he thought, although it was odd the way his hip sockets ached now. He hadn't realized that hip sockets *could* ache. Even when all his limbs had seized up after their climb out of Hession's cave, his hips had felt perfectly fine.

"You want to marry me?" Bandu asked suddenly.

"What?" he asked, startled. "Bandu, what made you think of that?"

She put an arm over his stomach and nestled closer. "Phaedra says after people make love they marry and promise not to have others. She says you marry me because you are good."

Criton stiffened. *I could kill Phaedra!* he thought.

"Phaedra said that?" he asked. "What did she tell you about marrying?"

"She says people make promise to Gods," Bandu said, looking up at him. "Why do you do like that?" She sat up.

"Do what?"

"Stop moving. Make body not soft anymore. Why?"

He shifted uncomfortably. "I don't know what you're talking about."

Her eyes went wide. "You are afraid! Why you are afraid?"

He rolled over and turned his back on her. "I'd rather not

talk about it," he said.

What did Phaedra have against him, that she would fill Bandu's head with thoughts of marriage? They were dangerous, so dangerous. Marriage had trapped his mother.

"We don't need to promise Gods," Bandu said, putting a hand on his shoulder. "I don't care about Gods. You can promise me."

"Forget about marriage!" he said, pulling away again. "Just go to sleep, all right?"

Bandu punched him in the back. "You want others!" she cried. "You not promise because you want others!" She slapped at his shoulder and side, making his skin sting and burn.

Criton sat up in anger, swiping back at her. Bandu recoiled. He had missed, thank the Gods! With these claws of his, he could easily have ripped the flesh from her body.

The look of shock and fear in Bandu's eyes horrified him. He jumped to his feet and ran off into the darkness. His head was pounding. It was her fault! Bandu had ruined everything! Phaedra had ruined everything! Why did they hate him so?

He ran on and on, until he could no longer hear her voice or even feel the stiffness in his legs. There was a fire in his throat, and he let it out in great billows of smoke and flame. A stream glittered before him in the moonlight, but Criton didn't slow his pace. He jumped, and did not fall. Soon he was past the stream, and still his feet did not touch the ground. An almond tree loomed in the darkness, and he rose through the air until he could graze its top. He circled a few times, then came to land on one of its branches. His head was still pounding. Marriage! Were they crazy?

After a time, Criton calmed down. How had he gotten up here? How had he done that? Would Bandu ever forgive him for running away?

Oh, Bandu. He had nearly struck her. Oh Gods, he could have killed her! Poor, beautiful Bandu! Psander's scroll had been right: he was a monster. How could he ever protect Bandu from himself? If this happened every time she made him angry, then how many fights, how many arguments before he lost control? Sooner or later, his ancestral evil would get the better of him.

He had to tell her. She would understand – she had to. He was dangerous. Surely, after this, she would want to leave him. The thought filled him with pain. He clutched the tree trunk, bowed his head, and wept.

She would be worried about him. He had to get back to her. Where was he? In the starlight, nothing seemed familiar. He wasn't even sure which way he'd come.

Criton carefully climbed down the tree, thinking wryly that Narky would be excited to hear about his flight. Now, which way was the camp? The fire had been little more than a pile of glowing embers by the time Bandu had asked him about marriage. He would not be able to spot the light from this distance. Criton left the tree and walked out into the darkness. Somewhere around here was that brook he had leapt over. Why couldn't he hear it now?

He never found the stream. He wandered about in the dark, getting ever more worried and frustrated with himself, as the night grew cold and windy. The wind was blowing out of the mountains, but it was more than just that. The rainy season would be coming early this year. By the time Criton gave up on finding the brook, he could no longer point in the direction of the tree either. He curled up on the ground, using a rock for a pillow, and drifted in and out of an uncomfortable sleep.

He awoke still in the dark, feeling something wet against his side. Oh Gods, what *was* that?

"Keep me warm," Bandu said. "The water is cold."

Bandu! How had she found him?

"I'm sorry I ran away," Criton said.

"I know," she said. "I'm sorry too. Keep me warm."

Criton put his arms around her, and wondered at her

cold, wet little body. She had found him. Somehow she had followed his trail from the camp, swum through the brook, and tracked him down here, all in the dark.

"How did you do that?" he asked. "How did you find me?"

"I find you anywhere," she said. "Keep me warm."

25
Hunter

Hunter could not sleep. It was not his fault – the clansmen had mobbed him. They had wanted to keep the horse, and they knew that it was Hunter whose purse held the islanders' gemstones. There was no other way – it was them or him. The first man had screamed as Hunter's blade slipped beneath his upraised arm and plunged into his chest. The second man had thought he could pounce on Hunter before he had freed his blade, but Hunter had slammed the rim of his shield into the man's throat and retrieved his sword while the second man choked to death with a crushed windpipe. The others had backed off then, and Hunter had led the packhorse away, looking warily over his shoulder. Two men dead, over a packhorse.

Hunter had trained hard for war. He had thought it would bring him glory and status and his father's respect. But Father was dead now, and there was no glory in killing strong men for the sake of an animal and some rocks. Those men had been fathers too.

The others never asked Hunter about his meeting with the mountain clan. They were glad to have the packhorse back, and they accepted his word that two men were dead with a kind of casual acknowledgment. To them, killing was what Hunter *did*.

Glory. How foolish he had been! There was no glory in killing fathers. The only thing Hunter had experienced that even resembled the pride he had imagined he would feel after a battle, was the way he had felt when he had rescued Criton from the Boar of Hagardis. When the boar was dead and Criton was still alive, *then* he had felt proud. He had *done* something. But as often as he told himself that those two men's deaths were not his fault, the fact remained that they had died, and he had killed them. If he had not gone back for the horse, those two men would still be alive, and Hunter would still be able to sleep at night.

He wanted to go home, back to the life he had had before, back when he had still known nothing about pointless death. He would pretend that glory still existed, and that his sword and armor were worth more than just the blood they could help him spill. Why couldn't he have stayed and been drowned along with his father? He could have died a happy fool, drowning in single-minded idiocy.

Oh Father, he thought, *you were right to be worried about me.*

The Oracle had promised his father that Hunter would have a long and meaningful life. Meaningful. If the Gods could fulfill a prophecy like that, They could do anything.

What now, though? Phaedra had said the Gods were still watching them – was there any hope of a rebirth for him? He thought enviously of the way Narky had burned his crossbow, but he knew deep inside that he could never throw away his weapons. The others expected him to protect them, and besides, he was just as attached to his blade as he was to his limbs. But was the sword a part of him, or was he a part of it?

After more days of travel than Hunter could bother to count, they came to the city of Anardis. The city was abuzz with action: it seemed that every man in sight was engaged in the work of building a city wall. Stones were piled everywhere, and young boys were struggling to push barrows full of them to the places where the men were working. A few of the men looked up and noticed the islanders, but they only pointed to one side and went back to their toils.

"Gate's that way," one of them said helpfully.

The islanders turned and followed the direction they had pointed in, though Narky protested at the waste of time. "Why should we find the gate," he asked, "when we can just walk through a wall? There are plenty of places where there's no barrier yet."

"It's a matter of respect," Phaedra told him. "They're working hard on that wall. You don't taunt them by stepping through it."

Narky shook his head in exasperated wonder. "If you say so."

There was only one man at the gate, a somewhat rotund elderly man leaning on a staff.

"Go away," he said. "We don't want wanderers here."

"We're looking for a place to rest from our travels," said Hunter, "and for my friend to heal from her injuries."

The old man looked them up and down. "Look here," he said, "you're those cursed wanderers of Tarphae, aren't you? Your island is gone, so you go about the land, bringing bad luck with you wherever you go. I hear you slew the Boar of Hagardis, and brought your bad luck to the prince of Atuna while you were at it. We don't need your luck here. Our city's had enough bad luck as it is."

"What city is this?" Phaedra asked, her face a mask of innocence.

"You've come to the once-great Anardis, girl. Great once more, as the king would have it. Time will tell, as to that."

"That same Anardis where Elkinar's Temple can be found?"

"Of course." The old man eyed her suspiciously.

"Thank the Gods!" Phaedra exclaimed. "I have heard

that the priests of Elkinar might be able to lift our curse. Where is His temple?"

"Inside," the man said warily. "Who told you that Elkinar's priests would lift your curse?"

Hunter wondered how she would get out of that one. He was not disappointed.

"Our curse can be lifted only through rebirth," Phaedra said confidently. "If anybody can lift the curse without killing us, it will be the priests of Elkinar. Please, let us in to see them."

The old man scratched his head. "Well, all right," he said. "I suppose they'll know what's best. But don't overstay your welcome, or you'll be very sorry."

"That's a new rumor," Criton said once they were within the gates. "Who's been telling people we're cursed?"

"The Gallant Ones," said Narky. "Nobody else would have gone around calling Tana the 'Prince of Atuna.'"

"Or blamed us for his death," Hunter pointed out.

"But how did you know what to say to him?" Criton asked Phaedra. "Who is this Elkinar? What kind of God is He?"

"He's the God of the Life Cycle," Phaedra answered. "Birth, life and death are His domain."

"Oh, just that?" said Narky, raising an eyebrow.

The Temple of Elkinar was not hard to find. It was a large building in the heart of the city, across from the king's palace. There were no windows in its sides, but the temple was crowned by a terrace, and from a distance one could see several trees and bushes growing there. Wisps of smoke rose from between the greenery, creating a strangely ominous effect. The plants were clearly very much alive, but Hunter still half expected them to go up in flames at any moment.

They helped Phaedra off her horse and she limped to the door, supported by Hunter and Narky. The door to Elkinar's Temple was built into one of the building's corners, and as they approached it, Hunter noticed for the first time something odd about the building's shape: the temple had only three sides. They were not approaching a normal corner, but rather the tip of a triangle.

The door was half open, held ajar at such an angle that its edge completed the triangle's point. They ducked through, and found themselves in a chamber filled with pillars. Each of the pillars was hollowed into a chimney, and the devotional lamps nestled within lit the room with an orange glow. The oil inside the lamps had been infused with some sort of spice, the smell of which permeated the chamber. Even with the door open, the atmosphere was suffocating.

"What is this place?" Criton asked. "It reminds me of something."

"Of the womb, perhaps," said a voice from up ahead. An elderly priestess was refilling one of the lamps with oil. The jug in her left hand shook somewhat as she replaced the lamp and moved onto the next.

"You have never been here before," she continued. "Welcome. I am Mother Dinendra, the senior servant to Elkinar. Have you brought a tribute to the God? Do you have a request of Him?"

Hunter found that the others were all looking at him. "Our request is for Phaedra to be healed," he said. "If you can help us, we will gladly pay an appropriate tribute."

The priestess nodded, her eyes still on her work. "And what ails the young lady?"

"A broken ankle," said Phaedra. "It's been a few weeks since I broke it, but I still can't walk."

Mother Dinendra put down her oil jug and took up the lamp she had been filling. She turned to look at them. "My eyes may be failing me," she said, "but you look like islanders! Where do you come from, that you would visit Anardis and its temple?"

"We come from Tarphae," Narky said. "But we're not cursed," he added hastily.

The priestess nodded and smiled. "Except with broken ankles," she said.

She handed Criton the lamp, saying, "Hold this," and disappeared between the pillars, returning a few moments later with a low stool. She lowered herself carefully onto its seat, and motioned for Phaedra to show her her foot.

"Does this hurt?" she asked, touching her ankle carefully. Phaedra winced. "How about this?"

After a close inspection, the priestess shook her head. "It is healing," she said sadly.

"Then what's the problem?" Narky asked.

Mother Dinendra let go of Phaedra's ankle and looked up at him. "It should have been set before it began to heal. I can try to set it now, but that will involve rebreaking it, and even then it won't be the same as if it had been set properly to begin with. In a few weeks, you should be able to walk again. But you will always have a limp, and I doubt you'll ever be able to run, or dance, or climb stairs without holding onto a wall."

"Oh," said Phaedra. She looked dazed. "Oh."

"You should plan on staying with us for a few weeks," Mother Dinendra suggested. "Travel isn't good for an injury like this."

Phaedra nodded absently. "Do you have any rooms where we could stay?" Criton asked.

The priestess chuckled awkwardly. "I would recommend the inn across the square," she said. "We servants of Elkinar sleep down below in the catacombs, as we call them. The air is heavy, there is no light, we do not keep fires, and the rooms are small and cold. There is an expression: Elkinar's servants live in the light, work in the womb, and sleep in the tomb. It is not a place for you."

"This is a life you chose?" Narky asked. "Why?"

"For some of us, it is devotion," Mother Dinendra said. "Some have more practical considerations. I confess I am of the latter kind. I joined the Temple of Elkinar to escape from the nobility. The king is my nephew, you see. My children would have been noblemen, but Elkinar's servants are forbidden from ruling, and their children follow in their line. Mine have scattered, though my grandson Taemon is a junior priest here. It is a better life than that of a noblewoman. The Temple sheltered me in its catacombs for a long time, until one by one all my seniors died and left me in charge. No matter. It is too late for my family to drag me into anything, and if they try, I can pretend to be senile. With every year that passes, I pretend less and less."

Mother Dinendra smiled at this little piece of self-deprecation. Hunter did not believe her for an instant. This woman was no more senile than he was.

"Let me set that ankle for you as best I can," the priestess said to Phaedra, "and I will have to send you on your way. If I do not finish with these lamps, Father Sephas will think I really am losing my mind."

She led them into a second chamber, this one better ventilated and better lit due to a number of angled shafts in the ceiling. There was a table here, and a few chairs, but the room's greatest feature was that it was lined on all sides with rows upon rows of shelves, most of them covered in scrolls or books. Mother Dinendra pulled a bucket of water from underneath the table, then tottered over to the far wall and pulled a sack from the bottom-most shelf. She lugged this to the table before retrieving a shallow, wide-lipped bowl from right above where the sack had been. Then she pulled over one of the chairs and sat down with some satisfaction.

"Damned fool," she said suddenly, rising to her feet again. "Forgot the rags."

A large pile of rags had been shoved into one corner of the room. Mother Dinendra gathered some of these and returned to the table. She poured a white powder from the sack, added water, and spent the next few minutes mixing plaster. Finally, she motioned with one plaster-covered hand to a chair.

"Sit," she said to Phaedra.

When she had done as commanded, the priestess handed

her the bowl and rags, pulled her chair closer, and sat down with relief. She patted her knee, and Phaedra placed her foot on it. Mother Dinendra grasped her ankle in both hands.

"This is going to hurt a little," she said.

Judging by Phaedra's reaction, it hurt more than a little. The elderly priestess grimaced and commenced dipping rags in the plaster and wrapping them around Phaedra's ankle. It was messy work, and by the time she had finished, her smock was covered in white droplets and more than a few handprints.

"There," she said finally. "Now let that set for some twenty minutes, and I'll be back when I'm done with the lamps. Do you read? Good. Then you won't lack for entertainment."

She left them and returned to the dark smoky chamber of the building's entrance.

"Maybe Psander can do something when we get back," Phaedra said hopefully. "Hand me one of those books, will you, Hunter?"

Hunter looked about him, more than a little overwhelmed. Codices, scrolls and papers were stacked every which way, separated by bags and jars of this and that, and the occasional candle.

"Which one?" he asked.

"How about that big black one over there?" She pointed to a black leather bound codex that lay on one of the lower shelves. He handed it to her.

"Oh!" she said, upon opening it. "It's annotated!"

"Oh?" Criton asked.

"How thrilling," said Narky.

"Well, it's not magic," Phaedra admitted, "but it's definitely interesting. Listen to this: 'When They started over, the Gods created water, wind and earth.' Why does the scroll begin thus? Chalinos says, 'Because in Their first creation, the Gods created wind and earth before water, and all the earth blew away.' Belerphon says, 'Because when the Gods created Their first world, it was so filled with love, joy and perfection that it exploded. The second time, the Gods built the world of sturdier stuff.' Polina says, 'Because when They created the first world, the Gods argued so violently over its contents that it grew dangerous and chaotic, and They had to abandon it and start anew.'"

"Is this supposed to make sense?" Narky asked.

"Shush, you," Phaedra scolded. "All of Elkinar's sages are weighing in on the same sentence! So much wisdom gathered in one place!"

"What original scroll are they all commenting on?" Criton wondered aloud. "Does it mention God Most High, do you think?"

Phaedra shook her head. "No, I don't think so. It's a scroll called 'The Second Cycle.' I imagine it goes on to talk mostly about Elkinar." She flipped forward a few pages. "Yes, it gets to Him almost immediately."

Narky snorted. "It doesn't sound like it does anything immediately. Can't they just let the original speak for itself?"

Hunter gave him a look. "You want an annotated scroll without any annotations?"

"I'd prefer a few pictures," Narky said, "but that would be a good start."

"You're stepping awfully close to blasphemy again," Phaedra warned him.

"I'm not mocking Elkinar!" Narky protested. "It's these sages who are wasting everybody's time."

"I'm sure there's a plain copy of 'The Second Cycle' around here somewhere," Phaedra told him. "It must be a very central work, if there's so much commentary on it. Go find it and stop interrupting me."

"And how am I supposed to find it?" he asked. "By smell?"

"Look!" said Bandu triumphantly. She had made a fairly convincing boat out of plastered rags. "It's the water leaf," she announced with pride.

When Mother Dinendra returned, she replaced the

books on the shelves and gave Bandu's sculpture a bemused look. Criton had been taking up scroll after scroll and book after book, looking for anything that might mention God Most High. Hunter noticed that Dinendra placed these back on the shelves in entirely new places, without so much as glancing at their contents.

"Go and rest now," the priestess said. "You can always come back if you want to read more."

They left the temple and crossed over to the inn that the priestess had mentioned. The proprietor clearly did not want them there, but when Phaedra said that Mother Dinendra had asked them to stay, he begrudgingly let them a pair of rooms at a somewhat inflated price. They stayed a few weeks, while Phaedra's ankle healed again and the weather grew wetter and colder. The inn was neither as elegant nor as comfortable as the one in Atuna, for the pilgrims that flocked to Elkinar's temple on holy days were not as wealthy as Atuna's financiers. Still, Hunter took the opportunity of being in a city to sell the last of his gemstones to a proper jeweler, and despite the innkeeper's prices, his purse was soon heavy with gold once more.

Going to the market was an unpleasant experience, though. Rumors about the islanders had spread about the city, and Hunter received dangerous looks from merchants and customers alike. He suspected that without the Elkinaran priests' implicit protection there would have been trouble.

He bought a razor and shaved his head again. The dead clansmen would be mourned by their loved ones, but they deserved his respect too. It would be inexcusable, he felt, to mourn those he had lost unexpectedly, but treat the men he had slain himself as if their deaths meant nothing to him. On Tarphae, mourners shaved their heads and waited a year before they were permitted to alter their hair's appearance again, whether by trimming it, teasing it up, or braiding it as Phaedra had once done. But with the killing of men, Hunter felt that his period of mourning ought to begin anew.

For it wasn't only those two men who had died that day: Hunter had also lost his sense of who he was. "Hunter" had lived for combat and for glory, but it turned out that the real Hunter didn't. So what *did* he live for? He wished he knew.

Over the next few days, Hunter and Narky often accompanied Phaedra to Elkinar's temple, if only to give Bandu and Criton some privacy. While Phaedra read in the library or discussed religious philosophy with the pear-shaped Father Sephas, Mother Dinendra encouraged the boys to help the younger priests tend to the rooftop terrace. They were glad to do so. Everyone but the priests seemed to believe that the islanders would bring doom and bad luck to Anardis. The temple was a welcoming enclave in a hostile city.

As the walls came nearer to completion, the tension in the city rose. While Phaedra was perusing the library one afternoon, and the others had already retired to the inn, Hunter asked Mother Dinendra about the wall.

The aged priestess shook her head sadly. "When I was a girl," she said, "Anardis was legendary for its impregnable walls. Then my father the king went to war with Ardis. He died in battle, slain by the king of Ardis' Dragon Touched general. My brother only learned that he was our new king from the Ardismen, after their army had surrounded our walls. He surrendered. He had to. The men of Ardis came in and tore our walls down stone by stone."

They climbed the stairs to the rooftop terrace, where Mother Dinendra picked up a watering can.

"Mind you," she said, "this was all before my nephew was born. By the time our current king was a boy, we'd been paying tribute to Ardis for years. But still he dreamed of meeting that Dragon Touched general in battle, and avenging his grandfather. Even when Ardis rose up against their king and slew all the Dragon Touched, it did not calm him. When he could no longer restore our city's greatness by killing, he decided to restore it by rebuilding the wall. I thought of warning him against it, but I don't think he would have listened."

"You think that building a wall will reignite the war with Ardis?" asked Hunter.

The old priestess smiled wryly, and plucked a weed. "How could it fail to? A city with a wall is a city that plans to be attacked. Once the wall is completed, the king will likely refuse to pay our yearly tribute. Then it will be war again. If my nephew had been alive for the last war, he would not so readily start a new one."

Hunter nodded. A few short months ago, he would not have understood. Now he did.

Phaedra's voice called out to them from the stairwell. Mother Dinendra left off her watering and went to see what the matter was.

"Do you mind if I borrow this for a few days?" Phaedra asked her, raising a scroll.

"Developments in Magical Surgery?" the priestess asked incredulously. "Take it. It's yours. Nobody uses those techniques anymore. I don't know why we still have that."

She turned back to Hunter. "It's funny how hatred can live on after its object is long dead," she said. "I think much of our city's hostility against you islanders comes from the rumor that one of you is Dragon Touched."

Hunter said nothing. A part of him wished the Boar of Hagardis had killed *all* the Gallant Ones.

"Although," the priestess went on, "many of our citizens worship Magor, just as the men of Ardis do. If it's true about your slaying Magor's sacred boar, then *their* anger at least can be justified."

"The boar died at our hands," Hunter admitted.

"Good riddance," said Mother Dinendra. "That beast was murderous and indiscriminate. It killed worshippers of Magor just as readily as it did anyone else."

She sighed. "Magor is a harsh and terrible God. His

followers are always dancing on the line between aggression and cowardice. The ones in our city, who watch you and your friends with smoldering eyes, today they are cowards. Tomorrow they may turn aggressive. Once Phaedra is able to travel, I would encourage you to leave our city and head south or east. Get as far away from Ardis and the Magor worshippers as possible."

"I'll tell the others," Hunter said.

When they were back at the inn, Hunter told them all that Mother Dinendra had said.

Narky seemed relieved, if anything. "She's right," he said. "We should go as soon as we can."

"Too bad!" said Phaedra, disappointed. "I'd have liked to spend a few more weeks here, just talking with Father Sephas. Mother Dinendra is very nice, but she's just a woman who tried to avoid politics by putting on a priestess' robe."

"Maybe," said Hunter, "but her political instincts are good. She's been listening to the rumors at the same time as she was protecting us from them. We're lucky she's Elkinar's High Priestess."

"Oh, I completely agree," Phaedra said. "It's just that I don't know if Elkinar's so lucky for it. Mother Dinendra isn't much of a leader or a theologian. Father Sephas is the one who's really running the temple. I think when seniority passes to him, the church of Elkinar will become much more than it is now."

"Dinendra *is* leader," Bandu corrected her. "Inn man only lets us stay when we say Mother Dinendra wants us to stay. You don't like her because she not read."

"I do like her!" Phaedra protested. "I was just – well, it's not important."

"It doesn't matter if you like her," said Narky. "She's right. We should get out of Anardis. The people here think we're bringing them bad luck, and they've heard that Criton is Dragon Touched. What more do you want?"

"Shh!" Criton looked terrified. "What if the innkeeper had heard you just now? We'd have a mob outside, screaming for my blood. Magor's worshippers are the ones who killed my people, remember? Phaedra, can you walk on that ankle yet?"

"I don't know," she answered. "The plaster bindings hold it in place so I can get to the temple and back without much pain, but they wanted me to wait another week at least before they tried taking the binding off."

They all sat in grim silence for a moment, considering this. They were glad they did. Now that nobody was talking, they could hear the shouting from outside. Bandu jumped up and opened the window's shutters.

"The Ardismen are here!" somebody outside was yelling. "The doom is upon us!"

26
Criton

They ran to the temple, practically carrying Phaedra in their hurry. Father Sephas let them in and barred the door behind them. Even in the short time it had taken them to cross the square, people had already begun pointing and shouting.

"There they go!" some had yelled. "The black cursebringers!"

"Don't worry," Father Sephas said. "There will be no mob. They'll have to run to defend the walls first."

He was trying to reassure them, but he had also barred the door.

"Have you heard?" Mother Dinendra asked, joining them from the stairwell. "Bestillos leads them."

Even in the orange light of the devotional lamps, Father Sephas went white.

"The wall is finished, isn't it?" Hunter asked. "Do you think it can withstand the Ardismen?"

Priest and priestess shook their heads. Mother Dinendra spoke first. "The Dragon Touched general who killed my father died at the hands of High Priest Bestillos. You have to understand: I am only High Priestess of Elkinar through seniority, but Bestillos is Magor's chosen. It has been prophesied that he shall never know defeat in battle, and he has proven the truth of that prophecy time and again."

Father Sephas' voice came out a whisper. "Wizardbane, they call him."

"The fear of him will tear down our defenses faster than any siege weapon ever could," Dinendra said grimly. "The king is a fool. He should have expected that Ardis would hear of his wall-building, and that they would not take the news lightly. Now Bestillos is here, and no man will stand against him."

"I'm glad I brought my spear," Narky said. "Is there a way out of here besides this door?"

Mother Dinendra shook her head. "We'll have to wait and see. I will go up to the garden. You should stay out of sight. When the city falls, its people will point their blame in two directions: at the king, and at you. Sephas, make sure that nobody is let in. Where are Taemon and Phadros?"

"Father Taemon was out visiting the sick this morning," he said. "Father Phadros is still with Terassa. Her labor began last night."

"They will have to stay where they are, then. It will be safer for them anyway."

With that, Mother Dinendra returned to the stairs and began to climb them, leaving the door in between open. The islanders went to sit in the library, but even Phaedra did not bother trying to read.

"If the city surrenders quickly and peacefully," said Hunter, "the Ardismen may execute the king and then take their tribute and go."

"In which case," said Narky, "the people of Anardis will blame us, and they'll surround this temple and scream for our blood."

"Dinendra does not listen to them," said Bandu.

"We'll all need to eat and drink eventually," Narky insisted. "She can't protect us here forever. Either she'll let the mob have us, or we'll all starve to death."

"But if the cityfolk resist…" Phaedra began.

"Then we'll be killed even sooner," Narky said.

"You're not helping," Phaedra snapped. "You sound like you think we should just give up and die. If you have any ideas for how we can get out of this, I'd love to hear them. If you don't, shut up."

Criton expected Narky to say something sarcastic. He expected Narky to mutter something angry, and spend the next few minutes sulking. Narky did neither. "I'm sorry," he said quietly. "You're right."

"If we had horses," Hunter said, "we'd have some chance of outrunning both the cityfolk and the Ardismen. Ardis is not known for horsemanship."

"Neither are we," Criton pointed out.

"I know horse," said Bandu. "You ride with me."

"Then Narky can go with me," Hunter said. "We'd only need three horses."

Phaedra sighed. "But how will we get the horses if we can't leave the temple? You couldn't fight your way to the inn, could you, Hunter?"

Hunter shook his head. "Not if there's a big crowd out there. Besides, if I did, it would be obvious what we were doing. We couldn't all mount horses in the middle of a mob. Even if there isn't one out there yet, I'd never make it to the inn and back without drawing an angry crowd."

Criton had to admit that Hunter was right. There was no way they could leave the temple without drawing tremendous attention to themselves. He wondered briefly whether Mother Dinendra or Father Sephas would be willing to try getting the horses instead, but he had to dismiss that idea. It was extremely kind of the Elkinaran priests to offer the islanders sanctuary, but they could not be asked to risk their lives for the sake of the foreigners.

Suddenly, Narky lifted his head. "Criton can do it," he said.

"What?" Criton asked, horrified. "No, I can't."

The others were staring at Narky too. "He can," Narky

insisted. He lowered his voice. "You can look like someone else. You hide your claws and your scales all the time, and make your eyes change color – why not change your skin too? If you thought about it, I bet you could make yourself look exactly like one of the priests. Then you could slip out of the temple without raising any suspicions. You could walk around a little, and when no one was looking, you could change again and look like the inn's groom, or even like an Ardisian soldier. If the Ardismen have taken the city by then, they'll be busy burning buildings and looting, and you can fit right in. They won't attack the temple, I don't think, because they're not really at war with Elkinar. You can lead a few horses over near the temple, and then in the middle of all the looting and confusion, we can jump out and ride away before anyone realizes what's going on."

The others' expressions had turned from shock to wonder, and they were all looking at Criton now. He wanted to protest, to say that it was impossible, but Narky was right. If there was sufficient confusion when the Ardismen breached the walls, this plan had a real chance of working. But it was only a chance, and what's more, it all rested on him. It was frightening to think that if Criton failed, it would doom them all.

"That could actually work," Phaedra said, sounding extremely impressed. "Gods above, Narky, that's ingenious!"

Narky smiled a rare smile, dipped his head in thanks, and looked a little too proud of himself.

"And you're right," Phaedra added. "They won't attack the temple. The same way that many people here worship Magor, most of the city of Ardis worships Elkinar as a secondary God."

"I'll do it," Criton said, though his stomach churned. "If it's the only way, I'll do it."

"You'll have to get the timing right," said Hunter. "Wait until the Ardismen have breached the walls, and no one in Anardis will be watching the temple. If you look continental, you'll be able to walk right over to the inn and get the horses. That should be the easy part. The hard part will be for us all to get out of the city once we've *got* the horses."

Criton nodded. Something told him this was much easier said than done. "What if Anardis lets them in without a fight?"

"Then the Ardismen will march right into the square," Phaedra said. "Someone will probably tell them about us, but they'll be more concerned with the king at first. They'll probably drag him out of the palace and execute him. Magor is no God of mercy, and His prophet is leading the Ardisian army."

"That should still give some time for you to slip out and bring us the horses," said Narky. "Especially if you look like an Ardisman."

"I've changed my appearance before," Criton said, shaking his head, "but I don't know if I can make it look like I'm wearing armor or anything like that. I'm not Psander."

"Of course not," Phaedra said reassuringly. "We understand that. If the Ardismen are let in peacefully, you shouldn't have to fake any armor."

"We'd better know what's going on outside, then," said Narky. "I'll go up to the terrace and ask Mother Dinendra. I think if I stay low, nobody will be able to see me from the ground." He left the room.

"You know," Phaedra said, once he had left, "Narky's a lot smarter than I gave him credit for."

Criton nodded, and began working on his appearance. Once he had set his mind to the task, it did not take long before his skin was appropriately pale and the others were looking at him in admiration.

"You're a brave man," Hunter said.

Narky returned a very short time later, slightly out of breath. "They're already in the city!" he said. "Peacefully, Ravennis be thanked. You'd better get out there while everyone's distracted."

Criton nodded. There was a knot in his stomach. Feeling slow and heavy, he re-entered the dark pillared chamber and made his way toward the entryway. Bandu followed him and Narky made to follow as well, but Phaedra held him back. Criton heard her begin to explain, as the door shut behind Bandu, that the two of them wanted a moment alone.

Father Sephas had recovered from his initial shock, and had extinguished most of the lamps in the chamber of pillars. If anyone were to break in through the door, they would have to stand there in the doorway for quite some time to let their eyes adjust, or else blunder recklessly forward into pillar after stone pillar. The priest was now standing at one of the two remaining lamps, holding a pen and a prayer slip. When he was finished writing his prayer, Criton knew, he would burn it so that its smoke could reach the heavens.

They reached the door to the outside world, and Bandu touched his shoulder. "If we live," she said, "you marry me later?"

The knot in Criton's stomach tightened. Really? They were going to have this conversation now? This was the last thing he needed.

"Bandu," he said. "I love you. I love you so much, I – I don't want anything to change. I never want us to change."

He hoped she understood. He gave her a quick kiss, and unbarred the door. "What are you doing?" Father Sephas cried out, but by then it was too late. Criton slipped outside, and the door shut quietly behind him.

It was terribly bright outside, but Criton did not give his eyes time to adjust. He had to get away from the temple door before anyone noticed him there. He backed along the temple's wall away from the square, reaching out his arm to steady himself. When he could see a little better, he was relieved to find that nobody was looking. He stepped a few paces to the left and then strode back toward the square, trying to look natural.

When the pounding in his ears subsided a little, he finally heard the great commotion that was all around him. People were yelling, crying, cheering and laughing, and a few steps later, Criton could see why. The army of Ardis had just reached the city center, and their front rows were congregating around the palace gate, banging their spears against their shields and cheering. The anguished cries were coming from the citizenry, and as Criton neared the inn, the reason became clear. The palace gate had been torn down. Soon their king would be dragged out and punished, bringing shame on the entire city.

The Ardisian soldiers hollered and whooped, shaking the whole world with their commotion. A number of them were holding back the horrified crowd, which surged against them in a combination of anger and despair. For the time being, Criton went unnoticed.

He reached the inn, and found no one guarding the stable. There were some six horses there, including the packhorse. As quickly as he could, Criton went about the business of putting saddles on three of the riding horses. He transferred the islanders' saddlebags to one of these, leaving the packhorse to chew its oats contentedly. If they were to make a getaway, they would need horses bred for speed.

Nobody had given him any trouble yet, thank the Gods – no! No. If God Most High still lived in the heavens, then He was the one Criton wanted to thank. The men who had killed Ma's family were just outside the door, cheering on the humiliation of their neighboring city. Criton wanted to make fools of them all, and when he did, it would be as a worshipper of God Most High.

As casually as he could, Criton led the three horses out of the stable. The crowd had quieted, to his dismay. Everyone was standing still, watching the two men who stood at the palace gate. The one in king's garments was kneeling, a circlet of gold gleaming from his bowed head. Then there was the other one, the one whose robes were red as blood, whose spear was barbed and whose voice rose above the silence of the crowd to assert the king's guilt. Bestillos, High Priest of Magor.

"Behold your king!" this man cried. His gray hair blew in the light breeze, and his eyes pierced his audience. "Behold the man whose arrogance has brought your city to its knees. Until today, we demanded only a small tribute from Anardis. It was not so much to ask. But this foolish man bade you rise up against us, to build a wall, as if any wall could hinder the power of the great city of Ardis. This man led, and you followed. You, who are so weak that your gates could not withstand a single man's voice. Kneel, all of you, as your king must kneel."

To Criton's horror, the crowd began to follow the priest's orders. If everyone knelt, how would he ever reach the temple without being noticed? Criton was still far enough from the door that he could never get there in time if he made a break for it. To blend into the crowd, he too would have to kneel.

With the reins still in one hand, Criton sank to his knees. The king was shaking, he noticed. The king was weeping.

The red priest continued his speech. "The king bears the guilt of a city," he said. "Let the guilt of Anardis be purged!"

With that, High Priest Bestillos lifted his barbed spear above his head and plunged its point down into the king's back. The king screamed in agony and the crowd gasped, some women and children covering their ears. The king's screams seemed to go on and on, and they only got worse when the priest wrenched his spear back. But even when the king's cries had died out, Bestillos did not stop there.

"Bring forward his wives and children," he ordered his men.

A man in the crowd near Criton jumped up and tried to run away from the sight, his eyes filled with tears. He had not taken a single step before the butt of an Ardisian spear struck him in the back and sent him crashing down again.

The crowd was forced to watch in horror as, one by one, the High Priest of Magor executed the king's two wives, three concubines and fourteen children. By the time he reached the youngest, the gathered citizens of Anardis were all weeping. So was Criton.

"We're next," he heard a woman in the crowd whisper.

When the youngest of the city's royal line was dead and still, High Priest Bestillos turned to one of his captains. He whispered something to the man, who turned and gave orders to his lieutenants, as the word was passed along through each rank of soldiers.

Criton did not want to see where this was headed. He rocked back from his knees to the balls of his feet, and began inching toward the temple. Yet he had not traveled more than a foot before the red priest's gaze suddenly fixed on him. Bestillos' eyes widened, then narrowed again. The priest did not only see Criton; he *saw* him. The pale skin, the soft hands, everything that was fake about Criton fell away before the priest of Magor's gaze.

"That one!" the priest shouted, pointing. "Kill him!"

To Criton's great luck, it seemed as if half the men in the crowd thought Bestillos had pointed at them. Men rose everywhere and tried to escape through the crowd, many of them finding themselves impaled upon spears within moments. Criton jumped to his feet and sprinted toward the temple, dragging the horses along behind him.

"Monster!" one of the Ardismen cried, leaping toward him through the crowd. Criton looked down at his hands for a split second and found that they were claws again. The priest had not only seen through his disguise – he had torn it clear off.

Criton had nearly reached the temple by the time any soldiers caught up with him. *Forgive me,* he prayed to his people's God, and when the soldiers barred his way, he roasted them. The living ones scattered then, and ran burning through the crowded tumult and confusion.

Criton arrived at the temple door just as it opened and his friends rushed out. Then it was onto the horses, faster than seemed possible, with Criton clinging to Bandu's back and the others helping Phaedra onto her horse before practically leaping onto theirs. Hunter swiped a few spear points aside as they all wheeled around and made for the city gate.

"Dragon spawn!" Criton heard the priest's voice shouting from behind him, and he turned his head to see the barbed spear flying toward him through the air. As far as the priest had thrown it, still its aim would be true.

Criton never knew how she did it. Even in retrospect, he didn't see how it made sense. But somehow, Bandu's arm shot out and she slapped the spear out of the air. One moment it was about to pierce Criton's heart, and the next moment it was falling to the ground, harmless. They sped away.

When they reached the city gate, some twenty soldiers were waiting there. Hunter only spurred his horse, and Bandu and Phaedra followed his lead. Criton raised his head and sent a burst of flame heavenward. Hunter's sword beat aside a pair of spears and sliced through one of the soldiers' necks. The rest scattered.

Then the city walls were behind them, and they were riding away southward as swift as the wind. Criton held tightly onto Bandu as the ground flew by underneath them. Even with the horror behind them, they could not ride fast enough. Smoke was rising now: the city was burning. Criton prayed that the Temple of Elkinar, at least, would be free of smoke and slaughter. It was hard to imagine that it would.

When they came to a rest, Criton climbed off his horse and collapsed to the ground. Bandu dismounted too, whispering in their horse's ear and wiping off its foamy mane with her hand. The saddlebags on Hunter's horse turned out to have a brush inside, and he gave the horses a more thorough grooming.

"I can't believe we made it," Narky said.

Criton just shook his head. He couldn't believe…

"Bandu," he said, "how did you do that, with the spear?"

Bandu turned to him. "Do what? What you say?"

"I saw you reach out and knock Bestillos' spear away. It would have killed me otherwise."

"My hands are on the how-you-call-them all the time," Bandu said, indicating the reins.

"I saw the spear fall," Phaedra put in helpfully, "but nobody touched it. I thought it got blown aside by a sudden wind."

"Yes," Bandu said. "Wind. Not my hand."

She said it with finality, and Criton took that to mean that he should close his eyes and breathe slowly and try to stop feeling so dizzy. He had been breathing too fast, and riding too fast, and – no, it was none of that. It was the screaming of the children.

27
Narky

In his mind he had apologized to Criton a thousand times. Whether he had meant to or not, Narky had suggested that Criton's ancestors were monstrous beings that deserved their enemies' hatred. How could he have thought that Criton would not take such a thing to heart? Narky, of all people, should have understood what it was like to have one's sires maligned. Everyone he knew from childhood was dead and gone now, and he was *still* trying to escape his identity as Narky the Coward's Son.

How could he even face Criton now? The plan Narky had asked him to carry out had been more than dangerous; it had been absolutely suicidal. Any man in Criton's position who had a single shred of selfishness would have run for his life the minute he had stepped out the temple door. If Narky had been in the same position, he was sure he would have given up on the others and fled the city as quickly and quietly as he could. It was a horrible thought, but it was true.

Yet Criton had followed the plan through, even when his disguise had been compromised, even when the man who had killed his family was pointing straight at him and ordering his death. Criton's loyalty and bravery were staggering.

How could Narky look him in the eye, after what he had said and after what Criton had done? Apologizing would only remind Criton of their earlier argument. Perhaps it would be better to let those words die a quiet death, foolish and forgotten. Yet how could he know that they would even *be* forgotten? Maybe Criton would never forget. Maybe bringing it up and apologizing was Narky's only way to be forgiven.

He wished he could be sure. He wished he knew what to do. He wished there was a way to find out what Criton would think if he apologized, short of actually apologizing and learning the answer the hard way. The closest thing he could think of was to ask Phaedra.

"Apologize for what?" Phaedra asked, when he brought his question to her. It was nighttime, and he had stayed up after his watch was over to talk to Phaedra during hers. "What did you say to him that requires an apology?"

Narky had forgotten that Phaedra had not been present for that particular quarrel. He squirmed now, as he was forced to explain. Phaedra looked horrified when he told her what he had said, and though she listened to him explain his internal conflicts on the matter, her mind was clearly made up long before he had finished.

"You have to apologize," she said.

"You're sure?"

"I'm sure. Even if Criton *has* forgotten, that's the kind of thing you should apologize for anyway. Criton hardly knew anything about his ancestors until he read that scroll. It filled him with self-doubt, and then while he was trying to make sense of it, you hit him where he was most vulnerable. You have to apologize, Narky. There's just – you have to."

Narky sighed. "I thought so. Thanks, Phaedra."

For what must have been the first time, Phaedra smiled at him. "I'm glad that you're trying. I didn't like you at first, but I think you've really changed. For the better."

"Really?" Narky beamed back at her. He had wanted so

badly to become a new person after Ravennis had forced him to examine himself, and had not felt that he was living up to his hopes. But Phaedra had noticed a difference. Gods bless her, Phaedra had noticed a difference.

There was not much time to rest. As soon as the sun rose, they broke camp and continued southward. Narky doubted that the High Priest of Magor would abandon his victorious conquest just to chase Criton across the continent, but Criton clearly thought otherwise and for once, Narky did not argue. He was still trying to find the right time, the right way, the right context in which to say he was sorry. The thought of apologizing while everyone else was present made him want to beat his head against a rock.

He would have to do the same thing he did with Phaedra, and speak to Criton during his night watch. Narky yawned. If he kept staying up in order to talk to people one-on-one, when would he ever sleep? No, that was selfish. He could always sleep later.

Criton opted for the final watch that night, and because he was too unfocused during the discussion, Narky ended up with the second. Second watch was the worst. His sleep would be interrupted before he could derive any benefit from it, and he knew he would have to wake up a second time in order to speak to Criton and, if he fell asleep after their talk, a third time only an hour or two later.

When Bandu woke him up for his own watch, he sat staring bleary-eyed into the fire, wondering how he would ever wake up once he lay down again. Without anyone shaking him as Bandu had done, he would have to rely on his body to awaken on its own. He sighed and picked up his water skin, draining it in one long string of gulps. If that didn't wake him up later tonight, nothing would.

The water performed its task admirably. When he had finished emptying his bladder, Narky shambled over to where Criton was sitting, looking tensely out into the night.

"I can't help but feel like he's coming after me," Criton

said, out of nowhere. "He wouldn't, right? He'll stay in Anardis until he's done making his point. I know that's what he's doing, but I *feel* him chasing me."

"Do you think that comes from magic?"

Criton considered this. "Bandu says the wind told her Tarphae would drown, so I guess premonitions like that are possible. But do you think he'd follow us without dealing with Anardis first?"

"I doubt it," Narky said. "I actually meant, do you think it comes from *his* magic? If everyone is so afraid of him that the whole city of Anardis surrendered without a fight, maybe some of that is magical."

"Huh," said Criton, looking thoughtful. "You could be right. I feel so… hunted."

They were silent for a time. Criton kept opening his mouth to say something, then closing it again. Narky stood uncertainly, not sure whether to move on with his business or wait for Criton to speak.

"Um," Narky said, finally sitting down with a thud next to Criton. "For what it's worth, I'm really sorry about the things I said earlier. Your ancestors in Ardis, and all of that. If they were anything like you, they were good people. The best people. That scroll was full of lies, just like you said."

Criton nodded, his expression blank. It took him some time to speak. "You were right though, I can never know for sure."

Narky squirmed. "But the scroll said you were all pure evil by nature. That's just obviously not true. You could have left us. You could have run away when you had the chance, instead of risking your life to come back for us, with horses and everything."

Criton looked sick at the very suggestion. "You think I could have betrayed you all like that? Betrayed Bandu? I could never. Never."

"You didn't even think about it, did you?" Narky asked enviously.

"Who would have?"

"Most normal people would've at least considered it," Narky said. "We were so scared back there. I thought for sure we'd all die. I think if I'd been in your place... I think I would have left."

Criton looked disgusted. "You really would have, wouldn't you?"

That look of disgust made Narky want to stand up for himself. He might be a coward, but thinking of saving oneself from mortal danger by abandoning one's friends was not *uniquely* cowardly! Surely it wasn't! Criton was the unusual one. Why couldn't he just take the compliment?

"I don't know," Narky said. "I never got the opportunity, so I'll never really know if I'd have taken it. But it wouldn't be crazy for someone to do that. It was crazy not to. What was the chance we'd all make it? More likely we'd all have died and you'd have died with us. Look, what I was trying to say was, you're a good person. Brave and loyal and all that. And I'm sorry about the scroll. I didn't really think it was true, but I thought it might be, and I said so. I'm sorry."

Criton did not say anything for a minute. Then, finally, he nodded. "Thank you," he said.

It seemed like that was all Narky was going to get out of him. If he'd hoped to be forgiven or absolved, that would have to wait for another time. It didn't matter. At least he had said what he wanted to say, and he wouldn't have to say any more about it. Narky returned to the tent, and fell asleep almost as soon as he had laid his head down.

Waking up was exactly as unpleasant as he had expected. The next day dragged by dreadfully, and the only part of it that Narky enjoyed was lying back down again that night. The plainsfolk on the way south were still closing their doors to the islanders, so they relied on Criton to disguise himself and buy their supplies on his own. Bandu often wandered away while they were waiting for Criton, eventually rejoining them with no explanation. Though

Narky had seen more of Criton's magic, he knew that Bandu's must be progressing just as rapidly. Criton claimed that she had power over the wind now, a possibility that she did not exactly deny.

"Power is wrong," she would say. "Is not power."

She did not, however, supply any alternative explanation.

Narky did not speak to Bandu much. They had an understanding, as he saw it: neither of them would ever be able to really relate to the other, so why bother trying? As long as they didn't need anything from one another and didn't get in each other's way, all was golden.

During those times when Criton and Bandu were away and Hunter was busy sharpening his sword, Narky and Phaedra found plenty of time to talk. Phaedra had finally removed the plaster bindings around her ankle, and she stretched and exercised her foot while they spoke in an attempt to strengthen it. Narky mostly asked her about making friends and being polite, and she was generally happy to answer. She did not always answer him gently and she did not always answer succinctly, but she was always honest.

He wished he had been able to talk to her sooner. If he had had Phaedra to guide him before, he might not have made such a fool of himself over Eramia, and then things might have been different. He might not have insulted Ketch, or goaded the boy into humiliating him, and then... and then he might have stayed on the island and died like everyone else. Much though he wished he could blot Ketch's murder from human memory, it had also saved his life. Fate had given him a chance to reform. As long as no one found out about Ketch, he would be fine.

If only they weren't on their way to Psander.

It made sense, of course: Psander could shield them from Magor's gaze, and from His servants' pursuit. Narky couldn't argue with that. He couldn't even blame Phaedra for looking forward to their next meeting with the wizard.

"The best healers in the world say I'll never walk properly again," she said at one point. "Maybe Psander can do better."

"Do you like her because she reads?" Bandu asked. She was sitting nearby, eating some figs that she had no doubt stolen from that orchard a few miles back. Criton was away, buying food for the rest of them.

"Phaedra wants her ankle healed," Narky corrected her. "She might agree with Psander's goals too, but that's not the same as liking her."

"I do like her!" Phaedra protested. "At least, I sort of do."

Narky turned on her. "Really?"

"Well, I mean, we'd never be friends," Phaedra sputtered. "I don't think she likes *me* very much."

"Who cares if she likes you?" Narky nearly shouted, causing Hunter to finally stop scraping his sword against that bloody rock of his and start paying attention. "Why would you even *want* her to like you?"

"Because," said Phaedra, "she's a great woman."

"She's a blackmailer!" Narky cried, and shrank back in horror at what he had let slip.

"She is not," Phaedra insisted. "She's certainly tried to buy us with her knowledge, but that's not the same. I don't blame her for any of her decisions, even her dealings with the Gallant Ones. She needs our help."

"Sure she does," said Narky. "But you didn't just say you forgave her, you called her 'a great woman!' What makes her so great, her magic?"

"It's not the magic," Phaedra said. "It's that... it's... ugh, I don't think I could explain it to you."

That stung. She didn't mean that her explanatory abilities weren't up to the task. She meant that he wouldn't understand. "Try," he said.

"It's not going to be a quick answer," Phaedra warned.

Narky snorted. "When is it ever?"

She frowned at him, and he realized he'd offended her. "Sorry," he said. He tried his sentence again, this time with a smile. "When is it ever?"

Phaedra chuckled a little despite herself. "All right," she said. "But I warned you.

"My father was a merchant. He started as a merchant, that is, but he did very well and became a financier. Everyone said he was a great man, and my parents expected me to live up to my name as a great man's daughter. They always said that I could do anything in life, go great places, whatever I wanted. But what they meant was that I'd be able to marry well.

"They taught me to read, and make dresses, and do sums, but it was only so that they could tell suitors that I was clever and learned. When I tried to talk about all the interesting things I'd read in my father's books, they were afraid that I was learning *too much*. And you know a part of me started to believe them?

"What if I was so smart that nobody wanted to marry me? The only reason they wanted to teach me was so that I could be a useful, accomplished wife to some nobleman or something."

Hunter looked shocked. "My father was thinking about matching you up with my brother."

"Kataras?" said Phaedra, looking pleased. "Gods, that would have made them happy. Anyway, I don't think my parents expected me to be anything other than a good wife. What else is there for a woman to be?"

Narky shrugged. He had never really thought about it.

"*That's* what's special about Psander," Phaedra said. "She's not just powerful. She has huge plans for herself, and they have nothing to do with marriage. She got her power on purpose, by studying for it – not because she wanted to impress anyone. She *assumes* that her having power is legitimate. And you know, it *is*. That's what I like so much about her. My parents taught me to be worthy of a great man, but they never taught me to be a great woman. I never even knew that was possible, until I met Psander."

Bandu scratched her head. "If there is great man, why not great woman? It's of course!"

"Not really," Phaedra told her. "Or at least, I hadn't thought so."

"But woman God is strong as man God, no?"

"Maybe," Phaedra answered, "but the Gods aren't the same as people."

"Then Gods are no use," Bandu said. "Don't say what to do, don't help, and fight all the time. Gods are no good!"

"Shh!" Narky shushed her. "What's the matter with you? They're always watching us! You want to get struck down?"

"I want Them to stop watching," Bandu said. "What They care? I'm so small, why They even watch me? Maybe They don't."

"She doesn't mean what she's saying," Narky said, closing his eyes and hoping Ravennis would listen.

"I do mean," Bandu insisted, folding her arms.

"The Gods don't watch over Silent Hall," said Hunter, looking up at the sky. "I hope we get there soon."

Narky followed his gaze, and found the clouds growing thick and dark overhead. Was it just the rainy season starting early? Or were the clouds gathering for them?

28
Phaedra

The lightning came before the rain. The first bolt struck some hundred yards away, so close that the hair on Phaedra's arms stood on end in reaction to it. By the time her ears had recovered from the blast, the rain was coming down in heavy sheets that felt like stones. Hunter and Narky scrambled to take down the tent. The horses had gone mad with fear, and were trying desperately to free themselves from the lone tukka tree to which they had been tied. Phaedra limped over and tried to calm them, but had to retreat to avoid being trampled. She looked to Bandu for help, but the girl had disappeared into the rain.

The second bolt of lightning fell behind them, somewhat farther away but just as loud. Phaedra felt her heart stop briefly at the impact. Had the Gods sent this storm as a punishment? To which one should she pray to keep them safe? What could she possibly sacrifice?

Another flash, another crack. Phaedra had to wipe the wet hair from her eyes, and even then she could not see far. Hunter and Narky had taken the tent down by now, and Hunter was vainly trying to calm the horses. Where had Bandu run off to? If anyone could calm the animals, it would be her.

It took many long minutes for Bandu to return, dragging Criton along behind her.

"We have to get to Silent Hall," Hunter shouted at her. "Can you help me with the mounts?"

Bandu nodded, and sure enough, the poor beasts began to calm down as soon as she approached them.

"Let's go!" Narky yelled, and he took one of the horses' reins and led the way.

"I need help!" Phaedra called after him, but by then Hunter was already at her side. He flung her arm over his shoulder and supported her as she tried to walk, leaving Bandu and Criton to lead the last two horses.

It rained the rest of the evening, and all that night. Criton led them toward the village where he had been buying supplies, and they snuck into a barn to sleep. The storm did not weaken overnight, and they started off again before dawn the next morning. They trudged through the mud for three days, and for those three days the flood never ceased. But at least the thunder and lightning had abated.

Was Mayar of the Sea trying to drown them? Had Atel the Traveler forsaken their journey? Even if Phaedra had had the time or the animals with which to make sacrifices, she could not have guessed which God she ought to appease. Perhaps the Gods did not even intend this storm as punishment, but as a normal change of season. Narky joked that the Gods did not mean to punish them at all, but rather to reward the plants.

They traveled in muddy misery for six more days, following Bandu's intuition, or perhaps her sense of smell. In the rain, Phaedra couldn't have told one hillock from another, let alone led her friends in search of a fortress that was quite literally invisible. Yet Bandu seemed confident, so they followed her lead.

To Phaedra's amazement, Bandu came through for them. On the evening of the sixth day, with the sounds of thunder echoing in the distance, Silent Hall suddenly appeared before them out of the mist and rain. The sight of Psander's fortress had never been more welcome. Even Narky looked relieved.

Criton pounded on the gate. Had a voice called down to them in response? With the wind blowing as it was, and the rain beating down against the stones, any such voice would have been completely drowned out. They strained their ears for some time in vain. Criton went back to assaulting the door. Could anyone even hear them?

Suddenly, the gate opened. There stood Psander, gazing amusedly at Criton's still upraised fist.

"I heard you," she said. "And what's more, I would have known you were here even if you hadn't been trying to knock the place down. I do have wards of alarum, you know."

"Oh," said Criton.

"Well, come in," said Psander, standing back. "If you get any wetter, you'll have to use fish as towels."

They led the horses into the passage under the tower, wiping their faces with their hands.

"You're a woman today," Narky pointed out.

"Yes," Psander said. "The great wizard Psander spends much of his time holed up indoors nowadays. I'm his maid, Persada. It's easier that way."

"So it does exhaust you to use magic," said Criton, sounding relieved. "I thought it was only me."

"No, that's quite common," she reassured him. "And illusions are substantially harder to keep in place than transformations of the type you seem to favor. I would do the same as you, but I find actually *being* a man to be so uncomfortable that I'm willing to make the extra effort to avoid it. But I take it, then, that you have been practicing?"

Criton nodded, and Psander looked pleased. "I'm glad to hear it. Forgive me for asking, but since you are all here, may I assume you have something for me?"

Irritation bubbled up in Phaedra, try as she might to

suppress it. Psander had not even *noticed* her limp! Or worse, maybe she had noticed but didn't care. Phaedra put her hands on her hips and tried to stand straight.

"We do," she said enigmatically, or so she hoped.

"I'll be glad to give you fair compensation for your troubles," said Psander. Her words were measured, but there was excitement in her eyes. Excitement, and hope.

"I'll have the villagers care for your horses," she added. "You'd better go inside and dry yourselves by the fire."

They did as she said, taking their packs and the saddlebags with them.

"Fair compensation," repeated Narky. "Not likely."

They huddled around the fire pit in Psander's otherwise empty dining hall, feeling safe at last. The warmth from the fire made them so sleepy that by the time Psander came back, Hunter and Bandu had already nodded off and Narky looked to be well on his way to joining them. Phaedra could easily have let herself drift away too, but she wanted to talk to Psander tonight. There were things that had to be said and questions that had to be asked, preferably without interruptions.

"Oh," Psander said, when she appeared in the doorway. "Perhaps we should leave our business for tomorrow. You all look like you could use a night's sleep in a warm bed. I'll find a few braziers for you to take up to your rooms."

The wizard was as good as her word, and soon the islanders were shambling up the stairs to their bedrooms, each carrying a brazier full of burning embers. It was funny, Phaedra thought, while she was showing Bandu how to warm her sheets without burning them, but Silent Hall seemed to have become a sort of home to the islanders. It wasn't their real home, of course, but there was no questioning the fact that these beds had sat unused during their absence, awaiting their return. However harsh or unwelcoming the world became, Silent Hall would always be open to them.

As soon as Bandu was safely in bed without having set her sheets afire, Phaedra slipped out of the room and went to find Psander. She found the wizard in the library, just as she had expected, except that Criton had beat her there. Criton, with his long, healthy strides. Why couldn't *he* have helped Bandu with her bedsheets? The two of them were lovers, after all.

Criton and Psander both looked up as Phaedra entered.

"And because my defenses here are built on far more than that," the wizard said, continuing whatever sentence she had begun before Phaedra's entrance. "Hello, Phaedra. My mask, Criton, as you call it, is made by concentrating my own small field of magic. It's much the same principle by which you transform yourself. This fortress, on the other hand, is made mostly of reworked God magic. The great power of magic theory is, among other things, in allowing an academic wizard to reuse the magic of others. My defenses here are powerful enough to overcome your Wizard Sight because they're made of much stronger stuff than my own puny self. The Boar of Hagardis was only the latest sacred beast harvested for its divine power. I'm sure that raises more questions than it answers, but there you have it. Now, Phaedra, how can I help you?"

"Oh, um, well…" said Phaedra, unsure of where to start. "I have a lot of questions, but…"

"So does Criton," said Psander. "I have now answered one of his questions, so I suppose I can answer one of yours."

Phaedra took a deep breath. "My ankle broke," she said, "and it healed wrong. The priests of Elkinar did what they could, but I still can't even walk properly. Can you fix it magically?"

Psander looked at her pityingly. "I'm afraid I can't," she said. "There were once those who could: healing wizards who were beloved of even the lowliest peasants. But they were the first to feel the Gods' ire. Even before I began my studies, the healing wizards were already being persecuted.

They practiced their techniques on the dead so that they might learn to heal the living. The priests called this a desecration, and purged the world of its best healers. By the time I could rightfully call myself a wizard, healing magic had become a lost art."

"Well, I brought you a scroll on healing magic from Anardis," Phaedra said, showing it to her. "Will this help?"

Psander scanned it excitedly for a moment, but then shook her head. "If your appendix had burst, this scroll might have saved your life. I am grateful for this, but I'm afraid it won't help with your ankle."

"Oh," said Phaedra. "I'm... a cripple, then."

Psander nodded. "I'm sorry."

Criton scratched at his scalp. "You told us before that you were an expert in God magic. Aren't some of these Gods supposed to be healers of diseases?"

Psander's face grew suddenly contemptuous. "Whole lifetimes have been spent studying just one aspect of one God's powers," she said. "God magic is a vast field. Yes, I am an expert in Godly magic; specifically, I studied the magic of movement and travel, and I also made some promising discoveries about the ways that Gods mark Their territories. That's what I was studying before the purge, anyway. These days, I'm more of an expert on hiding. But really, even the Gods do not seem to be experts on each other's powers. I have studied Them for most of my life, but I'm only mortal."

"Did you study Atel then?" Phaedra asked. If there was any God that Phaedra felt qualified discussing, it was Atel.

"I continue to study Him even now," said Psander. "Atel the Traveler haunts my dreams. He is an infiltrator of boundaries, a God who ignores His peers' territorial markers and who will worm His way into every crevice of the world sooner or later. If my doom ever comes, it will arrive on one of Atel's roads."

Phaedra only stood and blinked, trying to let that sink in. Atel: the humble traveler, the barefoot God. The spy.

Psander, who spoke openly of the Gods' weaknesses and did not hesitate to send hunters after Magor's sacred beasts, lived in fear of Atel. Phaedra was not qualified to discuss any God, it seemed. She knew nothing of the Gods.

Criton was the first to speak, and it was easy to see that he had been waiting for some time to ask his next question. His voice was nearly a whisper. "Do you know anything about God Most High?" he asked.

"The dragons' God?" said Psander. "I cannot say I know much. But my mentor, who studied dragons, always insisted that He was not dead. His was a minority opinion, you understand, but he claimed that the dragons' God was only dormant somehow. 'Hiding His face,' I think, is how he used to put it. I doubt any of his work survived, but if it did, it would be in the ruins of his tower near Parakas."

She lifted a hand, as if anything could stop Criton from getting excited at her words. "I would caution you against venturing there," she said. "Mayar of the Sea rules in Parakas. Karassa's father, Magor's brother. His servants guard the fallen tower day and night, to prevent anyone from exploring the ruins in search of gold. My mentor's tower was full of artifacts, including golden statuettes of dragons that he had collected over the years. When I came to gaze upon the ruins, I discovered that the men of Parakas had dedicated the tower's riches as a sacrifice to Mayar, and would let no one near. I don't recommend you try. We have a few days, I think, before this rain stops. When you regroup in the morning, perhaps I will be able to point you in some more fruitful direction."

Psander picked up a scroll that had been open on a lectern, and began thoughtfully rolling it closed. "You should both go to bed now," she said. "There will be time to answer all of your questions in the coming days. Right now, you look half dead. If you collapse from exhaustion, you will be of no use to me."

"You know," Criton said, as they made their way back

to their rooms, "every time I think she's being genuinely kind or generous, she says something like that to change my mind. I can see what Bandu and Narky have against her."

Phaedra yawned. "I think it's another one of her masks," she said. "I think she's afraid to show that she likes us."

"I don't know," Criton said doubtfully. "Anyway, I know where we're going once this storm clears."

Phaedra stopped in her tracks, right in the middle of the stairwell. "You can't be serious," she said. "Psander just told you it's guarded! Besides, by tomorrow she'll have thought of somewhere else to send us. If you want to know more about dragons, ask her for a scroll by that Dragon Knight person. I'm sure you've earned it, after everything we brought her."

Criton looked up at her and shook his head. His eyes were glowing gold. "Psander said her mentor was an expert on dragons. Whatever writings she has, they're nothing compared to what we'd find in the ruins of that tower. That's where we have to go."

Phaedra sighed wearily and went back to limping down the stairs. "We can talk to the others about it," she said, "but frankly, I'd rather stay here and read. Last time we went looking for your dragons, I was the one who paid."

29
Criton

At least Bandu didn't object. "I go where you go," she said. They were all congregating in Phaedra's room, discussing Criton's plan to visit the fallen tower of Parakas. Phaedra was lying on her bed with Narky sitting by her feet. Criton and Hunter stood, while Bandu made herself comfortable on the floor.

"I don't understand," said Narky. "Why do you insist on going to these places? When we were following Phaedra's lead, we went to an abbey. We visited a bunch of pious old men and talked about their religion. When it's up to you, we climb down steep cliffs in the dark and get attacked by giant ants!"

"You can't blame Criton for the ants," said Phaedra.

"Well, I can blame him for the climb."

"*You* don't climb," Bandu pointed out, and Narky glared at her.

"You're right, it is dangerous," said Criton. He clenched and unclenched his human hands, a nervous habit.

"You don't have to come with me," he went on. "Fact is, I don't want to be safe. I want to learn about my ancestors, and their descendants, and their God. I want to find out where they all went, and I don't care where that takes me."

"Psander knows what happened to the dragons," said Narky. "But she knows that learning about dragons is all you care about, so the longer it takes her to tell you about them, the more she can get you to do for her."

"That's why I want to go to her mentor's tower," Criton said. "She can't control what we find there, or how much we learn. For once, we won't be dependent on her to teach us what we need to know."

For a moment, he thought he might have convinced them. But then Phaedra said, "What if Mayar sent the plague?"

The others stared. "We would be walking right into His hands," Narky groaned.

"We don't know that He sent the plague," Criton objected.

"True," said Phaedra, "but we do know that the ruins were dedicated to Mayar by the people of Parakas. It's too dangerous, Criton."

Narky looked horror-struck. "Wait, the ruins belong to Mayar? Even if Mayar *didn't* send the plague, He wouldn't just sit by and let us despoil His sacrifices! If there's anything that could make a God angry, it's that."

Criton tried to object, but Hunter cut him off. "We've made enough enemies among the Gods as it is," he said with finality. "If you go, you'll have to go alone."

"Criton never goes alone," Bandu said defiantly. "I go where he goes."

"Neither of you should go!" said Phaedra. "Let's just ask Psander about the dragons' extinction. I'm sure she'll tell us all about it. She was very open with the two of us last night."

Criton looked at her incredulously. Psander had given them *some* information, but *very open*? Phaedra's admiration for the wizard was getting the best of her.

"We'll see," he said.

When they did ask Psander, the wizard gazed up from

her reading with a weary expression. Had she slept at all last night? Criton had never seen her look so tired.

"The extinction, eh?" Psander said. "Well, that all depends. Phaedra gave me an interesting scroll last night, but what else have you brought me?"

When Phaedra showed her the mushrooms and the ore, the wizard became suddenly excited. She leapt up from her seat and cried, "Give those to me!"

For the first time, Phaedra looked alarmed. She hesitated, and Criton took advantage of her uncertainty. "Tell us about the extinction first," he said.

Psander pressed her lips together in overt frustration. Her eyes did not leave the items in Phaedra's hands.

"Very well," she said. "The last of the dragons died nearly two hundred and fifty years ago, in the year 7385 by the common reckoning. She died in battle. Against a God."

This was not what Criton had wanted to hear. He looked at Bandu, and found her gazing sympathetically back at him.

"Gods do kill dragons," she said sadly.

"Yes," said Psander. "The War of the Heavens, we call it now. It lasted for nearly a century and ended with the death of every last dragon in existence."

"How did the war start?" Phaedra asked.

Psander sat back down again, with a sigh. "That's impossible to know. The Gods won the war, so of course the surviving sources all claim that the dragons started it. It's possible that they did, of course. They were arrogant creatures, without a doubt. But I'd rather not rely entirely on the winning side's story."

"Did the dragons' God participate in the war?" Hunter wanted to know.

"Not in any noticeable way," said Psander. "It is written that the dragons expected God Most High to triumph over His enemies, but the dragons' God seems to have been conspicuously silent, even when the war was only just beginning."

Criton finally recovered enough to speak. "So they fought a holy war for God Most High, and He abandoned them. He went silent, and the other Gods slaughtered them."

Psander smiled wryly. "Slaughtered? I wouldn't put it that way. The casualties were not exclusively on the dragons' side."

"Gods died in the war?" Phaedra asked disbelievingly. "The dragons killed Them all on their own, without help in the divine realm?"

Psander nodded. "I presume nobody told you this about the War of the Heavens. Of course they wouldn't. The Gods do not want it thought that They can be defeated by mere terrestrial beings. But the war tore a temporary breach in the mesh, and for a time it was possible for Gods and dragons to clash openly in the heavens. The dragons were annihilated, but the Gods did not come out unscathed. Several were destroyed, starting with Hormul the Desiccator, God of droughts and the desert."

"And there were others after Him?" Phaedra asked. "Which other Gods died? Any I might have heard of?"

Psander raised an eyebrow. "As a matter of fact, yes. Caladoris the Mountain God was the first general of the divine army. When He fell to the dragon Hession, His body became the Calardian range. Accounts from before the war describe the area as hilly country, with the occasional true mountain, but also vineyards and even farms. All that changed in 7320, when Caladoris came crashing down to earth. The mountain clans live on the corpse of the very God they worship."

"But then Hession's cave…" said Hunter.

"Is the deathblow that the dragon Hession inflicted upon the God."

Criton lightly slapped his forehead. "I assumed Hession had lived there. The mountain men might even have said so. I thought we would find some relic of the dragons, some kind of remnant of their lives–"

"–When in fact you were stepping into a gaping wound," Psander finished. "You climbed down into it then, searching for evidence of dragons?"

"That's where I fell," Phaedra said, nodding. "I nearly died in that cave."

Psander nodded. "Yes," she said impatiently, and held out her hand. "Now if you don't mind, I will take those off your hands. I have work to do with them, after which there will be plenty of time for us to converse further. You are welcome to stay here for as long as you like, and I will give you access to my library. You may read any text that you can reach, provided you put everything back when you have finished with it."

When she had gone, Narky whistled. "A dead God," he said. "What do you think calardium is, then? Caladoris' blood? I guess they don't call it a vein of rock for nothing."

Hunter nodded along thoughtfully. "Do you think the mountain men know? They called the calardium 'sacred stones,' but they did sell it to us. I can't imagine anyone knowingly selling his God's blood for white quartz."

"They didn't seem like very thoughtful people," Phaedra pointed out. "They certainly didn't look like the type of people who would study history or theology. They might not even know why the calardium is sacred to their religion. They probably believe their God is still alive."

They considered this silently for a time. Criton could see now why Psander had wanted calardium ore: a God's blood must contain a tremendous amount of power. What new ward could the wizard make out of such power?

"Phaedra," Criton asked, "why do you think she needed the mushrooms? The calardium seems obvious now, but what's so special about blueglow mushrooms?"

"I don't know, exactly," Phaedra admitted, "but they were growing on a pile of dead bodies. There were all these dead people down there, rotting and sprouting mushrooms. It was awful. One of the farmer ants came right by me, to harvest the mushrooms."

She shuddered. "I'm lucky to be alive."

She had never spoken about her fall into the ants' nest before. Now Criton knew why. Her experience had been even more horrific than he had realized.

"Did you say *farmer* ants?" asked Narky, realizing, at the same time as Criton did, who the clansmen's mysterious 'farmers' were. "Those inbred bastards."

"And the mushrooms were growing out of dead bodies?" Hunter asked. "Human bodies?"

Phaedra nodded.

Criton drew in a sharp breath. "Psander said earlier that people all have their own fields of magical energy. If the mushrooms draw that out... you don't think Psander's going to kill the villagers, do you? Just to harvest their latent magic?"

"No, of course not!" Phaedra snapped, looking horrified. "She wouldn't do something like that! It doesn't even make sense!"

"I wouldn't put it past her," said Narky. "It would explain why she wanted all these people here."

"No!" cried Phaedra. "She invited them here for their protection, and because she can't go outside to buy food or supplies. She needs them so that she won't starve, that's all."

"Are you sure she can't just summon food with magic?" Hunter asked.

"I'm sure," said Criton. "Magic exhausts her too. Even if it's possible to summon food, it would be a huge waste of energy."

Hunter's hand fell instinctively to his sword. "Would you bet all the villagers' lives on that? Who knows how Psander's magic works? We have to make sure she doesn't kill anyone."

"She's not going to!" Phaedra insisted.

"How you know?" asked Bandu.

"I just – she wouldn't –" Phaedra sputtered.

Criton let his body revert to its natural state, his claws emerging once more. "It can't hurt to check with her," he said.

But when they looked for Psander, she was nowhere to be found. Their climb to the top of the staircase yielded only a locked door, and as much as Hunter knocked, it never opened. They stood there a moment, unsure of what to do. Criton exchanged a glance with Hunter, both embarrassed to have been stymied by a closed door.

"Do you smell something?" asked Narky.

A wisp of blue smoke curled up from beneath the door. It smelled foul.

"Oh Gods, let's get out of here," pleaded Phaedra.

They retreated to the library. "There's got to be something in here about blueglow mushrooms," Narky said. "Maybe we can find out what she's doing with them ourselves."

Phaedra glanced from him to the walls with a sarcastic look, but soon she was limping from bookshelf to bookshelf, checking titles and gathering a steady pile of manuscripts. Hunter did not seem the least bit interested in this task, but he went to help Phaedra carry her load. Narky sat down in a chair.

"Do any of those really look promising?" Criton asked. "I don't even know where to start looking."

He turned to Bandu, who was walking beside him. "This is ridiculous," he said.

She was not even looking at him. "Bandu?" he said, trying to get her attention. But rather than acknowledging him, she suddenly turned and began to run.

Phaedra had collapsed onto the floor. Hunter dropped his pile of books and knelt over her. "Phaedra! Are you all right?"

The girl's body convulsed as Criton neared. What was wrong with her? Was she sick? Was the smoke from earlier getting to her? Had Psander somehow booby-trapped one of the books?

Bandu understood the situation long before Criton. Without a moment's hesitation, she fell upon Phaedra and gave her an enormous hug.

"What's going on?" Narky called out, rising from his chair.

"O Gods," sobbed Phaedra, "not here, not in front of everyone! I'm sorry," she said, waving impotently at them, "I didn't mean to do this."

"What's the matter?" asked Hunter.

"I'm a cripple!" the girl cried. "I can't even carry my own books!"

"You don't have to," said Hunter.

Phaedra only sobbed louder. "You don't understand! I'll never dance again – I can't even walk properly. I can't get on a horse by myself anymore. Psander can't do anything, and, and, *this wasn't supposed to happen to me!*"

Criton did not know what to do. He couldn't hug her the way Bandu could, and between her and Hunter there was little room to kneel. He simply stood there, feeling useless.

"Psander must be able to do something," Narky said, finally drawing near. "Couldn't you ask her if–"

"We asked already," Criton told him. "Last night. She doesn't know how."

"I don't want to be a cripple!" Phaedra wailed. "I'm no good to anybody like this! My parents would be ashamed of me."

"That's not true," Hunter tried to reassure her.

Phaedra laughed ruefully, tears still flowing from her eyes. "Oh, yes they would. Who would marry me now? I have no money; my family name means nothing to anyone; I'm not pretty anymore – I can't even walk straight!"

"You're very pretty," Criton said, and Bandu glanced at him but said nothing.

Phaedra shook her head. "I'm nothing. I'm nothing."

"You're smart," Hunter told her. "You're brilliant and quick-witted, and you know all about–"

"Who cares?" shouted Phaedra. "What good is any of that, if even *Psander* can't fix my leg?"

After that, nobody knew what to say. It was Bandu and her hug that carried the day in the end. After a few minutes of silence, Phaedra squeezed her hand and thanked her, and began to dry her eyes.

"I'm sorry," she said. "I didn't mean to just collapse like that, like a stupid, weak–"

"Like me?" said Hunter.

That stopped her. She blinked uncertainly up at him.

"It's all right," he said. "It was bound to catch up with you sometime."

Finally, Phaedra smiled a little. "Thanks, Hunter."

They lifted Phaedra to her feet, and Criton helped Hunter gather her books. "Take to rooms," Bandu commanded them. "This is a bad place."

They did as she said.

For two weeks, the clouds above Silent Hall never cleared. The courtyard became such a puddle of mud that the villagers began eating all of their meals in Psander's great hall, and some even slept in the entryway. The islanders saw Psander only twice during this time, since the wizard only emerged from her chambers once a day to eat, and often before dawn. The second time they ran into her, Narky had the wherewithal to ask if she planned to plant blueglow mushrooms in murdered villagers. Psander only shook her head absently and muttered, "No no, that won't do; I'd run out." She never specified which resource she was talking about.

As might have been expected, Phaedra spent her time reading. She did not, however, read aloud these days. The boys did not have much to do until Narky discovered a shelf full of maps in Psander's library, after which they spent their days familiarizing themselves with the landscape as best they could. There was one map that particularly disturbed Criton. It was a map of the continental cities with the territories of each God marked in a different color. On the far right edge of the map was written *Mayar – the Sea*. On the other three edges, it said *Magor – the Wilds*.

Bandu, in the meantime, seemed to have contracted some illness that left her feeling tired and uncomfortable. She ate little, and made constant use of her chamber pot. Criton worried that the Gods had heard her blasphemy after all, and had inflicted her with the seeds of this malady before the islanders could find refuge at Silent Hall. He wished he could help, but she would not even let him touch her. Like an animal, she became very defensive when sick.

Actually, the weather was oppressive for all of them. Narky seemed to be always sniffling or snorting, and Hunter had developed a cough. Phaedra rarely left her room. Only Criton, it seemed, still felt healthy, and his health belied his misery. Bandu worried him, and the clouds worried him, and Psander definitely worried him.

He wished they could leave, but Phaedra said that they should wait until the first sunny day, to be sure that the Gods were no longer looking for Bandu. He couldn't argue with that.

At the end of two weeks, Bandu called for him. He found her sitting up in bed, looking a little better than usual.

"Sit," she said. "Look. No blood now." She presented him with her chamber pot.

Criton sat down at her feet, but tried not to look at the pot's contents. "What do you mean, 'no blood *now*?' Was there blood before? Has your illness gotten that bad?"

"No," she said, "no, is young."

"What?" It was beyond his imagination to guess what she was trying to say.

"No blood, is young," Bandu repeated uselessly, and strangely she smiled. "It is good," she said.

"If you say so," said Criton, "but what do you mean about the sickness being young?"

"Not sick, young!" Bandu said, looking exasperated. "No blood! Young!"

Criton put out his hands to stop her. "Bandu, you'll have to calm down. You're too excited to make any sense. You have to use enough words to make your meaning cl–"

"I make young!" Bandu laughed, slapping at him. "No blood! Six weeks and no blood!"

Criton's heart stopped beating.

30
Bandu

He wasn't happy. He wasn't happy! What was wrong with him? He should be smiling and proud, but instead he looked sick and scared. What was wrong with him?

"How could you…" he said. "How could we… what are we going to do? We've been so stupid!"

"No," she tried to tell him. "No, it is good! Not stupid."

"What do you mean?" he cried. "You can't… I can't… this is terrible!"

"No," she insisted again, "not terrible. I want it."

She burst into tears. Why wasn't he happy? He had *wanted* to mate with her! What did he think would happen?

"I can't believe…" he sputtered again. "I have to think about this."

Then he turned and left the room.

Bandu's tears would not stop flowing. Had she made a mistake? He *wanted* it, she kept saying to herself. He *wanted* it.

She threw her chamber pot across the room. Wicked man! Wicked, stupid man! Would he ever come back? She wanted him to come back and hold her and say he was happy and that their young would be strong and healthy and that he would always protect them with her. That was what she wanted; that was what she had expected. Why had he run away?

She was still crying when Phaedra came in. "Bandu!" she said. "You're pregnant?"

Bandu could not think about new words now, she had to find out why Criton hated her. "He is not happy," she wailed. "He is a wicked, wicked man!"

Phaedra put an arm around her. "What happened, Bandu?"

"I tell him we make young, and he leaves me!"

"Bastard," Phaedra said. "I don't know what's wrong with him, Bandu, but I'll go and talk sense into him. He has no right to treat you like that."

"No, stay with me," Bandu begged her. "Go later. Stay now."

Phaedra nodded vigorously. "Whatever you say, Bandu. I'm here for you."

"I throw that," Bandu confessed, pointing to her overturned chamber pot.

Phaedra grimaced. "We can take care of it later."

They sat together a long time, while Bandu laid her head on Phaedra's shoulder and cried. Phaedra wanted to go yell at Criton, but Bandu wouldn't let her. What she needed was her company.

She did wish Phaedra would stop talking sometimes. Phaedra kept trying to make Bandu feel better by saying things like, "Don't worry, he'll realize what an idiot he is, and he'll come crawling back to you. He has to. He has duties to you now."

Bandu did not want him to crawl, and she didn't understand why Phaedra would suggest it. Didn't Phaedra understand? What Bandu wanted to do now was to leave this room and go find him. She needed him.

But Phaedra would not let her go. "No, Bandu," she said. "You have to make him come to you. It was awful of him to walk out like that, and you can't let him think he can do that to you. He has to realize that there are consequences when he hurts you, or he'll do it again."

Bandu understood, but that only made it hurt more. She knew that Phaedra wanted her to win, because Phaedra was a good friend. But Bandu didn't want to win. All she wanted was for Criton to come back.

"If I go get us some food," Phaedra asked, "will you promise to stay here?"

Bandu nodded, but Phaedra wasn't fooled. She opened the door, walked to the next room and knocked.

"Narky," Bandu heard her say. "Could you do me a huge favor and bring us some lunch? I can't leave Bandu right now."

"All right," said Narky's voice, and then Phaedra was back in the room.

"You'll thank me," she said.

Bandu nodded meekly. She felt so tired, all of a sudden. And she was hungry, terribly hungry. "I want goose eggs," she said.

"Narky's already gone down," Phaedra told her, "but maybe he'll bring you some. I wouldn't mind a boiled egg either."

Bandu shuddered. "No boiled," she said. "I want old way, like with Four-foot."

Phaedra looked confused. "What do you mean, 'like with Four-foot?' Oh Gods, do you mean raw?"

"Raw is not cooked?" asked Bandu. "Yes, raw."

"Well," said Phaedra, looking horrified, "we'll see."

Bandu's stomach growled. She hoped Narky would hurry. "I need to eat," she said, her hands on her stomach. "Now."

"There's not much we can do but wait," Phaedra began to say, but then she looked at Bandu more closely, and her eyes widened. "Are you all right?" she asked. "Bandu, you look terrible!"

Bandu was about to vomit. She could feel it. She was dizzy and nauseous, and her eyes wouldn't focus. "I am sick," she mumbled, afraid to open her mouth too wide in case something came out.

Nothing did come out, though Bandu did not feel any better until Narky arrived, carrying a plate piled high with mutton.

"We can't eat all that," said Phaedra, but what did she know? Bandu did not say anything to correct her – she just ate. The mutton smelled heavenly, and by the time Bandu had started on her second piece, her nausea and light-headedness had subsided. She would have to make sure to eat whenever she felt sick, she thought, ripping the meat off a shank bone with her teeth. Eating made everything better.

When Bandu had finished, and her plate held only a pile of bones, she lay down on the bed to rest. "I sleep now," she told Phaedra. "You can go."

Phaedra raised an eyebrow. "You're sure?"

Bandu just sighed and closed her eyes. She was so tired, and sleeping would be a good way to wait for Criton to come back to her. If he ever did come back.

When she awoke at sundown, Phaedra was still in her room, sitting on the windowsill and reading. The room had been cleaned, and her chamber pot was under her bed once more. But the two of them were still alone.

"He is not here," said Bandu, heartbroken.

"No," said Phaedra, her eyes still on the curled animal skin in her hand. "I sent him away while you were sleeping."

Bandu jumped up. "Why you send him away? That is wrong!"

Phaedra finally lifted her eyes to Bandu. "You needed your rest," she said. "And besides, I thought it would give him more time to feel sorry."

Bandu stood up. "I bring him."

"No!" cried Phaedra, leaping for the door. She stood in front of it, arms spread wide. "No, no. You really shouldn't."

Bandu motioned her out of the way. "I do. Now."

Phaedra bowed her head. "All right. Or I can go and find him for you, and tell him you're ready to speak to him now."

Bandu nodded. She needed a little time anyway. She didn't know what she would say to him yet.

When Criton came in, Bandu was still trying to decide whether to be angry with him, or happy that he had come back to her. She sat on the bed and stared at him, wondering what he was thinking. Criton stood there in the doorway, staring right back at her.

"This is my fault," he said at last. "We never should have slept together."

Bandu did not cry now, but her heart sank. "You want it with me before," she said.

"I know," he said, "but I should have resisted. I'm not... I'm not ready."

"I am," she said.

"Why?" Criton asked. "You're even younger than I am! At least, I think you are. How could you want this? It'll tear us apart."

"*You* tear us apart," she told him angrily. "Every time I am happy, you are not happy. Why do I want you?"

He came closer and sat on the floor at her feet. "I don't know," he said sadly. "I don't know why you would want me at all."

"You are good," she reassured him. "But you are always wrong with me. When I am sad, you are good to me. When I am happy, you are not good."

"It's not because you're happy," he said. "I want you to be happy. It's just... you don't understand. Everything goes wrong when you have children."

"How you know?"

Criton just looked at her, until she thought he would never answer. Then he said, almost in a whisper, "Because my ma told me. She was happy until she had me."

Bandu didn't care what Phaedra would think. She slipped off the bed and held Criton to her. He hadn't meant to hurt her. He was just broken.

"The young has your eyes?" she asked.

He nodded. She kissed his neck and sat down on the floor across from him, leaning her back against the bedframe.

"Your sharp hands too?"

"Probably."

"And your, your..." she rubbed her forearms.

"Scales? Yes."

She smiled at him. "Good," she said. "That is what I think before."

He let out a long sigh. "You really want this?"

"Yes."

"I don't understand you," he said, "but I love you."

"Then I am happy," she told him.

They mated, and Bandu was happy to feel the tension leave his body. When they lay together afterwards, she stroked his shoulder and asked, "You are afraid of marry because your mother marry?"

He looked at her thoughtfully. "I suppose so. Yes. She told me that being married had made her happy at first. But if they hadn't gotten married, he wouldn't have been able to keep her locked away. She had nowhere to go after she married him."

Bandu nodded to show him that she understood. "But you don't want others?"

"No. But I still don't want to marry."

She kissed him on the shoulder. "I understand," she said. "If later you want, then we marry." She rolled over and closed her eyes.

She was almost asleep when Criton spoke again. "I'm really afraid," he said. "I don't know what I'll be like when we have a child. What if it changes me the way it changed Ma's husband?"

She heard, but was too sleepy to put words together.

"I'll be a terrible father," he whispered.

"You are a good man," she mumbled. But even as she fell asleep, she knew that he was still awake. He would be awake for a long time.

31
Narky

Judging from the sounds next door, Criton and Bandu seemed to have already made up. He wished they would be quieter about it. If *he* were ever in a similar situation, he… well, never mind. He'd probably be as loud as he damn well pleased. That didn't mean he had to excuse them for their noise, though.

He crossed the hall to Phaedra's room. Since their return to Silent Hall, Phaedra had taken the room that had once been Criton's, while Criton moved in with Bandu. To Narky's surprise, he found Phaedra sitting there and eating bread and soft cheese.

"A big plateful of mutton wasn't enough for you?" he asked.

Phaedra looked up ruefully. "Bandu ate it all."

"Why didn't you go eat while she was sleeping then?" He had heard the altercation between her and Criton over whether to awaken Bandu.

Phaedra sighed. "There wasn't time. I had to clean her floor, or it would have smelled like a privy all week. And it took so long to find a bucket and rags in this place that I was afraid Criton would go in and wake her up if I dawdled."

"Well, they're both awake now," Narky noted.

Phaedra nodded, looking concerned. "I hope he really

apologized to her."

"I just hope we don't have to wait around here until she has her baby," Narky said.

"Oh Gods," said Phaedra. "I hadn't thought of that. Do you think she's fit to travel?"

Narky snorted. "You're asking me?"

"Why not?" Phaedra said. "You've been pregnant just as many times as I have."

They decided to wait until the next day to ask Bandu how she felt about traveling. She rose before them, however, and search though they might, they could not find her.

"She can't be missing," Criton said in disbelief. "It doesn't make sense."

"Did she say anything to you when she got up?" asked Phaedra.

"It was really early," Criton mumbled, scratching his head. "I think she said something about being hungry."

They asked several villagers if they had seen Bandu, but the townsfolk only stared sullenly at them. "Psander might know," said Hunter. "She eats her breakfast early enough, she might have seen Bandu."

"Maybe they're in the library," Phaedra suggested. "I hadn't thought to look there, since Bandu doesn't read, but it's possible she's talking to Psander."

Criton shook his head. "She wouldn't just go and talk to Psander. She hates Psander."

"We should find Psander and make sure," Narky said, his suspicions aroused. "She's always talking about how fascinating Bandu is."

They rushed to the library, and finding it empty, practically flew up the stairs to the locked door that had impeded them earlier. This time, Hunter slammed on the door with all his might, and when it did not budge, Criton pulled him out of the way and breathed fire at it. When that had no effect either, he tore at the wood with his claws until finally Psander opened it. The wizard stood there a moment, holding a necklace of thin wire and looking extremely irritated. She was wearing a long, thick gray robe reminiscent of armor, and Narky noticed patches of soot on both the robe and Psander's hands.

"You had better have a very good reason for interrupting my work," the wizard hissed.

"Where's Bandu?" Criton demanded.

Psander held his angry gaze without flinching. "I haven't the slightest idea," she said.

"Did you see her at breakfast?" Phaedra asked.

Psander stood for a moment in silence, and Narky had the distinct impression that she was considering whether to lie or not. At last she said, "I did. We did not speak long, however, and I have no idea where she went afterward. I came back here to continue my work."

"What did you say to her?" Criton asked, his voice shaking.

"Very little," the wizard replied curtly. "I offered advice on her pregnancy, as someone with some experience in the matter. She refused my offer of help."

"How did you know she was pregnant?" Narky could not believe that Bandu would tell Psander her news willingly.

"From her magic," said Psander. "It's becoming radical. It's quite obvious. I'm sure you'll understand when you find her."

Criton looked worried. "What do you mean, 'radical'?"

"Stronger, wilder, uncontrollable – extremely unpleasant. For those who are used to controlling their magic, pregnancy scrambles everything. The magic of early pregnancy is a purer form, heavily swayed by one's feelings. It's supposed to get better in the fourth month, but I wouldn't know. I never got that far."

"What happened?" asked Phaedra.

Psander regarded her coolly. "Two months of torture, and then a bloody mess."

"How awful for you!" Phaedra gasped.

Psander shrugged. "Frankly, I was relieved when it happened. For two months I had had to give up all my research. My magic had become impossible to work with. Books changed their texts around me. Experiments failed in absurd and disastrous ways. I could do no work; I couldn't even read. It was miserable. I was glad when it was over."

"Who was the father?" Narky asked. He wondered what kind of a man would have slept with Psander.

Psander frowned severely at him. "That is an extremely personal question, besides being completely irrelevant, and I have no intention of answering it."

"All right," said Narky. "You're sure you have no idea where Bandu went?"

"None," Psander replied, with a wave of her hand. "I offered her a room underground where she could be observed and cared for while keeping her wild magic away from my books, but she did not seem too keen on the idea. She ran off somewhere. Go find her yourselves."

With that, she slammed the door shut. The islanders retreated down the stairs. "Where to next?" Narky asked.

"Out," said Criton. "If Bandu had an argument with Psander, she'd leave here quick as she could."

"Right," said Hunter.

They had to pause when they reached the courtyard, to give Phaedra time to recover from their frantic pace. As they stood there, puffing, Narky finally took some notice of the village that had sprung up within the courtyard. It was strange, perhaps, how little he had bothered to think about the people whose food he ate each time he came here, but the fact was that he had taken them completely for granted. The villagers had done their best to ignore the islanders ever since their association with the Gallant Ones, and it had been so easy for Narky to return the favor.

They were thriving here, he now realized. They had erected permanent houses to replace the tents, and their sties, pens and chicken coops nearly filled the courtyard. He wondered where they had gotten the lumber, out here on the plains. Perhaps Psander had summoned it for them, just as she seemed to have conjured the rest of Silent Hall out of nothing. The houses had mostly been built around the well near the far wall; the tower and gate of Silent Hall had been left unencroached upon. Perhaps none of the villagers dared live quite that near to Psander.

When they stepped out through the gate, Bandu was nowhere to be seen. It was the first clear day in weeks, and the plain stretched out for miles before them. But though they could see many a flock and shepherd, none of the figures in front of them resembled Bandu in any way.

"She can't have traveled more than a few miles," said Hunter. "She hasn't been gone that long."

"I don't see her, though," Narky said.

"Let's circle the wall and check the other side," Phaedra suggested.

They did just that, tromping through the tall grasses that abutted Psander's fortress. Progress was slower than Narky had imagined it would be, since they had to step gingerly around some thorny caper bushes that seemed to reach out for their legs at every opportunity. About halfway around the wall, it dawned on Narky that the thorns really *were* reaching out for them. Even when the breeze died completely, still these dreadful plants swayed toward every limb that drew too near.

"The thorns–" he said.

"I think they're capers," Phaedra pointed out. "Ouch!"

"I know what they are, Phaedra," Narky said. "They're going for us on purpose."

Hunter drew his sword. "I'll clear a path."

The caper bushes tried to avoid their fates by pulling away from the sword, but that only further convinced Hunter of the need to eliminate them. Something about those shivering plants horrified Narky. What kind of a plant could express fear like that?

The possessed thorn bushes grew thicker the further they went, until finally the islanders came upon a vast thicket of them, in the middle of which sat Bandu. She looked up as they approached, tears in her eyes.

"Bandu!" Criton cried, "Are you all right? Stay there."

Hunter hacked a path toward her as quickly as he could, but the plants seemed to change strategy now. They curled around his blade after every swipe, until he could barely yank it back for another stroke. In the meantime the bushes on either side of the beaten path drew their thorny limbs nearer and nearer, and belatedly Narky realized that he and the others were in danger of being flayed alive.

"Stop," said Bandu, lifting her hands.

Hunter obeyed, and so did the thorns. "I make them," Bandu shrugged apologetically. "I don't know how."

She whispered something to the thorn bush next to her, and a wave of rustling sticks and leaves rippled outward through the thicket. The bushes between Bandu and the others splayed their limbs outward, clearing a narrow path.

"Since when have you been able to do this?" Phaedra asked in wonder.

"Since now."

Criton reached Bandu first, and drew her into a hug. "I was afraid Psander had kidnapped you," he said.

Bandu shook her head and drew away. "She want me, but I run here. She is afraid to go outside, so I am safe."

"If you're so safe," said Narky, "then why all the thorns?"

"She doesn't feel safe," said Phaedra empathetically, and Bandu nodded.

"She wants to watch me," Bandu said, and shuddered. "I don't go back inside."

"Bandu," said Criton, "you can't just stay out here for nine months. Psander has experience with this sort of thing; maybe we should trust her this time?"

The thorns thrashed in anger, and Bandu shook her head. "Psander is wicked," she said.

"I think we should go to Gateway," said Hunter, finally joining in the conversation.

They all turned to him in surprise. "What?" Narky asked.

"Gateway," Hunter said. "Where the wizards used to study fairy magic. Bandu's magic is getting stronger, and even Psander doesn't know what'll happen. She just wants to watch and find out. But she said earlier that there used to be a whole community of wizards researching fairy magic at Gateway. Even if it's in ruins, at least those ruins weren't dedicated to any Gods."

"That's a good idea," said Phaedra. "But where *is* Gateway? Psander never said."

"No," said Hunter, "but I found it on one of her maps. It's southwest of Parakas and the dragon tower, in some kind of a forest where the trees were drawn differently. It's not on the coast, so we can stay away from Mayar's territory."

"Sounds fine to me," said Narky. He would go anywhere if it meant they could avoid angering more Gods.

They looked to Bandu, who nodded. "All right," said Phaedra, "Gateway it is. But we have to get our things from inside before we go. And we should bring plenty of food with us this time, in case nobody wants to sell us any."

They packed as quickly as they could, leaving Bandu by the gate outside. They could have used her help, but she refused to go inside under any circumstances.

"I never go back to her," she said. The horses whinnied and tried to back away from her, perhaps sensing some angry ripple of magic.

Hunter reached for the reins of the nearest horse. "Psander won't hurt you," he said, simply but forcefully. "If she did you any harm, she'd regret it."

"Besides," said Phaedra, trying to sound equally certain, "she wouldn't experiment on you without your consent."

Bandu looked skeptical. "I stay outside," she said, and the horses calmed down just as suddenly as they had been spooked.

They were already a few miles down the road when Criton said, "Damn. I meant to ask her about the spear."

"The spear?" repeated Narky, confused. "What spear?"

"Bestillos' spear. He threw it at me, and I could have sworn I saw Bandu knock it down. Phaedra said it was just the wind, though. I thought Psander might help me make sense of that."

"I do have a theory," Phaedra said. "You have the wizard's sight, and I don't. If Bandu were to do something very suddenly and forcefully with her magic, do you think your eyes might literally see her hand in it?"

Criton's eyes widened. "Huh," he said.

"But can you really control the wind?" Narky asked Bandu.

The girl shook her head. "Control is bad word. I not control. I listen to wind. For years, I listen to wind. Now it listen to me."

Narky gulped, while Criton looked pleased. Pleased! Had the thorn bushes taught him nothing? Bandu couldn't control her magic anymore! The more power she had, the more dangerous she was to them all. If the wind had to obey someone's orders, Narky would have rather it obeyed *anyone* other than the crazy girl with the erratic powers and the poor grammar. The very thought of it chilled him to the bone.

Or was that just the wind?

32
HUNTER

The weather barely improved as they traveled away from Silent Hall. They camped under the spitting sky and awoke to an overcast morning, drizzling and gray. And yet, traveling felt very different this time. The others deferred to Hunter now, as the one who had studied Psander's maps most closely. Leading his companions across the countryside, he felt for the first time as if they looked to him for more than just his skill in battle. It was a good feeling.

Phaedra had lapsed into moody silence. Hunter hoped she wasn't torturing herself, thinking about her crippled leg. In many ways, her situation was much like his. She had had a bright future back in Tarphae. Now she was being forced to rethink her life.

He had to cheer her up somehow, but he didn't know how to begin. What could he say that could possibly distract her from her troubles?

"Can you tell me more about the Gods?" he said.

Phaedra blinked at him. "I don't... I don't know. I have more questions than answers right now."

Hunter pressed on. "What kind of questions?"

"Well, who weakened the mesh during the War of the Heavens? How? Did the Gods create the mesh, or is it primordial? Is there another mesh between the fairy world and the world of the Gods?"

Hunter nodded. He wished he could think of something to say, but he was out of his depth. Luckily, Phaedra had not run out of questions.

"Is the fairy world the 'first world' I read about in that annotated Second Cycle? If so, what *really* happened to make the Gods decide to create another world?"

"I don't know," said Narky, "but I'm starting to think they shouldn't have. This world is ugly."

"Only because there are no more dragons," Criton said. "*If* there are no more dragons. I don't believe they were all killed."

"Why not?" asked Narky. "*Everybody* says they're gone, even Psander. Besides, how could any dragon have survived the war with the Gods?"

"I don't know," said Criton. "I just feel it."

The pitying look Phaedra gave Criton made it clear what she thought of his intuition. Still, Hunter thought, it was good for Phaedra to pity someone other than herself.

"What I don't see," said Narky, "is how the Gods could go and kill all the dragons, and then fail to kill God Most High. Weren't those dragons the equivalent of all His fingers? I mean, compared to the dragons, the Dragon Touched couldn't have been more than a pinky's worth. If the dragons' God really is dormant the way Psander said He might be, why did the other Gods let Him live?"

"Because God Most High isn't just any God," said Criton, with heartfelt certainty. "He's more powerful than all the others; otherwise, He wouldn't really be God Most High. If losing the dragons could put Him in real danger, He would have fought for them. I think the dragons angered Him somehow, so He let them get themselves killed in a war without even worrying about the danger to Himself. He must be vastly more powerful than the other Gods."

Phaedra's pitying expression had never left her face.

"Or," she said gently, "Psander's mentor could have been wrong. Psander did say that his was a minority opinion."

Criton shook his head. "No. God Most High is alive. He just needs to see that His worshippers are still faithful to Him. Then He'll awaken, and the other Gods will be in trouble."

Phaedra shrugged. "Maybe," she said, trying to be kind.

Hunter led them southward across the plains, veering west at one point to avoid the forest before drifting back eastward. They stopped to eat every time Bandu became hungry or nauseous, which was often. Hunger and nausea seemed to go hand in hand for Bandu. The worst part was when she insisted that the smell of salted meat made her sick, and that Criton would have to find her something fresh to eat.

"We haven't passed a town in days!" Criton complained. "Where am I supposed to get you fresh meat?"

"Hunt," she told him. "I eat sheep or goat or cow or bird or rat or *anything*, but not old and salty!"

Criton came back almost two hours later with a single charred rabbit, blackened on the outside and raw on the inside. "I'm sorry," he said, as he presented it. "I've never hunted before."

Bandu ignored him completely until she had gnawed every last piece of meat off the rabbit's bones, and her hands and face were smeared with blood. "Ooh," she said, burping and sitting down on the ground. "Next time I wait for you to cook."

A few days later they came to a place where the plains ended and a forest of tall broad-leafed trees stretched all the way to the mountains. Here Hunter turned them eastward. They would travel this way for a day or two, he decided, before journeying south again. On second thought, considering how long it had taken them to go this far, perhaps two days of eastward travel would not be enough. Should they go east for a third day, or a fourth? He wished he could have brought the map with him.

After two days of further travel, Hunter decided that

three would not do. They were stopping too often, mostly to satisfy Bandu's heightened need for both food and rest. Narky muttered in irritation at the girl's frequent demands, but Hunter did not mind Bandu's presence. She was better than he at finding good, sweet water here in the forest. Considering the length of their journey, he doubted they would have been able to manage it without her help. By his estimation, their travels would last well over a month, and there were simply not enough towns in their path for the islanders to avoid foraging.

After the fourth day they turned southward again, and their pace slowed even further. The trees and undergrowth grew thicker the farther south they went, and the rain escalated from drizzle to downpour. Far from providing protection, the leafy boughs above only served to convert all rain into oversized drops, which splashed startlingly on the islanders' heads at every third step.

Bandu's magic began to govern their movements. When she was hungry or tired, the trees and bushes conspired to block their path. Her hunger radiated from her little body and spooked every animal within miles, so the islanders took to hunting only in those few moments when Bandu was *not* hungry. At last, after nearly two months of travel, Hunter deemed that Gateway must be near. The trees here were taller and broader than before, with enormous leaves that seemed designed to catch the rain. Bandu grew even more unsettled, but that struck Hunter as a good sign.

"We're in the right area," he told the others. "Now all we have to do is find the ruins themselves."

"And that ought to be easy!" Narky said sarcastically.

Criton sniffed the air. "Bandu, do you smell something? You're better at this than I am."

Bandu shook her head emphatically, tears suddenly pouring from her eyes. "I only smell mushrooms!" she wailed.

"Are you hungry again?"

She nodded sadly. "A little."

"Well then," sighed Criton, "I guess I'll have to learn how to follow the magic myself."

He took a deep breath, and pointed. "This way," he said.

After three days of following Criton's nose, even Hunter had to admit that he had doubts about his friend's tracking abilities. Then, to his surprise, Phaedra stopped them short.

"It's here," she said.

"I don't know," said Criton. "I don't feel anything different here."

"It's here," Phaedra repeated. "The trees here are younger, and the only older ones I see, there and there, have burn marks on them."

Hunter followed her gaze. "You're right," he said. "What should we do? Dig?"

"Let's see," said Narky, and he began crashing through the undergrowth toward one of the burned trees. He tripped and fell partway there. "There's a stone here!" he shouted.

Criton and Bandu followed him, inspecting the grounds while Hunter helped Phaedra down from her horse.

"This is really strange," Phaedra said. "I expected far more ruins. These stones look like they must be part of the foundation."

"This one's a corner stone," Narky called, standing some way ahead.

"If this is the foundation," said Criton, "what happened to the rest of the tower?"

Phaedra shook her head. "I don't know."

A sudden fear struck Hunter. "How do we know these are really the ruins of Gateway? This could be anything."

"Bad here," said Bandu. "Very bad here."

"I think that means we're in the right place," said Narky. "Let's dig a little and see if anything useful got buried."

They had brought no shovel, but did their best with their hands, tearing away at the moss and trying to break through the tree roots using shards of broken rock.

"Nothing," Bandu kept repeating. "Nothing here. This is a wicked place."

Phaedra looked at her curiously. "What are you feeling? Is it the God magic that destroyed the tower, or the wizard and fairy magic that used to be here?"

But Bandu just shook her head and insisted that this place was wicked.

The rain, thankfully, had stopped for now. They excavated some more, but found little besides rocks, bugs, and tree roots. "There's something useful around here somewhere," said Phaedra. "I can feel it."

"I sure hope so," Narky replied. "Because if this is it, we'll never learn anything besides what Psander wants to tell us. Can you imagine if we'd risked our lives going to that dragon tower Criton wanted us to go to, and all we found was this?"

Criton did not look pleased at the suggestion. "There's plenty to be found at the dragon tower. Nobody would place guards over a useless pile of rocks."

"Oh," said Narky, "well, at least that explains why there are no guards here."

"Shut up, you two," Phaedra snapped. "We've spent all this time getting here; we're not going anywhere until we've looked under every last stone. There must be something around here that can teach us about Bandu's magic, or the fairies, or *something*. As long as we have food and fresh water, we're staying."

"We'd better put up the tents while there's still light out," Hunter said.

They followed his suggestion, and soon all three tents were standing apart from each other among the ruins, wherever the islanders could find level ground. The new tents, which Narky had been wise enough to commission from Psander's villagers during their stay at Silent Hall, were of greatly inferior quality. The villagers had made them out of oiled goats' wool, and they stank. During their travels, the near-constant rain had been interrupted by a brief dry spell, and this had been enough to partially felt the wool such that the tents had shrunk considerably since Criton had bought them. They were also extremely heavy.

After a somewhat heated discussion, they left the old tent – the one that Narky had bought from the Gallant Ones – to Phaedra. Criton and Bandu shared one of the goat tents, as Bandu called them, and Hunter and Narky took the other.

"Hunter," Narky asked that night, just as Hunter was about to fall mercifully asleep, "how are you so selfless all the time? Phaedra could easily have taken one of the smaller tents. You practically gave her the big one yourself. How do you stay so damn gallant?"

Hunter sighed and opened his eyes. "I'm a nobleman," he reminded Narky. "That's just how I was raised."

"Oh, come on," Narky said. "All noblemen act that way?"

Hunter turned to him. "My brother did. He was always generous, especially with girls."

"All right, sure," said Narky, "but wasn't that just so that he could get them in bed?"

Hunter rolled over again, and tried to close his eyes. Why did Narky always think the worst of people? It was so ugly. Could he be right? Kataras had been so much more social than Hunter, and his friends were all older. Hunter didn't really know what his brother did with his time. Sparring with swords was the only thing they had ever really done together, but Kataras had stopped doing even that once Hunter began beating him.

"I don't know," he said to Narky, and hated himself for it.

"I wish I could be like that," Narky said. "I wish I could just do things for people naturally, without feeling like an idiot."

"Why would you feel like an idiot if you were being good to people?" Hunter asked. Gods, how he wished he could just sleep.

"I don't know," said Narky. "It doesn't come naturally to me. I feel like if I started acting all generous, people would wonder what I wanted out of them."

Hunter simply shrugged, and hoped that the conversation would end there. Thankfully, it did.

Over the next few days, Hunter took on the task of hunting for food while the others excavated the ruins. There were a few nearby streams where he could fill their waterskins and watch for prey. Narky, Criton and Phaedra all seemed to find digging exciting, and Bandu generally watched them from a distance, muttering to the horses and trying to wrest back control of her magic. Judging by tonight's new moon, she must be entering her fourth month of pregnancy by now. Hadn't Psander said the fourth month was better?

If anything, Bandu was acting more anxious than ever. Hunter could hear her at night, agitatedly insisting that this place was wicked even as Criton tried to calm her down. Tonight, Hunter almost agreed with her. A cool mist was rising from the ground, and the stars seemed to shine more dimly without the moon. They were all a little hungry, because Bandu's fear had scared away every animal but their horses, who would have fled too had they not been tied to a tree. Her magic was growing stronger. Even Hunter could feel it.

There was something insidious about this mist. Hunter could have sworn that it had been thicker around Bandu's tent. The thought chilled him. Maybe he should go outside and check.

When Hunter stepped out, he had to blink a few times to make sure he wasn't dreaming. Bandu and Criton's tent had completely disappeared at the center of a vortex of swirling mist.

"Narky!" he cried, ducking his head back into the tent. "Get your spear and get out here! Something's happening!"

By the time Narky stumbled out, the vortex of mist had expanded even further. White tendrils spiraled out from the center, enveloping the tents, the ruins, the forest. Hunter shivered. The stars had faded away.

33
BANDU

There was a box in her head, and the lock was broken. She could not remember what was inside, but she knew that as soon as she opened it, she would realize that she had known all along. She hadn't made the box herself; she was sure of that. *They* had put it there.

The box was old. How long had it been hidden there, in her head? A long, long time. A long time. Definitely before Bandu, and maybe even before Two-foot. Yes. The box had been put there when she still had a real name. A name she hadn't given herself.

Father. Father had given her a name. Maybe the name was inside the box! But she knew that couldn't be right. No, the box held something much scarier than her name.

It whispered to her, quiet words that she could not quite hear. It wanted her to open it. It had been waiting so long to be opened.

She could almost touch it, though she didn't want to. The closer she came, the more it frightened her. That muffled voice went on from inside it, asking her, begging her, commanding her to let it out of its prison. She would, she knew she would. She couldn't help it. The voice would wear her down with its unheard demands and promises.

She could resist it for now, but she couldn't last forever. No, she couldn't.

Why even bother resisting? The longer the box stayed shut, the more she would fear it and the longer it could control her. She ought to rush forward and fling it open with all her might, just like that! Then it couldn't frighten her anymore. Whatever happened then, it would happen, but she would not be afraid. She really ought to. Touch it. Open it.

Still she hesitated, like a child stepping into a cold river. She *should* jump in quickly, but instead she went slowly and awfully, one toe at a time. She had to open it. She would open it. She could not bear to open it.

The box was underneath her hands now, and quiet though the voice sounded, she knew it was screaming. Her fingers felt the broken lock, rusted and crumbling and useless. She should just do it. One swift motion of the hands, and it would be over. But no, she couldn't. She could only move slowly.

She slipped her fingers under the lid and slowly, slowly lifted it.

Wicked child! said the voice.

Book III

Prophecy

34
The Fairy Captain

The moons were aligned for them tonight, for the first time in oh so many years. The captain could almost taste the sweet flesh of children on her tongue. There was no better flavor than that of innocence.

Eleven steeds, eleven riders stood on the brink of the Other World, the cursed favorite. Soon the hunt would begin. Tonight they would dance in the halls of the mighty.

Raider Two began the incantation. "Let the elders feast once more upon the young," said he.

"Let those who were abandoned seize their bounty," spoke Raider Three.

"Let rash creators grieve their favorite children," sang Raider Four.

"And we shall claim that which we've been forbidden!"

"And we shall steal a dream from every county!"

"And we shall suck each prayer from their gasping lungs!"

The captain raised her sickle high, and the others fell silent. "The Gateway opens," she said now, just as she had said throughout the ages. "Eleven riders step across the boundary. Elven raiders take what should be theirs. Eleven riders revel in their suffering. Elven raiders teach their world to fear!"

She slashed the air with her sickle and the mists rose, just as they had risen a hundred years ago, and a thousand. The raiders slowly drew their nets out of the air, clutching the reins with their free hands. How they had waited for their hunt to resume!

The ring of steel met their ears. "–And get out here!" someone shouted from up ahead. "Something's happening!"

Raider Two raised an eyebrow. Who could possibly be waiting for them on the young side? The tower had only fallen twenty-two years ago – had the godserfs really forgotten their loss so soon? Or was this some new trick the Goodweathers were playing on them?

"Phaedra!" shouted another voice. "Criton, Bandu! Are you all right?"

Raider Five looked to the captain. "Sickles?" she asked.

The captain considered. The voices sounded delightfully frightened. Perhaps they were not elves but only frightened godserfs, like the ones who had built the tower. She still had fond memories of slaughtering those terrified men after their unexpected journey through the boundary. She was glad they had returned to this gate.

"Nets," the captain said. Even if these voices really were a Goodweather trick, capturing them might be a good deal more fun than a battle. The raiders could always cut them to pieces afterwards.

Two dark figures emerged from the mist, clinging to each other most wonderfully. How easy it was! Raider Five cast her net, and soon the couple was trapped underneath the silken wires. They screamed and cried out, the trapped ones, as the raiders circled round.

"Another!" shouted Raider Eight, and soon his net too had fallen, this time on a lone figure that had come running out toward them with a great jangling sound. How terrifically disorganized these runners were!

Within minutes, the raiders had caught another two figures and determined that there were no more. The glow of the nets revealed these five to be dark-skinned youths, wide-eyed and frightened.

"Godserfs!" laughed Raider Two. "Tonight, they come to us!"

"These are too old," said Raider Nine. "Shall we quarter them?"

"Embowel them!" suggested Raider Ten.

"They're younger and stronger than the others were," Raider Four pointed out. "We could enslave them."

One of the godserfs was sobbing now, the little one who shared her net with the tall scaly one. The scaly male tore uselessly at the net, obviously unaware of its powers. There was a flash of light from inside. "Nothing's working!" he cried, with growing horror.

The captain laughed. "Godserfs, indeed. Leave them for now. Our hunt must not be forgotten. They will still be here when morning dawns. We can plan our games during the hunt, and play when we return."

The raiders cheered, already thinking of wonderful games to play with their captives. What a pleasant evening this would be!

But first, the hunt. The captain gave her orders, and her raiders galloped behind her through the boundary. A delicious catch awaited them on the other side.

35
Criton

"Are they gone?"

The dark silence seemed to answer Narky's question. No crickets chirped here. No wind rustled. A fairy couldn't have hidden here without the islanders noticing, anyway: the elves' white skin had shone in the darkness with its own ghostly light. Even so, only after a minute of listening in silence did Bandu lift her head.

"They are gone," she exhaled. "They don't know me!"

"How would they know you?" Criton asked. "Bandu, have you been here before?"

The girl nodded. "Yes," she said. By way of explanation, she added, "I opened the box."

"You opened a box?" asked Hunter, from somewhere up ahead. "Is that what brought us here?"

"I don't know," Bandu replied. "Maybe gate opens before. Maybe I open gate by mistake, because of young. I don't know."

"If you've been here before," asked Narky angrily, "then why the hell didn't you tell us?"

In the dark, Criton felt Bandu put her hands on her hips. "I don't know then," she said defiantly. "I only know when I open the box. Remember is in the box."

Narky made a frustrated sound. "Criton, can you translate? What the hell is she trying to say?"

Before Criton could say anything, Phaedra interrupted. "Where did you find the box, Bandu? At Gateway?"

"At Gateway, in my dream," Bandu explained. "The box is in my head."

"You made it up, you mean?" asked Narky.

"I don't make it! *They* put it there! They put in all the young, so when they send back, nobody remembers."

"Nobody remembers..." Phaedra pondered. "I think I understand you, Bandu. You're saying you were here as a child, but the fairies locked your memories of their world in a mental box, so that they were hidden from you until now? Until you found the box in your head and opened it?"

Bandu nodded in the darkness. "Yes."

Phaedra whistled. "Well, that explains why you can do some fairy magic, but couldn't explain why! Your memories of the fairy world were hidden from you. If they do that with all the children, it even explains why none of the sage Katinaras' writings mention his abduction. Oh, wow."

"What?" asked Narky.

"Well," Phaedra said, "that means that none of our lore about the fairies comes from people who have been here. The children who have come back from this world don't remember anything about their time here."

"So what you're saying," Narky pointed out, "is that we don't know a damn thing about this place, or about the people who just captured us."

"Bandu does," said Criton. "She opened the box."

That struck them all silent again. They were looking toward Bandu, he was sure of it. Now that his eyes had had some time to adjust, Criton realized that he could see the outline of the net that had caught him and Bandu. It twinkled with its own starlight, as if made somehow out of the night sky itself. When he squinted, he could see the nets that had caught the others too. No wonder he had been unable to tear these cords! How could one tear the sky?

"Bandu," Criton asked, "do you know how to get out of these nets? I didn't see any weights on them when the fairies threw them, but now it won't budge, no matter how hard I pull. It's like it's attached to the ground!"

"Yes," Bandu answered sadly. "If you are inside then no good. Nets move only if you pull from out there."

Narky and Hunter both seemed to be verifying this for themselves. "Great," said Narky, giving up first. "What now?"

Phaedra shuffled around in the darkness behind them, perhaps sitting down. "Can you tell us some of what you remember, Bandu? The more we know, the better."

"I don't have many words," Bandu answered slowly, "and it is many, many words to tell."

"Don't bother trying," Narky snapped. "We never understand you anyway, and I, at least, don't have the energy to waste making sense of you. It's bad enough being caught in a net and waiting for a crowd of Kindly Folk to come back and chop us to pieces."

"Narky!" Phaedra scolded. "What's the matter with you?"

"Oh, I don't know," he shouted back at her. "Maybe the fact that I'm going to die horribly! You heard them talking! They're going to torture us and kill us as soon as they come back from their hunt. We're going to die in front of a bunch of little kids, and if any of those kids survive their time in this Godforsaken place, they won't even remember us!"

"Shut up, Narky," said Hunter.

"Make me," Narky retorted. "You can't get out of your net any better than I can."

"You don't know that they'll kill us," said Hunter, sounding more defiant than hopeful. "We should be thinking about what we can do to keep them from killing us, not giving up before they even get back. You wanted to give up back in Anardis too."

Narky did not respond, and they stood some time

without speaking. Hunter made some attempt at cutting the net with his knife, to no avail.

"Bandu," said Phaedra. "Does your magic still work in there? I heard Criton say his didn't..."

"Nets are too strong," Bandu told her.

"Oh." Phaedra was clearly disappointed. "But what *can* we do, then?"

"Sleep," said Bandu. "Wait." And she lay down.

Criton sat beside her, trying to plan an escape. He imagined the others were doing the same. If a fairy took the net off for just a moment, he might be able to... no. There were eleven fairies, with magic and weapons. They would anticipate a struggle. If they meant to kill him, kill him they would. Still, his hopeful imagination would not let him rest. His mind constructed elaborate fantasies in which he escaped, tore the fairies to shreds, and rescued Bandu and the others. He couldn't help it. To his dying breath, he would imagine himself a hero.

Bandu! She was carrying his child. Their child. How could their lives end like this? How could he die without ever seeing his son smile, or hearing his daughter laugh? He wanted this life with Bandu. Oh God of Dragons, he wanted this life!

He sat down beside Bandu and stroked her thick tangled hair. In mourning, the islanders' hair had all grown into short but aggressive mats. "I wish I could have married you," he whispered.

She opened her eyes. "You want to marry now?"

"Yes," he said wretchedly. "I do."

In the dim light of their shimmering prison, he saw her smile.

"We marry," she said. "You never want others?"

"Never."

She sat up. "I don't want others. So now we are marry."

"I guess we are," he said, feeling oddly better.

"That's it?" asked Narky, butting in. "You're not going to

give her anything, or swear any vows in front of Gods, or any of that?"

"I know some wedding vows," Phaedra offered, "if you want to repeat them after me."

"Shut up, all of you!" Criton scolded them. "This isn't your wedding!"

But Bandu just laughed.

Criton sat up straight. "I'm going to get us out of here," he said.

The ground was soft and moist. His claws tore through it easily. Soon his hands would pass under the net, and then…

His hands did not pass under. The unbreakable cords extended even here, below the surface. The net had grown into the ground somehow! The fairies were no fools. When they returned from their hunt, the islanders would still be here. Criton sat back down with a thud, and began to weep.

36
Narky

The fairies returned just before dawn, as the sky was turning from black to deep blue. Seven of them had nets dragging behind their pale horses. Frightened children looked out between the cords with desperate eyes. The captain's net held twins, a boy and a girl, who clung together and did not lift their eyes to the strangers.

"See how we have returned!" the captain gloated, and her skin shone an even brighter white than before. "With you, we have thirteen."

"We only need eleven," her lieutenant said nastily.

"Let two of us go then," Narky suggested. Somehow, he felt an overwhelming need to challenge these beings.

The captain laughed. "Perhaps we will, Godserf, perhaps we will. Shall we play a game for your freedom?"

Her cavalry had come to a stop, and the captured children stared silently at the islanders. All of them were pink and pale, Narky realized. He wondered what they made of him and the others.

"What sort of game?" asked Hunter.

"The game of wounds," answered the lieutenant with relish.

"No," said Bandu suddenly. "Riddles first. Play the riddle game."

The elves stared at her, surprised and annoyed. The captain raised an eyebrow high up her forehead. "You know of the riddle game?" she exhaled. "And you challenge us? Very well. We will win, and you will die."

"How about if we win?" asked Criton.

"Then you are safe for eleven days," she said. "Raider Two, you may begin the game."

The lieutenant bared his teeth at them. "Lovely," he said. "The Godserfs catch it. The Godserfs do it. The Godserfs are it."

Damn it, Bandu, thought Narky, *why did we ever come here? What have you gotten us into?*

"How many guesses do we get?" asked Phaedra.

The fairies burst into hideous laughter. "One," said the captain.

"Can we consult with each other?"

The captain shook her head.

Narky felt his heart sink. "Then how are we supposed to decide who gets to answer the riddle?"

"Whoever answers first," said the one called Raider Two.

"Give us a minute then," demanded Phaedra. "We need silence to think."

Narky tried to think about the riddle too, but it was impossible to concentrate. These horrible beings would happily kill them over a single wrong answer. Kindly Folk indeed.

"I think I have it," said Phaedra.

"Have what?" asked the captain, twinkling.

"The answer. It's prey, isn't it? 'Godserfs' is your word for humanity. We catch prey, we pray to the Gods, and to you, we are prey."

The elves tittered. "So you are," rumbled Raider Two.

"Our turn now," said Bandu. "Phaedra, now you say riddle."

Phaedra looked a bit startled. "Me?" she asked. "Does it have to be me, because I answered theirs? I don't have any good riddles. I only have mysteries."

"Ask one then," suggested Criton.

"Well, all right." Phaedra cleared her throat. "Um, so, the mesh between the worlds. What is it made of?"

"Sky, of course," answered the captain. "My turn."

Narky found it hard to keep down his frustration. They would lose this game and die as a consequence, but at least Phaedra would learn more about the universe first!

The elf captain cleared her throat. "It is the dream of civilization," she began. "A kingdom without it cannot stand long, yet for one of you, it would mean death. What is it?"

Concentrate, Narky thought to himself. A necessity for civilization, something people wanted, which would nonetheless kill one of them? Which one? Could fairies see the future? Or the past…

Narky's blood ran cold. Oh, Gods. The fairies could read memories, just like Psander! Would his past never truly be behind him? The others looked at each other, clearly unsure of the answer to the fairy's 'riddle.' Of course they didn't know. It wasn't a riddle at all: it was a trap.

"Well," said Phaedra. "This would be more of a guess, since I'm not really sure about that last bit, but… I don't know, should I? I have an idea, but if anyone else has a more solid one…"

"You guessed right on the last one," said Hunter. "I don't think any of us are better at riddles than you are. Go ahead, Phaedra. We trust you."

Oh Gods, she was going to kill them all!

Phaedra took a deep breath. "All right," she said. "Well, I think it's–"

"Justice," said Narky, interrupting her. "The answer is justice."

Phaedra stared at him, horrified. They all did. Then their eyes shot to the fairy captain, who sat calmly upon her horse, looking utterly composed. She said nothing for a few moments, smiling mildly at the islanders whose lives hung in the balance. She was milking their fear for all it was worth.

"Correct," she said at last. "It's your turn now."

His turn? What could Narky say? If the captain could read his memories, surely she could read his present thoughts too! Posing a riddle he knew the answer to would be tantamount to giving up his turn entirely. The fairies held an outrageous advantage over them.

There was only one thing to do: like Phaedra, he would have to ask a question to which he did not know the answer. He felt guilty now about how frustrated he had been with her for trying to satisfy her curiosity. She had done the right thing, after all. And in case the fairies were able to answer him too, he may as well ask a question that really mattered.

He held the captain's gaze defiantly. "Tell me this," he said. "Is the dragons' God dead?"

"Of course not," said another of the fairy women. "If He were dead, the sky would crash down once more upon the earth, the worlds would run together like flowing rivers, and all who are living would perish in a flood of pure magic. All this may yet happen, but it has not happened yet."

"Huh," said Narky.

"I knew it!" Criton cried, reveling in the news. At least he would be happy, before the fairies killed them.

"We have toyed with them long enough," the captain declared. "Finish this, Raider Eleven."

The elf woman who had answered Narky's question nodded her fair head. Her silvery white hair, which grew all the way down to her hips, jingled when she nodded. Eleven tiny silver bells had been woven into it. Was it a sign of her greater importance? Lesser importance? He didn't know. All he knew was that the sound enchanted him, hypnotized him. He wished he could run a hand through her hair… pull her head toward him… kiss her forehead…

"Why do we call you 'godserfs'?" she asked. Her voice thrilled him.

"Because–" began Criton, but Bandu suddenly elbowed him in the gut and he doubled over, coughing.

"Don't talk!" she shouted. "Narky, Hunter, don't talk!"

Her words confused him. Why did she not want him to speak? He knew the answer – he could see it on the elf's lips. "Because I love you," he wanted to tell the fair-headed maiden, and why shouldn't he say it? It was the truth.

"So beautiful," he heard Hunter mumbling to himself. No! He must not speak! If Hunter answered the elf first, she would be his!

"Because I–"

"You do not have the Gods!" screamed Bandu, before Narky could finish. He and Hunter stared at her, dazed.

"They make your sky a wall," Bandu continued, "and They do not watch you here. They say you are not for them. You call us godserfs because always Gods tell us what to do, but never tell you anything."

The elf maiden's eyes flashed, and her charm dissolved. She had almost succeeded, Narky realized with sudden horror. If Bandu had not recognized their danger, the elves would have won and the islanders would have been executed right here, in front of these children.

Bandu did not even wait for the elves' angry mutters to die down before confronting them with her own riddle. "When my young comes," she said, "what name do I give?"

The fairies' anger dissipated in an instant, replaced by malicious glee. "Your riddle breaks our rules," gloated the captain. "A riddle must have a single answer, but yours does not. Whatever name I say now, you will change your answer accordingly. You have forfeited the game, and your lives are ours."

"You are wrong," said Bandu. "I choose already, and never change. But you don't see because I don't see."

The fairies were clearly just as confused by this answer

as Narky was. "What are you saying?" the captain asked. "If you had chosen a name already, we would see it!"

"No," said Bandu, smiling. Smiling! By now, the first rays of sunlight were peeking over the horizon, revealing her face in all of its glowing triumph.

"When I am little like them," she said, indicating the captured children, "your kind puts a box in my head. I can't remember what's in. When Gateway opens, I open box and see all remembering about elves. But after I take remembers out, I see riddle game. So I keep the box and put my young's name inside. Only one name inside, but I don't remember it, so you don't see!"

The fairy captain seemed to darken in front of Narky's eyes. "Impossible!" she cried.

"You don't answer the riddle?" confirmed Bandu. "Then we win. If you take away net, I can open the box and show you."

The captain looked to her followers, who only looked back at her sullenly. Their skin really did seem to be growing darker as the light began to dawn on their world.

"She could be bluffing," offered Raider Two.

The captain nodded, though she did not look hopeful. "Release her," she said, with a limp wave of her hand.

Raider Two grimaced and reached for the net that covered Bandu and Criton. It sprang back into his hand.

"Now," said the captain. "Prove the truth of your words."

Bandu nodded, and closed her eyes. "I do now."

For a moment, all was still. Then, suddenly, the captain cried out. "How dare you?" she shrieked. "Your child will be Goodweather? How dare you!"

Once more the net came hurtling down, but this time Bandu and Criton were ready. Bandu jumped one way, Criton the other, and at the same time a burst of flame shot up toward the elves' steeds. The elves pulled hard on their reins to avoid the fire, and their horses trotted obediently sideways without so much as a surprised whinny.

"Run!" Bandu screamed, as the elves drew their sickles.

Criton took a quick, frightened glance back toward the nets and then ran between the horses, breathing flames in all directions. The fairies clearly did not know what to make of his dragon magic. They shielded their faces with their arms as Criton passed them, and cried out when their sleeves caught fire.

"Burn them!" Narky shouted. "Burn the bastards!"

The elves beat helplessly at their clothes, their cries growing ever shriller. Atop their horses, they were in a very poor position to extinguish the flames.

At last the captain raised her burning arms. "Die," she commanded of the flames. "Choke and suffocate. Our bodies and our air shall not nourish you. Die!"

The flames obeyed her. The other elves followed their captain's lead, and soon the smoke was billowing off their limbs and dispersing in the morning breeze. But Bandu and Criton had already disappeared into the forest.

"Hunt them down!" cried Raider Two, shaking his sickle in the air. "They cannot hide from us!"

He spurred his horse, but the captain raised her hand and the horse did not move. It just stood there, blinking.

"No," the elf captain told her raiders. "The girl is involved with the Goodweathers. They may be waiting for this opportunity. If we leave our quarry only half protected, the Goodweathers may snatch them away from us."

"Captain," purred Raider Eleven, "send me after them. They will come to me."

"No," the captain said again. "The fire-breather's mind is closed, and the girl was able to hide secrets from us – she will resist you too. Eleven Godserfs remain to us, though three are old. We will take these and ride for Castle Illweather. Immediately."

Raider Two grimaced, but he rode over to tug at the net that held the twin boy and girl. "Walk," he said.

By the light of day, the fairy world's terrain was becoming

visible. This was a hilly country, lightly wooded except to Narky's left, where the forest grew thick and deep. The trees here were unfamiliar, with leaves that looked like oversized wolf paws.

"Narky," Phaedra called softly. "Hunter, look behind us."

They did as she said, and gasped. The ruins of an enormous tower stood behind them, huge and ominous in the daylight. How, during their stumbles through the mist, had they avoided crashing into any of those waist-high stones, or tripping over the rubble?

"That's where we came from last night," said Phaedra. "That's the real Gateway."

"Quiet!" shouted Raider Two. He was a surly one, that tall elf. By now, his fair skin had turned the color of Narky's, and his hair was black as coal. Even the bells in Eleven's hair, Narky noticed, had turned from light silver to blackest iron. The fairies, it came to him, were only called that because nobody had ever seen them during the daytime.

One of the raiders grabbed a hold of his net and began to drag it along the ground. Narky had to run to keep from getting swept up.

"Some Kindly Folk you are," Narky spat up at the raider. "You're not even Fair Folk half the time. You were no match for Criton and Bandu. Eleven days is plenty of time for them to free us."

"Silence," the fairy growled. "The game does not protect you as much as you think."

"Oh, sure," Narky laughed meanly. "Threaten us all you want, up on your horses there. You couldn't even catch a pregnant girl."

"Stop," commanded the fairy captain, sliding off her horse. For a moment, Narky wasn't sure what was going on. Then she turned back toward him, and began advancing rapidly. With a single motion, she drew her sickle from her side and slashed it through a hole in the shimmering net.

His eye, his eye! The pain was so sudden and so great that

Narky was unable to fathom it. The voice that screamed so horribly must be his, he thought, as his hands shot to cover his wound. His vision blurred and then ceased entirely as his eyelids shut against the pain.

"You said you wouldn't harm us if we won!" roared Hunter. "You said we'd be safe for eleven days!"

The captain's boots crunched as she turned on her heel and went to climb back onto her horse. "My hand slipped," she said mildly, and remounted her steed while Narky's left eye bled into his hands.

37
Phaedra

Having determined that the remaining islanders possessed no magic, the fairies finally released them from their nets and let Phaedra help Narky with his slashed eye. They took Hunter's sword and armor, and Narky's spear, and threw them back toward the ruins like garbage. For once, even Hunter didn't seem to care about his gear: all he and Phaedra cared about right now was Narky.

There was little to be done at this point, besides keeping pressure on the wound and hoping it wouldn't get infected. For the sake of having done *something,* they tore off one of Narky's sleeves and wrapped it around his head.

"Will we have to burn it?" Narky asked, babbling a little in his fear. "We have to, don't we? If we wait, it'll be just like with Bandu's wolf… oh Gods, can't I ever leave what I've done behind?"

"I don't know if we have to," Phaedra told him. "I remember the Atellan friars said to keep wounds clean, but did they say we had to burn every wound? And anyway, I don't have anything to burn it with."

"We do," said Raider Two. He was blacker than night now, blacker than any skin ought to be. His eyes and teeth stood out like pearls among coals. He snapped his fingers, and a poker materialized out of the air. Its end was glowing red.

Narky held Phaedra's hand tightly. "I don't want to die here," he said.

"I don't want to do the wrong thing," she answered. "I don't even know if this is necessary."

"Do it," he commanded her, though he looked terrified. "If I get infected here... do it."

She nodded, and took the poker from the grinning elf. Narky lay down, and Hunter held his arms out of the way. They were both trembling. Phaedra carefully framed Narky's eye with one hand, and touched the poker to the wound.

Narky did not scream long. By the time she was done, he had long fainted. She nearly fainted, herself. That sizzling, crackling sound, and the smell... she hoped she would one day forget all of this, though she knew that was not even remotely possible. She wanted to vomit. She wanted to die.

She threw the poker aside, and Hunter retied the sleeve-bandage around Narky's head.

"Can we carry him on one of your horses?" he asked.

The fairy captain shook her head. "We will drag him behind," she offered meanly.

"No," said Hunter. "I'll carry him if I have to."

He struggled for a moment to lift the unconscious Narky over his shoulder, but he was soon steady on his feet once more. Thankfully, the fairies did not force the humans back into their nets after this. Instead, they released their nets into the air, where they shimmered briefly in the sun before disappearing.

"Make no attempt to escape," the captain warned the children, "or we will catch you and skin you and roast you all for tonight's feast."

The children stood there, trembling. They were so young – none older than six, Phaedra thought. The fairies led them eastward, toward the horrible glare of the rising sun. Phaedra tried to reassure the children as they marched through woods and fen and shallow streams, but the children did not talk to her. They were all continental, and they feared the islanders' black skin. Perhaps now that the fairies had darkened, they thought the islanders were related to them.

The fairies' skin surprised her. She could hardly believe that these beings had been given a name that only fit them for a few hours each day. It felt silly to even think of them as fairies at this point. She would have to devise a more appropriate name for them. Changelings, perhaps.

After nearly half an hour, Narky woke up and asked for water. Hunter was relieved to set him down – it was a marvel that he had managed to carry Narky this far. The elves threw Narky a waterskin, which he promptly failed to catch. He sighed and picked it up off the ground.

If the children had been wary of Phaedra, they were terrified of Narky. The one-eyed black man loomed like a monster in their eyes, and they all did their best to avoid walking beside him. Narky didn't seem to mind. He slogged after the fairies without a word, head bowed, and did not even look at the children.

Phaedra wondered at his secrets. In answering the elf captain's riddle, he had admitted that justice would mean his death. Why would it? Was it for the same crime that he had committed against Ravennis, the one that had nearly killed him already? Or was Narky's past so sinister that his repentance to Ravennis would not suffice?

It worried her. She was starting to like Narky. Yes, he could be rude in conversation, but at least his eyes never glazed over when Phaedra spoke. What if he was secretly a rapist, or a murderer? She had always thought of him as a private person, but now she had to admit that he was altogether secretive. The boy never spoke of his life before the boat. He had never told them what sin had sent Ravennis' messengers after him, and he had called Psander a blackmailer. With what was she blackmailing him?

She couldn't ask him. There was so much she couldn't

ask. Her mind was bursting with questions – for Narky, for Bandu, for the fairies – but she couldn't ask any of them. Narky was silent and brooding, and Bandu and Criton had vanished into the forest. Phaedra was too afraid to ask the fairies anything, after what they had done to Narky.

After a second hour of walking, the children began to stumble and lag behind. They were just too small; their little legs had to move twice as quickly as the islanders' in order to keep up. The fairies grinned down at them maliciously, as if relishing the punishment they were about to inflict. Some of the children began to cry. In response, Hunter picked up a sobbing little boy and sat him upon his shoulders. That ended the sobs for a time, but it hardly made the journey easier: soon all the children wanted rides on Hunter's back.

Luckily, the fairies did not force them to go a full third hour without rest. Phaedra couldn't have made it that far, with her uneven gait. As it was, pain radiated from her hips up through her back and all the way to her neck. She was surprised she hadn't collapsed yet. But now, after maybe a half hour of Hunter switching between different children on his shoulders, they were all allowed to sit and rest their legs over a meal of water and an unfamiliar green fruit. The fruit had a thick spongy peel, and the inside came apart in large sections. The fruits were barely sweeter than lemons, and at first the children refused to eat them. They relented when they saw Raider Two reach for his sickle.

Since encountering Hunter's generosity, the children were beginning to look at Phaedra differently as well. She was no longer suspect in their eyes, but a potential friend and benefactor. But they still avoided Narky, who only scowled when he saw them.

"How far is it?" one of the girls asked their captors.

"Ten thousand steps," said the elf captain.

"Twelve thousand shuffles," said the one called Raider Four.

"At our pace," said the angelic Raider Eleven, "only 'til noon."

Phaedra thought Raider Eleven must be even more beautiful in the daytime than she had been at night. Her flawless black skin contrasted strikingly with her silver clothes, and gave her an appearance that was more divine than human. She looked like a cruel goddess.

The green fruit could hardly be called filling, but soon the travelers were once more on the move. At first their pace nearly matched the one with which they had set out, but soon the many little legs began to give in, and the children started looking even at Phaedra's shoulders as potential resting places. Phaedra was forced to refuse their pleas: her ankle bothered her already, and her limp was having an impact on her hips and back as well. She wished the islanders' horses had passed through the Gateway with them.

Her heart sank when she realized how much had been left behind with the horses. The tents, their blankets, their food. Flints and torches. Even if the fairies let them go, how would they ever survive in the wilderness?

The sun was high in the sky when the captain let them rest once more, in a shady grove between hills. "Rest and prepare yourselves," she said. "We shall arrive within the hour, and then the real games will begin."

Hunter lowered a girl called Delika from his shoulders, and they all sat down heavily on the moss. Delika was the most gregarious of the girls – it was she who had asked the fairies how much further they had to go. The children's personalities were starting to emerge through their masks of fear, so that Phaedra was beginning to get to know them. The other girls were Tella, whose twin was Tellos, Adla, Temena and Caldra. Tella was a shy one, too shy even to ask Hunter for a ride. She gazed up at him with awe and envy as the others took their turns, but still she said nothing. She and her brother were olive-skinned like the Atunaeans or the Parakese, and her hair was straight and long.

Temena and Adla turned out to be sisters, though it was hard to tell which was the elder. They couldn't have been more than a year apart. They were the shortest of the girls, and the skinniest. Phaedra doubted they had ever been well fed.

Caldra's name and yellow hair identified her as belonging to a mountain village. She was slender and graceful, and her voice was high and light. Before today, Phaedra would have said she was like a little fairy.

Then there were the three boys: Tellos, Rakon, and Breaker. Tellos spoke a good deal more than his sister, enough for Phaedra to detect an Atunaean accent. He was somewhat ill mannered, always pulling at Hunter's shirt and demanding to be next, but he had such an adorable little face that Phaedra found him charming anyway. Rakon was the youngest of the children, and the one who needed rides most frequently. He had very dark hair for such light colored skin, which to Phaedra's mind made him look sickly. Breaker was a fisherman's son who seemed used to spending time without his parents. He was a sweet, quiet boy, which was practically a miracle considering his name. Phaedra wondered what his parents could have been thinking, giving a boy a name like that.

Phaedra spent their brief respite getting to know the children, telling them stories about the islands and their relations to the continental cities, and hoping that they would get over their fear of black skin. Hunter's rides had been priceless in that regard, opening them up to the possibility of trust and friendship. Talking to them gave Phaedra something to do besides worry.

After a few short minutes of rest, the fairies pushed them onward. They crested the hill, and then another, and finally found themselves looking down upon Castle Illweather.

The castle was like no structure Phaedra had ever seen. The stones, if there even were any, were so covered in moss, ivy and tangled vines that not a spot of gray was visible anywhere. The castle seemed to have been built – or, rather, grown – in a pentagonal shape. Where the corner towers should have stood, there were instead five massive trees. Even the lowest branches of these towered above the ground, many of them integrating into its walls and roof. Above the castle hung a single, angry stormcloud that twisted and swirled, but never swept on. Ill weather indeed.

The elves drove them toward the gate – or toward the place where a gate ought to have been. There was no true gate here, only a portcullis of writhing vines. The sight reminded Phaedra of Bandu's caper bushes.

They reached the vines, and the elf captain called for them to halt. When she spoke, it was to the castle itself. "The captain of the Illweather Raiders requests entrance," she said.

The living gatehouse creaked and groaned horribly, to which the fairies listened with patience.

"We bring with us eleven godserfs," said the captain. "Three are old."

Again, the gatehouse creaked and rustled in disapproval.

"That decision is neither yours nor ours to make," the captain said, apparently in response to the rustling. "We will let the prince decide."

The gatehouse accepted her words with a reluctant groan, and the vines whipped apart from each other with a great cracking sound. Phaedra shuddered. The gaping passage that lay ahead felt ominously alive. It was not just letting them in, she thought, as they advanced down the passage: it was swallowing them whole.

Inside, the halls of Castle Illweather were dank and smelled of fungus. A blanket of mushrooms on the floor looked very much like blueglows, except that these mushrooms emitted a pale green light and did not *seem* to be growing out of corpses. As the fairies led them through the castle, Phaedra noticed their skin reacting to the darkness by turning a luminescent white again. Interesting.

Deeper and deeper into the castle they went, twisting this way and that between walls of knotted roots and clinging fungus. They did not come across any more elves, but Phaedra sensed them nonetheless, waiting in hungry anticipation, just out of sight. Or perhaps it was the walls that waited.

Hadn't one of the Elkinaran sages claimed that the first world fell apart because of an excess of love and goodness? Too much love and goodness. The thought almost made Phaedra laugh.

What would the fairy prince choose to do with her and the others? Would he have them enslaved? Executed? To what degree were the fairies bound by the rules of Bandu's riddle game? It was supposed to protect the Godserfs for eleven days, but the fairy captain had taken Narky's eye anyway. Obviously the elves could still harm them. What *couldn't* they do? Could they just not kill the humans? What if Narky died of an infection?

Surely, Bandu wouldn't have suggested the riddle game unless it had *some* kind of power over the fairies. Perhaps they would learn more when they came before the prince.

But they never did come before the prince. Instead, the elves brought them to a large windowless room, its only entrance guarded by a gigantic, wicked-looking thorn bush. The bush parted down the middle when they approached, flattening its spiky branches to the sides of the entryway to let them enter. As soon as all the humans were inside, the branches sprang back to block the passage.

"Rest now, sweet little ones," said the captain. "We will return as soon as our prince has spoken."

With the thud-thud of hooves slowly fading away, Phaedra turned back to the cluster of frightened children. Sweet little ones... those words made her shudder. She couldn't help but feel that the fairies meant them literally.

38
Hunter

They sat for an hour or more, awaiting their captors' return. Phaedra tried to teach the children a game to keep them occupied, but she explained it poorly and they became restless and frightened again. Hunter lay on his back with his eyes closed, listening to Phaedra's winding explanations and wishing his whole body didn't ache so. Offering to carry little Rakon had seemed like such a good idea at first, but what had Hunter known? Once he had offered a ride to one…

He hoped his back would recover soon, but somehow he doubted it. He suspected that it would ache for at least the next day or two, and quite possibly longer. It was a frightening thought. The fairies would never willingly let them go, so if they wanted to survive, they would have to break out somehow. How would Hunter run or fight if his whole body was stiff?

He wished he still had his sword, though he doubted he would have been able to fight their way to freedom. The elves bore their weapons confidently, and those elvish sickles did not strike him as ornamental. The sharply curved blades extended from shafts almost three feet long, making them well designed for one-handed use when mounted in battle or two-handed use on foot. They were practical and deadly. Hunter might know nothing about elves, but weaponry was another matter.

He didn't really expect to break free. He longed for his sword because sharpening it had always calmed his nerves. Without it, all he could do was lie there and try not to go mad with fear.

He opened his eyes and took a good look around. This room was damp and alive, its floor covered in a bed of moss and mushrooms. There was a gurgling pool of water at the far end, fed by some subterranean spring. The walls were made of dirt and roots – roots so thick and tough that Hunter doubted he could have cut his way out even if the elves had left him an ax. With a sudden thought, he rose to his feet again, walked over and thrust his arm into the pool of water. No, it was no good. The deeper parts were not nearly wide enough for a body to slip through. Even that most dangerous of escape plans was impossible.

The thorn bush rustled and parted and all eleven raiders entered, sickles in hand. Hunter jumped up with a jolt. He had not even heard their footsteps!

"The feasting games begin tonight," the captain announced. "They will last eleven nights, and on the twelfth, one of you shall be named Apprentice, and another, Feast."

She turned to the islanders. "You are too old for feasting, but neither shall you be servants. Our Prince has decreed that on the twelfth night, when your victory in the riddle game is but a memory, you are to play the game of wounds for the feasting crowd whilst Illweather drinks your lifeblood. Come now, little ones."

The elves ushered the children out of the room.

"Well, great," said Narky, finally breaking his silence. "So they're going to kill us, after all. Glad Bandu made such a difference."

"Eleven days is a long time," Hunter said. There was at least *some* hope of escaping. Bandu and Criton would come to their rescue…

And then they would be caught and killed. These fairies were not like the soldiers in Anardis: they had experience with magic, and powerful magic of their own. At most, Bandu's powers were a shadow of theirs. How could he ever expect Bandu or Criton to defeat a living castle full of elves? The best thing to hope for was that the two of them would stay away from this place, and maybe even live to find a way home.

"This place is horrible," moaned Phaedra. "I wish… this place is horrible."

"It's even worse than the stories made it sound," said Narky, wincing and putting a hand over his eye covering. "They don't just use kids as slaves, they eat some of them. And I thought *Psander* was bad."

"I think," Phaedra said, "that the absence of the Gods drove them mad."

"Maybe it drove them madder," Narky replied, "but if they weren't trouble to begin with, how come the Gods abandoned them?"

Hunter thought about that. "Maybe they were too magical," he said.

Phaedra nodded. "That's certainly possible. I think their nets are made out of the sky, just the same as the mesh between the worlds. With magic powerful enough to manipulate the mesh, the Gods might have seen them as a threat."

"If They find some humans threatening," Narky said, ruefully, "the fairies must have terrified Them."

"Narky!" cried Phaedra.

He sat up. "What?" he said. "They've abandoned this world, Phaedra. They're not watching here, any more than at Silent Hall. Except here the wards are foolproof, because the Gods put them up Themselves."

Phaedra sighed. "I don't understand you," she said. "You pray to Ravennis when you need something, but when you think no God is watching, you blaspheme against the whole pantheon!"

"That's true," admitted Narky, turning contemplative. "That's not very good repentance, is it? Why did Ravennis even spare me? I'm a lost cause."

The Gods were mysterious beings, Hunter thought. That was what Father used to say. Father, whom the mysterious Gods had not spared.

"What kind of horrible games do you think they're playing with the children?" Phaedra asked.

"I don't know," said Narky. "I don't want to know."

"I wonder if Bandu won the games," Hunter said, thinking aloud.

"What?" asked Narky.

Hunter fingered his empty scabbard. "The captain said when the games are over they'll name one child their apprentice. If they teach their apprentice magic, that could be how Bandu learned."

"Could be," said Narky, shrugging noncommittally. "I'd like to know how she got away from them when she was that young."

"They might have let her go after a few years," Phaedra suggested. "It sounds like that's what happened to the sage Katinaras as a boy. The elves keep calling us old, so they must bring all the children back after a while – the ones that are still alive, I mean."

"I don't know," said Narky. "Psander said the sage was, what, ten or something when the fairies sent him home?"

Phaedra nodded. "Nine, I think. He was six when he left."

"Right," Narky went on, "but she doesn't talk anything like the fairies, does she? She talks like someone who hasn't had to say anything to anyone for a really, really long time. Ten years, maybe. I think she escaped from here on her own somehow, not too long after she got here. I don't think they brought her back on purpose."

Phaedra didn't answer. When Narky got to thinking, he was *smart*. Being here with these fast thinkers made Hunter feel like a clod. He'd felt this way around Phaedra and Narky before, but not so strongly. Maybe having Bandu around had made it easier not catching onto things too quickly. Now he felt alone in his struggle to keep up.

"Could you tell us a story?" he asked Phaedra. "Anything that's not about fairies."

Phaedra nodded. "I'll tell you more about the sage Katinaras. He didn't live on Tarphae all his life, you know. When he was still young he sailed eastward, visiting all the islands of the archipelago and collecting myths and oral histories. He went as far as the land our ancestors came from, the great continent across the ocean. When he came back and told the people what he had learned, they rejected his teachings and cried for his blood, and he had to flee Karsanye. But the king respected his knowledge and had him secretly brought back to live in the palace, writing his philosophies out of reach of the mob."

"What did he say to make them want to kill him?" Hunter asked. "I've never read any of his writings, but everyone knows he's Tarphae's most famous sage. Was he hated throughout his life?"

"Just about," Phaedra said. "After he died, the young king who had grown up in his presence undertook the project of redeeming his name. He kept Katinaras' original writings in a vault, and had only the least objectionable portions copied and distributed. The rest of his writings took generations to filter out into the world, and they're still considered radical by those who have read them. I think if my father had known what they were, he never would have collected them. But he thought, like you, that owning the full works of Tarphae's greatest sage was more prestigious than subversive."

"All right," Narky said, "now I'm curious. What's so dangerous about these writings?"

"Oh, lots of things," Phaedra answered cheerfully. "He challenged nearly everything we believe about the Gods. He argued that Karassa is not Mayar's daughter, but a former rival. He said that in the eastern islands and on the coast of the great continent, Karassa is the sole Goddess of the Sea, and that when our ancestors came to Tarphae and began dealing with the peoples of the western continent, there was a great struggle for supremacy. At that time, Atuna was not yet the great naval power it is now. As the continental cities grew in power and their influence spread into the westernmost islands, Mayar began to gain over Karassa as the God of the Sea and Karassa became a mere local Goddess. In the east, Her power is greater."

"So She's not Mayar's daughter?" Hunter asked.

"Not according to Katinaras. In fact, the sage claims that the Gods have neither parents nor children, and that all familial ties between them were invented by men in order to explain allegiances and rivalries between cities. So Mayar and Magor are not really brothers, nor are Atun and Atel. They just have aspects in common, and their worshippers are usually allies in war."

Narky whistled. "That really is radical. Is any of it true?"

Phaedra shrugged, but her eyes shone. "It's hard to know, isn't it? Do you see why all this fascinates me?"

They nodded dumbly.

"There's more," Phaedra said triumphantly, lowering her voice as if someone might be listening. "Katinaras claimed that the Gods are not male or female, They are creatures of pure magic. The sexual distinctions between God and Goddess were also invented by men. He writes that They have consented to these human notions of sex only because it makes it easier for us to pray to Them, and to believe in Them. It's worth it for the power we give Them."

"I wonder what Psander thinks of that," Hunter mused.

"Me too," said Phaedra. "One day, I'll ask her."

"Sure you will," Narky said, returning to his gloomy state. "When we reach the underworld. We're not getting out of here alive."

"Bandu and Criton are out there," Hunter reminded him. "They'll come to break us out. We just have to be ready."

"Oh, really? Ready how?"

"Well rested, for one thing," Hunter answered, lying down on his back again. "I've been carrying people all day, and not all of them were little."

That quieted Narky down. They spent the next few minutes in silence. "The fairies can read minds," Narky said at last. "Do you really think Bandu and Criton will be able to rescue us, against enemies like that?"

"I know they'll try."

Narky sighed. "You're right. They're going to get themselves killed."

"You can't know that," protested Phaedra. "They beat the fairies once."

"They ran for their lives," said Narky. "The only way we beat the fairies was at the riddle game, so unless you think that's going to come up again..."

"Well," Phaedra said, "is there any other way to get out of here?"

They turned to look at the thorn bush, almost in unison. "There's no way," said Narky. "We have no armor and no protection."

Phaedra nodded and sighed. "We have to try, though."

Hunter swallowed. "I'll go first," he said.

He stepped gingerly closer to the entryway, practically on tiptoe. When he was about four feet away, the plant started waving its thorny branches in his direction. *This isn't going to work,* he thought. Still, he pressed on. He reached out toward the branches, hoping to catch a hold and keep the thorns out of his way. The branches waved and rustled sideways, away from his outstretched hands. He edged closer. With each step, the bush further contorted itself to avoid his grasp. Maybe it would let him through! Within a step or two he would reach a place where he might be able to leap through to the other side. He carefully lifted his foot, inched it forward...

With a snap, the branches closed in on him from all directions, ready to tear the flesh from his bones. Hunter threw his whole body backward, covering his head with his arms. The thorns tore at his arms, legs, back and sides, ripping holes in his clothes and clawing at his flesh. Then he was out of their reach, lying on the ground and bleeding from a thousand scratches.

"Oh, Gods!" cried Phaedra, hobbling over to him. "I'm sorry, Hunter, oh I'm so sorry! We should have known!"

"We did know," Hunter reminded her. "But I had to try anyway. It was worth the risk."

"If you say so," said Narky. "Better you than me. Good thing you covered your face."

"Right," said Hunter. "Phaedra, stop. There's nothing you can do for me. I was already hurting all over anyway."

Phaedra shook her head, tears in her eyes. "You're so brave. I shouldn't have made you go."

"You didn't," Hunter told her. "I volunteered. It wasn't a bad idea to try."

Narky snorted. "It was a terrible idea."

They did not try again.

The elves came back a few hours later, bringing eight tired and battered children with them. Miserable as the children looked, Hunter was glad at least to see that they had all returned, and with every limb intact. As far as he was concerned, that had hardly been a foregone conclusion.

"Sleep now," Raider Eleven recommended. "We will rouse you early tomorrow morning for your first full day of the games. Tonight was only a taste."

The children did not even complain. Instead, they simply lay down on the moss and closed their eyes. The raiders left again.

"No dinner?" asked Narky. Their stomachs had been grumbling for at least an hour now.

"No dinner," repeated Hunter. "You don't think those green mushrooms are edible, do you?"

"I'm almost willing to try," said Phaedra. "If they're not growing out of corpses, that's good enough for me."

"Maybe we should wait 'til tomorrow and ask the elves," Hunter suggested.

"Maybe," said Phaedra, looking hungrily at the floor. "No, you're right."

But the fairies woke them so early the next morning that nobody had the wherewithal to ask. By the time Hunter even noticed his empty stomach, the elves had already marched off in two lines with the children huddled between them.

Phaedra splashed her face with water from the pool, then drank some. "Oh Gods," she said. "It's awful here."

Narky's stomach growled so loudly Hunter could hear it. "That's it," he said. "I don't care if they're poisoned, I'm having mushrooms for breakfast. At least I won't die with an empty stomach."

With that, Narky picked a small green mushroom off the ground by the pool and ate it. Hunter and Phaedra watched as he chewed the mushroom, swallowed it, stood for a moment in careful consideration, and then reached for another. So far, he seemed completely unharmed. And he was eating.

With their stomachs feeling the way they did, there was no more room for caution. Soon all three of them were plucking mushrooms from the ground by the handful and unceremoniously stuffing themselves with glowing fungi. Within minutes they were lying on the ground, clutching their abdomens and wondering if they'd been poisoned after all.

"Why are they so filling?" asked Narky miserably. "I feel like I just ate half a cow."

"I know what you mean," said Hunter. He thought his stomach might burst. How many mushrooms had he actually eaten, though? Ten? Twelve?

Phaedra rolled over with a groan. "It's the magic," she

said. "It feels like the mushrooms are expanding in my stomach. Ugh. This whole world is unbearably magical."

"Unbearably magical," Narky repeated, his words interrupted by a sudden loud belch. "You've got that right."

"We shouldn't have more than a couple each for lunch," Hunter said.

"Don't even talk about lunch," Phaedra advised. "I think I might skip dinner."

They almost did skip dinner. The children returned just when Hunter was starting to consider eating again, and their arrival put off all thought of edible mushrooms. As soon as the fairies left them alone, Delika suddenly turned and shoved Tellos to the ground.

"I should have won today!" she shouted, jumping on top of him and beating at him with her little fists. She was crying. "You killed me, you killed me!"

Hunter quickly pulled her off the boy, but he could see that the damage was done. The children were enemies now; the fairies had seen to that.

"Stop, Delika," he said, holding both her wrists in one hand while warding the boy's sister off with the other. "Stop, all of you!"

Phaedra had reached them by now, and helped him by pulling the twins away toward the other side of the room. The others looked sullenly from one side to the other, wary of every little rival.

"What do you think you're doing?" Phaedra said. "We're all humans! Who cares what twisted games those monsters are putting you through? We have to stick together, don't you see that?"

"They'll eat the weak one!" Delika shrieked. "You're the weak one! You're the weak one!"

"That's it!" Narky shouted, standing up. The startled children went silent immediately. They hadn't heard Narky speak since he had lost his eye.

"If I see you fighting again," he said, gazing down at the

little ones with his one good eye, "I'll strangle you all and let the fairies decide which one's a dead servant and which one's a meal."

The children's eyes widened fearfully. They believed him.

"There's a chance," Hunter said, trying to de-escalate, "that we'll all make it out of here alive. But we have to be ready. We can't fight with each other. If our friends come to get us, we'll have to be healthy, and strong, and ready to run in whatever direction they tell us to run. You need to help each other whenever you can, so that we'll all be strong. Do you think you can do that?"

They all nodded, still looking at Narky. "We won't fight," Tella said meekly.

"Good," said Phaedra. "Now, did they feed you out there? Are you hungry?"

The children nodded again, more vigorously this time. "They gave us some," Breaker said, "but they only had four plates."

So the elves were making the children fight over scraps of food, without ever telling them that parts of their prison were edible. If only Hunter still had his sword…

"I might have thought something like that," said Phaedra. "It's all right, though, you can eat here. These mushrooms are very filling, so you may each have one."

They ate gratefully, and there were no more fights. Later, Hunter even saw Delika patting Tellos on the arm, though he never heard her apologize. Between the hope of escape and fear of the one-eyed Narky, the children made no more trouble. They passed the next evening in peace, and then the next. Hunter was relieved not to have to break up any more fights, but the passage of time worried him. It was hard to be completely sure how much time was passing, but he counted a new day each time the fairies brought the children back from the games. Four such days passed, and five, and six, and Bandu and Criton still made no appearance. Had they been captured? Hunter could not believe that they would have abandoned him and the others. It was not like them. Where could they be?

On the eighth day, he really started to worry. On the ninth and tenth he was sick with fear. On the eleventh day, the islanders fasted and prayed to every God they could think of, even though they knew that no God was listening.

39
BANDU

She was not glad to have her memories back. She had held them mostly at bay throughout their escape, but in the forest the horrors of her childhood sprang upon her all at once, clawing for her attention. It made her wish she had never opened the box.

She had been alone and starving when the fairies captured her and brought her to their castle. She had fought for her food harder than the other children had fought for their lives; in the end only she had emerged with both. They had made all the children attend the first feast, but after that, they had been allowed to stay away until their own times came – all except for her. As the winner she had been forced to go to every feast, to serve the queen her wine and amuse her with forced smiles and graceless dancing. The elves took a particular delight in the weaknesses of human children. It assured them that the Gods had made a mistake.

The cruel memories flooded Bandu's mind, vision after vision and sound after horrifying sound. This time as before, Goodweather was her anchor. She thought of the great den that had whispered to her in the dark, and her strength returned. It was Goodweather who had told her of the Gods' abandonment, Goodweather who had taught her how to speak to the world and how to listen. And it was Goodweather who had opened the gate for her, and told her when to run.

Bandu opened her eyes.

"Bandu!" Criton cried. "Are you all right? What happened?"

She shook her head. "I am here now. They are gone?"

"I think so. Should I climb a tree and check?"

She nodded, and soon heard what she already believed: the fairies had gone. They had taken the children and the other islanders and marched them off to Illweather. Criton wanted to follow them, but Bandu stopped him. They had eleven days before the fairies could slaughter their friends. It was time they might need to learn how to open the gate.

Criton was studying Bandu's face as they walked back toward the ruins of Gateway. "What happened when you were here before? When you were a girl?"

Bandu did not answer for a time. Where could she even begin? "My father takes me to trees," she said, "and he leaves me there. I tell you before. The Kind Folk catch me then, when I am alone. They take us to Goodweather, and make us do... I don't know how to say. I live, but they make me work and they say I am wicked. Only Goodweather is kind to me. Goodweather opens gate and says run, so I run. After I go through the gate, I hear the wind's voice for the first time. It is kind too, and it tells me how to get home. It brings me to the sea, it tells me which water leaf to hide in. But I don't go back to father. I go to trees and live there."

They arrived at the ruins, where they found Hunter's sword and armor lying on the ground, not far from Narky's spear. "Who *is* Goodweather?" Criton asked. "Why do you want to name the – our... *child* that?"

Bandu sat down on a stone and put her feet up on another. "I'm tired," she said. "Goodweather is not a man, he is a big den where Kind Folk live. Very big, and old."

"A den? Do you mean like Hession's cavern?"

She shook her head. "Like Silent Hall. But bigger, very bigger, and old and alive. I don't know how to say. But he talks to me, and teaches me, and tells me when to run. So now I live, and I want to name the young Goodweather."

Criton sighed. "I guess we can talk about that later," he said. "But if we're staying here instead of following them, what exactly do you think we should do?"

She was about to answer, but he stopped her before she could. "No," he said. "I know you want us to find a way to open the Gateway again. But how? Where do we start?"

"I don't know," she confessed. "I stay here and try things. You look inside. Maybe animal skins help, if you can find and read."

"Oh," said Criton. "All right. Good thinking."

He wandered off to pick through the ruins while Bandu scratched her head and tried to decide how to begin. She had never witnessed the sky in between the worlds being opened – Goodweather had done it for her somehow, but she had not seen it, and the fairies had been on this side while she was on the other. All she knew was that the fairies' nets dissolved when the gate closed, and she thought that must be because the nets and the gate were the same thing. If she could only pull a net or two from the air, the gate would open.

She reached out her hand and tried to feel for a break in the sky-mesh, a place to slip in a finger and pull. There was nothing. She closed her eyes and tried again, but she already knew it was useless. If it were that easy, the elves would do it more often. They loved the taste of children.

The elves liked to speak in poetry before they did anything big. Would Bandu have to do the same? She didn't think she could. It was hard enough for her to speak *without* rhyme or rhythm. She did not have that word-music in her. What could she do then, besides keep trying and hope that Criton would find a way to help her?

Goodweather. Somehow, she would have to ask

Goodweather. Was there a way to do that without the elves catching her?

Maybe she could ask another tree to take a message – an old tree, with roots deep enough to touch the roots of the world. It was worth trying.

Back out to the woods she went, leaving Criton where he was, consumed with his search. The plants around Gateway were all too young, but the deeper into the woods she went, the older the trees became. She wondered if any of them remembered her, from when she had been here as a girl.

"Do you remember," she asked the tree beside her, "when a little girl runs here before, all alone?"

The tree, a big solid elfinoak, said nothing at first. Bandu did not give up. "Many seasons ago," she told it.

Finally, the tree made a low groan and roused itself. *A little girl?* it asked. *Like you?*

"Yes, me," she said, "but smaller. This small." She lowered her hand, guessing at her size then.

Hmm, said the elfinoak, *I have seen many like that, I think.*

"This one is alone," she said.

A lonely girl, the tree pondered. *Other than you? I can't remember.*

"Goodweather asks you to help her."

My children will protect you, the castle had said. And indeed, when she thought of it, she could remember the trees coming to her aid as she ran. There were animals in this forest, animals that had wanted to eat her. There had been a big blue cat with teeth longer than Bandu's little arms, and it had made no sound at all until a dead branch had knocked it to the ground in mid-pounce. Remembering it now, Bandu put her back against the tree and looked around nervously. Maybe she should have brought Criton with her.

The oak rustled its leaves thoughtfully. *Goodweather, you say? I know that name. But from where? A relative, maybe?*

Oh, thought Bandu. This tree had no memory. It might

be better to ask a younger plant, but would a younger one be able to deliver her message?

"Do you touch the roots of the world?" Bandu asked. It was a phrase she had heard the fairies use, and she did not think they were only being poetic.

The roots of the world? Yes, I believe I do.

"Then Goodweather can hear what you say to him," she said hopefully. "Can you say his friend is here, the girl who runs away? Say I need help with open the gate again."

I can say those things, the tree assured her, but she repeated her message anyway.

She went back to Gateway feeling a little better. If anyone could help, it would be Goodweather. She hoped the message reached him.

40
Criton

Criton picked through the ruins looking for something, anything, that could be useful. It was hard to know where to look – Gateway did not really resemble a tower anymore. Without its foundations, it must have collapsed immediately upon entering this world. The fallen stones were already overgrown in places, covered in lichen and ivy and dead leaves. Once, he saw a scrap of parchment peeking out from under a rock, but upon struggling to retrieve it, found that it was only a shred of scroll containing a few scribbled words.

"...of the syllables suggests fairy influence..." said the longest string of words, and below that, "to request his opinion." At the bottom of the scrap was the single, half cut-off word, "ight." Criton threw the parchment back on the ground and kept looking.

Goodweather. She wanted to name their child Goodweather. And why shouldn't she? Criton hadn't even wanted the baby. What right did he have to argue with her about names?

Still, Goodweather? What sort of a name was that? His baby, a Dragon Touched baby, should have a dragon's name. Hession, maybe.

Wait, what was this? Some pieces of splintered wood,

rotting among the rubble – the remains of a bookshelf! Criton knelt on the ground, picking at the scraps. Yes, there were books underneath, leather-bound codices that flaked when he touched them. He carefully lifted one of the covers…

An enormous centipede scuttled out of the book and onto his hand. Criton yelped and shook his arm, and the book tore through the middle, its contents falling to the ground in a pile of dust, mold and insects. The centipede had disappeared. Criton swore and stood up, frantically brushing his hands across his skin and trying to reach his back to make sure that the bug hadn't gotten back there somehow. His hands found nothing, but his whole body tingled as if completely covered in tiny legs. Had he flung it off without seeing it fall?

He shuddered, wondering if he dared try another book. He stuck out his foot gingerly, poking at the other covers with his toe. They must all be bug-infested, he thought. Time and the elements had caused the pages to disintegrate.

Still, it must be possible to salvage some of the writing. The area he was standing in now seemed to contain part of a library; surely *some* of these books must be intact. He knelt again, and began to dig. Most of the stone blocks around here were far too heavy to lift, but by clearing the dirt away from underneath them, he could try to recover anything that had been trapped when the tower fell.

After some twenty minutes of digging, his efforts finally bore fruit. With a final tug, he pulled a sealed copper scroll tube from where it had been wedged underneath a gigantic building stone. The case was green with rust and terribly bent, but he managed to tug the end off and retrieve the scroll, proud to have found anything of value among the ruins. He had begun to wonder if Psander had somehow gathered every single useful book that remained in existence. This find gave him hope.

Elven Numerology, read the scroll's top line. "Bandu!"

Criton shouted. "I found something that might be useful!" He sat down on yet another mossy block and began to read.

"In studying the numbers most significant to the fair folk," he read, "no number matches the number eleven in frequency. The number appears everywhere: in the years between elven raids, in the syllabation of elvish poetry, even potentially in the number of children kidnapped in each raid.

"While child disappearances have been attributed to elves all throughout history, the only sightings ever confirmed by multiple reliable witnesses were recorded in 7382, in the waning years of the War of the Heavens; in 7503; and most recently in 7569. The intervals between these confirmed raids, as Zaradon points out, are all multiples of eleven. It is possible, of course, that raids have been much more frequent than recorded. Zaradon has posited that fairy raids may occur as often as every eleven years, although he has so far been unable to produce solid evidence to that effect."

Criton rubbed his eyes. Whoever had written this scroll had tiny, cramped handwriting that forced him to strain his eyes to decipher every word. There were even smaller notes scribbled in the margins, and combined with the obtuseness of the sentences, it made for very slow going. He wished Phaedra were here. She would have pored over this scroll and picked out all the useful parts. Without her, he had no choice but to soldier on.

"Besides the question of raids," he read, "the number eleven also appears in poetry attributed to the Kindly Folk, generally in the syllabation of each line. However, the authenticity of all such fairy poetry has been called into question of late. Mage Saphon has suggested that what was once credulously termed fairy poetry is an invention of bards and minstrels, an opinion that has gained some standing in recent years."

Criton's mind was going numb. He yawned and skipped ahead.

"While the number eleven is by far the most prominent, three and its multiples also appear to be relevant numbers to the Fair Folk, much as they are to humans. It is a strange fact that although accounts of fairy kidnappings – including those not confirmed by reliable witnesses – contain significant variation, the rare tales of a child's return always follow the same pattern: a child formerly thought kidnapped by elves returns to his bed precisely three years later with no recollection of the time spent away from his family. Although only four unique variations on this tale have been recorded, the cases bear such a striking similarity to each other that the three-year timeline of return cannot readily be dismissed."

Enough – Criton could read no more. He was getting a headache. He stood up, scroll in hand, and went to find Bandu.

Bandu was standing at the edge of the rubble, repeatedly thrusting her arm into the air, curling her fingers around nothing, and yanking her hand back to herself as if burned.

"What are you doing?" Criton asked her.

She sighed and sat down. "I try to take sky net from the air," she said, frustration in her voice. "No good."

"I found a scroll," Criton said, showing it to her. "It's awful to read, though. It's all about numerology."

Bandu looked at him blankly. "What is nume, nume, what?"

"It's about numbers," he explained, "but I don't think it's said anything useful yet. I guess I'll have to read to the end to make sure I don't miss anything important before I go looking for more. The thing is, I don't think I even want to find any more scrolls at this point. This stuff is so hard to read, Bandu!"

She reached for his hand and squeezed it reassuringly. "You can read," she said. "You are strong and good."

He squeezed her hand too, and sat down next to her. "How do you feel?" he asked.

"Hungry."

Criton nodded. He was hungry too, now that he thought of it.

"This gate is not the same," Bandu said.

"How has it changed?"

She shook her head. "Not changed. It's a not-same gate. The gate I come through before is another place."

"So they have different gates? If this one won't open for us, should we try another one?"

"No," Bandu answered. "How do we find other one? If we are lost, our friends do not live."

Criton nodded, and they sat a moment in hungry silence. Not all the hunger in his belly was really his, Criton realized with a start. The feeling was radiating so strongly from Bandu that he could feel it in his own stomach. It tasted of her.

"I'd better find you something to eat," he said, standing up.

Bandu nodded. "I find Hunter's things," she said, pointing. Sure enough, Hunter's sword, dagger, armor and shield were gathered in a small pile alongside Narky's spear. "I move them here, so we don't forget."

"Oh, good."

"The reading helps?" she asked.

Criton sighed. "Maybe," he said. "As I said, it's all about numbers. It talks about some discussions between wizards about the timing of the fairies' raids and that sort of thing. One of them thought that the fairies kidnap children every eleven years. The author didn't agree with him, I think, but if the elves kidnapped you when you were the same age as those kids, and they're back again now, the eleven year thing might be right. I don't see how knowing that really helps us, though."

Bandu thought about it. "Read more," she said at last. "But first bring food."

He stood to go, but for a moment, Bandu held his wrist.

"Be careful," she said. "Animals here look almost same, but they are not the same. Don't let them eat you."

Criton smiled weakly. "I'll be fine."

He wandered into the forest, more afraid than he liked to admit. Every noise sounded menacing to him; even the wind on his back made him spin around nervously. He thought he heard the sound of water up ahead – that at least was promising. He and Bandu would need fresh water, and so would the animals.

There were also fish in the stream. Criton could see them darting this way and that, and though they were mostly small, fishing did seem a good deal safer than hunting. Criton knelt down by the water, slowly dipping in his hands and waiting for a larger, unsuspecting fish to pass between them. This might take time, but at least it wasn't especially dangerous.

At least so he assumed until the fish noticed him. Within seconds, a crowd of them were swarming around his arms, biting him with their tiny teeth. One of Criton's scales was ripped off, and then another, drops of his blood running into the stream in little clouds. He stumbled back away from the water, and still the fish clung to him. God Most High, they could bite!

He breathed fire at his own arms, anything to stop those little teeth. To his relief, the fish fell off him in a small pile. There were a good ten to fifteen of them, but he still thought they would be less of a meal for him and Bandu than he had been for them.

He glanced back into the stream, where his blood had caused a frenzy. The remaining fish were ripping each other to shreds. Then a larger fish came by and swallowed them all, drifting away placidly. Criton picked up his catch and fled back to Bandu, feeling sick.

They spent several days at Gateway, and each day Bandu insisted that they should stay a little longer. Goodweather would help somehow, or perhaps Bandu would have a breakthrough and find a way to open the mesh herself. The scroll on numerology, when he finally finished reading it, did not help matters. She kept insisting that the barrier would be easier to open on the third day after their capture, then on the sixth day, then surely on the ninth, and when that passed, on the eleventh. Finally, Criton told her she had to stop trying. Ten days had passed since their triumph in the riddle game. If they didn't rescue their friends soon, it would be too late.

"You go," she said. "Maybe when you bring them here, then I know how to open."

"Bandu," he said, as patiently as he could. "I can't go by myself. I need you, and so do they. I don't know anything about this world. If I go alone, I'll be caught and killed right along with the others."

"No," said Bandu. "You are strong and smart, you can help them. I need to stay. If we go together and help them and we all run, how that helps if I don't know how to open gate?"

"I do understand what you mean," he answered, "but if I track those elves down to their hall without even a plan for what to do when I get there, I'll just get myself killed. You think I can rescue everyone on my own? How?"

She looked at him silently for a long time. "They go to Illweather," she said. "I am sure. They are so angry when they see I name young Goodweather. I never go to Illweather before, but if Illweather is like Goodweather..." She trailed off.

"Yes?"

She took a deep breath. "Goodweather tells me once, he has only one seed every many many years, eleven and hundred and thousand I think. If Illweather is like him, he does anything to save seed. You steal and say you burn it, and I think Illweather is afraid and does what you say him to do. He helps you and shows you others and keeps elves away. If he doesn't, you burn."

Criton frowned. "Illweather and Goodweather have seeds? I thought you said they were fortresses, like Silent Hall?"

"Like Silent Hall, yes," Bandu said, frustrated, "but not same. They are also trees and thorns and mushrooms and parts of sky also. Seeds are important for them."

"I'm sorry, Bandu," he said, "but I don't understand you at all. If they're fortresses, how can they also be plants and sky? Are you saying they're fortresses made out of trees and mushrooms?"

"Yes," Bandu sighed. "Is not really right, but almost. Right enough. If you take seed, then Illweather wants it back and maybe will help you."

Maybe. "And where would I find this seed?"

Bandu looked uncertain. "I think up very high. Goodweather says his seed falls when he is ready, so it has to be up."

"All right," said Criton. "That's something to go on, at least. If Illweather has only one seed, and if I can find it, and if Illweather doesn't betray me somehow. Is there something you were planning to do in case that didn't work?"

Bandu shook her head. "If that doesn't work, then I think some other thing when I am there."

"I thought so," he said, sitting beside her. "That's what I'm worried about. If I don't have you there with me, who will think of a backup plan? I'm afraid, Bandu. You know this place, and I don't."

He was finally getting through to her, but that only seemed to make her sadder.

"You need to go," she said, "and I need to stay. Or they die."

"I know," he told her. "I know. I just wish I had you with me, and I'm… afraid."

"Take Hunter's sword," she said. "I love you."

Luckily, the fairies and their prisoners were not hard to track, even after a week and a half. The group had made such deep and wide impressions in the greenery that Criton simply followed their path until he came to a hill that overlooked the castle Illweather.

Now he understood what Bandu meant about the fortress that was also plants and a piece of sky. A dark cloud hung above the castle, concealing the tops of the enormous trees that were its corner towers. Criton swore softly to himself. Bandu thought Illweather's seed would be somewhere near the top, which meant it would be hiding at the end of a limb in the middle of a stormcloud. She had said it without certainty, but he was sure she was right: Illweather needed no deception to keep its seed safe – its natural defenses would be more than sufficient.

But then… what if deception really was among the seed's defenses? The thought of climbing all the way up one of those towering trees only to discover that the prize was hidden elsewhere – Criton could hardly bear to think about it. Yet what else could he do? If the castle possessed as active a mind as Bandu seemed to think it did, he would likely get only one chance to search for the seed before Illweather began to fight against him, one way or another. Dare he risk the climb?

Perhaps he didn't need to climb. A few months ago he had flown, albeit a very short distance. Maybe he could manage it again.

He slowly bent his knees, trying to remember exactly what he had done before. He couldn't remember now – it had all been a blur at the time. He tried jumping. Nothing happened. He jumped again, imagining his body soaring upwards as he did so, but he fell right back down to earth, the same as ever. What was the trick? What had he done before that he was not doing now?

He closed his eyes and tried to remember that night. He had been angry, he thought, about something Bandu had said. He had been running away from her, and from his troubles, and he had gotten lost. No, on second thought, it was only after the flight that he had gotten lost. What was it, now? What had he done?

He remembered the feeling of jumping without falling, of letting his anger and his anxiety carry him away. Yes, he had been anxious. That must have been the night that Bandu had first brought up the question of marriage. How that had frightened him then! It was not really Bandu that had frightened him, but the thought of being like his mother – of being married to a man who would beat Criton until his whole body was a useless broken thing, just because of what he was. Criton chuckled darkly to himself. How could Bandu ever have become that man in his mind? It seemed so absurd now.

Ma's husband had made him afraid to breathe, lest a spark escape into the open. He had been afraid to explore, in case that man found him under the bed and broke his ribs again. Only his transformations had ever brought him safety in that house, by allowing him to look more human. The rest of his magic had been suppressed, hidden behind his fear and his rage. Bandu's talk of marriage had brought back the fear of the man who had beaten him, and with that fear came the magic.

Criton opened his eyes. He was still on the ground. Not for long. His mind still held the memory of his childhood, and he turned it to his purpose. Yes, he had it now! He took a third leap into the air, and this time, his body floated slowly back down to the ground. It was the thought of that man that had done it. From here, it would only take practice.

After a few more attempts Criton managed to stay aloft, floating a foot above the ground. If only Ma could see him now! He raised his eyes heavenward. It was time to find that seed, and rescue his friends.

He shot upwards through the air, climbing ever higher. The cool wind beat at his face as he neared the living castle, bringing tears to his eyes. He would be there soon, he thought, and then the wind would not sting him so. Yet as he approached, he could see the tree-towers swishing their branches angrily in his direction. The castle had spotted him.

And then, suddenly, there was a blinding light and a deafening boom. Criton swayed backwards and covered his eyes, dazed. Every hair on his body was standing on end. A warning shot, he thought. This dark stormcloud was not hanging above the castle, as he had believed at first: it was a *part* of Illweather.

He reconsidered his position. At any moment, the castle could strike him down with a bolt of lightning. If he got any closer, it certainly would. But if anything, the castle's reaction to his presence suggested that he had been right about the seed's location. How, then, would he reach it?

One fact, at least, encouraged him: the castle could not read minds. Had it read his mind, it would have known why he was there and killed him immediately. Criton looked down thoughtfully at the castle's base. If Illweather could not read minds, then perhaps it could be fooled.

He took one last look at the nimbus above, then turned and dove back down toward the main bulk of the castle. Closer and closer he came, plummeting ever onward until he was almost at the gate of vines. He changed directions then, and hurtled at the base of one of the corner trees. As soon as he reached it, he began to climb again. Would the castle be willing to strike at its own body in order to keep Criton away from his goal? There was only one way to find out.

The air grew heavy around him as he rose once more toward the cloud. His hair and skin tingled. Lightning. Criton grasped the trunk with his claws and stopped flying. As soon as he had touched the bark, the air lost its tension. From here on, it seemed, he would have to climb upwards on the strength of his own arms. It began to rain.

Criton dug his claws into the wet bark and clung there, waiting for the rain to stop, or else for his arms to weaken and for him to fall to certain death. His clothes grew heavy with water. It was foolish to hope for an end to this rain, he knew. This was no passing shower: it was raining on purpose. The castle would wash him off, and then…

He was a fool. Why had he stopped flying? Just because he had to touch the tree's bark didn't mean he had to climb up it the hard way. Criton gathered up his magic once more, and his body returned to its earlier weightlessness.

Light as a feather, he sped up the wet trunk hand over hand until he reached the lower branches. Yet just as he was passing the first signs of foliage, the tree began to writhe, curling its branches back on themselves and trying to slap him off. Criton ducked as the first massive limb struck the trunk above him with an enormous cracking sound, and he had to hurriedly scramble around the trunk to the other side when the branch swept down toward him. He could not stop there either, because more woody arms were reaching for him all the time. Criton took a quick breath and corkscrewed up the trunk as fast as he could, clambering away from each assault only just in time to face the next. Twigs scratched at his face and tangled themselves in his matted curly hair, snapping off as he climbed ever faster and ever farther, desparately trying to avoid the tree's limbs. It seemed to Criton as if each attack came closer to hitting him. The twigs and leaves lashed him even as the thicker wood of the main branches swished over his head or at his feet. Criton forgot about his friends, about the elves and the children – even about his destination. There was nothing but the climb.

The trunk and branches began to thin as he neared the top, but Criton was still unable to rest. The shorter branches up here were close enough to connect when they lashed out at him, beating him mercilessly as he climbed. Then, just like that, Criton reached the top of the tree and could go no further. He held tightly onto the treetop and swore. Had he missed the seed somehow, or was it growing on a different tower?

He was just considering climbing down again when the whole tree convulsed and tried to hurl him into the air. He clung madly to his handhold, rainwater splashing into his eyes, his nose, and his mouth as the tree attempted to cast him into the storm. A flash of light and a crash of thunder rendered him momentarily senseless. Then came another, and another, and his claws began to slip. He knew he would soon let go, and then the castle would strike him dead and throw him to the ground like a burned moth.

The top of another tree loomed out of the dark vapor, reaching out to slap him away. It missed the first time, but Castle Illweather need only try until it succeeded. It lashed out at him again, and again Criton somehow managed to avoid getting brushed off by a limb. Lightning cracked nearby once more, and the tree that had attacked him out of the clouds became suddenly, sharply visible. Near the top of this other tree, hanging off a high branch, was an enormous acorn. And here Criton was, hurtling toward it.

He had no time to think. Moments before the two trees slammed their upper branches together, he let go of his hold. He only barely had time to steer himself toward the acorn and reach out his hands before he hit the other tree with full force, crashing through the foliage toward his goal. His clawed hands grasped wildly about and by some miracle caught onto the acorn's stem. Then his new tree was snapping back the way it had come, carrying him along with it.

When the tree came to a sudden halt, the whiplash nearly lost Criton his hold again. Still, he held on. The castle finally seemed to have realized what he had done and where he was, and it paused in sudden indecision. This was all Criton needed. He reached one hand down toward his belt and drew Hunter's sword, and with all his strength, slashed at the acorn's stem. Then, his only connection to the tree broken, he fell, plummeting toward the castle roof with his prize clutched under his arm.

41
Illweather

Thief! The Ancient One cried out in anguish. Its body shook with its rage, so hard that the creatures inside it threw their arms up in terror. *Thief!* cried Illweather. *Catch it!*

The elf prince asked where the thief was, what it had stolen. Illweather hated the elves. They always had to know everything. Illweather wanted to tear them open and drink their blood, but that was forbidden.

Catch the thief, the Ancient One screamed, *or you will regret it!* Elven curiosity could not get in the way of action. If they delayed too long, the seed would be gone forever.

But wait! The thief was not fleeing as expected. It had landed on the lower body instead, and was demanding to be let in. Perhaps the elves would not be needed after all. Illweather reached out a thorny vine and caught the thief by the leg, squeezing and squeezing. It would not escape now! Its blood and decaying body would sustain the Ancient One until the next sacrifice.

A burst of heat met Illweather's senses, burning at its body's surface. What was this? The thief could breathe fire? It was threatening to burn the seed! Illweather snatched back its vine. It could not risk losing its only seed. The blood of thousands had gone into that seed, blood of elves and of their little cousins alike. No new one would grow, not for a thousand years. The seed was everything.

The thief kept making demands – let me in, release my friends – but Illweather ignored it for now. The thorns had drawn blood, blood that did not taste familiar. Was this a new kind of creature? It tasted most like a little cousin – the elves' little cousins tasted the sweetest – but its blood was colder and a little bitter, like a lizard. Perhaps it was a bigger cousin, like the ones that the elves planned to sacrifice tomorrow. Illweather preferred the little ones.

The elves were finally responding to Illweather's call. The Ancient One felt them inside, spurring their mounts through its chambers toward the gate. Where was the thief now? their captain wanted to know. *Up. Find it. Kill it.*

The thief stamped its foot and breathed its fire. It was counting to ten, and then it would burn the seed. The count had already reached seven. The elves were too slow. Illweather could not afford to wait for them. It had to stop the count.

With a painful shudder, the Ancient One opened its body to the thief. A big, inviting hole awaited the invader, and it climbed in unsuspecting. As soon as the thief was safely inside, Illweather closed itself once more, noting the relieved sigh of the creature that held its seed. The foolish thing thought that Illweather was protecting it from the elves.

The thief snuffled around in the gloom, asking about its friends. *You will never see them,* Illweather told it. *Now you are inside me, and I can kill you whenever I please. Release my seed, and I will let you live.*

Illweather could not feel the thief quaking or trembling, nor did it hear any oaths or cries or labored breathing. The thief only shifted its weight a few times and asked again for its friends.

Foolish creature, Illweather hummed, *you do not understand. I have lived since before this world, before the elves, before the youngest of the Gods. You caused me pain when you took my seed, but in time, I will grow another. You have only one life, little thief, and I can take it from you. Give me my seed, and you can go.*

Illweather moved a limb aside, just enough to let a shaft of light back into the chamber. The thief started in surprise and scuttled away from the light. It must know that the elves were on their way – it was not as foolish as it seemed.

Illweather hated to let this impertinent creature live even a moment longer, but it had little choice. Only the seed was important. Even the elves did not truly understand. They had not been there when the Gods had torn the mother-tree in two and fashioned a world out of its body. They knew the seed was important, that their whole world was built upon Illweather's roots, and the roots of its brother-tree. They knew, but did not understand. They understood only that the Gods had made *them*, and left *them*. They were foolish, selfish things. And they were too reckless to be trusted.

Illweather spoke to the elves, who were already climbing toward the place where the thief had stood. It told them that the thief had flown off in the direction of Goodweather, and they believed it. Off they went, the trusting little idiots.

The thief stood still, listening to the receding hoofbeats. *They are gone,* Illweather told it. *Leave me my seed, and no elves will catch you.*

The creature heaved a sigh of relief, but only repeated its demand to see its friends. How Illweather hated it! *The bigger cousins,* Illweather demanded from the elf prince, *sacrifice them to me now.* The thief could see its friends – once they had been slaughtered.

But the elf prince refused, making some excuse about a game. Impertinent fool! What did Illweather care about the elves and their games?

I give you the count of nine, Illweather told the thief. *For each three, I will eat one of your friends, the bigger cousins.*

The thief did not answer. It only walked toward one of the chamber's walls and blew fire at it. Show me to my friends.

Finally, Illweather realized the infuriating truth: the thief was not listening, because it did not understand. None of Illweather's threats meant anything to this creature. It could only understand elf speech and cousin speech.

What then could Illweather do? If it killed this creature or ignored its requests for too long, the seed would burn.

Very well. First, Illweather would deal with this creature's impatience. The Ancient One shifted its limbs to create a passage for the thief to wander. A twist here, a turn there – the thief could believe it was making progress. Illweather kept the passages shifting, so that this creature would not recognize its aimlessness. Good, good. It was time to devour the cousins.

The elves had ceased their games when Illweather raised the alarm, and now three of them were leading the little cousins back to their cell. Illweather could feel the tramping of all those little feet down its halls – delicious little feet. As soon as the elves left them alone, Illweather would consume them and the bigger cousins alike. Their blood would be sustenance, their flesh fertilizer. The Ancient One had only to wait. Soon, the elves would leave…

The elves did not leave. They remained in the room to gloat about catching the thief, even while the thief was still wandering about on the floor above them. Stupid, arrogant fools.

The thief stopped moving. It was standing in the portion of hall that was above the cousins' cell, listening silently. Had it heard the elves' voices? If it demanded to pass through the floor now, it would find all of its friends still alive and well, and Illweather would not be able to slay a single one without risking its seed's destruction. Illweather could not wait to find out. They all had to die, now.

The trouble was those elves again. If they had so much as a moment's warning, they could force Illweather to stop. They would have to be completely stifled, even before their cousins were. As they stood speaking to the young ones,

Illweather carefully raised a trio of vines through the cell's floor. The vines curled upwards behind the elves, slowly gaining height, and then snapped forward and caught each elf around the mouth, preventing any cry. Success!

But then, disaster! Even as the vines curled around the elves' limbs and immobilized them, one of the cousins rushed forward, snatched an elf's weapon, and beheaded it with a swift, clean blow. The head, freed from its gag, cried out "stop!" while Illweather was still bringing the ceiling down to crush the cousins. Illweather froze, powerless to resist the command. Then the elf head whistled, and Illweather's failure became complete.

At the whistle, the elf prince felt its kin's distress and stood up.

"Illweather," the prince cried. "What treachery have you done? Of old it has been your curse to serve us. Move no more today, neither vine nor leaf nor root.

"Find out what has happened," the prince then commanded its brethren. "We will see how Illweather is to be punished."

Punished? The fools! The seed would be lost, and the succulent cousins with it! The cousins might now be staring wide-mouthed at the screaming head, but already the thief was prying its way between half-descended roots to reach them! They might even escape, and the seed with them! The elves would be punished too. Oh yes, they would be punished too. Illweather hated them. It hated them all.

42
Phaedra

It all happened so quickly. One moment the elves were laughing at them, torturing them with the knowledge that their rescue had failed; a second later, the elves could speak no more. The castle's thorny vines gagged them, and then quickly wrapped themselves around the elves' limbs. Hunter did not hesitate to take advantage, diving forward and disarming Raider Two even before the elf's sneer could leave his face. Phaedra looked away as Hunter swung the blade, shutting her eyes against the world until vertigo forced her to open them again. The floor was shaking, and the elf kept screaming.

When she opened her eyes, the roof was plummeting down at them. Phaedra fell to the floor, covering her head with her hands. To her surprise, the ceiling did not crush her. Instead, with another shriek from the elf and an angry groan from above, the roots froze in place halfway to the floor. Raider Two's cries, however, continued. Phaedra followed its voice and realized to her horror that the shrieks were coming from his disembodied head.

"Curse you, Illweather!" screamed the head, even as the blood ran out through its neck. "What have you done? Godserfs! The Godserfs have escaped! Come and catch them, tear them to pieces, crack their bones and drink their blood!"

Nobody responded. The elven lieutenant glared up at Hunter. "May you be cursed for as long as you live, Hunter of House Tavener! And you, Phaedra Merchantsdaughter, may your life be brutal and short!"

Wordlessly, Narky bent over and seized what remained of Raider Two by the hair. He stood, spun around once and flung the head away with all his might.

"May you die at the hands of your friends, Kanarke Coward's Son!" Raider Two howled as he sped through the air. Then his head landed, bounced twice, and, still cursing and howling, fell with a splash into the pool of water at the far end of the room.

"One day they will learn–" the elf sputtered, his head bobbing up sideways for a moment before sinking below the surface with an infuriated gurgle.

Hunter took a step back, hesitating before attacking the other two elves. Immobilized as they were, they did not seem to pose any threat at the moment. Besides, it no longer seemed clear that fairies could be killed. If a beheaded elf could still curse and scream, then what good would stabbing them do?

"Let's get out of here," said Narky, raising his voice above the chorus of sobbing children.

Hunter nodded, took another step back, and hit his head on a tree root. He turned around, blinking without comprehension. "The roof caved in!" he exclaimed. "When did that happen?"

"The question is," said Narky, "why did it stop? Was it something the elves did? Either way, we should get out of here as soon as we can. The castle's obviously trying to kill us."

"Which way should we go?" Phaedra asked. "If any of the other elves heard him–"

"Wait," said Hunter, shushing her. "I thought I heard

something. Quiet down, everyone."

Sure enough, as soon as they stopped speaking they could hear something above them, scratching at the semi-collapsed ceiling. Hunter circled the lowest roots, sickle in hand, waiting.

"Over there!" cried Narky, pointing.

A foot was descending through a hole in the roof, long, dark-skinned and callused. Criton! Soon his waist appeared, and then his whole wonderful self came floating down through the hole as if his body weighed little more than the air around him.

"Thank God," he said. "I thought I heard you. I feel like I've been wandering around in here forever. Do you know the way out?"

"How did you get in?" Narky asked. "Where's Bandu? Isn't she with you?"

"She couldn't come," Criton said. "She's still trying to open the gate for us. And I came in through the roof, so that wouldn't do *you* any good. What happened down here?" He had finally noticed the elves.

"Illweather tried to catch them and crush us," said Narky. "It's only done half the job so far, but let's not wait for it to finish."

"Suits me," said Criton. "Out through that thornbush? Oh, and Hunter, I brought your sword."

Considering Illweather's potential for motion, the thornbush had become strangely inert. Criton and Hunter swapped weapons and began hacking a way through it, leaving little but broken stems where a formidable guardian had once stood. Phaedra beckoned the children, and they all followed Criton and Hunter out into the hallway.

"Which way from here?" asked Criton.

"I'm not sure," said Hunter. "We took a lot of turns to get here, and that was days ago."

"They take us that way for the games," Delika piped up, pointing left.

They went right.

It did not take them long to reach a fork, one that Phaedra did not recognize in the slightest. "I think we must have come in the other way," she said.

"Let's take a left here," said Narky. "If we do our best to keep going in a straight line, we should at least reach an outer wall at some point."

Hunter nodded. "The left hand hall it is."

They walked on, taking the occasional left or right turn but always heading in more or less the same direction. To Phaedra's surprise and relief, they did not come across any fairies on their way. Narky, however, did not seem relieved in the slightest.

"This is wrong," he said. "It's too easy. There should be *someone* around here."

"I don't know," said Criton. "I heard a group of them ride off while I was trying to get in here. I didn't ever see them, but it sounded like it might have been a pretty good number."

Narky did not look convinced. "Huh. Still doesn't feel right, though. Ambush, maybe?"

"Well," said Phaedra, "all we can do is be careful." As she said it, she stepped in something sickeningly soft. She looked down to find horse droppings scattered throughout the hall.

"We're getting closer to the gate!" she cried excitedly. "There are horses around here somewhere."

"And thank Ravennis for that," said Narky. "Without horses, we wouldn't get more than a mile from this place before they caught up with us. I hope there's a carriage, or a cart or something, or we'll have to leave the kids behind."

"He's joking," Phaedra told the children.

"Right," said Narky. "I'm joking. If it's a little selfishness or death, I'll take death, thank you. All I'm saying is, if it's between them being caught and *all of us* being caught, why shouldn't some of us choose survival?"

Hunter spun around and glared at Narky, looking angrier than Phaedra had ever seen him. "You're going to die, Narky," he spat. "Sooner or later, you're going to die. Wouldn't you rather die a decent person?"

His words struck Narky like a blow. Phaedra thought she saw tears welling in his eye, though they never fell. Hunter turned and stalked off down the hall.

"Don't worry," Phaedra told the little ones. "We'll all get out of here safely. Just follow Hunter."

In Illweather's dank, windless tunnels, it did not take long for them to smell the horses. They followed their noses until they came to the indoor stable, where two elven grooms stood attending to some six or seven horses. When they saw the humans in the archway, the grooms snatched up a pair of unused sickles and charged, shouting an alarm as they did so. Hunter impaled one with a smooth thrust, then let go of his sword and yanked the sickle out of the groom's hands. With a flexibility that surprised Phaedra, he then lifted his leg high, planted a foot on the groom's chest, and kicked him away.

Criton, in the meantime, only barely managed to fend off the first two blows against him before Hunter spun around with the sickle and lopped off the second groom's arm. The elf screamed until Hunter gave him a vicious crack over the head with the butt end of his new weapon, and the groom collapsed in a heap.

The other elf had by now pulled Hunter's sword halfway out of his body, but his arms were too short to finish the job. He was still pulling at the blade when Narky snatched the sickle from the severed arm on the floor and rushed forward, bludgeoning him over and over until he too lost consciousness.

"They take a lot of killing," noted Criton.

"You haven't seen the half of it," Narky told him.

Phaedra hadn't shut her eyes this time, afraid to look away. She thought she might be sick. She bent over and put her hands on her knees, staring at the floor and waiting for her nausea to subside. She almost tipped over due to her uneven legs, but somehow she kept her balance.

"What are you looking at?" asked Delika, who had come to stand beside her. The little girl gazed wonderingly at the ground, as if it held some mysterious wisdom that only big people could see.

Phaedra smiled despite the churning in her stomach. It was sweet that Delika should assume all of her actions were so purposeful.

"Nothing," she said, before suddenly realizing that she was wrong.

The moss of the floor had a deep groove in it, where a cart must frequently have rolled. She followed the groove with her eyes to the far end of the horse stalls, and saw there the edge of a chariot peeking out from behind the last live-wood stall. Excitement bubbled up inside her, banishing her nausea completely. She limped past the stalls as quickly as her lame leg would allow.

It was beautiful. The front of the chariot featured a fantastical design in gold and silver leaf, but the lovely part was its size. It could have fit a driver and three well-armed men, even with a barrel for spears or arrows in the middle.

"Look!" she cried, with sudden hope. "Delika, Adla, all of you, come here!"

The children ran to her, and Hunter looked over and said, "The prince's chariot?"

"It's perfect!" she told him.

Sure enough, all eight children could fit aboard with Phaedra, if they squeezed. Hunter and Narky fastened a pair of horses to the front while Criton tried and failed to find saddles for the other horses. There were none. In retrospect, that shouldn't have been surprising: the elven raiders had all ridden bareback.

Even without saddles, Hunter and Criton had no difficulty climbing on. These horses were unnaturally docile. It was as if the fairies had sucked the spirits from them and left only the shells behind. The horses did not buck or snort or whinny, only placidly followed where they were led. As convenient as this was, it still bothered Phaedra immensely.

Narky did not immediately climb onto his horse as the others had done. He stood beside it hesitantly, looking back at the two remaining horses that waited patiently in their stalls. Then he walked over to the stalls and swung the elvish sickle at one of the horse's legs. Phaedra gasped as the horse fell forward, its hot blood soaking into the mossy floor. But still the horse made no sound of protest, nor did the second one shy away when Narky approached it to repeat his grisly task. It was not really cruelty, Phaedra tried to tell herself as Narky swung the blade once more. These horses were more vegetable than animal.

When he was done, Narky dropped the sickle and climbed onto his mount, wiping his hands. "We can't have them following us," he said, defiantly fixing Phaedra with his one good eye.

"I know," she said. "It's just… I know."

"Let's go," said Hunter.

He gave his mount a kick and it sprang into a light trot. Phaedra shook her reins, and the chariot followed. They rode through the halls, following the trail of wheel grooves and old horse droppings toward the entrance. Soon they began to hear the elves, seemingly from all around them. Was it some unnatural echo, or were they being surrounded?

"Don't slow down," warned Hunter. "If they're ahead, we'll need to break through."

She thought she heard Narky snort at Hunter's statement of the obvious, but she said nothing. She knew what Hunter really meant: he did not believe he could prevail in another fight. He wanted to make sure they did not rely on him.

They spurred the horses on, bouncing down the hall as the soulless animals hastened their steps. Then they turned a corner, and Phaedra's pulse quickened.

The gate was ahead, closed but unprotected. From the right, a crowd of elves rushed toward them, led by their prince. He looked like a minor God, his clothes lush and dark upon skin of blazing white. A tiara of gold nested upon his silver hair, its brilliance reflecting the unnatural glow of his skin. It hurt to look at him.

"Stop!" he cried, and Phaedra's hands began to pull on the reins of their own volition. Even Hunter reined in his horse, and the humans lingered uncertainly while the elves approached.

The prince held out his hand expectantly. "You have something that belongs to us. Give it back."

He did not promise them anything in return for their compliance, only stood there with complete authority, knowing that they could not help but follow his commands.

"Give it back, Criton," Phaedra heard herself saying.

Criton held tightly to the head-sized acorn, still somehow trying to resist. Phaedra wondered at his strength. Then he raised the seed high and breathed fire upon it.

The elves cried out and charged toward them, and the prince's spell was broken.

"Go!" Criton shouted, dropping the seed and digging his heels into his horse's hide.

Phaedra shook the reins and her horses began to trot placidly forward, as if urgency was completely foreign to them. The others might make it to the gate before the elves cut them off, but at this rate, the chariot never would.

She never knew what got into her. One moment she was impotently shaking the reins, and the next, she was a madwoman, leaping half out of the chariot to scratch and bite at the horses' rears. Her nails dug into their hides as the animals finally began to canter and then to gallop.

Had it not been for the children, Phaedra would have fallen off and been crushed as the chariot rolled by. But they caught her legs and pulled her back, her stomach and chest connecting painfully with the chariot's lip. She clung there as the horses sped onward, their reins flapping loose and free.

To Phaedra's great luck, the elves were too focused on Illweather's seed to attempt to cut her off from the gate of vines. The gate was already badly damaged by Hunter's sword, but now its destruction became complete. The chariot crashed through it, snapping the strong vines like deadwood, flinging debris to all sides. Phaedra sat aching in the back, watching Illweather fall farther and farther behind. They were free.

For now.

43
Narky

They rode until the horses were covered in foam and they were sure no elves could catch up on foot, even by magic. Narky was glad for his decision to eliminate the other mounts; it had bought them this brief rest.

"A whole bunch of raiders left Illweather while I was breaking in," said Criton, reining his horse in. He wiped some white frothy sweat from its mane with the side of his claw. "I thought they might be looking for me, but then they rode off. They must still be out here somewhere; we shouldn't rest long."

Hunter nodded. "Understood."

They had no brush and no blanket with which to do a better job wiping off their horses' sweat, but Hunter took off his shirt and used it as a rag. Narky winced when he saw Phaedra admiring Hunter, less discreetly than she probably imagined. It reminded him of Ketch, somehow.

But why should it? He had thought that Eramia might love him; that was why her attachment to Ketch had hurt him so. The thought that she would prefer Ketch over him had been unbearable. But it was not that way with Phaedra. Narky had never had a chance with Phaedra. She was too pretty and well bred. He was beneath her, and he knew it.

Hunter finished his work and draped the shirt over his shoulder. "We shouldn't push them much further," he said. "We can go the rest of the way at a trot."

"Right," said Phaedra.

When Hunter turned away, she stuck out her tongue. "Oh yuck," she confided to Narky. "My mouth still tastes like horse."

He looked at her curiously. "Why?"

She seemed strangely surprised and embarrassed. "You didn't – oh." She waved him away. "Never mind."

They rode onward, following Hunter's advice of letting their horses trot even though the beasts made no conscious indication of weariness. If it hadn't been for the foam at their mouths and on their hides, Narky might have thought the flight from Illweather had been effortless for them.

Narky took the lead now, while Criton fell back to speak with Phaedra and Hunter. Words from their conversation drifted forward to him as he rode.

"…Found a scroll… ousand two hundred and ten… understand it better," said Criton's voice, followed by Phaedra's reply of, "…to see… it with Bandu? I don't… her experience… unlikely to be completely… to look at it myself."

He rode ahead a little. It sounded like the kind of conversation best left to others. There was only one question that interested him right now: had Bandu found a way to open the gate? If not, how would he and the others get out of this Godforsaken world?

In his estimation, they were now only a mile or so from the ruins. The trees were thinning, and certain clumps of them began to look familiar. If they ever made it back to their own world, Narky thought, he just might kiss the ground. Only Anardis had felt this dangerous, and at least there they had had some powerful friends. Here they had no friends, only burdensome children. Narky could hardly wait to be rid of them.

He wondered how things would change when Bandu

had her baby. Would she and Criton leave them and settle down, in some dark and lonely wood perhaps? Or maybe only Bandu would drop out of their group to raise the child on her own in the wilderness? That certainly seemed possible, knowing her. She would not want her son or daughter to grow up tame and comfortable, living any halfway civilized life.

A shout from behind pulled him out of his reverie. The fairies had spotted them! Narky could see a group of them some distance behind, galloping toward them. He gave his horse several kicks, as trot turned to canter turned to gallop. They were coming! Oh Gods, they were coming!

Hunter's words came back to him. If he fled just like this, without a thought for the others and their safety, would he really deserve to survive? What good had all his repentance done him if he was still the same old Narky Coward's Son? He looked back as he rode, and saw the way the chariot was falling behind, and the way that Hunter and Criton were honorably staying with it. Hunter had already drawn his sword. Although the fairies were still a good distance behind, they were gaining rapidly. It would probably be a fight, then.

Narky reined his horse in. If he was to die today, let him die something other than a coward. He waited until the chariot had reached him before spurring his horse once more. There were at least twenty elves chasing them, led by the same captain who had captured them eleven days ago. A fight would be useless. Narky could see Hunter in his mind's eye, turning to face them with his sword only to be decapitated and dismembered by those elven sickles. The image stuck in his head as he rode on beside the chariot. It would happen that way, he knew. There were just too many of them.

When he next looked behind him, the fairy captain was a mere horse-length away, with her companions spread out to either side, forming a vee. With a blood-chilling war-cry, the elves raised their sickles high above their heads.

The nets flew.

44
Bandu

She sat among the stones and cried, fearing for Criton. How could she expect him to succeed without her help? Even if he could find Illweather's seed, he would not be able to talk with the castle. How could he use the seed to save the others without being able to hear what Illweather was saying? She wished she could be there with him.

And if he did succeed, even without her, what then? It would not take long for Illweather to tell the elves that its seed was missing. The elves would chase them, and without Bandu's help, how would they ever get away?

She shouldn't think about that right now, she told herself. Criton was strong and smart. He would find a way. The important thing was for Bandu to open the gate.

She sighed and tried to concentrate. She could almost smell the power of this place. It was growing now, on this eleventh day since their capture. But feeling the power's presence and understanding how to use it were two different things. She closed her eyes and tried to feel for the netting again. There it was, brushing against her fingertips! But as soon as she curled her fingers, it was gone.

She tried over and over to get a hold of the mesh, but it kept slipping away. Her motions were not as graceful as the elves'. Her fingers were too… too… she did not know the word. They weren't too big, but they *felt* too big.

Finally, her little finger found a wrinkle. She would do it; she would open the gateway on her own! But when she tugged, she found that she was too weak to tear the mesh away. Her arms were all right – it was something else. What the others called her 'magic' was not strong enough. She finally understood that word now. Magic was the ears with which she listened to the wind and to Four-foot. It was the voice with which she told the plants to grow. And it was the strength that was too weak to open the gateway.

But what could she do, then? Only wait. If Criton came back to her, she would show him how to feel for the mesh, and together, maybe, they could tear off a piece. She could hope, at least.

After a time, she thought she heard the sound of horses in the distance. Empty, elvish horses. Was Criton riding one of them?

Her heart sank when the elves appeared through the trees. So Criton had lost. Criton was gone. And she might never live to see her young.

Wait! These were not Illweather's elves. She recognized their leader as the one who had caught her in his net so many years ago. The captain of the Goodweathers. So Criton and the others might not be lost after all! Perhaps if Bandu lay still, the Goodweather elves would go away.

No such luck. The elves rode straight for her, fanning out as if expecting an attack. Their captain peered down at Bandu suspiciously. Then he smiled.

"Well, what have we here? Our own little one, whom we lost some ten years ago! What say you, brothers? Shall we thank our little troublemaker for showing us which gate the Illweathers have been using?"

Bandu could not speak. The terror of those days had come back to her all at once.

The elf captain laughed. "Very clever, as always, asking

the trees for help. The slow way, the quiet way. We almost didn't notice. But we don't trust the trees anymore, not since Goodweather helped you escape. We had words with the castle, child, after you left us. Our Goodweather was strangely fond of you. I don't know what the old shrub was thinking.

"You are such a *wicked* child," the captain went on. "You disappeared right at the end of the window, when we could not follow you. Eleven months and eleven days after we first rescued you from the woods of your little island, you snuck out and left us without so much as a parting word!"

"You kill the others!" screamed Bandu. Why was he taunting her again? Hadn't he done that enough, those many years ago? "You kill them and you eat them!"

"And they were delicious," the captain agreed. "But we would not have eaten you, little one. You earned your life in the games, don't you remember?"

The other elves guffawed and chattered their teeth. Bandu remembered them, though she had not seen much of the Goodweather Raiders after she won the games. They never spoke, because they had no tongues.

"I remember," said Bandu.

The captain grinned. "But all is well now, because you have come back to us. And you might even provide us with a tasty little morsel, if we wait patiently."

Bandu gasped, and the Goodweather captain laughed again. "What brings you back to us, little one?"

She felt him prying into her mind, dragging at her secrets… she felt him, and she put a wall in his way. The elf's eyes widened, and Bandu stared him down. She was growing stronger with practice.

"My mate brings me Illweather's seed," she said. "If he comes, you take the seed and let us go."

"If he comes," said the captain, his mouth tightening, "we will butcher him before your eyes. Then we will take you back to Goodweather, so that the castle can drink your blood and suffer."

She had thought he would say something like that. "Maybe Illweather elves come with him."

The raiders chattered their teeth again. "After him, you mean?" smirked the captain. "I'm sure they will, if he stole their castle's seed. When they do, we will be ready for them. We will catch them and cut them to pieces, and leave your unfortunate lover 'til the end. Or are there others? Has he gone to rescue Illweather's prey? He has, hasn't he? If the children come with him, they will make a most triumphant prize. To feast on Illweather's quarry! Oh, that would be too sweet!"

The raiders clacked their teeth once more, and did not stop this time. They knew how the sound frightened her, and they relished her fear. Louder and louder they became, until Bandu could tolerate it no more.

"Stop!" she screamed, and the horses stamped and snorted with her distress. A tree root broke out of the ground at her call and tangled itself around the leg of the captain's horse. With a mighty crack, horse and rider fell to the ground.

The elf tumbled off his horse and rose gracefully to his feet, still carrying his sickle. With a smooth motion, he snatched a sky-net out of the air and threw it over Bandu. She made to dodge, but he was too fast for her.

"You have grown," the captain spat. "Godserfs like you should never grow."

"Come close," said Bandu, reaching for where Hunter's knife lay on the ground beside her. "You should be like others, without tongue."

The captain turned to his horse, and finding its leg broken, cut its head off. "Take up your nets," he commanded his raiders, "and leave your horses here. We're going to set a trap for our little one's mate."

They left her there, sitting and waiting for the sun to set. She could see their limbs changing as they walked away, springing twigs and leaves as their clothes turned to bark.

By the time Criton and the others came back – if they ever came back – the Goodweather elves would look like nothing more than a clump of bushes. It was too much to hope that Criton would see through their disguise. He and the others would be caught, just like they had said. For the first time, she hoped her friends were being chased.

She sat there, waiting for the worst to come. The sun beat strong over the ruins. It would shine in Criton's eyes when the elves attacked him. She began to cry. The elves had their sky-nets, and the nets would not miss. Here she was again, trapped and useless. She could not even warn him.

This was a terrible world. It was here to torture her, to make her feel stupid and weak and to take everything she loved away from her. It was teasing her, even now. The Goodweather elves had pulled their nets out of the air, just the way she had failed to do. She could not escape or even move, while all around her the mists were growing.

45
Hunter

The first net flew past him toward the pursuing elves. It had come out of a bush – he was sure of it. Had it been meant for him, or them? Hunter did not wait to find out. He turned his mount and rode hard toward whoever was hiding there in the undergrowth. He squinted against the sun. Was it just him, or was the bush itself moving? Its twigs and branches seemed to dissolve before his eyes, leaving… could that be Bandu?

No, he realized at the last moment. It was an elf. He recovered as quickly as he could and swung his sword, but the elf was too fast. He – or was it a she? – ducked his blade and with a single motion sliced off one of the horse's hind legs. Hunter's stomach plunged as his mount collapsed under him. Without any stirrups to entangle his feet, he managed to fall from the horse without any of his limbs getting caught underneath. He rose just barely in time to block the elf's first blow, but the force knocked his sword from his hand. He dropped to the ground as the elf raised the sickle, and then was sprayed with blood when one of his Illweather pursuers rode by, decapitating his aggressor.

Hunter crouched, shielding his head with his hands. What was going on here? Afraid to stand and come within mounted sickle range, he crawled forward on hands and knees to retrieve his sword, looking around and trying to determine what all this meant.

The new elves, the bush elves, were outnumbered and unmounted, but they had caught some eight or nine Illweathers in their nets and were more than holding their own. They were taking advantage of the afternoon sun to dismount and dismember every rider they could find. The trapped elves made even more noise than the ones engaged in battle: they whooped, jeered and shouted advice at their fellows, who seemed to ignore them completely. As far as Hunter could see, none of the islanders had yet been captured in the sky-nets. Perhaps these new elves expected to deal with the humans after the battle was over.

Hunter crawled a little farther forward, still squinting at the scene behind him. To his relief, all of his friends seemed to be alive so far. The horses had not fared as well. One of the ones that pulled the chariot was already dead, with the other uncomprehendingly attempting to drag both corpse and chariot all by itself. Criton's horse too had been slaughtered, but Criton had been able to fly up into a tree before his attacker could catch him. Narky was still riding an uninjured mount, but to Hunter's surprise, he soon wheeled it around to help Phaedra. Maybe Hunter's words had had an influence on him after all.

"Run!" Narky yelled at the children, dismounting beside the chariot. "Run! Get out of here! Make for the Gateway!"

They did as he said, running away on their little legs while Narky helped Phaedra onto his horse. "Go," Hunter heard him say. "The rest of us will meet you there. At least, I sure as hell hope we do."

Hunter did not know how many bush elves had started this fight, but now there were only six. The Illweathers were faring little better, however. All but five of them were either captured or dead, though as Hunter watched, one of them rode down and butchered a bush elf to even the score.

But Hunter's eyes were on the two captains.

The Illweather captain's horse was among the fallen, and she was facing off with her counterpart, their blades flashing. They moved almost too quickly for Hunter to understand, slashing and blocking and parrying and evading. Hunter realized suddenly how lucky he was that the only elf he had had to fight on his own had been a groom. These two were so fast that their movements were a blur.

Then in an instant it was over. The captain of the bush elves made a beautiful cut at the Illweather captain, but instead of parrying the blade, she parried his arm. The bush captain's arm flew off his body, and a second later, so did his grinning head.

"A rare win, captain," laughed the head, as it rolled back toward the islanders. "Next time, the pleasure will be mine."

Hunter jumped to his feet and ran. There was nothing he could hope to accomplish in a fight against speed like theirs. Narky had come to the same conclusion, and was already a few paces ahead of him. Criton flew above, doing his best to stay out of reach. They fled as fast as they could, hoping that the remaining ambushers would buy them just a few minutes before the Illweathers could give chase. Hunter ran, and did not stop for breath.

It did not take long to catch up with the children, small as they were. Hunter snatched up little Breaker as he ran, speeding through the undergrowth with the boy slung over his shoulder. Then, finally, the ruins of Gateway came into sight.

The stones were shrouded in a thick mist, spinning and swirling just as they had done a week and a half earlier when the islanders had fallen through into this world. It was a welcome sight, this time around.

"Bandu!" cried Criton, coming down for a landing. "Bandu, are you still here?"

"I am here!" her voice answered, from somewhere within the mists. "But they catch me in a net now. Where the Goodweathers are?"

"Still fighting the Illweathers," said Narky. "Is the gate open?"

"Yes," Bandu wailed, still concealed by the mist. "Take net and open gate is all same thing. But I am in net still here! I can't go out to you!"

"Wait for me," yelled Criton. "I'll find you and get you out of there!"

Hunter put Breaker down and stretched his weary left arm. "She can't do anything *but* wait," he heard Narky mutter.

Criton vanished into the fog just as Phaedra rode out of it, soaking wet. "The gate is open!" she shouted. "I've just been to the other side! It's open! Follow me!"

Hunter looked back and gulped. The other children were still running toward him, with three mounted elves already in pursuit. The Illweather captain rode in the middle, with a male elf on one side and the ethereal Raider Eleven on the other. Their sickles were dripping blood.

"There!" cried Criton triumphantly, shrouded in mist and apparently unaware of the situation, "Now stand up, and – what's all this you're – oh no, we don't have time to worry about…"

"Follow Phaedra!" Hunter shouted at the children. "Narky, you too. I'll go last…"

Tella had fallen. The poor girl had simply tripped over her own feet as she ran, tumbling to the ground and skinning her knee. Her tumble was so perfectly childlike that in any other context it might have been endearing. Instead, it spelled disaster.

"Go!" Hunter repeated, running toward the fallen girl. "Everybody, go!"

He reached Tella as she was rising unsteadily to her feet, tears in her eyes. "I've got you," he said, sheathing his sword and lifting her off the ground. Then he sprinted back toward the mist, cursing silently to himself. The elf captain was so close behind them now that he doubted he would make it. In fact, he was sure he wouldn't. What would they do to him? The riddle game probably meant nothing as a protection against their blades, but if it did, he was sure to find out soon enough.

The thundering hooves were shaking the ground beneath him, but he dared not turn his head. He poured his last, desperate energies into his sprint, even while his legs began to feel as if they were made of wood.

A net flew out of the mist ahead, hissing through the air. Hunter ducked as he ran, and it passed overhead. He heard the captain's cry from behind him, screaming out a furious curse while Hunter's numbing legs carried him out of the clear air and into the fog. On and on he ran with Tella clutched in his arms, until he could hear the others' calls once more and felt the sweet rain on his face.

46
Criton

Criton had only just pulled the sky-net off Bandu and taken Hunter's armor from her hands when the girl lurched to her feet, snatched the net away from him and threw it with all her might. "*Now* we go," she said.

When they stumbled out of the mists, it was raining heavily. The wet forest and mossy stones welcomed them with a benevolent inertness – one that he had always taken for granted before. All around him, other bodies were crashing through the bushes, falling and springing up again – running for their lives.

"Find cover," Hunter shouted. "They're still coming!"

Criton and Bandu staggered forward together, collapsing at last behind a huge mossy cornerstone. Hopefully the fairies would not find them here. He wished he had a horse for them to ride away on – surely even a regular horse could outrun an exhausted elven one. He wondered what had happened to the horses they had left here.

The sun was just setting dull and gray behind the rainclouds when the captain and Raider Eleven rode out of the mists, holding their nets at their sides.

"Hurry," said the captain. "We don't have long before the sun here sets and the barrier closes again. Hurry! The prince will be furious if our quarry escapes."

Raider Eleven nodded, her newly pale skin shining as if with the light of the unrisen moon. She whistled once, a low whistle that made Criton feel queasy.

"Come out, little ones," she sang, her voice high and intoxicating. "Follow my voice, little things."

They would not be able to resist her call for long, Criton knew. *He* could barely resist it, and the call wasn't even directed at him. The children would come to her, and they would be eaten.

Suddenly, Narky came into view, leaping onto a rock with his hands outstretched before him. "I am a child strangler!" he shrieked, his voice cracking. His burnt out eye socket gaped menacingly in the semi-darkness while his good eye darted wildly about.

"Come out like the elf says," he cried, "and let me get my hands around your little necks!"

The elves hissed furiously at Narky. He gave them a sarcastic salute. He certainly looked like a madman, but would the children be frightened enough to stay in hiding? They had been imprisoned with him for over a week, after all, and he hadn't strangled any of them.

For now, no children emerged. Of course! The memory-boxes! Narky had figured that the children wouldn't remember him at all, and that they would find his figure frightening. And so far, at least, he was right.

Raider Eleven made a frustrated sound and tucked her net under her left arm. She reached for the sickle that was slung over her back, but the captain stopped her.

"There's no *time*," she hissed. "Lure the children. I'll deal with him."

With an impossibly smooth motion, the captain retrieved her own sickle and spurred her horse toward Narky, who jumped down from his rock and tried to run away. Raider Eleven resumed her call for the children, but this time Hunter jumped up.

"I cut children to pieces!" he shouted, standing on the other side of the tower's foundation. "Come out here and I'll skewer you!"

With a grunt, the elven captain veered off and charged now at Hunter, allowing Narky to escape into the woods. Hunter also turned to run as the captain bore down on him, and once again Raider Eleven took up her song.

"Come to me, children!" she trilled, her voice sweet and ethereal.

With a silent prayer to God Most High, Criton shot into the air. "I come from the seed of dragons!" he shouted, breathing fire in all directions and turning the nearby raindrops to steam. "Come near me, and I'll burn you!"

With a look of disgust, the fairy captain turned away from chasing Hunter and cast her net into the air. Criton had no chance to avoid it, but in the end he didn't have to. The twinkling sky-net faded as it neared him, disappearing into the growing darkness. Both elves cried out in anguish. Their time was up. They turned their horses and galloped back through the misty gate. Within moments, they were gone.

Criton could hardly believe the islanders had won. As soon as he had touched down upon the earth again, he fell to his knees and kissed the muddy ground. He was safe. They were all safe.

The children, though, remained in hiding. "Rakon!" Criton called out. "Tella! We didn't mean it – we're not going to hurt you! You can come out now! Adla? Delika?"

"How do you know my name?" asked Delika, from the boughs of a tree. How had she managed to climb all the way up there?

"The fairy riders who were here just now stole your memories," Phaedra said. "We've known you for over a week. We're your friends."

"I don't know anyone like you people," Delika insisted.

Phaedra winced. "Come down from there," she pleaded,

"and we'll tell you all about it if you like."

"Cold here," Bandu whispered to Criton. "Make fire and they come."

Criton nodded and went to recruit Hunter and Narky to help him gather firewood. It was all hopelessly wet, but they built a decent woodpile anyway, against one of the moss-covered building stones.

"All right," Criton said, "now step back."

When he breathed his flames onto the wood, he nearly choked on the smoke that billowed up from it. He took a step back, coughing. It took five attempts to get the fire started, and by then he was beginning to grow lightheaded. He sat down on a damp stone and put his head between his knees, while the fire crackled and hissed.

"Thanks," said Hunter, clapping a hand on his back. "You don't have to stay out here. It's been a long day – get some rest."

Criton nodded gratefully and rose, looking back for Bandu. As she had predicted, Phaedra was finding it much easier to coax the children out of hiding now that there was a welcoming fire for them to sit by. Bandu beckoned them over, pointing to the large tent that was, thankfully, still intact.

"When you are tired, sleep there. We find food tomorrow, after sleep."

The next morning, Criton awoke to find Narky in the tent with him and Bandu curled up at their feet by the entrance. Bandu was still asleep too, so Criton rose quietly and tiptoed past the two of them to leave the tent. Hunter and Phaedra were already up, as were several of the children. They were dressing a deer to be roasted on the fire, while Phaedra's elven horse stood nearby, placidly cropping the tall grasses among the ruins.

"Where was the horse?" Criton asked Phaedra. "I didn't see it last night."

Phaedra did not look up from her work. "I gave it a

slap when I dismounted. I thought maybe the elves would follow its tracks instead of looking for us here. Hunter found it by the stream this morning, just standing there."

Criton nodded, and helped them rebuild the fire. The rain had abated, though the sky remained uniformly gray. Criton doubted their clothes would dry today. The air was sticky.

When Narky came out for breakfast, Criton went back into the tent to see how Bandu was doing. The dress that had once belonged to Phaedra's nursemaid hung strangely on her body now, still too big in the sleeves, yet growing tight around the belly. Her pregnancy was really starting to show.

Bandu was in a cheerful mood. "We are not with elves now," she said happily.

She ate more breakfast than Criton would have believed possible. He did not blame her: the venison was heavenly. The others too were hardly shy filling their stomachs. Apparently, they had been living on mushrooms for days. Between the five islanders and eight children, they ate more than half the doe in one sitting.

When they could eat no more, they spoke of their next move. They were not well equipped for travel: they had only one horse, and no saddlebags. The woolen tents were too heavy to be carried easily on foot, so they would have to be left behind.

Then there was the problem of where to go. They could not travel far with all these children, at least not without more tents and horses. Even feeding them all would probably be difficult. Narky suggested that they find the nearest village and leave the children there. Naturally, his suggestion terrified the children. Terrifying them seemed to be Narky's specialty.

Criton asked them where they all came from. They answered him all at once, but Phaedra helped to clarify since apparently she knew them fairly well at this point. As

Criton had suspected, the fairies had gathered them from all over the continent. The twins were from Atuna. Adla and Temena hailed from some village near Ardis. Rakon was from Laarna. Caldra said she came from the mountains, but she could barely describe her home beyond that. Delika could only say that she lived in a forest village near a big river. Breaker was from Parakas.

Parakas. Criton had already told the others he wanted to go there; who could deny him now? Besides, it was closer than any of the other cities.

"If we go to Parakas first," he suggested, "we can travel north along the coast from there, to Atuna and Laarna. There should be roads and inns along the coast. We won't have to worry about tents."

"I don't know," said Phaedra. "Do we even still have money?"

"We should," Hunter said. "I didn't leave it with the horses, so unless someone else has been here in the last week and a half, it should all still be in the tent where you three slept."

"Really?" said Criton. "I didn't notice it there."

"What is wrong with all of you?" asked Narky, sounding nearly hysterical. "Last I heard, Mayar is still worshipped in Parakas. If Tarphae's plague was His doing, we'll be going straight to our deaths!"

"I'm not so sure anymore," Phaedra said. "First off, we don't know that it was Mayar who killed our people. Don't forget that we sailed away from Tarphae in a boat. The Sea God could have drowned us, but He didn't. The more I think about it, the more I think it must have been someone else.

"Even if it was Mayar, though, we will be in a less vulnerable place this time. Tarphae is an island, surrounded by His domain. Parakas is only a coastal city right on the edge of His territory, where His powers might come into conflict with others. So we have some protection there too."

"And some of the Gods are protecting us," Hunter added.

"That's what you told me in the mountains. They have a plan."

"Yes," Phaedra agreed, "though we're not really in Ravennis' territory over here, and He's the one who seems to have been watching us most closely. On the other hand, we don't know whether the God who cursed Tarphae cares that we're still alive. The rumors in Atuna were that King Kestan is being punished by having to live out the rest of his life on an island of corpses. He probably didn't know we made it off the island, so our deaths would have been no further punishment to him. We might be safe as long as we don't try to go back."

"Those are all great theories," Narky admitted grudgingly, "but would you bet our lives on them?"

"These children deserve to be brought home," Hunter said.

"Right," said Criton.

And if their homes take us past a library full of dragon lore, all the better.

47
Criton

Beginning their journey was a complicated affair. Even leaving two tents behind, there was still a lot left to pack. They threw a pair of blankets over the horse – the empty horse, as Bandu called it – and tied them there with rope from one of the woolen tents. It was not as good as a saddle, but it was a start. Hunter carried the canvas tent, all folded and bundled up on his back. He seemed surprised and pleased that Bandu had brought his armor back from the fairy world, and while the loss of his shield clearly upset him, he tried not to show it.

"There's so much to carry," he said, pulling the shirt of scales over his head. "I wouldn't have had room for it anyway."

Narky carried the remaining venison and their cooking supplies, and Criton took the tent stakes and the three blankets that were not already on the horse. After that they set out eastward, moving at the children's pace. The children slowed them down, but at least Bandu was no longer scaring all the game away.

After a week's travel they came to a winding river, which Hunter said should lead them to Parakas. "The city stands at a delta between the sea and the Parek River," he said. "The river is supposed to be lined with red settar trees, which I think is what those big ones are."

"Where did you learn all that?" Narky asked.

"There was a war a little after I was born," Hunter said. "My father told me about it. He was the king's champion when we allied with Atuna against Parakas."

Phaedra looked around at the rust-colored trees and nodded. "So this is the famous Parek," she said. "Just like in the myth."

"What myth?" Criton asked.

"There's a myth that Parek was once a great king," Phaedra said. "A greedy king. He only ever gave the Gods what was outright required of him, and no more. When Mayar had a special celebration for His daughter Karassa's birth, all the kings of the world raised sacrifices in special tribute to Him except for Parek. Mayar became so angry that he cursed Parek and turned him into a river, so that from then on he has brought the Sea God a tribute every day, in the form of river water."

"Huh," said Narky. "Now that you mention it, I know that story. My pa told it to me, when I asked how come he always sacrificed an extra lamb on holy days."

"It doesn't go well with Katinaras' theory," Hunter pointed out. "It assumes that Karassa really is Mayar's daughter."

Phaedra smiled. "If everyone agreed with Katinaras, he wouldn't be radical." She looked around and must have seen how confused Criton was, because she spent the next half hour explaining what she and Hunter meant.

They followed the river for another two weeks until the trees thinned and the sea became visible. The land here, fertile and well cultivated, sloped down toward the delta where the Parek met the sea. By the intersection of river and sea, just as Hunter had said, stood Parakas. Criton's eyes did not stay on the city long. He was looking for the wizard's tower.

That must be it! The ruins were a good deal closer to Parakas than Criton had expected – perhaps a mile or two at most. Psander's mentor must have had a commanding view of the city before he and his tower had fallen under the Gods' might. Criton shuddered as he imagined looking down from the tower to see an army gathering in front of a roiling sea. That final view must have been terrifying.

"Oh, good," said Phaedra, when she saw the city. "I'm tired of sleeping in the mud. Let's get to an inn!"

They hurried down through flowering apricot orchards and fields of wheat and barley, craving civilized life. But when they reached the city walls, the gates would not open for them.

"Move along," the olive-skinned gatekeeper called down at them. "We have no use for slavers."

"We're not slavers!" cried Phaedra. "We have no intention of selling these children! We're just here to take Breaker home."

"If that's so," said the gatekeeper, "send him forward and I'll let him in alone."

Breaker looked at them nervously as he approached the gate, but when it opened he darted in without so much as a glance behind him.

"All right then," said the gatekeeper. "Move along."

"Why can't we come in?" asked Narky. "We're not carrying a plague, you know."

"All the same, you'll stay outside," the man replied. "If you need a place to stay, ask Scypho by the seashore. Like with like."

"How do we get to Scypho?" asked Hunter.

Scypho's house turned out to be more of a shack, with cracked clay walls and a sod roof. It stood right at the edge of the shore, so close that at high tide the waters would come almost to the doorstep. Criton could see the uneven lines in the ground where the farthest waves had reached. A wisp of smoke rose from the house's central chimney.

Hunter knocked on the door. "Someone there?" a voice called from inside, and a short while later the door opened, revealing a bent old man. The children gasped even as Criton let out a sigh of relief: the man was an islander. Frizzy white hair grew out of his black scalp, and his dark face was lined with wrinkles that deepened when he beheld the crowd at his door.

"I thought I heard something," he said. "How can I help you all?"

Everybody spoke at once. The old man covered an ear with one hand, waving at them to stop. "Enough, enough!" he cried, "I'm only a *little* bit deaf."

He turned to Hunter. "Why don't you start?"

"We are refugees from Tarphae," Hunter said. "We met these lost children in the woods and are trying to bring them back to their homes. We brought one back to Parakas, but the gatekeeper wouldn't let us enter the city. He said we should see you instead. We're wet and tired from travel, and my friend is pregnant. We need food and horses and a place to stay before we start our journey up to Atuna, where these two come from. Can you help us?"

The old man looked behind him and then back at the travelers. "I don't have room for you all to stay here," he said, "and I have no money for horses. But come on inside for now."

They left the elven horse outside and crammed into his hut as best they could. There was barely enough room for them all to stand in there without anyone ending up in the fire. A small pot of fruit was bubbling over the fire pit, and Scypho went back to stirring it.

"It's been a long time since I had children in my house," he said. "The ones here in Parakas all grew up after the war. I'm the only black skinned man they've ever seen. They think I'll boil them."

Criton noticed Tellos and his sister sharing a glance. They didn't look entirely certain that the old man *wouldn't* boil them.

"There were more islanders here before the war?" Phaedra asked, sitting down on the dirt floor.

"Islanders?" Scypho repeated a bit scornfully. "I'm no islander, young miss. I was born and raised in Parakas. My children were born here, and my grandchildren. We had a fine house right in the center of town, with four rooms and a garden, and walls and floors made of stone. People came to us to have their shoes mended. Mine wasn't the only family, either. There weren't many of us, but we had a community here before the war."

Bandu sat on the floor beside the old man, and Criton followed her lead. It was so comfortable here in this house, even though there wasn't enough room for Hunter to sit down, and Phaedra had to hold Delika in her lap. Criton felt more welcome here than he had felt at any time since leaving home.

"Do you blame Tarphae for what happened?" Hunter asked.

The old man shook his head and poked angrily at the jam. It smelled like apricots. "Of course not," he said, sounding only half truthful. "Our neighbors were always itching to get rid of us. If it hadn't been that war with Tarphae and Atuna, it would have been something else. That's what my sons said, when they took their families and left. They said we were never wanted here, and it wouldn't do any good to stay. So I gave them my blessing and they went. They weren't wrong, but I'm too old to be sailing off and starting a new life on an island somewhere."

His voice was bitter, and Criton wondered why this place felt so welcoming. The little home that Scypho had taken for himself was full of the old man's misery, his loneliness and abandonment. Yet here, Criton could relax. The islanders had been traveling among continentals for most of a year now, and Scypho was the first one who did not stare. Their skin meant nothing to him.

Scypho stirred the pot one last time before lifting it off

the fire and placing it on the ground beside him. "There's some bread up on that shelf there," he said to Hunter. "It's not much to go round, but we'll have to make do. Yes, just tear off a little piece and pass it along. You can all dip it in here if you like."

"Why did you leave your old house?" Phaedra asked.

"It wasn't my choice," Scypho said. "I'll tell you that. They said I couldn't stay within the walls anymore. Have to keep the city pure and all that." He snorted. "I hear my old house is a brothel now."

"You still trade with the cityfolk though," said Narky. "I mean, you didn't pick those apricots yourself, did you?"

Scypho looked at him sternly. "No, I did not. There are still some people left in this city who would not stand by and see an old man starve, Mayar be thanked."

"If we gave you the money, could you arrange to buy us horses?"

Scypho lifted a bushy eyebrow. "Refugees who travel with piles of gold?"

"My father was Lord Tavener of Tarphae," Hunter said, "who led the island's forces in the Parakese War. He did not send me from home empty-handed."

"No," said the old man, looking him up and down, from his young noble face to his heavy purse and rusting armor. "I see he didn't."

"Please?" Phaedra asked him, holding Delika close. "We'll never reach Atuna without horses. We can't take a ship, because it might be Mayar who drowned Tarphae. We need your help."

"You want my help because you think my God is your enemy?" Scypho's hand went to the necklace of shark teeth that he wore as a symbol of his God. Then he sighed. "How many horses do you need?"

"Five," said Hunter, "but we have much travel ahead of us, and we'll need money for food and inn stays too. I think we can afford four."

"I hope you're wrong about being Mayar's enemies," Scypho said. "Of all the friends I've had, He's the only one who hasn't abandoned me yet."

He passed a hand over his eyes. "I'll see about the horses tomorrow. Where are you going to stay?"

Criton looked around. Temena had already fallen asleep, slumped against a wall. "Could the children sleep here tonight?" he asked. "We can set up a tent outside for the rest of us."

Scypho looked as if the very thought tired him. "Yes," he said. "I suppose that would be all right."

They put up the tent against one of the shack's outer walls. There was only barely room for four to cram in there, but Hunter volunteered to sleep outside this time. Criton was glad to have shelter for once. The islanders had slept out in the elements on the way down, and let the children sleep in the tent. It was easier to fall asleep, knowing that he would not be covered in dew the next morning.

Criton awoke to the sound of Hunter sharpening his sword outside. "Morning," Hunter said, as they all stumbled out of the tent. "Scypho's out buying us horses."

"Great," said Narky. "I can't wait to get out of here. This place is depressing."

The children were less sullen. They spent the morning on the beach, laughing and trying to see how far they could follow each receding wave without getting caught by the next one. Criton went and sat on a stone at the edge of the sand, watching them play. He envied them.

"They're sweet," said Phaedra, noticing his gaze but misinterpreting it. She came over and sat beside him. "Are you ready to be a father?"

He looked away. "I don't know what it is to be a father."

Scypho returned shortly before noon, leading a single horse. "My friend will try to find you three more by tomorrow," he said. "You'll have to suffer my company for another day."

They ate a midday meal, after which Criton asked about the wizard's tower.

"It's dedicated to Mayar, just like you say," the old man confirmed. "They have guards there day and night to make sure nobody goes treasure-hunting. Only my God's priests are allowed up there, to gather sacrifices for festivals and special events."

"Sacrifices?" asked Phaedra. "What kind of sacrifices?"

"Whatever they can find," said Scypho. "Furs, papers, scrolls, little carved statuettes – whatever the guards dig up, the priests burn it on the altar and scatter the ashes on the sea. It's amazing how many scrolls and things that dangerous old wizard had up in his tower. I always knew he was trouble, but now we know that he had a whole library full of blasphemies! Good riddance."

Phaedra looked horrified. "They burn scrolls?" she gasped, clutching her elbows as if suddenly cold.

Scypho looked at her sharply. "Of course they do, girl. The Tidefather protected us from that wizard for many, many years, and now the wizard's gone forever. I'd say a proper set of sacrifices is the least we can do."

"He was supposed to be an expert on dragons," said Criton, feeling sick.

"Dragons, yes," Scypho agreed. "The great lizards who thought they could fight the Gods. I'm glad I never had to live in those evil days."

"When is the next sacrifice?" Criton asked.

"We've completely lost track of time," Phaedra explained hurriedly.

"The Storm Festival is next week," Scypho said. "Five days, really. I used to prefer the Rain Ceremony, but now I look forward to the Storm Festival every year."

Criton nodded. The Storm Festival was the only one of the Sea God's festivals worshipped at the seashore instead of at the church of Mayar. Criton still remembered how Ma's husband had grumbled about having to stand cold and wet on the docks while the priest of Mayar made his prayers. He had complained about it, the cruel bastard, all while keeping his wife and Criton trapped in the house, unable to even see the docks from their window.

But Mayar's church would be inside the city somewhere. For Scypho, the Storm Festival would be the only one of Mayar's festivals that he did not have to worship alone.

"Five days," said Phaedra. "So they'll be building the seaside altar soon?"

"They will," Scypho said. "Probably tomorrow, or the next day."

"And the sacrifices?" asked Criton, his heart sinking, "When do they usually gather those?"

Scypho shrugged. "I don't know. Soon. That young priest, Pellos, usually gets them."

"Does anyone know where all the children went?" asked Hunter suddenly. "We'd better make sure they don't drown."

"Yes," said Scypho. "Go, all of you. It's been a tiring morning, and I need some rest."

They left him there and walked back onto the beach, where all seven children were playing harmlessly in the sand.

"I know what you're thinking," Hunter told Criton, "and it's too dangerous. We are *not* trying to rescue a pile of scrolls straight out of the hands of guards and priests and practically Mayar Himself."

"I can't believe they burn it all," said Phaedra, shaking her head with a stunned expression.

"I'm with Hunter on this one," said Narky. "We might not be happy about what they're doing, but the answer is not to get ourselves killed. We've had a *lot* of close calls. We shouldn't press our luck."

"You're right," Phaedra admitted. "But I still don't like it."

Criton said nothing. Now he knew better than to ask Hunter or Narky for help. But one way or another, he would not stand by and watch his heritage destroyed.

He passed the next morning in agony, while Hunter and Scypho went to buy the rest of the horses. In the meantime, Narky and Phaedra watched the children and talked, and Bandu tried to pull Criton into the tent to make love. He didn't go. He was feeling too tense, and besides, afraid though he was to say so, he was put off by her size. She was growing so quickly now, her body barely resembled the one he had grown used to. And they were, at best, halfway through this. He knew it was wrong, but what could he do about it? He felt the way he felt.

Bandu was insulted and hurt when he rebuffed her. She kept repeating, "Why you don't want me?" He had no answer for her, so instead he fled.

He walked uphill toward the tower for a time, then turned around and headed for the city gate. He had just arrived and was trying to decide where to go next when out stepped a man dressed in blue-gray robes, an empty sack thrown over his shoulder. This must be Pellos, the priest charged with sacrificing Criton's family history to the Sea God. Criton had to stop him.

"Excuse me," he said, stepping into the priest's way. "My wife is pregnant. Could you bless our baby?"

Pellos looked at him with surprise and alarm. Criton was surprised himself. Where had he come up with that?

"I am on an errand," said the priest. "I will make sure to come by when I have finished."

"I'm afraid she'll give birth soon," said Criton. "Please? It'll only take a minute or two. We're staying with Scypho."

"Oh, very well," Pellos sighed. "Lead the way."

Criton brought him back to the hut by the sea, frantically trying to think of a plan. When they arrived, he found Phaedra and Bandu outside the tent, conferring with each other while Phaedra worked on adjusting a spare dress for Bandu. He wondered what Bandu had been telling Phaedra about him.

"Gods, man," said Pellos, with surprise and irritation. "This girl is yet months away from giving birth!"

"Is she?" said Criton, looking to Phaedra for help. *Please distract him,* he tried to tell her with his eyes, *please, please distract him.*

"She miscarried once, at about this time," Phaedra lied, her eyes acknowledging Criton's request. "He worries a lot."

"You worry?" said Bandu, confused. "That is why you don't want me?"

"Well," the priest sighed, "I suppose I can bless your baby anyway. Come here, girl."

Bandu refused. She refused! "I don't want bless," she said.

"Stay," said Phaedra to Pellos, "we'll talk her into it. Criton, I don't think your presence is helping."

Thank you, he thought at her, and slipped away around the hut. As soon as the priest was no longer within sight, he began to run toward the tower. He suspected he had only a few minutes before Pellos disentangled himself from Bandu and Phaedra and came to collect the sacrificial relics. Criton closed his eyes, trying to picture exactly what the priest looked like. Yes, he thought he had it right.

When he looked down at his hands they were several shades lighter and a good deal smaller than before. He touched his face, and it *felt* right, at least. Now for the hard part. He had become an expert at transforming himself, but it would take an illusion to turn his ragged clothes into Mayaran robes. At illusion, he was a complete amateur. Still, if he could not do this, what was his magic good for?

He concentrated, thinking about the robe and trying to let his imagination extend itself out into the world. It worked, sort of. He did not think he had the color quite right, and his tunic did not rustle the way a robe ought to, but he thought this would probably do. He strode forward, silently praying to God Most High that the guards would not notice his mistakes.

There were half a dozen of them scattered around the ruins, looking bored. "Here he is!" cried one, and hopped to his feet.

"What have you found?" Criton asked him, trying to sound businesslike.

The guard gave him a funny look. "Are you all right? You don't sound normal."

Criton coughed and smiled and hoped that his racing heart was not audible. He might have looked right enough, but his voice and accent were all wrong!

He coughed again and shook his head. "Don't worry about it," he rasped, hoping that this would mask his terrible attempt at a Parakese accent. "Been like this all day."

"Oh," said the guard, still looking unsettled. "Well, the pile is over there, but you should have brought something to put it in. We found a few sculptures this time, and some precious stones, and of course more scrolls. You won't be able to carry it all in your hands."

Fool! Criton thought. How could he have forgotten that the priest had been carrying a sack?

"I'll make two trips," he whispered. "I'll bring the sack next time."

"Right," said the guard. Criton wished he wouldn't look so concerned. He suspected the guard would watch him walk back toward the town until he was out of sight.

He went to the pile of dug-up items and began collecting scrolls in his arms. There were five or six of them, some bulkier than others, and they fit poorly there. "I'll be back," he said, and hurried away as nonchalantly as he could.

He had not gone more than four steps before a scroll fell from his arms. As he bent over to retrieve it, another fell, and another. The guard with whom he had just spoken rushed over to help him, but when he handed the last scroll back to Criton, his hand passed straight through a piece of imaginary robe. The guard blinked, unsure of what he had just seen.

"Thanks," said Criton, and fled as quickly as he could.

To his relief, the guard did not follow. Criton practically flew down the hillside, and nearly cried out when he saw the real Pellos coming toward him. The priest was looking down at his own feet as he climbed up the hill. Criton dropped his illusion at once and transformed back into his usual human shape, hurriedly stuffing scrolls into his tunic.

"Hello," he said, when the priest looked up at him. He tried to use magic to look less lumpy, but the scrolls slid down toward his legs and he had to put his hand on his stomach and stand perfectly still to avoid letting them tumble onto the ground.

"How did you get all the way up here?" the priest asked with irritation, stopping to look up at him.

"Went for a walk," Criton answered, completely unsatisfactorily.

"Your wife refused to let me bless the baby," Pellos said angrily. "You and that dirty girl completely wasted my time."

"I'm sorry," said Criton. Why wouldn't the priest walk on? "Anyway," he said, "thank you for trying."

"Huh. Right," the priest said suspiciously. But he continued on his way.

Criton gathered up the scrolls and ran. His chest burned and his legs seemed to be moving faster than they were meant to, but he did not stop until he reached Scypho's little house, coughing and panting. Scypho and Hunter had apparently returned with the horses, and Hunter was fastening a new saddle onto the empty elven horse while Phaedra gathered the children for their first meal of the day. Criton stuffed the scrolls into one of the horses' saddlebags and waved his arms wildly at Phaedra.

"We have to go!" he wheezed. "Now!"

"Why?" asked Hunter, but when he turned around and saw Criton, his eyes widened in horror. "What did you do?"

Criton shook his head. "We have to go," he repeated.

"All right, let's go!" Hunter cried, turning to shout at the others. Bandu came hurrying out of the tent, and Narky ran out of the house. Criton helped Bandu onto a horse, then snatched up Tellos and placed him in front of her.

"Ride upriver," he said. "Keep away from the tower."

The others had all gathered round by now and were trying to figure out how they could mount four islanders and six children all onto the four remaining horses. "I can take two," said Hunter, "one in front and one behind. Narky, can you do the same?"

"Wait!" cried Phaedra. "Where's Delika?"

Criton lifted Temena onto his own horse and looked around. Delika was still standing at the edge of the sand, looking out to sea. The burning in Criton's chest became a sudden deathly cold. His theft had not gone unnoticed. A wall of water towered above the shoreline, dark and angry, dwarfing the little hut that lay before it. And then it crashed.

48
Phaedra

Delika screamed and ran for the horses as the water rushed toward them. Phaedra wanted to help, but she had already mounted the elvish horse with Rakon in front of her, and there was no practical way to be of use. "Go!" Criton shouted at her, and Phaedra kicked the horse without looking back again.

The horse did not get far before the water reached it, crashing against its legs and belly. Phaedra felt the swirling waters clawing at her legs, trying to drag her off the horse and under the murderous waves. She clung fiercely to the reins, her arms on either side holding Rakon in the saddle. For now, the horse stood firm.

She thought she heard cries around her, but she could not make out the words over the roar of the ocean. With a last tug at Phaedra's leg, the waters drew back toward the sea, preparing for a second, more devastating wave. Phaedra gave her mount a frantic kick and it sprang to life, cantering away from the beach as directed.

It was lucky this empty horse knew no terror. The other horses had gone completely wild, galloping away from the ocean without paying the least attention to their riders' direction. Phaedra saw Hunter's mare take him and two children off toward the tower, while a gelding charged upriver past Phaedra, carrying only Temena on its back. Phaedra gasped. That was Criton's horse.

The second wave struck with a crash even louder than before. Phaedra looked back in search of Criton, just in time to watch Scypho's shack get swept away.

She kicked her horse into a gallop, and still Mayar's fingers reached out for her, snatching at the horse's tail and dragging at its feet. Ahead and to her right, Hunter was trying to turn his horse toward the river and away from the tower and its guards, two of whom were firing arrows at him from Parakese crossbows while the others mounted horses in pursuit. At last Hunter prevailed over his mount, pulling hard on the reins while Caldra clung to his back and Adla bounced perilously in front.

Narky, also up ahead, looked back toward Phaedra. "There he is!" he cried.

Phaedra turned to find Criton breaking out of the water, a sputtering Delika in his arms. He flew upwards, already far behind them, but still the sea would not let him and Delika go. It reached for them, waves crashing higher and higher, and a large tangle of seaweed wrapped itself around his ankle and made to pull him down.

"Keep going!" Criton shouted, when he saw Phaedra looking. He had no disguise on, and the golden scales on his arms flashed in the sunlight. He shifted Delika under one arm, clawing at the seaweed. In the distance, the sea battered against the walls of Parakas, crowning its battlements in foam.

"Hold on," Phaedra told Rakon, and rode after poor Temena, who had completely let go of her reins and was hanging onto her saddle for dear life. Phaedra's elvish steed did not fail, and with a lucky grab, she caught hold of the other horse's reins.

When she had time to look again, Criton had escaped the sea's grasp. The limp seaweed still dangling from his foot, he soared skyward out of reach before finally turning toward Temena and his horse.

Phaedra had only just begun to feel relief when a splash of water struck her from the side. She turned back and stared. The Parek had overflowed its banks, its waters surging out toward her. The river was flowing backward. Phaedra shuddered and pulled away from the Parek into a sodden apricot orchard, watching fearfully as the mounted soldiers neared her, with the angry priest of Mayar at their head.

"Heathens!" Pellos cried. "Traitors! Cursed in the name of Mayar! You will pay for what you've done! Scypho will pay for hosting you!"

Phaedra looked into his face, his youth turned ugly with rage. Didn't he know? Scypho had already paid for helping them. He could pay no more.

Hunter was turning his horse back around to come to her aid, but it was no good: the tower guards were already between him and Phaedra.

"Stay back!" Phaedra yelled at them, bringing the elvish horse to a stop. "Or I'll tear your souls from your bodies and feed you to the waves."

The priest ignored her, but the guards pulled back on their reins. "A witch!" breathed one of them.

"Ride on," commanded Mayar's priest. "There are no more witches and wizards."

"But she's an islander," protested another. "Who knows what they still have over there?"

"She's just a girl trying to scare you," Pellos insisted. "I have stood beside her and spoken to her. She's no witch."

The guards looked encouraged. "Fool!" Phaedra shouted frantically. They were so close! "I only distracted you while my friend stole your sacrifices! You say there are no wizards now? Well, look there!"

The guards followed her finger with their gazes, and gasped in terror when they saw Criton flying toward them.

"Wizards!" cried one. "They're all wizards!" They fled back toward the tower.

Pellos looked frightened as well, but he did not turn around. "My God has killed wizards before," he said, "and He will kill wizards again. Die, abomination!"

He spurred his horse, and Phaedra panicked. She grabbed at her saddlebags, snatching up the first object she could find. It was a small copper pot. Pellos was nearly at her, his arm already outstretched to drag her off her horse. With a grunt, Phaedra swung her pot at the priest's head.

Pellos had only just caught her by her other arm when the pot slammed against his temple. He let go and fell from his mount with a lifeless thud, landing face down in the muddy grass. Phaedra wobbled, but she caught onto the elven horse's makeshift saddle with one hand and managed to steady herself.

Rakon, who had somehow not fallen despite Phaedra's flailing, turned round so that he could stare up into her face. "You hit him!" he said. "You hit him, and he fell over!"

"Well done," Hunter called from up ahead, his face displaying unguarded relief. He could never have helped her, Phaedra realized with a shock. With Adla in the saddle in front of him, it would have been disastrous to even try drawing his sword.

At last Criton and Delika arrived, drenched and subdued, and took their place on the horse with Temena. Bandu had gotten quite a head start on the rest of them, but now that Phaedra had time to look, she saw her some distance ahead, waiting for them. Criton glanced over at the Parek, which was still flooding its banks, its water creeping ever closer to them over grasses and tree roots.

"Let's get out of here," he said. "They'll probably send an army after us if they can."

By the time they stopped, most of the children were crying. The seawater had stalled a few miles west of Parakas, and the waters of the Parek flowed gently here, as if blissfully unaware of the chaos that awaited them.

"It's all right," Phaedra told the children. "We're safe now."

Her words did no good, of course. They were crying *because* they were safe.

"Everything's going to be all right," Criton echoed uselessly.

Tella looked up at them, her eyes still full of tears. "The old man..."

"He's in his God's hands now," Phaedra said, though her heart ached. "Many sages say that's the best kind of death."

"That's right," said Narky, holding his reins in one hand and awkwardly patting Tella on the head. "He's probably happy now. Happier than he was, anyway."

Tella looked skeptical, but she stopped crying.

Narky turned to Criton. "Well, I hope those scrolls were worth it," he said. "We're never going to be safe near the water again."

"They're worth it to me," Criton answered defiantly. In his mind, he had just rescued his ancestors themselves. Phaedra could see it in his eyes.

"Let's get a little farther from Parakas," she suggested, "and we'll see what you got out of there."

They cut north, away from the Parek. With five horses, the travel was not nearly as difficult as before. It became even easier when they came across one of Atel's roads. Shortly before sundown, they came to an inn marked with the God's mule symbol. The inn's middle-aged proprietors stared at them when they stumbled in through the door, but being true followers of the Traveler God, they took Hunter's money without question and showed them to their rooms. The beds here were enormous, large enough that the entire bedraggled party was able to fit into two of them. Phaedra fell asleep almost immediately.

The innkeepers made a fine breakfast. As a girl Phaedra would have found it bland and simple, but these days even bread and unsalted mutton seemed outright luxurious. Well satisfied after a good meal, they set out that morning at a more leisurely pace.

When they stopped to give the horses a rest, Criton gave Phaedra the smallest of the scrolls to read aloud.

"An Experiment in Biocontingent Luminescence," she read. "The intent of the experiment was to identify the biocontingent triggers with greatest amplitude and longevity. To this end, fifteen Phalasean lanterns of varied colors were set at three-foot intervals along the walls of a darkened room, with exposed side facing out toward the wall. A separate trigger was utilized for each of the lanterns, including name trigger, intent and proto-intent triggers, Parakian trigger, neohessionic trigger and diffuse simian biothermal trigger. A full list is reproduced below..."

Phaedra looked up from her reading. "Try this one," Criton said hopefully, handing her another scroll. "They can't all be like that."

She hoped he was right. How devastating it would be for him if the papers he had rescued were nothing but a collection of wizarding experiments!

"By Caruther," she read, at the top of this second scroll. "Being a Discourse on the Dragon Knight, His Prophecy, and the Controversy Thereof."

"That sounds more promising," said Hunter.

Phaedra nodded. "Much has already been written about the famed Dragon Knight, Hession son of Pilos, who explored the world nearly a century ago in search of the Dragons' Prisoner. For the purpose of this discourse, a brief summary will have to suffice."

"This story is boring too," Tellos complained.

"Go play with sticks," Criton suggested.

"Criton is right," Bandu said. "Bring sticks and I show you."

Bless her. Phaedra gave Bandu a grateful look and read on.

"As we know, the war between Gods and dragons put an end to all but the weakest of the flying lizards. Prior to the war, however, relations between the two sides were known more for their cold distaste than for any bitter hatred. The dragons worshipped their own God, whom they saw as lord above all others, and tolerated the other Gods as younger, weaker cousins to their own.

"The incident of the Dragons' Prisoner, taking place a mere decade before the war, was at one time thought to be a catalyst for the subsequent events; more recent research casts doubt on this notion, suggesting rather that the imprisonment involved a cooperation between several Gods and dragons, and may have been the last significant piece of cooperation ever to occur between these two camps.

"To this day, it remains a mystery what crime the Prisoner committed. Salemis of Hagardis had been a most venerated prophet of God Most High prior to his sudden fall from grace. Though the crime remains unknown, its consequences suggest that it was deeply transgressive, considering the list of those who came forward to punish him for it. As well as the entire Draconic Council, the Gods Pelthas (Justice), Caladoris (Mountains) and Magor (Wilderness) are specifically mentioned as co-conspirators in the Prisoner's downfall.

"But most mysterious of all is the fact that although Salemis was vanquished and imprisoned, not a single source mentions his prison's location, nor was his death recorded. It is this fact that inspired the ill-fated Dragon Knight to commence his quest.

"Though Hession son of Pilos traveled the world over in search of Salemis and his prison, inspiring many a song and legend, his journey began and ended in his hero's abandoned home, a cavern now known as the Dragon Knight's Tomb. Many claim that by the end of his journey the knight had gone insane with his failure, rendering his final words to his assistant the ramblings of a dying madman. We will discuss this possibility shortly, but it is incumbent upon us to review the exact words recorded by the squire, and dissect their potential meaning:

Let he who is fatherless find his true sire
And he with no wishes fulfill his desire
Let she who is darkest bring light to the people
And she with no church raise skyward her steeple
For I see the end now to all things once planned
When he who was murderer rescues the damned.

This prophetic poem, thankfully preserved, is subject to varied interpretation, with religious sources claiming–"

"Hold on," said Narky, interrupting. "Hold on a second. Is it just me, or could that whole thing be us?"

"What?" said Hunter.

Phaedra reviewed the poem again. "I don't see how."

"'He who was fatherless?' That's Criton!"

"Maybe," said Phaedra, trying to stifle her annoyance, "but can I keep reading? Even if – *especially* if – you're right, the sages' interpretation can do us a lot more good than just wildly speculating on our own."

"Read," said Criton, waving her on.

"All right, where was I? Oh, here. This prophetic poem, thankfully preserved, is subject to varied interpretation, with religious sources claiming that it was a reiteration of mythological events long past, while the faction of academics now called the Blasphemous Clairvoyants emphatically insisted that the Knight's words were spoken as a true prophecy of things to come, and that its first line referred to some future hero and not, as the priests imply, to the Knight himself in his arrival in the afterlife.

"There has also been much debate over the number of subjects described as 'he' and 'she' in the Knight's verse; in particular, whether the verses refer to five different people or to a primal pair of man and woman who must remake the world after 'all things that were planned' come to pass. For the most part, the Blasphemous Clairvoyants coalesced around the Theory of Five, while priestly sources promoted the more eschatological Pair Theory. It is my proposal that, considering the evidence I have presented elsewhere of sometimes intentionally shoddy and misleading work by priestly scholars, the religious authorities are most likely in error, if not participating in an act of deliberate obfuscation.

"I will not repeat the Clairvoyants' exhaustive study of the subject here, but indeed, can it come as any surprise that the Gods and their servants should stand in opposition to those who would accurately interpret verses that celebrate 'she with no church' and other such presumably Godless heroes? I think not.

"Let us not forget that the Dragon Knight, though best known for his wizardry and martial prowess, was one of the few fully human ordained priests of God Most High. Read these verses once more, then, and ask yourself, is this a grand religious tale about a husband and wife remaking the world, or is it a smaller prophecy about five individuals still to come, bringing one age to a close and ushering in another?"

"That's enough," said Criton, sighing and putting a hand to his forehead. "That's enough for now. I can't really concentrate anymore. I have no idea what he's saying half the time."

"It's really very simple," Phaedra told him. "He didn't think priests could be trusted to interpret the prophecy honestly."

"What did *he* think it meant?" Narky asked, knowing the answer but rubbing it in.

Phaedra sighed. "He thought it hadn't happened yet, and that it's about five separate people."

"It's about us," Narky said. "Read it again."

When she had done so, Hunter frowned. "I can't tell what it means. If all of these things come true, then what? What's 'the end to all things once planned?'"

"Who cares?" Criton asked gleefully. "It says I'm going to find him!"

"I don't think we can be sure," Phaedra said gently. "It's awfully cryptic. The second line contradicts itself, the third is vague to the point of uselessness, and the fourth is just confusing. And if you're so sure it's about us, who's the murderer?"

"What is murderer?" Bandu asked suddenly. She had turned away from the children, who were now hard at play. Delika seemed to be in a constant state of inventing new rules, to which everyone but Tellos was attempting to adapt.

"I am," Hunter said gravely. "I killed two men in the mountains."

"In self-defense," Phaedra pointed out. "That's not the same as murder."

Narky was silent, his good eye lowered to look at the ground. "Maybe it's not about us, then," he mumbled.

Phaedra's chest tightened, and her heart sank. She was no fool – she knew guilt when she saw it. Who had Narky killed? It was all coming together now: his secrecy, his hurry to leave Tarphae… he had never shown any remorse over the loss of their home, and now she knew why. Tarphae's curse had meant that he could not be pursued.

Should she say something? Narky might turn dangerous if he realized that she knew his secret, and thought he could keep her quiet. But was she ready to condemn him?

"No, you could be right," she said to Narky, trying to keep her face neutral. "Maybe Hunter considering himself a murderer is enough."

"It has to," Narky said. "I mean, Criton's not really fatherless either, but I still think that first line is him."

Criton glared at him, and Narky winced. "Sorry, that's not really what I–"

"Here," Phaedra interrupted, trying to keep the peace, "why don't I read another page or two? Let's see…

"An intriguing note brought up by Mage Tyrol of Gateway is that of the six verses in the Dragon Knight's prophecy, five have exactly eleven syllables. According to him, a poem of six verses with eleven syllables each would fit into a well-established pattern of elven poetry. It is conceivable, at least, that the third line was somehow altered before or during transcription. If indeed the Dragon Knight's prophecy takes the same form as elf poetry, the ramifications would be truly fascinating. It would shed a new light, for instance, on the other mad ramblings recorded by the Dragon Knight's companion, such as the repeated phrase in his account, 'There is a third side! There is a third side, but I cannot reach it.'"

"That *is* interesting," Hunter said, "but we should get going. Daylight doesn't last forever."

Criton nodded and went to help Bandu back onto her horse. "Maybe you can read the rest later, and just tell us about it? The language those academic wizards use is hard for me."

"That's fine," said Phaedra. She would need something to do before she slept, to help calm her nerves. She could not stop thinking about Narky. She had grown to like him, and it devastated her to think that he had killed someone in cold blood. Who had his victim been? What would make a boy like Narky kill?

Maybe he had been a different person once. Perhaps Ravennis had changed him. After all, the line from the prophecy was about a man being transformed from murderer to rescuer. If the prophecy was really about the five of them, couldn't that mean that Narky would redeem himself?

The scroll did help her get to sleep that night, though its single-mindedness irritated her. Despite his occasional assertions to the contrary, Caruther had been obsessed with proving that the priests who had contributed to the understanding of the Dragon Knight's legend and prophecy were all liars. There was very little of value other than what she had already read aloud.

It was the fairy angle that maddened Phaedra most.

As 'truly fascinating' as the idea apparently was to him, Caruther had never gotten around to explicating the connection between the Dragon Knight and the fairies. She tried to think about it as much as possible during the next day's ride – anything to avoid thinking about Narky and his unknown victim.

"The Dragon Knight could have gone mad," she pondered aloud. "That's always possible."

"What?" asked fair-headed Caldra, who was riding with Phaedra today. Bless her; she thought Phaedra had been talking to her!

"I'm talking to myself," Phaedra reassured her. "My father used to say that sometimes you have to talk to someone who really understands you."

"Oh," said Caldra, sounding lost.

"What's that you were saying?" asked Narky, riding up beside them with Rakon holding onto his waist.

Having his attention made Phaedra nervous, but she pressed on. "I was thinking about the Dragon Knight. Caruther mentioned, sort of in passing, that while the knight was dying he kept saying there was a third side, but that he couldn't reach it. Maybe the Dragon Knight really did go mad, but if he didn't, I was thinking that this 'third side' might be the fairies. The scroll kept referring to the dragons and the Gods as 'the two sides'; that was what made me think of it."

"So you think the fairies were also in on the plot to punish what's-his-name?"

"Salemis. I don't know for sure, but I think it's possible that's what the Dragon Knight meant."

Narky bit his cheek thoughtfully. "He said he couldn't reach it, right? Do you think he meant the prison, or the fairies' world? Or the Gods' world? There's nothing new about not being able to reach that."

"Narky!" cried Phaedra. "What if the dragon was imprisoned *in* the fairies' world? It would explain why no one was able to find the prison, and why the Dragon Knight would have been unable to finish his quest! The mesh between us and the fairies can't always stay open – that's why the captain and Raider Eleven had to give up on us! Criton, didn't you say you had a scroll about fairy numerology somewhere?"

Criton looked back at her, startled. "I left it with Bandu when I came to get you out of Illweather. I don't think she brought it with us."

"Can you try to remember what it said? I think it might help with finding the Dragons' Prisoner."

Those were the magic words, of course. Criton spent the rest of the day silently trying to remember what he had read. Bandu tried to speak to him once, but he told her he was busy thinking. She turned and looked back at Phaedra with a vengeful expression.

The two of them were having problems, Phaedra knew. The bigger Bandu got, the more Criton seemed inclined to avoid her. It was grossly unfair. Phaedra knew that he was struggling with his impending fatherhood, but that was no excuse to distance himself from his wife. She was having a hard enough time just controlling her own body.

Bandu's nausea seemed to have subsided, but she had grown so much that she barely resembled her old self. Her belly, which had been emaciated when Phaedra had first seen her, was growing by the day. Her tiny breasts too had easily doubled in size. Even her back seemed wider.

When they stopped at another inn that night, the islanders spent some time trying to determine what they actually knew about the barrier between their world and the world of the fairies. Criton's recollections of the numerology scroll, combined with Bandu's childhood memories, pointed at a barrier that fluctuated in strength depending on the amount of time since the previous breach. Without the right timing – or a truly vast amount of power – it was likely impossible to break through. That was a comforting thought. The barrier kept the fairies out.

They followed Atel's road for about a month, while Hunter's funds slowly dwindled into nothing. When the road split only a week or so from Atuna, they turned left, away from the sea. The right fork clung too close to the sea, and besides, Phaedra suspected that the left fork would take them to Crossroads. The Atellan friars barely charged for their rooms, and she had never felt as safe as she had among them.

Crossroads did not have the same effect on Narky. He kept back, muttering, as the new head friar came out to greet them, and he awoke twice in the night, crying out in pain and terror.

"The ravens!" he shouted once, loudly enough that Phaedra could make out his words from two rooms over. "He's dying!"

Phaedra did not want to embarrass him the next day by asking about his dream, but she did ask him how he felt.

"My chest hurts," he said, scratching at it through his shirt and wincing. "It itches, too."

He looked awful. His shirt was clinging to his body with sweat, and like the rest of them, his hair had grown over the months into a shaggy tangled mess. Then he wiped his forehead, and Phaedra noticed the blood on his fingertips.

"What happened to your fingers?" she asked him.

"My fingers?" he said absentmindedly, looking down at them in surprise. "Nothing."

"There's blood," she pointed out.

"Huh," he said. "I don't know where that came from."

The others were slowly gathering round, concerned. "Take off your shirt," said Hunter.

The shirt was still partway over Narky's head when he heard their collective gasp. "What?" he asked.

Somehow, even after all these months, Narky's scar had reopened. All across his chest, the symbol of Ravennis was bleeding.

49
HUNTER

"What does it mean?"

Phaedra shook her head. "I don't know. Narky, do you–"

"*I* don't know!" Narky cried. "It wasn't like this yesterday. It just happened!"

"It doesn't look very deep," said Criton.

Phaedra shook her head. "You're sure you don't have any idea why this would happen? What did you dream about last night? I heard you saying something about ravens."

"I don't remember!" he shouted, panicked. "I just remember that it was awful. It felt really *important* when I woke up."

She made a frustrated sound. "You have to be the only person who's had a prophetic dream and can't remember a single detail."

"Well, I can't," he said angrily. "I'm sorry if that bothers you."

"What you want now?" asked Bandu.

Phaedra began to say something, but Bandu hissed at her. "Not you," she said. "Narky. Where you want to go?"

Narky just stared at her for a moment, collecting his thoughts. "I want to go to Laarna," he said at last. "A priest of Ravennis or an oracle might help me."

"Then Laarna it is," said Hunter. "Atuna's on our way north; we can stop there to bring the twins home."

They parted with the friars and continued northwards, keeping to Atel's road. Narky became more jittery as the days went on, urging them to hurry. When they reached Atuna, he wanted to abandon the twins there and continue onwards without even stopping.

"That's not going to happen," Hunter told him. He felt bad enough for the way they had had to leave Breaker at the gates of Parakas. Besides, although Hunter did not like to bring it up, they were now completely penniless. As soon as Tellos and Tella were back in their parents' care, Hunter would have to sell his horse.

Still, Narky would go mad without something to do for the next hour or two. Hunter set him the task of getting a good price for the horse, while Bandu and Criton watched over the other children and he and Phaedra went to return the twins to their parents.

"I can't believe they're going to have a baby," Phaedra said, out of nowhere.

Hunter nodded, unsure of what to say. Criton certainly didn't seem ready for fatherhood, but that was not the kind of thing one said out loud. As for Bandu… he didn't know what to think about Bandu. The fact was that he found her pregnant body embarrassingly arousing. Her vast, growing belly captured his imagination completely, filling his head with thoughts that he would never, ever share with Phaedra. Her shape and her motions were so compelling. Bandu moved her round fertile body with such matter-of-fact strength that Hunter did not doubt she would make a capable mother. She seemed completely, beautifully ready.

They followed the twins' lead, trying to ignore the stares from passersby. Finally they reached a house of white imported stone in the wealthy Atunaean style, and Tella said, "This is it."

Hunter took a deep breath and knocked, wondering

anxiously about the parents' reaction to the sight of a pair of islanders with their children. He decided that they should not have a chance to think about it. As soon as the door opened, Hunter said, "Are these your children, my lady?"

The young woman who had opened the door simply stared at him, saying nothing. She had callused skin and short, straight hair, and Hunter could see immediately that he had made a mistake.

"That's not Mother," said Tellos, "that's Hindra. She's our slave."

"Tellos!" cried Hindra, breaking her eyes away from Hunter's and noticing the children. "Tella! Where have you been?"

"We found them in the woods near Parakas," said Phaedra. "We think they'd been kidnapped by fairies."

"Fairies," repeated Hindra. "Thank you for bringing them all the way back here. I know it must not have been easy. I grew up south of Parakas, in–"

"I'm hungry!" shouted Tellos gleefully. "Find me something to eat!"

"First to your mother," said Hindra. She turned to the islanders. "Please wait here," she said. "I'm sure they will want to reward you for your troubles."

They waited there, uncomfortably, while Hindra took the twins inside. A courtyard could be glimpsed past the half-opened door, with fig trees planted at artistic intervals and a stone fountain in the middle.

"I had no idea they were so rich," Phaedra said.

"Noble, you mean," said Hunter. "They must be, to own slaves."

"Not here," she corrected him. "Most of Atuna's noblemen died in the uprising, alongside the king. In Atuna, any wealthy family can buy the right to own slaves from the ruling council. You didn't know that?"

"I guess I did, but I forgot."

She eyed him quizzically. "You remembered all about the

trees near Parakas, but you didn't remember this? We're practically swimming distance from home here, in the largest city in the world! Your father must have talked about Atuna all the time!"

Hunter shrugged. "I didn't think about those things back then."

"But you thought about trees."

"I thought about war," Hunter snapped. "When people spoke of Parakas and its settar trees, they were speaking about war. *That's* why I listened."

Phaedra seemed taken aback, embarrassed.

"I wasted my life learning how to kill people," Hunter told her. "I didn't think about it that way, but that's what it was. I was just learning how to kill people. And I didn't even realize I was wasting my life until I actually killed someone the first time, up in the mountains. It's awful. It's even worse knowing it's the life I *wanted*."

"But Hunter–" she said sympathetically.

He didn't let her finish. "I know," he said. "You rely on me. If I didn't keep fighting, we'd probably all be dead. But I don't want to keep having to kill in order to live."

"Maybe one day you won't have to," she said.

He laughed ruefully. "But then what? It's all I know how to do, Phaedra. I don't know how to farm or be a merchant or a cobbler or an anything. I'm not really a nobleman anymore, not of a country that exists, but I don't know how to *do* anything!"

"You'll find something," she reassured him, "and in the meantime, we wouldn't be here without you. You didn't waste your life."

"My father thought I did," he answered her. "He worried so much about me wasting my life that he went all the way to Laarna to ask the Oracle what to do about me. And I haven't changed at all since then – I'm still doing the same old things. He'd probably be disappointed."

"No, Hunter!" she began, but she did not get to finish,

because just then the door opened and Hindra reappeared.

"The mistress wanted you to have this," the slave said, handing Hunter a small but heavy purse. "Thank you." She closed the door.

"How much was that?" Phaedra asked, as they turned to go.

Hunter glanced inside the purse. "Enough to have kept that horse," he said. It occurred to him that he would never have accepted this money back when he still had his nobleman's dignity. The thought was sad, but oddly freeing. It didn't matter anymore that the gift was a show of superiority: money was money, and the islanders could use however much of it they got.

Phaedra cocked her head to one side. "You're not the same, you know. And you're *not* just doing the same old things. For the Gods' sake, you're rescuing children!"

Hunter sighed. "I still feel the same on the inside. Lost and stupid. You know the happiest moment in my life was the day my father gave me this sword? I wanted a sword so badly. What am I supposed to want now?"

Phaedra shook her head, but she said nothing. Hunter became keenly aware that he was talking all about himself, and had not even asked her how she was faring.

"I'm sorry," he said. "I shouldn't complain so much. I still have my health."

"It's all right," she said to him. "I think you've lost more than I have. You lost your dream. I lost mine too, but I found a better one."

"You did?"

Phaedra nodded. "I'm sure you will too. It just takes time."

Hunter thought about this. He wanted to ask Phaedra what her new dream was, but the moment had passed, so he saved his question for another time. She didn't seem eager to talk about it, not yet anyway. Could she be right about him, though? Would he find another dream?

They slept in Atuna that night, at the same inn where

they had stayed so long ago. Narky objected to staying there, but the others overruled him.

"This was the first place we shared after that awful voyage," Phaedra said. "We have to stay here."

"No," said Narky, "we don't. This is the worst place I can think of to stay on the way to the Oracle of Ravennis. It's… it's bad."

"This is where we're staying," Criton told him. "We're tired, and it's familiar."

Narky kept grumbling, but he had already given up on changing their minds. The next morning, over a breakfast of flat bread and soft sheep's cheese, Phaedra suggested that they make a quick stop at the temple square before heading north toward Laarna.

"We haven't any of us made a sacrifice in a very long time," she said. "If we don't please *some* God, no one will protect us from the ones we've angered."

"That's true," said Narky, "but I want to get to Laarna as soon as possible."

To their surprise, the innkeeper interrupted them. "You're going to Laarna?" he asked, bringing them a new basket of bread and setting it down on the table. "Are you insane?"

"What do you mean?" asked Criton.

The man looked at them in disbelief. "Haven't you heard? Ardis has gone to war against Laarna. You'd be walking right into a battle!"

He left them looking dazedly at each other, wondering what to do next. Hunter saw fear on Criton's face. It seemed the red priest still haunted his dreams.

"We have to go," said Narky.

"Narky, we can't go," Phaedra explained gently. "We can't bring Rakon home to a besieged city! We should wait here until news comes."

Hunter agreed with her, but her words still made him uncomfortable. They reminded him of the last time they had stayed in Atuna – at this very inn – waiting for news.

"I have to go," Narky said. "Ravennis wants me there. If there's a battle going on, I have to join it."

Hunter could hardly believe those words had come from Narky. "You're a brave man," he said.

"No, I'm not," said Narky, wretchedly. "But if my choices are between a battle and a cloud of ravens, I'm going with the battle."

Criton shuddered. "Fair enough."

"I'm sorry," Phaedra said, "but we can't all go with you."

"Where is he going?" asked Delika, looking from one islander to another. The children had been eating with them this whole time, but she had only just started paying attention to the conversation.

"I'll go with you," said Hunter. "We can take a pair of horses and leave the others here in safety."

Criton nodded. "I'll come too. I don't like the idea of you fighting Bestillos alone."

"But where are they going?" Delika asked Phaedra.

"Phaedra can stay," said Bandu. "I go with Criton."

"Bandu, you can't!" Phaedra protested.

"It's too dangerous," Criton told her. "You're pregnant, Bandu. You can't just–"

Bandu stood firm. "Where you go, I go."

"WHERE?" cried Delika. "Where is everyone going?"

"Narky and I are going to Laarna," said Hunter, "to join a battle against Ardis. Criton, I think you'd better stay. Bandu won't let you go without her, and what if we don't come back? Stay here this time. We'll see you in a week or so, Gods willing."

Criton slumped his shoulders, but he didn't object. Hunter and Narky prepared to mount their horses, packing some feed and some dried meats in the saddlebags before setting off. Hunter left the purse, so that the others could stay at the inn during his absence. He also lent Narky his long dagger.

"If we're not back in two weeks," said Narky, "take the kids and go to Silent Hall. Psander's not safe, but she's better than here. We're too close to Mayar here."

Phaedra nodded. "Laarna is a port town too," she pointed out, "and if Ravennis is busy fighting with Magor, He might not have the strength to keep Mayar away from you. Be careful."

They set out midmorning, riding north along the coastal road. The cliffs rose high above the sea here, so for now they allowed themselves to follow the road, keeping an anxious eye on the waters below. When it grew dark they drew away from the cliffs and slept on a mossy bank. It rained during the night, and they awoke wet and frozen, shielding their faces from the droplets and trying to climb back onto their horses in the moonlight. If they could not sleep, at least they could make some progress.

They met a refugee the following day, staggering toward them along the road. "Turn around," urged the young man. His clothes were muddy and torn, and his knees and elbows scraped and bleeding.

"Did you fight in the battle?" asked Hunter.

The man stared back up at him defiantly. "He's a deserter," said Narky.

"We were losing," said the deserter. "There's no honor at the end of the Ardismen's spears."

"When was this battle?" Hunter interrogated him.

"Four days ago," said the man. "The battle was lost, I tell you! The red priest has probably burned the city by now."

They left him there and continued on their way. They did not meet many other refugees. Hunter suspected that armed riders such as Narky and himself would be avoided whenever possible. They did come across a group of ragged women once, and saw some dark-clothed people below them at the base of the cliffs, slogging wearily along the beach. Other than these, the road was empty.

It took them another day and a half to reach Laarna,

crossing through ravaged fields and burnt olive groves. Laarna's olives were well-known even on Tarphae – the loss of these trees would be felt for generations.

At last they found themselves atop a hill, looking down at the smoldering city in the distance. They rode on, their spirits falling. The battle was clearly long over. The battlefield lay well before the open gates, a scavenger's feast of corpses and broken arrows, riderless horses and smashed chariots, tattered standards and bloodied armor. The smell was sickening. Dogs barked and vultures took flight as Hunter and Narky rode among the dead, looking from side to side in horror.

"Look," said Narky.

Hunter followed Narky's finger, and found that it was pointing at a dead raven. Behind it was another. And another.

"The ravens?" asked Hunter.

Narky nodded. "They haven't been shot down. There are no arrows in them."

Hunter felt suddenly cold.

Within the city walls, some buildings were still burning. "Maybe someone is still alive in there," said Narky without hope.

The city turned out to be much like the battlefield, except that the corpses here included women and children, all speared and slaughtered. Hunter and Narky did not go near the docks, but the smoke that rose from that direction told them all they needed to know.

They wandered almost aimlessly through the wreckage of the town until they came to the collapsed building that had once been the Temple of Ravennis. The corpses of two women had been tied high onto the pillars on either side of the entrance. The one on the left had been young and beautiful, Hunter realized with some surprise. The other had been very old, and the ropes that bound her to the pillar had torn her skin. Narky saw them, and his eye filled with tears.

"Seekers of Wisdom," Hunter read above the gateway. "Readers of Fate. These must be the oracle priestesses. My father did say there was more than one."

"There were three," Narky whispered.

"What do you think happened to the last one?" Hunter asked, but Narky just shook his head and wept.

Hunter held out his hand. "Give me the dagger and let's cut them down from there."

They buried the oracles right in front of the temple, in as deep a grave as two men without shovels could dig. When they had finished, they sat down wearily on the temple steps.

Narky wiped his hands on his shirt and gazed about, looking lost. "What the hell happens now?" he asked.

"Now we go back to Atuna," said Hunter, "and we tell them what we saw."

Narky did not argue. They rode back in silence at first, stopping only once to rest their horses. Hunter wondered what they would do with little Rakon, now that his home and family were gone. What would they tell him?

As they were preparing to sleep beside the road, under the shelter of a lone tukka tree, Hunter asked Narky if he thought Ravennis still wanted him to do something.

"Want something?" Narky repeated blankly. He blinked a few times and then shook his head, as if coming out of a reverie. "Ravennis is dead," he said. "When crows fall dead out of the sky, what else could it mean?"

"I don't know," Hunter admitted, "but it's hard to believe."

Narky shook his head angrily. "It's not right. It doesn't make any sense. Ravennis was always there. He gathered us together, He sent us away from Tarphae… He saved me and you from the people we were. How can he be gone? How can the God of Fate be gone?"

Hunter had no answer, so he said nothing. No answer could have satisfied Narky anyway.

They reached Atuna around dinnertime, cold, wet, and hungry. Every head turned their way as they staggered into the inn. Rakon's eyes were already red from crying, but he took one look at them and burst into fresh tears. Apparently, the others already knew about Laarna's fate.

In fact, they knew more than Hunter and Narky did. A group of refugees had arrived in Atuna that morning; Phaedra told them about it over a welcome dinner of hot soup.

"They said that on the Festival of Destiny just under a month ago, the Oracle of Ravennis announced that a time of reckoning was on the horizon, a reckoning of Gods and men. The Gods would each be judged, and Magor would be judged most harshly. The priestesses said that His time was coming to an end. Within the year."

Hunter nodded absently. It was hard to get excited about the Oracle of Ravennis after what he and Narky had seen. "Magor seems to be alive and well so far," he said.

"He may have won the battle," said Phaedra, "but that doesn't mean it won't come true."

Narky turned away, hiding his face.

"Magor didn't win the battle," Hunter told her. "He won the war. Ravennis is gone."

"Gone?" repeated Phaedra.

"Gone. The Ardismen destroyed His temple and tied the dead oracles to its pillars. There were dead ravens all over the battlefield."

Phaedra looked stunned. "Well," she said, "that changes things. That changes things."

"Are you sure that means Ravennis is dead?" asked Criton. "It couldn't just mean He's been injured or something?"

Phaedra shook her head. "If His city is destroyed and His priestesses are dead, and His holy birds are falling dead out of the sky, then Narky has it right. The battles fought here on earth mirror the ones fought in heaven, and Ravennis' city was completely annihilated. The refugees thought the

Ardismen attacked them in order to punish the oracle, but it sounds like it was more than that. They were there to cut off Ravennis' fingers, and Magor did the rest."

Criton folded his arms. "So Ravennis announced that Magor was in trouble, and Magor went and killed Him. You'd think the God of Fate would see that sort of thing coming."

Hunter frowned at him. He thought Criton might be getting back at Narky for an earlier slight, and that bothered him. Narky had just lost his God. This was no time for vindictiveness.

"We're not supposed to outlive Him," Narky mumbled. "It's all wrong."

"That prophecy," Hunter said. "Did they say Ravennis would judge the Gods, or just that they'd be judged?"

"They didn't say," said Phaedra, at the same time as Criton said, "God Most High will judge them." They turned to look at each other, as if engaged in a contest of wills.

"They didn't say," Phaedra repeated again, forcefully.

"They didn't say," Criton admitted. "But it's obvious. He'll arise soon, and then Magor will pay for what He's done."

"But does the prophecy still stand?" asked Hunter. "If the God of Fate is dead, do His words still mean anything?"

"There's no way of knowing," said Phaedra. "They might, but they might easily not. It depends on the nature of this particular prophecy. If Criton's right, and Ravennis was predicting that God Most High would judge the other Gods, then Ravennis' death might have no impact on whether it comes true or not. But the prophecy could have been a boast on Ravennis' part, which would make it meaningless now that He's been defeated."

"Well, we'll have to find Rakon a new home," Hunter pointed out. The children had finished their dinners by now and were all huddling near the fire. Hunter was glad that the innkeeper had warned them away from all going to Laarna together. He shuddered to think that they had almost taken the children to the site of that massacre.

"Would the twins' family take him in?" Criton asked.

Hunter and Phaedra exchanged a glance. "I doubt it," said Phaedra. "They didn't come to the door themselves, even after they knew we'd brought the children back. We only spoke to a slave."

To Hunter's surprise, Criton gasped in shock. "They have slaves here? Real slaves?" He shook his head in wonderment, and – was that disgust?

"My mother used to tell me stories where the villains had slaves," he said. "I thought they were made up!"

"No," said Phaedra, "slaves are real."

Hunter nodded, relieved that she hadn't elaborated. The cooks and cleaners of House Tavener had all been slaves.

"So where now?" asked Narky, sounding as though he had very little interest in the answer.

The others all looked at each other. "Adla and Temena live near Ardis," Hunter said. "It might not be safe to go there. And Caldra and Delika don't exactly know where they live. We might have to find them all new homes, not just Rakon."

"We could ask the villagers at Silent Hall to take them in," Phaedra suggested. "But we might be able to bring Adla and Temena home, depending on how close it is to Ardis and what side it's on. Adla, do you know where your village is, compared to Ardis?"

Adla came over to them cautiously. "I don't know," she said. "It's close to the tune."

"What tune?" asked Narky. "What are you talking about?"

"That cave," she answered, "where the dragon man died. The tune."

Criton sucked in his breath. "She means the Dragon Knight's Tomb," he said, not even trying to conceal his excitement. "That's it – that's where we're going."

50
Bandu

Bandu felt the little arm pressing out against her belly, and she smiled. It felt funny and happy and alive, and it kept her from worrying. Goodweather was living and growing. So was Bandu.

They went the way Criton said, toward Ardis. After a few days of travel, they found the army's trail. It was wide and muddy, covered in food scraps and horse droppings and broken things that the Ardismen had thrown away. They tried to keep away from the trail, since they didn't want any scouts to notice them following it, but sometimes they would go over a hill or come out of a wood and there it would be again, a winding river of ugliness.

The men took turns walking, since they only had four horses now. They didn't have to hunt, at least, because Phaedra had bought them plenty of food in Atuna. She had also bought a wide canvas sail and some rope for them to use as a tent, which annoyed Hunter until the next time it rained. After that, he didn't complain about the money.

The journey was easy enough on her body, but it was still hard on her. She worried about Criton. He always said he loved her, but she didn't see it in his eyes anymore. At night, he didn't try to pull her away from the tent to mate, and he didn't seem to like it when she pulled at him instead. It frustrated her, because she did not want him any less than she had before. If anything, she wanted him more. But now, now that his young was starting to grow heavy, he turned away from her. He even closed his eyes when they mated.

She wanted to speak to Phaedra about it, but she never got the opportunity. Phaedra didn't want to talk about those things in front of the little ones, and they were always there, of course. One night, when Criton had already slunk away from her to fall asleep, she tried to wake Phaedra up to talk. Phaedra moaned and waved her away and didn't even open her eyes. Bandu sighed and lay down. It was a lonely time, even with a new person living in her belly.

She blamed Criton. He had promised to take care of her! Wicked man. She wished she could throw him away and want someone else instead, but she couldn't. Phaedra would have said it was because Bandu had promised not to, but that was wrong. It wasn't because of a silly promise. The trouble was that she loved him.

What was the matter with him? Maybe Phaedra would say that all men did this sometimes. Maybe she would say that Bandu should stay away from him again, as she had done at Silent Hall when Criton had first learned about the young. Maybe she would say… Bandu did not know what Phaedra would say. She wished she could find out.

They traveled another week, and Bandu could not take it anymore. She left him in the tent with the others, and walked out into the night. The woods welcomed her with that same comforting wind that once sung her to sleep. She found a guardian tree and looked up into its branches in the moonlight, her heart filling with sadness. She couldn't climb anymore, not with such a big belly. She was wider to the front than to the sides.

She missed Four-foot. He had never turned on her or rejected her, or made her feel so stupid for loving him. She wanted him back. When would Psander bring him back to her? He had been her only friend, but together they had been a pack. What was she with Criton?

She walked on until she reached a narrow brook. She had swum across a river once, to find him. What had made her so sure of herself?

She could hear him behind her now, crashing through the woods. "Bandu!" he was yelling. "Bandu! Where the hell are you?"

She waited for him to find her. When he panted into sight, she asked, "What is the hell?"

He shook his head at her furiously. "Why did you run off, so late at night? You could be eaten by animals, or captured by Ardismen – is that what you want?"

"I want you care about me!" she snapped at him. "You only care if I am dead?"

"Of all the stupid–" he began.

"You are stupid!" she shouted. "Always you want to learn about family, learn about family. Dragons not your family, stupid Criton!"

He slapped her with the back of his claw and she fell into the shallow water. She tried to jump to her feet, but she misjudged her weight and splashed right back down again. The stones at the bottom dug into her backside. She began to cry. "You are a wicked man!" she sobbed.

"I'm – I'm sorry," he said. He sounded shocked.

"You are wicked," she repeated, her tears dropping noiselessly into the stream. "Like your father."

Criton stepped forward, and his body blocked out the moon so that she could not see his expression. "I have no father," he said.

She smacked her hand against the water. "Everyone has father," she hissed. "You think everything only how you want. You don't love him so you say you don't have father. You don't love me so you say you don't have wife."

Criton didn't say anything for a moment, only knelt before her and held out his hand. "I do love you," he said finally, steadying his voice. "I'm sorry. I'm sorry. Please get up."

She did not take his hand, but stood up carefully on her own. "Why you don't want me?" she asked him.

"I do," he said, lying. "It's just – I'm not used to this."

"You are stupid," she told him.

"Yes," he agreed. "I am. I'm sorry I hit you. Please forgive me."

"No," she said. "You are bad to me. I don't forgive."

Criton sighed. "All right," he said. "But will you come back to camp with me?"

She shook her head.

"I'm sorry I hit you," he said again. "You're right about what I'm becoming. I don't know what got into me, I just couldn't… I lost control. I'll be good to you from now on. I want you to always be happy and I don't want… I don't want you to ever be afraid of me."

Why did she want to forgive him already? She shouldn't forgive – she knew she shouldn't. It was dangerous. She should tell the others and keep away from him, and bear her young on her own. If he could hit her once, he could hit her again. He could hit their young.

She fought with herself as he went on apologizing. He would never change. How could he change? His insides were angry. They always had been. What would it mean, if she forgave him? Would their young grow up to be angry like him? Would Goodweather say, 'I have no father'?

She followed him back to the camp, and sat while he built up the fire for her to dry herself. She knew she could not trust him, even though he was being good to her now. She knew it, but it did her no good. She needed Phaedra's help. She could not stay angry on her own.

He was a good man; that was the trouble. A good man, but a bad husband.

What should she do? She knew he would protect her and her young – from everyone but himself. Was that good enough?

She slept poorly that night, and not only because Goodweather kicked every time she lay down. She did not know what to do about Criton, and it frightened her. It frightened her to think of living without him as a mate, and it frightened her to think that he might hit her again. If he was not careful with those claws, one blow might kill. She trusted that he would try not to do it again, but could she trust him to succeed?

She dreamt that Goodweather grew to be a strong boy and that he and Criton were fighting. She feared for them both, but all she could do was watch them try to kill each other, hoping that they would fail. When she awoke, heart pounding, Goodweather was stirring inside her. She sat for a time, listening to the wind as it rustled against the canvas. Would her nightmares come true again? The wind gave no indication.

They rode onward, and this time it was Bandu who avoided Criton. He kept looking at her, longing and ashamed, while she tried to keep her gaze on the trees and hills ahead. She worried any minute that she might relent, but the hours went on and still she held strong. He had hit her, she kept reminding herself. She had to protect Goodweather.

The movements of the horse rocked her young to sleep while she rode, and Bandu only felt the little limbs within her when they stopped to eat.

"I think we're getting close," said Hunter. "We've gone a long way. I'm surprised we haven't come across any villages yet."

"There's smoke to the southwest," Phaedra pointed out. "That might be a village, or maybe even Anardis."

"Or a forest fire," said Narky.

"Which side of Ardis is your town on?" Criton asked Temena.

Temena shrugged. "We don't go to Ardis," she said. "Only Pa goes. He goes away in the morning and comes back at night."

"When he goes away in the morning," asked Hunter, "what side is the sun on?"

The two girls looked at each other. "That way," said Adla, waving her arm leftward. "I think."

"North of Ardis," said Criton. "We should start heading a little northwards now."

"Assuming the girls don't have it backwards," Narky added.

"Ardis is near the upper edge of the mountains," Hunter said. "I don't remember exactly, but I thought I saw a marker for a tomb on one of Psander's maps, northwest of the city. It might have been a badly drawn hill, though. It wasn't one of the better maps."

Phaedra sighed wistfully. "I wish we had Psander's maps with us," she said. "Actually, I wish we had Psander too. I have so many questions to ask her now, about Ravennis and prophecies."

Criton nodded. "Agreed."

"We don't need Psander," said Bandu. "Psander lies."

"That's not fair," protested Phaedra.

"It *is* fair," Bandu replied. Psander had said she would find a way to bring back Four-foot. That lie had never hurt more than it did now. "Psander is a liar," she repeated. "A wicked liar."

No one argued with her further. Phaedra knew she would never convince her, and Criton was afraid to argue. And Narky probably agreed with her.

Narky was starting to recover himself, Bandu thought. He was beginning to talk almost like his usual self again. Phaedra noticed too. She asked him once, gently, how he was dealing with Ravennis' death.

"Maybe He isn't dead after all," Narky said. "One of the oracles was missing."

Phaedra did not say anything. Narky's spirit was weak right now; she must have decided it was best to let him believe what he wanted.

They rode on, and soon the mountains became visible through the trees. "We're close," Hunter said that evening, while he and Narky were putting up their tent between two trees. "Just so long as we stay away from Ardis and its army, we'll be fine."

There was a warm wind tonight, unusually warm for the season. Criton nodded his head in sleepy agreement. "As long as Bestillos doesn't catch wind of us, we're all right. When we get closer to the sisters' village, I'll disguise myself and bring the children there alone."

He yawned. "If I can, I'll leave them all there while we explore the Dragon Knight's Tomb. No sense in having them underfoot."

They finished with the tent, and Bandu lay down underneath the canvas. The warm weather was making her drowsy. Even Goodweather did not awaken, despite her lack of motion. Good. She needed some sleep.

The men did not even build a fire that night. The travelers all joined Bandu in the tent and lay their weary heads on the moss and grass and dried guardian tree spines. *Go to sleep,* the wind seemed to whisper to them. *You're all tired. Go to sleep.*

Bandu startled for a moment, already beginning to dream. Something was not right. Was it her imagination, or had the grass been stroking her hair on purpose? For a moment she hung between sleep and wakefulness, unsure where reality ended and her dreams began. But the air felt so warm, and her young so peaceful and still, that she soon closed her eyes again. Bandu drifted off to sleep, and doubted no more.

51
Hunter

The woods were calling to him in a lady's voice. *Hunter,* they murmured. *I am here. Come to me.*

He rose dreamily to his feet, looking down for a moment without comprehension at the sword and armor that still lay on the ground. *Leave them there,* whispered the voice. *You won't need them. Come and find me.*

He did as she asked, picking his way over his sleeping companions and stepping out into the cool woods. The warmth of the night had subsided, though the chill was not enough to bother him. He followed the lady's voice to a little stream, where he saw the moon reflected in a thousand ripples. *Just a little farther,* said the voice. *I am here.*

Hunter took off his ragged shoes and stepped barefoot through the shallow waters, crossing over to the other side. He walked as far as the treeline, guardian tree spines sticking to his feet. The night grew darker and darker. When he looked up, the moon had disappeared.

There was a splash from behind him. Hunter spun around, tripping over his feet in the dark, and fell to his knees. A woman was standing in the brook, her skin and her robe shining such a brilliant white that for a moment Hunter thought the moon had come to earth.

"You are Hunter," the woman said. Her voice rippled in the air, and he heard her as much with his skin as with his ears.

"I am," he responded, his voice sounding faint and distant in comparison.

"You may rise," she said, turning her palm upward in a regal gesture. He stood, compelled.

"Come back to the water," she said, beckoning.

Hunter did as he was told. When he stepped into it this time, the water had grown strangely cold. "Why am I here?" he asked.

"You are delivering something for me," the woman said.

Hunter nodded, his throat dry. "What?" he croaked.

The shining lady took Hunter's wrist in her left hand, twisting outward so that his fingers uncurled themselves. When he blinked, her right hand held a flower. She placed it in his palm.

"This is for my love," she said. "Take it to him, that he may not forget his promise. I have not forgotten mine."

"Where do I find him?" Hunter asked. "What is his promise?"

"Take it to him," the woman repeated.

Hunter awoke with Criton pulling him out of the stream.

"Hunter!" cried Phaedra. "He's alive!"

"Where is she?" Hunter sputtered. "Where did she go?"

"It's a miracle you fell face up," Criton told him. "What were you doing out here?"

He sat Hunter down on the water's edge, and the others all gathered round. Even the children were there. Hunter wondered why that surprised him. He supposed he'd forgotten they existed.

"There was a lady," Hunter told them. "She glowed white."

The others looked at each other in alarm. "A fairy," said Narky. "There are supposed to be water fairies too, you know. They drown people."

"She gave me a flower," said Hunter, looking down at his hands. His right hand still held the white rose.

"Give it here," commanded Criton. "If a fairy gave it to you, it's probably dangerous."

"I don't think she was a fairy," he protested, still holding on tight. The lady had given it to *him*. Only he was meant to carry it. "She didn't feel like a fairy. And she didn't try to kill me or anything."

"We found you in the river," Narky pointed out. "I don't think we can assume she meant you no harm."

"Did she say anything to you?" asked Phaedra.

Hunter nodded. "She said the flower was for her lover, and she said something about a promise. I think I'll hold onto it until we find him."

Bandu knelt to inspect the flower. "You know where he is? Who is he?"

Hunter shook his head. "I don't know. I did ask where he was, but then I woke up here."

"Is he all right?" asked Rakon.

"Yes," said Phaedra. "Yes, he's fine." She didn't sound convinced. "We should take watches when we sleep. This shouldn't happen again."

Narky glanced about, searching for something. "Where are your shoes?"

Hunter looked down at his bare feet in mild surprise. "I don't know," he said. "They must have been washed downstream."

"Not need shoes," said Bandu. "Need to go. This is not a safe place."

"I'll walk this time," Criton offered. "You ride."

When they broke from the treeline later that day, they found the Calardian range much closer than Hunter expected. The mountains rose halfway into the sky, and Hunter could even see Ardis at their base when he squinted. The army's trail wound toward the city, its track of mud and litter visible for miles.

There was no way to avoid being seen, traveling as they were through vineyards and farmland. The best they could do was to stay as far as they could from the shepherds and the farmers along the way, hoping in vain not to stand out too much. It was no good: a band of islanders and continental children all riding together were bound to turn heads. But Hunter's armor still glinted in the sunlight, and for now, nobody stopped them.

It took them a full day's travel to reach Adla and Temena's village. "All right," Criton said, when they were perhaps a mile away. "You all wait here, and I'll take the children the rest of the way. Hopefully the girls' parents won't mind watching the other three while we go to the tomb."

His skin and hair transformed themselves as he spoke. By the time he took Caldra and Temena's hands and began to walk toward the village, he looked as blond and northern as they did.

They waited tensely for Criton's return, growing more nervous with each passing minute. What could be delaying him so long? Perhaps the red priest had been awaiting him in the village. Or had word not yet reached the Temple of Magor that a group of islanders had been seen traipsing about with a crowd of continental children in tow? How long would it take before the riders came upon them, or before some enterprising farmers decided to capture the Tarphaeans by themselves?

And still Criton did not come. Hunter nervously loosened his sword in its sheath, his eyes scanning the horizon. No soldiers yet. Wait, what were those spots in the distance? Riders? Oh, no, never mind. On second glance, they looked more like sheep.

At long last Criton appeared. "What took you so long?" Narky nearly shouted at him when he arrived.

"I'm sorry," said Criton. "When I brought Adla and Temena to their parents, the girls' father said his sister was barren, and maybe she and her husband would want to raise the other three as their own; but she was out at market, and her husband was off digging a well with his brother, so… right, that's not really important. The point is, we don't have to pick them up again when we come back. They've been adopted! That's worth waiting for, isn't it?

"And," he went on enthusiastically, "I got directions to the Dragon Knight's Tomb. Adla's father said we could reach it by nightfall if we rode hard."

"Right," said Hunter. "Climb on."

They rode for the mountains, but fast as they went, the sun set well before they arrived.

"Hold on," said Criton. "I've practiced this." He held out his palm, and a small pinkish light appeared there. He blew on it gently, as if reviving an ember, and it brightened before their eyes.

"That should do," he said. "Hopefully we'll be there soon."

It didn't take long after that. They reached the mountain where Salemis had lived just as the moon became visible over the mountains. They rode up as far as they could, then dismounted and led their horses the rest of the way. When they reached the cave mouth, they tied their mounts to a few saplings and entered in the dark.

The cavern was large and their footfalls echoed loudly and unevenly. For a moment, Hunter was sure he heard someone else moving up ahead. He peered into the darkness, but it was no good: Criton's light had grown weaker, and it only shone brightly enough for them to avoid stumbling on the rough floor. There were deep gouges in the stone where perhaps a dragon's claws had once dug in, and the cave floor had a slight downward slope. After some mostly aimless wandering, they found an area of even ground on which to lay their blankets.

Hunter's ears strained to hear those other footfalls, but he heard nothing. He took a deep breath and let it out slowly. He was imagining things. Just because they were close to Ardis did not mean that the High Priest of Magor was around every corner.

It was odd, though – once they had all settled themselves on the floor, he thought he could hear someone's shallow breathing coming from a little further into the cave. But when he sat up, he didn't hear it anymore. He stayed there, listening silently, until his sleepy mind began to wander and his eyes started to shut of their own accord. As a last precaution, he leaned forward and laid his armor out on the ground before him. If anyone approached in the night to kill them in their sleep, maybe the sound of the murderer stumbling over the armor would awaken him. It was the best he could do, for now. He fell asleep with sword in hand.

52
Narky

They awoke at dawn with the sun in their eyes. The cave's entrance stood in the east, and the rays poured in upon them and their surroundings almost blindingly. Narky rose, blinking, and looked around.

Ever since he had lost his eye, distances had become very hard to judge. Even so, the cave seemed awfully big to him. It must extend halfway into the mountain, he thought.

"Well," said Hunter with relief. "We survived the night."

"Of course we did," said Criton, his eyes glowing. "Now let's find Salemis! If the Dragon Knight started and ended his quest here, he must have believed this was the most likely place to find the Dragons' Prisoner."

Criton's face was overflowing with confidence, and Narky felt a little ashamed. What made Criton think that he could succeed where the famous Dragon Knight had failed? The prophecy, that was what. The one that Narky had suggested was about them. Now he worried that he had gotten Criton's hopes up for nothing. Yes, it seemed the islanders had been a part of Ravennis' plan – but so had been the judgment of Magor. Apparently, Ravennis had not been as powerful or all-knowing as Narky had thought.

"You think we can find a path to Salemis here in this

cave?" Narky asked. "All we have to go on is that Phaedra thinks he's in the fairy world. And I don't know about you, but I don't ever want to go there again."

"There's the knight's tomb," said Phaedra, pointing. "We should start there."

Narky followed her finger with his eyes. Far ahead, deeper in the cave, stood a stone sarcophagus made of the same color rock as the rest of the place. It had blended in so well that Narky hadn't even noticed it until Phaedra pointed it out. For that, Narky cursed his missing eye again. Even as he stared straight at it, the tomb seemed to disappear into the background.

"That's strange," Hunter said, as they approached. "I thought the Dragon Knight died with only that one friend beside him. There's no way he made that sarcophagus all on his own."

"He didn't," Phaedra assured him. "The assistant covered his body with stones, but the Dragon Touched later transferred the remains to this sarcophagus. Caruther described the Dragon Knight's Tomb toward the end of his scroll. He wrote that the Ardisian Dragon Touched made copies of the knight's journal, and then laid the original in the tomb with him. It's too bad we can't take a look inside."

"Why we can't look?" asked Bandu.

Phaedra opened her mouth to respond, then shut it again. In the meantime, Hunter walked slowly around the tomb, frowning. "Did the scroll say anything about people giving the knight tribute after his death?"

"No," said Phaedra. "Why?"

"Because," said Hunter, stooping behind the tomb, "there's a cup of wine here."

He rose and placed it on the tomb, a goblet of green blown glass, elaborately etched. "I *thought* I heard someone here last night."

Narky ran his hand along the top of the sarcophagus. "There are some wax drippings on here," he noted.

"Someone was doing a whole ritual before we came by."

Phaedra shivered. "Maybe they were trying to speak with the dead."

"Or command them," Narky suggested. "I wouldn't put it past the Ardismen."

"No," said Phaedra, "not the Ardismen. Whoever it was wasn't supposed to be here – otherwise, they wouldn't have hidden from us. Maybe it was a wizard."

Hunter looked surprised. "I thought Psander was supposed to be the only wizard left."

"No," Phaedra said, "she's just the only *academic* left. Don't you remember? She said that the other people who call themselves wizards these days are fools, and don't know anything about magic theory."

"No wizard could live out here," said Criton. "The red priest of Ardis would catch them. He has the Wizard's Sight. He was ready to kill me the moment he saw me."

"Ardis is close," answered Phaedra, "but it's not as if this place is on the way from there to… well, to anywhere, really. I doubt that Bestillos visits the tomb very often. If the wizard goes into hiding whenever he hears someone coming, he could avoid the priest for years."

Criton didn't look particularly satisfied with that answer, but he let it go.

"Well," said Narky, "whoever it was, he's not here now. The important thing is to finish whatever it is we're doing and leave before the priest finds out we're here. So what's the plan? Are we opening this coffin?"

The others all looked to Phaedra. "Wouldn't that anger the Gods?" Hunter asked.

Phaedra hesitated. "I don't know," she said slowly. "I don't *think* so. The only God who would care, I'd think, would be God Most High, and He's supposed to be dormant. If He is, we should be perfectly safe. And even if He awakens, He might not mind so much as long as we don't desecrate or rob the body. If what we're trying to do is find and free

Salemis His prophet, it's probably all right for us to do everything within our means. We should make a sacrifice to Him afterwards though, if Criton can go back into town and buy us an animal."

"All right," said Criton. "Let's do this then."

It took all three of the men, struggling mightily, to lift the stone slab off the top of the sarcophagus and slide it onto the floor. It landed and tipped over with a terrifying crash that made Narky jump.

"Well," he said, "if there's anyone nearby, they won't have missed that."

The Dragon Knight's bones lay still clad in his armor. The armor was made of interlocking bronze plates that were probably meant to resemble dragon scales. An enormous sword lay diagonally across the body, positioned that way so that it could fit into the sarcophagus. Narky gasped despite himself. Even so long after his death, the Dragon Knight made for an imposing figure.

Just as Phaedra had said, a leather-bound codex lay under the knight's right hand. She stared at it there for a moment before raising her eyes to the cave's ceiling.

"O God Most High," she said. "O God of Dragons, we ask for Your patience, and lenience, and forgiveness for what we are about to do."

She took a deep breath, and reached for the book. Slowly and carefully, she lifted one side of the volume. The bones slid off, clattering haphazardly against steel and stone. They didn't really resemble a hand any more, Narky thought. He considered putting the bones back in order, but then thought better of it. It was probably best just to pretend they looked fine.

Phaedra stepped away from the sarcophagus and opened the book. "What does it say?" Narky asked her.

She waved him away. "It'll take time to get through all this," she said.

Narky sighed and turned away. He had expected the

worst when they decided to come this close to Ardis, but he hadn't expected to feel bored. He spent the morning sitting at the mouth of the cave while Criton went to buy a sacrificial animal and Hunter rode off to live up to his name. Bandu sat beside Narky for a while, but as neither of them felt like starting a conversation with the other, she soon left to start one with the horses.

Hunter returned first, then Criton. After eating, they sacrificed Criton's goat on a makeshift altar, burning the entire carcass upon Phaedra's suggestion. Narky didn't argue, but he secretly wondered what difference it would make. What was the chance that a single improper sacrifice would wake a sleeping God?

Narky was still thinking about the likely pointlessness of their sacrifice when Phaedra suddenly said, "That's her! It has to be. Hunter, this is amazing!"

They all turned to her in surprise, and she began to read aloud. "Again I asked, from whence came the Dragon Touched? How could humans, children of the Gods, ever have bred with creatures whose strength was enough to fell those who dwell in the heavens? It is impossible. The human frame is too weak. But now the answer seems clear to me: the Dragon Touched did not come from a union of dragon and man. They came from a union between dragon and God.

"Can there have been any greater crime than the coupling of a dragon and a Goddess? For I am now sure that this was the Prisoner's crime. Why else would Gods and dragons come together to punish him?"

"Which Goddess was it?" asked Hunter.

"I'm getting there," Phaedra answered.

"Well, get there faster," said Narky.

"Fine," she huffed. "I'll skip ahead. Let's see... all right. 'The mention of Tarphae's children in the Book of Awakenings suggests to me that the Goddess in question may have been Karassa.'"

"WHAT?" Criton exploded. "*Karassa*?"

Phaedra nodded vigorously. "Isn't that amazing? Apparently this Book of Awakenings was an ancient dragon text, full of myths and prophecies. So he thinks that Karassa was Salemis' lover! Do you realize what that means?"

"That the plague *was* meant to kill us after all," said Narky. "If the other Gods suspected that a group of Tarphaeans would free Salemis, they would do their best to kill every last one of us."

Phaedra looked taken aback. "I hadn't even considered that," she said. "What I meant was–"

"That the woman in the forest was Karassa," said Hunter.

Phaedra nodded vigorously. "Exactly. She may always be depicted as green or gray, but a Goddess can appear however She likes. You met a Goddess, Hunter, not a fairy. If Karassa was the mother of the Dragon Touched, then all *kinds* of things start to make sense. For one thing, we know who Her lover is. And it sounds like She expects us to find him!"

Hunter looked confused. "But if Karassa is the mother of the Dragon Touched, how did they all end up in Ardis? Wouldn't Tarphae be their ancestral home?"

"Not necessarily," Phaedra said. "Salemis is the one who was punished, and his home is near Ardis. So maybe he was the one who took ownership of the Dragon Touched to begin with, and they lived near him. The Dragon Knight guessed that the Goddess was Karassa based on entirely different sources from those discussing Salemis' crime. It's possible even the Gods didn't know which of them had created Criton's people."

"Really?" said Narky. "That doesn't seem likely."

"Why not?" she asked. "The Gods can shield people and information from each other. Otherwise, Ravennis could have squashed the red priest before he ever reached Laarna. If a God is protecting someone, it will take a lot to smite him anyway. That's why They rely on people to kill each other most of the time."

"But if all the Tarphaeans are dead except for us and maybe the king, and Criton is the last of the Dragon Touched, then why hasn't some God gone and killed Karassa yet? The plague cut off all her fingers, didn't it?"

"Not if Katinaras was right," said Phaedra. "If Karassa is the major eastern Sea Goddess, Tarphae may mean little to Her. She could have lost a battle at Tarphae without being completely overwhelmed."

"Did the Dragon Knight have any thoughts about how to find Salemis?" Criton asked.

"Nothing we didn't already know about. I still think our best bet is the fairy world, if we could only get there somehow. But if your scroll on numerology was right, then the barrier between the worlds will be unbreakable by now. We've missed the window."

"I don't know," said Narky. "I don't trust that scroll. It said that the barrier only opened every eleven years at the earliest, right? We *know* it was wrong about that. We managed to get back out after only eleven *days*. Bandu, how long were you in the fairies' world the first time before you got away?"

"Eleven months and eleven days before Goodweather says run."

Criton visibly shuddered. "I don't think I'll ever think of that number the same way again. It bothers me every time."

"Right," said Narky, "but my point is, these elevens seem to show up much more often than that scroll said they would. Let's face it: the scroll was wrong. That barrier isn't as strong as everyone thinks."

"Or maybe," suggested Hunter, "it's been getting weaker lately."

"Oh, Gods!" moaned Phaedra. "Don't even say things like that!"

"It's possible," he insisted grimly.

"It is," Criton agreed. "But again, that doesn't help us find Salemis unless we can actually tear the mesh. Bandu, did you ever figure out how to break through?"

Bandu shook her head sadly. "No. I am not strong enough. The elves do it, when they take the nets. Needs strong magic. Speak magic."

"Great," said Narky. "So we're stuck, then."

"There *has* to be a way!" Criton cried in frustration.

Phaedra looked depressed. "If there were, wouldn't the Dragon Knight have found it? He was one of the greatest wizards of his age, and that was before the purge of the academics!"

"There has to be a way," Criton repeated, sounding deflated.

They lapsed into a sullen silence, and Narky's eye was drawn back to the cave. He wondered what made people like Criton keep trying and trying, so long after he had given up on things. He supposed it was his coward's upbringing that kept him from being so optimistic. Still, better *not* to be like Criton, torturing himself over things outside of his control. Whatever Criton's successes, he would never be happy or content.

Then again, would Narky? He couldn't say he'd ever been happy yet. So what advantage had his fatalism ever really given him?

"Karassa's flower," said Hunter suddenly, pulling it from where he had tucked it in under his belt. The rose had not wilted at all since Narky had first seen it.

"She gave it to me because She knew we were looking for Salemis," Hunter said. "It has to be more than just a flower."

They looked at it in wonder. It was like some key, a key to the heavens. "How do we use it?" asked Criton, looking downright greedy.

"I don't know," said Hunter, "but She wouldn't have given it to me unless it was useful."

"Give it to me," said Bandu. She reached out her hand.

Hunter gave it to her. Bandu sniffed it, then knelt down

and ran her hand along the ground. "Not good here," she said. "Dirt is bad here."

She turned, squinting at the mouth of the cave. She pointed upward. "There is better." She put the rose between her teeth and began marching up the slope.

They followed her lead, climbing up the mountainside until Bandu stopped, taking the flower from her mouth and panting heavily. They were standing on the edge of a precipice, right above the cave. Narky could see their horses cropping the scraggly mountain weeds far below.

Bandu knelt again, only inches away from the cliff's edge, and began to dig with her hands.

"Careful," warned Criton. "If you dig too much, it could collapse."

Bandu ignored him. She planted the flower in the rocky ground, propping it upright among the dirt and stones. Then she stepped back.

Nothing happened. "Need something else," said Bandu. "Dirt is right here, dirt is good, but need something else."

"Dragon magic," suggested Phaedra. "If it took a conspiracy between the Gods and the dragons to imprison Salemis, it'll probably take something similar to get him out again."

"So what do I do?" asked Criton. "I don't think I should burn it, should I?"

"Try bleeding on it," Narky suggested. "It seems like the kind of weird thing Psander might have you do."

Criton frowned and looked back to Phaedra, but she only nodded in agreement. He sighed. Wincing, he dug a clawed finger into his left arm. Blood welled up where he had pierced the skin and slowly trickled toward his hand.

"I don't think you scratched deep enough," said Narky. "That's all going to dry up before it even reaches your fingers. Why didn't you start at the wrist?"

"Shut up," said Criton. "You're not the one who has to cut himself."

Narky rolled his eyes. "I'd rather do it right the first time than have to cut myself twice."

Instead of answering, Criton crouched down over the flower and tried to brush it against his arm. It was a clumsy, awkward-looking motion, but he did at least manage to smear a red mark onto the white petals. "There," he said. "What now?"

Phaedra shrugged a little. "I guess we might need something from the fairy side too, if they were in on the conspiracy. Bandu? Can you think of any–"

Without a moment's warning, Bandu squatted by the flower and hiked up her dress. Narky looked away as soon as he could, but he still ended up seeing more than he ever wanted to. When Bandu was done urinating she stood up, looking pleased with herself.

"*That's* what you have for the fairy side?" said Phaedra, shocked. "Bandu, a *Goddess* gave us that flower! That's the most disgusting, irreverent..."

She trailed off, and her eyes widened. The flower was steaming. Vapors billowed up from it and the rose itself seemed to dissolve into the haze. Within minutes, the cloud of steam was so dense and so wide that it hid the mountains from view.

Narky laughed. "I can't believe that worked! Bandu and her magical piss!"

"I think that's a tunnel up there," Criton said.

"Where the cliff was?" asked Hunter.

"Yeah, Criton, you go first," Narky suggested.

"All right," Criton answered, without a trace of humor. "That makes sense. If I fall, I can catch myself and fly back up to join you."

There were no objections. Criton took a couple of small steps forward, obviously trying to muster enough courage to step off the cliff's edge.

"Go ahead," Narky heard him mutter to himself. "Just get this over with."

The fog was so thick now that Narky could hardly even see him as he took his final steps over the edge. He didn't need to. Criton gave a sudden startled cry, immediately followed by a loud thud.

"There's no cliff here," he groaned. "I just tripped on something, that's all. Damn. You'd better watch your step."

Carefully, Narky followed. It was dark in the tunnel, and he found Criton more by feel than by sight. When he did find him, he crouched and helped him to his feet.

"It smells just like Illweather in here," Narky said, sniffing the air. "I hope we don't end up staying long."

"Let's see," said Criton, his pinkish light springing up in his palm.

The tunnel was made entirely of gnarled tree roots. Narky couldn't even see any dirt, though the air was so moist and dank here that dark patches of mildew were visible on every surface.

"Let's go find a dragon," said Narky.

Criton stared at him blankly for a moment. Then, inexplicably, he laughed. "For a moment there," he said, "I thought I was dreaming."

The tunnel stretched endlessly into the distance, fading out of view past the range of Criton's light. When the others had joined them they set off, climbing for hours – or at least it felt that way – over, under, and above the giant tree roots that sometimes appeared right in the middle of the passage. Finally, Hunter held up a hand to stop them.

"Do you hear that?" he asked.

They stopped climbing and listened. At first, Narky could hear nothing. Then he finally noticed the low, rhythmic rumble just at the edge of his hearing.

"What *is* that?"

"It sounds like breathing," said Phaedra. "Salemis must be close."

Narky felt a chill coming over him. "You're sure he won't eat us, right?"

"He won't eat us," said Criton. "Keep going."

The rumbling grew louder as they continued on, like an approaching thunderstorm. With each step Criton became visibly more excited, while Narky only grew more nervous. It had actually been quite comforting to him to think that the giant fire-breathing serpents of yore were extinct.

"I wish my mother could see me," Criton burst out.

Narky only managed a 'huh' in response. The breaths from up ahead were growing ever louder, and for once Narky wished the Gods could see them here. They could use some divine protection right about now.

The tunnel ended abruptly, blocked by a wall of golden scales, each the size of Hunter's lost shield. Narky winced. With each booming breath from above, the scales intermittently strained against the roots, creaking horribly.

"What part of him are we even looking at?" Narky asked.

"I don't know," said Criton. "I'm… what if we can't even wake him?"

"Talk to him," Bandu suggested. "He only listens if you talk."

Criton shook his head, though it seemed more in wonderment than disagreement. "Um," he said, cautiously approaching the heaving wall of scales, "my name is Criton. It's an honor to meet you. I'm one of your… I'm one of the Dragon Touched. A descendant. My mother's name was Galanea–"

"No, no," said Bandu. "Like this." She walked up to the wall and pressed her palm against one of the scales. "We are here," she said. "Wake up. We are here to help you."

Even Narky could feel her magic this time, rippling out through her hand and pouring from her mouth, filling all the air with its current. Gods, but that was strong. Psander must have been right about pregnancies and magic. Narky made a note to himself not to cross Bandu if he could help it.

With a terrible groan from the passage walls, the dragon stirred.

53
Salemis

He dreamt that he had been buried alive, and when he awoke he found that it was true. The roots of the Gods' ancient nemesis entwined him, coaxing him even now to close his eyes once more and sleep, sleep forever. But no. Someone had called him. After all these years, someone had finally come.

The prophet shook himself free of the plant beast's spell and snapped off the roots that had wormed their way into his mouth. "Make room," he suggested to his captor. Then he lit the roots ablaze.

The walls of his prison retreated before him, and he shook himself free. His whole body ached. He stretched his wings until they touched against the ceiling, uncurled his tail, and craned his neck until it made a satisfying cracking sound. Then he looked around to find the ones who had woken him.

They were there, five tiny human figures cowering in a nook by his side. One had scales and claws and smelled of fire. Salemis smiled to see one of his love children here. Yet it was not the dragon child that had awoken him – it was the little pregnant one. There was something about all five of them that seemed strangely familiar, as if he had dreamt of them once but could not remember the dream. As he looked down at them, straining his mind to recall the dream in question, he realized that they were afraid.

"Don't be frightened," he told them. "Speak."

Still they stood, petrified, until one of the males spoke up in the high pitched tongue of humankind. "Well, Criton," he said. "You're the one who wanted to meet a dragon. Say something."

The dragon child Criton took a deep breath, but still said nothing. Finally, he burst out, "I've been looking for you all my life."

Salemis was amused. All his life? How old was this child?

"I have been here a long time," Salemis told him. "How long have you been searching?"

"Since I was small," said the child. "At least eleven or twelve years."

Eleven or twelve years! How sweet its earnestness!

"I believe I have been here a good deal longer than that," Salemis said gently.

"We know," said one of the females, a maiden. "You've been here almost four hundred years, since before the war."

The prophet felt his spirits sink. He had almost forgotten. "The war that killed my kin," he said grimly.

"How did you know about that?" asked the one who had goaded Criton.

"For many years," Salemis told them, "it was all I dreamed of. I felt it when Hession slew Caladoris, and I felt it when Hession fell. I felt all of them."

His words hung heavily in the air. "That is all long gone," he said at last. "And there is one whose death I anticipated, but never felt. How fares my love?"

"She lives," said the other human male, the one who had so far been silent. "She spoke to me in a river, and gave me a flower that helped us reach you here. She asked me – well, commanded me, to tell you that She had not forgotten Her promise, and that you should keep yours."

Salemis felt a flood of relief at his words. "She is well then," he said. "That is all that matters."

"I don't know that She's well," said the blunt one, the one with only one eye. "There was a plague on Tarphae. We're all that's left of Her people there."

"Tarphae?" asked Salemis.

"Karassa's island," the maiden clarified.

An image of Karassa swam into his mind, tall and gray like an angry wave. "What were my love's people doing there?" he asked.

"We lived there," answered the blunt one, as if this was somehow obvious. Salemis found it altogether puzzling. For one thing, he did not understand why this purebred human would include himself among his love's people. And what could have brought them – all of them – to Karassa's island?

"We were lucky to have been on a boat to Atuna that day," said the maiden, trying to explain. "The plague struck during Karassa's festival. We were the only ones who escaped, other than the king. We don't know what happened to him."

"Until Karassa gave me the flower," said the quiet male, "we thought She might be gone too."

The truth suddenly struck Salemis, so hard that he nearly bathed them in mirthful flames. "Karassa is not my love," he told his confused visitors.

"What?" cried the maiden. "Then who was it that gave Hunter the flower?"

"Eramia, of course," said Salemis. Her name flowed so sweetly off his tongue. "Eramia is Love Herself, and Her people are my people: the dragon children, whom we made together."

The humans all looked at each other, their expressions revelatory. "Eramia," breathed the one-eyed male.

The quiet male, Hunter, turned to the maiden. "But if it's this Love Goddess and not Karassa who sent us here, does that still explain the plague on Tarphae? I'm confused."

"Me too," the maiden admitted. She turned back to Salemis. "Were we at least right about the Dragon Touched? Did the dragons and the Gods punish you for fathering them?"

"They did."

He did not elaborate, and the little ones had the grace not to press him. Even now that they were all gone, his kin's betrayal stung. He wondered if the war had been their punishment.

He looked down at the one called Criton, and at the human girl who, from the smell of her, carried Criton's child. *Is this what You meant,* he wondered, *when You said that my people would live on until the world's end?*

God Most High did not respond. He so rarely did. *I thought You meant the dragons,* Salemis silently admonished Him.

"Um, Salemis?" asked Criton suddenly. "Is God Most High asleep? He hasn't been active since they imprisoned you."

"The Gods do not sleep," the prophet answered him, "least of all God Most High. But even so, one might never see His works in a lifetime. To Him, the ages of the world pass in the blink of an eye. The lives of humans could pass as if unnoticed."

"But you're His prophet," Criton said. "If you come back with us, that should get His attention well enough, right?"

Salemis pulled idly at a root. "The sky between the worlds is too strong for me," he explained gently. "Eramia's help might have been enough to open a crack for you to slip through, but I am far too big for that. It took the entire Draconic Council and three powerful Gods to send me here, and that was with help from the Yarek."

The humans looked at each other in confusion. "What is Yarek?" asked the pregnant one.

Salemis gazed down at her with tenderness. "Before this world came to be," he told her, "the Yarek was the Gods' greatest enemy. God Most High defeated the Yarek in ancient times and tore its body and soul in two. Then He built the first world out of His adversary's body, upon these roots that form the world's skeleton. The Gods and my kin brought me here, but it is the Yarek that opened its arms to imprison me. Above the ground, its kind and cruel halves hold an unending rivalry; but down here, all the roots intertwine."

The girl nodded. "Goodweather and Illweather," she said.

"Yes," Salemis agreed. "So they call themselves now. But in their dreams, they are one. They have been growing stronger since I was banished here, feeding off me as I slept. Even if I had once had the strength to tear through the mesh myself, I cannot do so now."

The maiden shook her head in frustration. "Surely there must be *some* way to get you out of here! Eramia wants you back, I'm sure. Maybe if you threaten Illweather, it will help too."

These humans were so sweet in their optimism! Their determination made Salemis feel sad and old. "No," he told the maid. "I do not have the power that the council had, nor does Eramia have the power of the three Gods who imprisoned me. If we relied on the Yarek's power to make up the difference, it would gain a toehold in your world. Its power is best left contained."

"What about Goodweather?" asked the pregnant one. "Goodweather is kind to me. If Goodweather has toes in our world, it is not bad."

Salemis remained silent, considering. "Possibly," he said at last. "But even with help from the Yarek's kinder half, it would take more than Eramia's working to part the sky widely enough for me to fit through. God Most High could do it single-handedly, if He would, but that is not His way. He demands much from His followers. You would need to go back and find more help."

"Psander could help," said the one-eyed one.

"Why would she?" asked the quiet male. "We'd have to

be able to offer her something."

"She's desperate to keep out of the Gods' sight," the loud one replied. "If she thought she could climb in here while Salemis was climbing out, she'd be sure to help us tear the mesh."

"Narky!" cried the maiden. "You wouldn't trick her into coming *here*? To the fairies' world? It's more dangerous than home!"

"Not for her," said the one called Narky. "How long do you really think she can stay out of the Gods' sight? If Eramia's been watching us for any length of time, She's seen us disappear whenever we reach Silent Hall. Ravennis probably knew about Psander for months, and it was just her luck that He didn't want to do anything about it. I think she'll jump at the chance to get away from the Gods once and for all."

They were seductive, these little ones. Salemis was starting to believe that he might once again walk the earth, and see Eramia face to face. They could resume their marriage where they had left off – no longer in secret, but standing proud before the heavenly council with God Most High as their protector.

Salemis could see his return in his mind's eye. The lower Gods would be disorganized now – They would not be able to contain him. The Gods had not known cooperation since the war. He had dreamt of their struggles with each other, and his dreams never lied.

No, with Eramia at his side and God Most High above, Salemis would never again find himself outmatched. Caladoris, Pelthas and Magor had caught him off-guard last time, it was true. But Caladoris was gone now, and it had taken the Mountain God's special genius to bring the Gods of Justice and the Wild together.

Here he stopped himself. Could this really be what God Most High wanted? For the sky's barrier to weaken and the worlds to intermingle? For the Yarek, long defeated, to rise again in the new world?

The humans had continued talking while Salemis sank into his thoughts, and when he emerged, the boy called Narky was crossing his arms and smiling.

"You have to admit it's about us, though," he said. "If Salemis doesn't count as Criton's true sire, I don't know who would."

True sire. The words were so familiar, somehow. Yes! He *had* dreamt of these children before – but that must have been hundreds of years ago! He remembered it well now: a human knight had come searching for him in his dreams, dying and desperate. The words had come to Salemis then, and he had relayed them to the dying knight. A set of verses, yes. What had they been? In his dream-state it had all seemed so clear.

"We talk to Goodweather," the pregnant girl said. "He helps us. Goodweather is kind – is not bad in our world. Better than Gods."

"Don't say that, Bandu," the girl Phaedra scolded her. "Goodweather might be the good half, but it's still half of a primordial beast. If it took God Most High to defeat it, then even the good half would be dangerous in our world."

"Worse than Magor?" the girl retorted. "Worse than Mayar? Gods are not so good. Gods hate us. Goodweather saves me. Goodweather is my friend."

"God Most High will judge the other Gods soon," said Criton. "That's what the Oracle of Ravennis said."

"Maybe Goodweather is part of the judgment," one-eyed Narky suggested. "Or maybe Salemis is. Bandu is right – our lives under the Gods haven't been all that great. They certainly haven't been safe. If Goodweather is as kind as Illweather was awful, then its presence can only be an improvement. Besides, our prophecy was about changing the world, wasn't it? 'Ending one age and beginning another,' or however it was that that scroll put it. So let's do it! If Salemis' return will wake up God Most High, with us on His good side, I say we do whatever it takes to make that happen."

"It's not just about our benefit," answered Phaedra, but she didn't rebut him further.

"I trust Bandu's judgment," said Criton, giving the girl a longing look that Salemis found curious.

"All right," said the male they called Hunter. "How would we get to Goodweather, to ask for its help?"

"The Yarek can hear us as we speak," Salemis told him. "We need only ask."

The prison walls twitched in anticipation. When Salemis asked them for help with the barrier of sky, they answered immediately: *If you plant my seed in the new world and help it grow, it shall tear a hole in the sky large enough for you to pass.*

Salemis passed the message onto the humans, only to find that Bandu, at least, already understood. "How do we get seed?" she asked.

The roots offered to send it down to them, but Bandu shook her head. "No good," she said. "We talk to both now, all together. We don't know maybe it sends Illweather seed. We need to go up and see Goodweather alone."

This girl was clever, and she knew the ways of the elves. Salemis was pleased that his descendants would come through her.

"If the roots will let us through," he suggested, "I will carry you up and we shall verify it together. Would you accept that?"

Bandu nodded and the ceiling gave way, parting to let the sun shine in upon them. It was miles to the surface, but that hardly mattered. Salemis reached out and gently lifted Bandu in his claw.

"I will be careful," he reassured Criton. The boy looked like he needed it.

"Wait for us here," he told the others, and then with a few beats of his wings, rose up toward the sun.

Higher and higher he climbed with Bandu in his grasp,

until at last they burst out into the sky. The castles became visible as he rose further, easily distinguished from one another by the weather that hung over each.

"You are wise for such a young child," Salemis told Bandu, as they approached Goodweather.

The girl said nothing, or perhaps her answer was lost in the wind. When they reached Goodweather, a crowd of fairies rushed out of the castle to stare at them, pointing and gibbering in fearful confusion.

"Burn them," said Bandu. "They are wicked."

"I know," Salemis answered. "This whole world is wicked. The Gods didn't build a mesh at first between them and this world. It filled with too much magic, and all its inhabitants were driven mad. In the end, God Most High had to build a solid firmament to spare the lower Gods from its chaos.

"Even so, I will not burn these elves. The time for killing will be upon us too soon as it is – I will not start it early."

He could sense Bandu's disapproval, but it did not bother him. She was still young. She would learn.

He landed on Goodweather's roof and set Bandu down there. "We are here for the seed," he told Goodweather.

But can I give it to you? the castle asked. *You know what this world is made of. Illweather's seed was endangered some months ago, but the elves recovered it. The planting time is nearly upon us. If I give you my seed, Illweather's roots will outgrow mine and my influence on this world will diminish. Balance must be maintained.*

"You agreed to the bargain before," Salemis pointed out.

The leaves twitched. *Where you spoke to us before, our beings are intermingled. Illweather wants to accept your bargain. That alone makes me wary. Illweather always strives for power, never for balance. Keeping balance is my greatest mission.*

Bandu sat cross-legged on the mossy roof and ran her hands along its surface, almost caressing it. "You are kind to me before," she said. "You save me. I want you strong always. But you are wrong, Goodweather. You are wrong."

I am not wrong, little one, the castle maintained. *Balance is essential.*

"No balance now!" Bandu insisted, growing frustrated and pounding the moss with her hands. "Where is balance? Illweather is wicked. Elves are wicked. Even animals here are wicked. Only you are good!"

"The girl is right," said Salemis. "This world was lost to madness a long time ago. But Illweather has no say in the new world. Even the elves hardly touch it, except now and then. In the new world, your influence will be felt. The new world needs balance too."

I will need permission, Goodweather confessed. *Without the queen's blessing, the seed cannot grow. God Most High has punished us by making us subservient to these creatures.*

"Then let her come up to speak with us," Salemis said, his eye on Bandu as she hurriedly stood up. She looked terrified.

The queen of the Goodweather elves emerged from a staircase in the center of the living castle's roof. Though her beauty meant nothing to him, even Salemis felt her power. The scent of it tickled his tongue.

"To what purpose have you called me, Goodweather?" she asked, gazing up at Salemis without much concern.

This emissary of God Most High wishes to return to his land, to plant my seed in the younger world and tear a breach in the heavens so that he may escape.

"I see. And what does he offer us in return?"

"People," said Bandu, coming around Salemis' side. "My world has people who want to come here and do not know you. Children, and big ones like me who can make more."

"Well," laughed the queen, "if it isn't our very own wicked little thing, all grown up. You would sell me your kin, for the sake of this dragon?"

Salemis felt the clash of wills as Goodweather's queen forced her way into Bandu's mind, and Bandu beat her partially back. "They have a wizard," the girl admitted. "She saves them from you, I hope. I hope, but I don't know. You don't know too. If you help, then you see. Maybe you eat the wizard and her people. Maybe they eat you."

The fairy queen smiled and nodded. "You offer me a war with children of your land, and a chance to grow my own supply. I accept. Plant your seed, Goodweather. May you reap the fertility of the young world just as I mean to."

She turned away, waving a dismissive hand to Goodweather. A moment later its acorn fell, landing almost in Bandu's lap. Bandu scooped it up and rose unsteadily to her feet. "Thank you," she said to Goodweather. To the queen she said, "I hope you lose."

They left then, before anything could get in their way.

"You did well," Salemis told the girl.

"I know," she said.

When they returned, they found Criton and the other humans waiting anxiously in the mouth of their narrow tunnel, squinting upwards as if afraid they would miss the dragon's arrival. When Salemis set Bandu down next to them, their relief was palpable.

"Here is Goodweather's seed," Bandu said, presenting it.

"Great," said Narky. "So all we have to do is plant it?"

"And infuse it with Godly power," Salemis agreed. "Eramia will help, but I don't know that Her strength will be enough. It took three Gods to get me here; it will probably take at least two to let me out. I'll widen the breach from this side, once the job is started."

"Will a hole that big take long to repair?" Phaedra asked. "We wouldn't want our world exposed to this one for too long."

"The sky repairs itself," Salemis told her. "Even a small hole cannot last very long – a larger one will collapse even sooner."

"In that case," said Narky, "we'd better get out of here. If the way back closes on us now, we're all in trouble."

Salemis agreed. "Good luck," he called out, as they disappeared back into the tunnel. "I will be waiting."

54
Bestillos

The High Priest of Magor finished with the sacrificial knife and threw it on the platter for cleaning. "Magor is not concerned with wizards," he said.

"He would be if He knew more about this one," said the Atunaean. "It's the wizard Psander who ordered the Boar of Hagardis slain."

Bestillos turned to face him, wiping the blood off his hands. The grizzled nobleman met his gaze without blinking. "The wizard promised my prince that he would retake Atuna for us if we brought him the boar's carcass," he went on. "I had deep reservations, but I followed my prince's orders."

So the truth was coming out! Bestillos reached back down toward the platter, playing idly with the knife's hilt. "It was Tana, then, that killed the boar?"

The Atunaean shook his head. "No. It was the islanders Psander hired to help us."

Bestillos stared at him, as images of the black dragonspawn rose before his eyes. "Tell me about the islanders," he said.

The Atunaean smiled, happy to deflect attention from himself and his compatriots. "There were five of them," he said. "Three men and two girls, and not a one of them over sixteen, I should say. Tarphaeans who left home before the plague. Suspicious, I'd call it."

It was the same group, Bestillos was sure of it. The dragon spawn had ridden behind a girl during their shameful escape from Anardis.

"One of the girls was a tracker," the Atunaean continued. "Ugly girl, but useful. The other one was good-looking and useless."

"I'm not interested in the girls," Bestillos told him. "Tell me about the others. There is a tall one, yes?"

The Atunaean looked at him suspiciously. "You've met them before?"

"No, no, only seen them from afar."

"Well then," said the gray warrior. "You probably know that the tall one is Dragon Touched. He hid it well, but he changed when the boar came at him. Other than him, there's the one that actually killed the boar, though I'd say it was more luck than anything else. He didn't even have a weapon 'til we gave him a spear. The last one has his sword and his fancy shield and scaled armor, and thinks he's really something with them. Acted like the big protector for the others, but I didn't see him do anything in the fight. If it were me, I'd worry most about the Dragon Touched and the ugly girl."

The priest of Magor smiled. "No man worries me. Only tell me where I can find them."

"I can't say for sure," the other man answered. "After all, that was months ago. But I'll say this: the islanders are young and homeless, and Psander is a clever man. He probably still has them running errands for him, just like he did then."

Bestillos considered this. The Atunaean clearly held a grudge against this Psander, and would likely say anything to bring about the wizard's destruction. But wizards were second only to the dragon spawn as abominations before the Gods. He would have to die, even if he no longer consorted with the accursed islanders.

"And where does this wizard live?" Bestillos asked.

"South of here," said the old hearthman, "in a fortress that cannot be seen until you stand at its door. Raise your army, and I will guide you."

The younger acolytes had finished with the ritual and were now looking at them, waiting for their leader's command.

"I will sleep on it," Bestillos said. Magor often came to him in dreams.

The Atunaean nodded and withdrew, saying that he would be ready to ride southwards at the priest's earliest command. Yet that night, as the first dry winds of the season blew in from the north, Bestillos did not dream of wizards. He dreamt instead that he had gone out hunting, and that in his absence a fire had sprung up in the fields of Ardis. *If only I had not gone out,* he thought in his dream, *I could have stayed and extinguished the fire.* When Bestillos awoke, he rose and called for the Atunaean.

The old warrior met him at the temple door, horse and arms at the ready. "We will not ride today," Bestillos told him, "nor tomorrow. Magor spoke to me in a dream. The dragon is coming to us."

The Atunaean's face registered skepticism and disappointment. "Why would the islanders come here? Even they must know that you would kill them."

"They are coming," Bestillos said. "I have seen it."

"So what do you want me to do, then? Just wait around?"

Bestillos eyed him coldly. "I don't care what you do with your time," he said. "I will go nowhere until I hear word of the islanders' arrival."

"And the wizard?"

"–Does not seem to be going anywhere," Bestillos replied. "His time will come as well. First, the last remnants of the dragonspawn must be eradicated."

The warrior slouched off despondently. Bestillos watched

him go. They had never impressed him, these Gallant Ones. If they had been as brave or noble as they told themselves, they would have stayed in Atuna to fight and die – or else to conquer. Even now, this man's revenge against his wizard enemy was a weak one. Only a coward would seek aid from his old foes instead of trying to slay the wizard himself.

For two days, Bestillos waited. On the third day, news came. A group of islanders had been traveling northward through the outskirts of the city, a small crowd of children in their wake. Bestillos called for the Atunaean and raised a pig of thanksgiving to Magor. The pig's squeal was short and loud when Bestillos slaughtered it, a good omen. He burnt it to a cinder, relishing the smell.

"Charos is here, Holy One," announced one of the lower acolytes while the first ashes were still blowing in the air.

"Charos?" asked Bestillos.

"Yes, Holy One. Charos the Atunaean, of the Gallant Ones."

"Ah," said the High Priest. "He is outside? Let him wait. Bring me my spear, and have Peskas saddle the black mare. I'm going hunting today."

Hearthman Charos drew in his breath when he saw the red robes and the spear. "They are here, then?" he asked.

"They are here."

They rode east, taking two skilled hunters with them. Mageris was one, Balkon the other. At each farm, the inhabitants pointed them northward. "They've been avoiding Ardis," said Charos the Atunaean. "At least they're not total fools."

"It is foolish for them to be anywhere in Hagardis at all," Bestillos told him. "The whole region is unsafe for the slayers of the boar."

Charos nodded and licked his lips. Had Bestillos' words made his mouth go dry? The priest smiled to himself. That was as it should be.

They continued northward, following the islanders' trail.

"Where are these fools going?" asked Balkon.

Bestillos looked westward, to where the mountains of the Calardian range loomed ever closer. He thought he knew.

The last village brought confirmation. A stranger had been to town, and brought with him a gaggle of children from all across the continent.

"Was the man an islander?" asked Mageris.

"It doesn't matter," Bestillos told him. "The dragonspawn can change their skin. Tell me," he added to the nervous villager, "where are these children now?"

There were five of them, a boy and four girls. "These two are mine," the villager said. "I don't know where the others came from."

Bestillos ignored him, gazing down at them. They were all about five years old – afraid of him, but too young to know how frightened to be.

"Tell me," he said. "Why did the islanders come here?"

"They were bringing Temena and Adla home," said one of the girls, a dark haired little thing. "They wanted to take us all home, but they didn't know how to get there."

"But they left you all here," said gray Charos. "Why the hurry?"

"They wanted to go to the tune," said another girl, either Adla or Temena.

Their father hastily clarified. "The fellow who brought them asked for directions to the Dragon Knight's tomb," he said. "I think he was planning to go there next."

The Ardismen looked at one another. "Paying his respects?" suggested Balkon.

"How long were you traveling with them?" Mageris asked the girls.

"A long way," said the first one. "The sea tried to eat me, but Criton saved me and we flew away!"

"They're all full of stories," said the villager apologetically. "Don't believe a word of it."

Bestillos ignored him. "The Dragon Knight's tomb," he commanded his companions.

When they had mounted their horses, the priest turned to the father one last time. "Question them thoroughly," he said, "and make sure they have not fallen under the islander's sway. If this Criton's influence upon them remains, I will be back."

The villager acknowledged the warning with a gulp. "I'll drive away their influence if I have to beat it out of them," he said.

"I hope so," said Bestillos, with a curt nod. They rode for the mountains.

They reached the Dragon Knight's tomb just before sunset, climbing up through the yellow glare with their hands over their eyes. When they had almost reached the mouth of the cave, Bestillos put up his hand to stop the others. Four horses were standing idly outside the cavern, loosely tied to a bush.

Bestillos smiled. "We have them," he said.

55
Bandu

The climb back did not feel so long, now that Salemis was behind them.

"I still can't believe it," said Criton. "We have the Yarek's seed now, and we're bound to have Psander's help. We're going to rescue Salemis!"

He was so happy now. Why shouldn't he be? This was what he had wanted, the chance to be a rescuer and to pretend that a dragon was his father. But what did it mean for Bandu and for her young? She carried big Goodweather's acorn in her arms, and little Goodweather inside her. Which one would Criton cherish?

"It's amazing," said Phaedra, stumbling along beside her with an arm over Hunter's shoulder. "I always knew that dragons were huge, but I never really realized what a... what a lesser order of being we are."

"How do you mean?" asked Hunter.

Phaedra panted a little as she walked. "That hissing sound he made – that wasn't speech. He was using magic to make us understand him. Just like Bandu does with animals."

Hunter nodded. "Right. I see what you mean."

"Back to Psander, then," said Narky happily, "and for once, she'll be doing as much for us as we do for her."

When they reached the end of the tunnel, they stopped. The entrance had shrunk while they were gone. A dim light poured through the narrow hole in the roots, soft and subdued. There was barely room to crawl through one at a time, and even as they watched, the roots slithered and tightened further around their exit.

"Let's get out of here," said Narky.

"Bandu goes first," Criton insisted. "She's the only one who can't slip through sideways."

It was true. Turning sideways would only have made Bandu wider now, the way her belly stuck out. She crouched and squeezed through, her arms out in front of her.

It was around sunset outside, though the mountain stood between her and the view. When she turned, the flower that had stood at the cliff's edge was completely gone. She went back to inspect it, then suddenly stopped and fell to her knees. There was a man standing at the mouth of the cave. A man with a spear.

She made to peek over the edge a second time, but just then Phaedra stepped out of the tunnel and stood beside her. Bandu grabbed her skirt and pulled her to the ground.

"Someone looks for us," she whispered.

She crawled forward again on her hands and knees, leaving Phaedra to warn the others if she could. The man with the spear was standing next to their horses, keeping watch. So far, he was looking down the mountainside instead of up it.

Phaedra managed to get Criton to stay quiet, but Narky stumbled as he came out of the tunnel, and the watchman heard him. His body stiffened, and Bandu pulled out of sight just as he began to look upwards.

"Oh please," Bandu whispered to the wind, "don't carry our sounds to him."

Above her head, the hole in the mesh was nearly gone. Before it could close completely, Hunter dove out of the shrinking tunnel and crashed to the ground beside her.

Bandu held her breath, but nothing happened. Then the man below called out to whoever was in the cave.

"What is it?" asked a harsh man's voice.

"I think they're close," the watchman replied.

"Did you see them?"

"No, but I thought I heard something."

"Where?"

"I don't know. It was gone almost as soon as it started."

Bandu sighed in relief and silently thanked the wind. The man below sounded frustrated. "It's getting dark," he said, "and they've left all their horses and equipment here. They'll come back soon enough. Here, bring the horses inside. When the islanders come looking for them, we'll be waiting."

"But what if they don't come looking?" asked a third voice, a rough, gravelly voice that sounded somehow familiar.

The other man laughed. "They won't get far without their food and their waterskins. We can track them by the light of day. And if all else fails – well, in that case we can try your wizard."

"Who *is* that?" whispered Phaedra. "I've heard that voice before."

"It's Bestillos," answered Criton, looking almost yellow. "The high priest of Magor."

Phaedra's eyes widened. "Gods protect us," she said.

There was a clopping of hooves from below, and the men's voices grew more distant. "Let's get out of here," whispered Hunter.

"We're not going anywhere near that cave," said Narky, "not until we can be sure they're not looking."

Criton seconded his opinion. "We'll find another way down," he said.

Their climb away from the cave was torture. It would have been impossible for her without Criton and Hunter's help. In order to avoid passing the tomb's entrance they had to go up the mountain for a while before heading back down again. The sun had long set by the time they were once more on level ground. They did not stop then, but continued traveling by the light of Criton's magic. In that dim light, Criton's eyes begged her for forgiveness. It weakened her, that look. With people nearby who so unashamedly meant to murder her, how could she stay angry with a man who had only hit her by mistake, when he was weak and afraid?

"I think I know who you were talking about," Hunter told Phaedra, as they continued down the mountainside. "You were talking about the one with the raspy voice. It sounded familiar to me too."

"That was Hearthman Charos," said Narky, "of the Gallant Ones. I bought a horse and our tents off him."

Phaedra groaned. "Bestillos said they'd try the wizard if they couldn't find us – Charos is going to lead him straight to Psander!"

"We should get to her as soon as we can," suggested Criton, "before Bestillos can raise his army again."

"Not a chance," said Narky. "We can't go by the roads. We can't even go back the way we came – too many people saw us that way. If we stay in the open, he'll track us down. He might track us down even if we don't."

Hunter nodded. "We have to go through the mountains," he said.

"What?" cried Phaedra. "Bandu and I can't climb over the Calardian range! And even if we could, that would take months!"

"What else can we do, Phaedra?" Hunter hissed back. "Narky's right. The red priest tracked us to the Dragon Knight's Tomb, and he has our horses now. The mountains are the only place we can go where he's not twice as fast as we are. If he doesn't follow us, *then* we can worry about Psander."

They traveled on through the night, and did not stop

until their march became a climb once more. The mountains loomed before them in the darkness, and Bandu shivered. It would be cold up there, and their blankets were still in the cave.

Bandu's belly weighed on her, and her feet felt as if she was pounding them flat. Her back ached. Yet onward they climbed until the sky began to brighten again and their legs could take them no further. Criton found them a sheltered nook to sleep in, and they all huddled there together for warmth.

And then, just when sleep was finally falling upon their eyes, the young inside Bandu woke up and began to squirm and kick. She moaned and shut her eyes tight. Would the torture never end?

Whether she slept, she could not say. She felt the priest of Magor tracking them, or else she dreamed that he was. He could smell the magic on them, smell Criton's fire and Bandu's pregnancy and Goodweather's seed, and he would chase them down until he had caught them all on the end of his spear. He was catching up with them already. She could feel it.

She rose and shook the others awake. "We go now," she said.

They did as she told them to, yawning and rubbing their eyes as they stumbled up the mountainside. They had not slept long, and by noon had broken past the treeline and could stare back down upon the plains of Hagardis. Bandu could not see the riders below, but she could still feel them. She begged the wind to scatter the islanders' scent, but she doubted that that would be good enough this time.

"Phaedra," she said. "I need talk to dead Mountain God. How do I do?"

"What?" Phaedra asked, startled.

"Mountains need to help," Bandu told her, "or we all die. Magor's priest can smell us. He is chasing."

Phaedra looked both horrified and confused. "But how

could Caladoris help us with that, when He's been dead for hundreds of years?"

"Dead God still is strong," Bandu answered. "Only does not wake up. Salemis says Yarek is dead, is broken and cut in two pieces, but Yarek is only not strong like before. And maybe one day Yarek is fixed."

"I don't know," Phaedra said dubiously. "I don't know anything about what will happen 'one day.' Eschatology never really appealed to me. None of it seems reliable."

"I don't know what you say."

Phaedra sighed. "I don't know anything about the end times. You could be right, or you could be wrong. I do see what you're saying, about primordial beings like the Gods being in some ways indestructible, but even if a God's death is more like a long sleep, I still don't see how you can hope to communicate with a dead one."

Bandu shook her head, disheartened. She had hoped that Phaedra would know.

"There's another way," Criton said suddenly. They all turned to look at him, and he sat up straighter.

"Another way to get Bestillos off our trail," he clarified. "He's tracking us. He can feel our magic, just like we can feel his."

"Are you saying we should split up?" Narky asked incredulously.

"Not all of us," Criton said. "Just me. I'm the one Bestillos wants. I'm the one he's following. But I'm also the one who can fly. I can move around these mountains much faster than you can, and send Bestillos off in the wrong direction. By the time he realizes I'm throwing him off, your trail might be cold. I'll rejoin you in two weeks, if you make a big enough campfire for me to see from the air."

"Right," said Hunter. He reached out to shake Criton's hand. "Good luck."

And just like that, Criton was gone.

Their travels grew no easier, for all that the feeling of

being followed abated. In the mountains, the others relied on Bandu completely. It was she who found them water and game, and showed them which plants were safe to eat. It was she whose magic kept the wild animals at bay.

At the same time, she knew she was slowing them down. She could hardly go a few paces without her belly seizing so that she had to stop and rest. It felt as if the weight of the world was on her shoulders – and on her bladder. That was the other thing. No matter how often she went, it seemed as though she could never relieve herself enough.

Criton rejoined them after two weeks, looking hungry but triumphant. "I think it worked," he said.

"Let's give it another two weeks before we start celebrating," Hunter answered.

They continued southward, grateful for the warmer weather of the dry season. Yet even when Hunter's two weeks were up, they had barely made any progress toward Silent Hall. Phaedra was even slower here than Bandu, and when the climbing got steep, it took two of the boys beside her to keep her from falling. How many miles had they traveled? It was hard to say, but Bandu doubted they had gone very far past Ardis. They came across a tribe of mountain people, but they had nothing to trade for food or shelter, so they had to simply move on. Phaedra asked if any of these clansmen had lost a daughter named Caldra, but none had.

Another week went by, and another. The weather grew hot and dry, and finally Hunter said that they could leave the shelter of the mountains and find a road again. It took them the rest of the day to find a gorge that led out to the plains, where they washed their dirty faces in the river and lay down to rest at the water's edge.

That night, it happened. Bandu awoke, her stomach a solid ball of pain. A moment later the pain was gone, but it soon returned with a terrible cramping sensation. Her young did not kick or move – it seemed to have slid down inside her while she slept, finding a place to hide from her tensing muscles.

Another jolt from her stomach, and she sat up sharply. Her back was beginning to ache, but for now, this did not bother her. All she could think of was Criton.

Should she wake him? He would try to take control, she knew he would, and she did not want that. But didn't he deserve to know?

Another contraction. No, Criton could wait until after. He would only trouble her now, and she did not have time for trouble. Phaedra would be more sympathetic... but would she be useful? Bandu was sure that she would have a lot of advice to give – advice that she had never tried out herself. Hunter was kind and gentle, but he seemed afraid of her body. He might be a wonderful help, but she could not risk it.

Narky? He knew more than he said about these things. He had helped her with Four-foot, and he had grown up in one of the farms by the forest. He would have seen sheep give birth, and maybe helped them... but no. Even though Narky might be the best one to help her, she knew how much it would hurt Criton to have another man there beside her instead of him. No, she could not ask Narky. She would have to do this herself.

She rose, gasping for breath, and tottered forward in the dark. She had to get away from them all, far enough so that they would not awaken until she had finished. She staggered through the night, stopping now and then just to clutch her belly and breathe. It was such an urgent feeling, that feeling in her belly. It was much more than pain. It was a force.

She sank to her knees and planted her hands on the ground, drawing strength from the steady earth. Wave after wave came upon her, each one longer than the last, and with less time to rest in between. Her dress bothered her, so she took it off. She lost track of time after that, with her mind focused entirely on her belly and her breathing. This was lasting hours, she thought, during a brief moment of clarity. Then another wave struck, and she stopped thinking.

At some point in the night, the feeling shifted. It became harder, more painful, more frightening. Her legs were wet, and she could not remember when or how they had gotten that way. She thought someone might be screaming, though she could not think who. When she felt she could take no more, she crawled forward and sat in the river.

The water should have been icy cold, but instead it steamed off her skin in roiling waves, filling the air with vapors. Her body was about to burst from the bottom up. She felt it straining, ready to tear at any minute. Then she reached down through the bubbling water, and felt a head.

It did not take long after that. She bore down as the current swept over her, and soon the head gave way to shoulders and torso and a behind, and Bandu caught the little creature and pulled it from the water.

It was a scaly little thing, its arms and legs covered in slippery armor. It was a girl. And as the first rays of sunlight fell upon her head, she began to cry.

56
Phaedra

They found Bandu with blood on her mouth and a baby at her breast, sitting by the water's edge completely naked. Criton rushed forward, anxious to see his wife and child, while Narky looked at his feet and Hunter tried very hard not to stare – with little success.

"She's beautiful!" Criton exclaimed. "Are you all right, Bandu? What happened to your mouth?"

"I am good," Bandu answered. "Everything is good. It's over."

"But the blood," insisted Criton. "Bandu, there's blood on your face and hands."

She nodded. "I was hungry," she said.

"Oh," said Criton, sounding disgusted. "Well, she's beautiful!"

An hour or two later, while Criton and Hunter were helping Bandu hobble along behind them, Narky said, "You know, I think that's the ugliest baby I've ever seen."

"Narky!" Phaedra huffed disapprovingly, but she secretly agreed. Baby Goodweather was undeniably hideous. Her whole body was a patchwork of skin and scales, her head was cone-shaped and bald, and her nose was too big for her tiny face. An ugly stump of cord extended from her belly, ragged at the end where Bandu had apparently bitten it off. But that didn't matter. It was clear that her parents loved her, and it would not do to make fun of her. Besides, she wouldn't look like this forever. She might even grow into that nose one day.

Bandu could hardly walk now, even with support. Phaedra didn't blame her for it, of course, but there was no doubt that it slowed them down. Even as close as they were to the edge of the mountains, they only barely made it onto the plains before nightfall. Dimly lit to their north, a familiar walled city sat leaking smoke from many a chimney. Anardis. It seemed that Bestillos had not destroyed the city completely after all.

"This is no good," Narky said, as he and Criton built the fire for their camp. "At this rate, it'll be months before we ever reach Psander. By the time we get there, Bestillos will have sacked the place."

"Bandu can't walk any faster," Criton scolded him. "You want to carry her?"

"No," said Narky, "but we could get a cart from a farm or something. That way we can at least move at a real walk."

"We're out of money," Hunter reminded him. He was sitting to one side, sharpening his sword against a stone.

Narky rolled his eyes. "I'm not talking about buying a cart, I'm talking about taking one."

"You mean stealing," Phaedra said.

Narky returned her gaze sternly. "This is war," he answered her. "Or it's basically war, anyway. Psander is probably under siege as we speak, and if she's not, she will be soon. If we want her help freeing Salemis, we're going to have to find a way to get to her before Bestillos puts her head on a pike."

What could Phaedra say to that? He was right, of course. It made no sense for them to travel at Bandu's pace, or at Phaedra's for that matter.

"You don't like stealing from poor farmers, is that it?"

Narky asked, misconstruing her silence. "These are the same poor farmers who shut their doors to us on our way to Anardis. They don't deserve your sympathy."

"You're right," Phaedra told him. "You're right."

"You and I can find a cart tomorrow," Hunter suggested. "Criton can stay here just in case, and spend some time with his daughter."

Criton thanked him and turned to Bandu and Goodweather, smiling. Bandu smiled back, a guarded, tentative smile. Phaedra was glad to see that smile. She hoped the two of them would reconcile soon. She didn't know how the troubles had started, but their strained relationship had been wearing at her nerves.

When Hunter and Narky returned the next day, they were driving a horse and cart piled with blankets and some meager food supplies. Hunter looked grim.

"The army of Ardis passed here two weeks ago," he said. "They didn't leave much for us to take. Even if this cart lets us go at the same speed they do, Psander and the others with her could easily be dead or starving by the time we get there."

"In that case," said Criton, "let's go now. There's no time to just stand here."

They loaded Bandu and her baby onto the back of the cart, and Criton joined her there while Phaedra drove the horse. The other two walked silently alongside. Nobody but Criton and Bandu seemed to have anything to say, and they spoke only to each other. Well, to each other and to baby Goodweather.

The next two weeks were brutal. For one thing, Goodweather never slept except when the bumpy motion of the cart rocked her to sleep. The rest of the time she would wail, at night waking up everyone but Hunter. At these times, when Bandu or Criton was trying in vain to rock as soothingly as a horse-drawn cart, Phaedra began to resent that enviably deep sleeper who still lay on the ground beside them. Why couldn't Hunter be awake and miserable just like the rest of them? A childish part of her wanted to wake him up.

Goodweather also soiled herself constantly. Without any swaddling clothes for her, the mess was uncontainable. Being wet inevitably woke the girl up – screaming, of course. Bandu handled the wetness better than she handled the screaming. Eventually the baby would nurse to sleep, at which point everyone could nap fitfully until the next time the baby awoke, an hour or two later.

And it was not only baby Goodweather who made their journey difficult. The closer they got to Silent Hall, the more oppressively Psander's fate seemed to hang upon them. Whenever Phaedra thought ahead, she imagined the smoking ruins of Silent Hall splayed across the ground just like the stones that had once been Gateway. The image filled her with dread.

The Ardisian army's path became heavier and more noticeable the farther they went, and its trash heaps and old campfires seemed to grow fresher by the day.

"We're catching up," Narky said. "That's a good sign."

"True," said Hunter, but he did not seem pleased. When Phaedra asked him what worried him so, he pointed out the number of fire pits in the campsite.

"The army's been growing as they go further south," he said. "Look at all those fires! Bestillos is pressing half the countryside into his service. I'd say he has at least two, three thousand men."

"Well," said Narky, "I guess that explains why they're moving slower than we are. How long do you think it'll take us to get there at this point? A week?"

Hunter nodded. "That sounds about right. In three days we should leave the cart and start walking. We'll want a couple of us to scout ahead too, so we don't walk straight into the enemy."

They did as he suggested, abandoning the cart on the road

three days later to break across the countryside. During the day, Criton and Narky scouted ahead while Hunter stayed behind to protect Phaedra, Bandu and baby Goodweather. Since Bandu's arms were occupied, and Hunter might have to draw his sword at any moment, it fell to Phaedra to carry the elder Goodweather's acorn. Phaedra marveled at how heavy and dead the seed felt. One would not have thought that this inanimate thing had the power to tear a hole in the world.

They took watches at night, though they did not light a fire for fear of being seen. Baby Goodweather continued to interrupt, of course. On the second night, Narky complained that she was sure to alert the Ardismen. "Can't you keep her quiet?" he asked.

"What do you think we've been *trying* to do?" Criton snapped at him. "Do you think I *like* to hear her cry?"

"Well, you'd better do *something,*" Narky retorted. "It's only a matter of time before we get close enough for the Ardismen to hear us."

"If they hear her cry," Bandu answered him, "what they think? They think somewhere is young. They don't know it's us. We don't have her before."

"That's true enough," Phaedra agreed. "There's no reason for them to think that a crying baby is a sign we're close by. If we're lucky, no one will investigate."

"Right," said Narky, "because nobody will wonder what a baby's doing right outside a besieged fortress."

"If you have any ideas for quieting her down," said Criton, "we're all ears. Otherwise, shut up."

Phaedra winced. The lack of sleep had them all on edge. It was certainly having an influence on her: she found herself snapping at Hunter the very next afternoon, for the crime of having yawned. Her attitude obviously confused him, and why shouldn't it? She was only angry at him because he slept so peacefully.

They passed through familiar woods, sleeping under the

new moon, nervous in the knowledge that Silent Hall was only a couple of days away. That night even Hunter woke up to the sound of Goodweather's voice.

"Is this normal?" he asked, infuriatingly. "She's so much quieter in the daytime."

"She sleeps when I walk," Bandu told him. She was rocking from side to side as she spoke, patting the baby's back all the while. Phaedra thought she was being remarkably patient with Hunter, all things considered.

"I see," Hunter said, and then, "We should travel by night."

Criton sat up, rubbing his eyes and looking at Hunter despairingly. "I don't have the strength to go anywhere right now," he said.

"We don't have to," Hunter told him. "We just need to stay awake now, and sleep tomorrow during the day. Then we can start traveling again tomorrow night."

"What good will that do us?" asked Narky. "Besides making us fall behind by another day, that is?"

"At night," said Hunter, "an army has no scouts. They just have watchmen who stand at the edges of the camp with torches. They'll be much easier to spot at night than we are. We won't be in any danger of walking into them by mistake."

That decided it. They stayed up together that night, and took their watches during the day instead. The change was not easy. Only Goodweather seemed to adjust well to it. For Phaedra, stumbling through the night on her uneven legs, it was torture.

Yet for all that, it worked. When they came upon Magor's army, it stood illuminated by a hundred fires, visible from miles away. The army lay all in a ring around the dark patch of land where Silent Hall stood invisible.

Phaedra heaved a sigh of relief. "Psander's still alive," she said.

"Right," agreed Criton. "If she wasn't, her wards would

have fallen. We'd see the fortress from here."

"Plus the army wouldn't be sticking around," Narky pointed out. "But how do we get in there?"

"I don't know," said Phaedra, "but we have to find a way. Otherwise, no place will be safe for us."

"We'll find a way," Criton said. "We have to manage somehow, or the prophecy won't come true. Since the prophecy's about us, we can't fail, can we?"

Phaedra sighed. "I thought I explained this earlier. Prophecies don't always come true. A prophecy is just a message. Sometimes it's not much more than a boast. Gods can promise Their servants success, but if They change Their minds or lose some conflict, none if it will come true. We're as mortal as anyone else, no matter what a prophecy says."

She did not have to see their faces clearly to know that they were crestfallen.

"Great," said Narky. "Now I *definitely* feel ready to walk through the Ardisian army. Thanks, Phaedra."

"We go now," Bandu said. "I ask wind to keep us quiet, but I don't know if it does, so you be quiet too."

"Fine," Narky sighed. "No use putting it off. If we die, we die."

Without a word, Hunter unclasped his belt and began removing his armor. The scales fell to the ground with a clank. He stood there for a moment, his face blank, and then grimly refastened the belt.

Phaedra stared. Hunter had *always* worn that armor. It had been shocking when the elves took it from him, and even then Bandu and Criton had recognized its importance enough to bring it with them during their escape. The armor had been a part of him. He had worn it in the heat and in the cold, in the mountains and on the sea. Of course he could never have worn it through the enemy camp, but it almost hurt thinking how much this journey was costing him.

Goodweather was still sleeping when they arrived

at the edge of the Ardismen's camp. They stopped just beyond the reach of the firelight, trying in vain to prepare themselves for the danger that they were about to step into. The watchman to their left looked half asleep, blinking slowly underneath his raised torch. To the right, another soldier vigilantly scanned the darkness, firmly clutching his spear. The gap in between them was wide, but was it wide enough? The islanders looked silently at each other, their eyes questioning. Hunter gave a curt nod.

They stole forward, keeping slightly to the left and walking carefully, toe-to-heel, to avoid making noise. Phaedra did her best to copy the others, but she was highly conscious of the way her legs stumped along more loudly than those of her friends.

The soldier swayed, then suddenly started. He had almost dropped his torch. The islanders stopped in their tracks, holding their breath. The watchman's eyes darted first away from them, then straight ahead…

He sighed and looked down at his feet. "Idiot," Phaedra heard him mumble to himself.

They crept on as silently as they could. A few more paces, and they were in the camp.

"Gods," Narky muttered. "I think I almost pissed myself there."

"Is that you, Kinar?" the guard called out to him. "Magor be thanked. I'm falling asleep here."

They hurried away. In the dark of the camp, they could move more freely. They rushed past horses and tents, making their way as quickly as they could toward the second ring of torches. Here again they had to stop, ducking behind a tent.

The men who watched Silent Hall stood much closer together, and they did not sleep. The wizard's castle was still invisible, but the soldiers nonetheless remained focused on the clearing where it stood. Phaedra could see all of them from here, those who stood nearby with their backs to the islanders and those who stood far distant, keeping watch from the other side of the unseen fortress.

"How do we get past them?" Phaedra whispered.

Nobody answered her. That shouldn't have surprised her, she thought. It wasn't possible. It simply wasn't possible.

In the stillness, Goodweather began to stir.

They stood, helpless, silently pleading with the little one to fall back asleep. She did not. Her cry pierced the air and the watchmen spun around, searching the dark camp for the sound's origin. The tent that hid the islanders from their view moved slightly, as whoever lay inside it woke up and started moving about. Hunter drew his sword.

He leapt out of the shadows and charged the guards, uttering no battle cry. The others followed him, running with all their might, too fast for Phaedra to keep up. She stumbled along behind, her terror growing with each footfall.

"Who's there?" called one of the soldiers, just before Hunter drove a sword through his belly. The man let out a horrified cry, dropping his spear and torch in confusion. In an instant, Hunter had spun away from him and rushed the next soldier, while Narky, Criton and Bandu charged past the dying man into the empty field where Silent Hall surely lay. They were all too fast for Phaedra. Her feet plodded dumbly beneath her, so slowly that she hardly seemed to be moving at all. They would catch her! At this pace, even the men awakening in the camp behind her would have the chance to catch up.

Hunter dispatched his second opponent and glanced despairingly in her direction. He knew she would not make it. She could see it in his eyes.

He did not have the time to help her. Soon another two soldiers were upon him, their torches burning on the ground while their spears lunged out at him. Phaedra shut her eyes and ran.

A hand caught her ankle and she fell to the hard dirt, a

startled shriek escaping from her lips. Goodweather's acorn dug into her stomach where it had fallen beneath her, and she gasped for breath. The hand would not let go. The first man Hunter had impaled stared up at her. He was mouthing words she could not recognize, and his face flickered in the light of his fallen torch, the unseeing face of a man about to die.

She kicked him. She kicked him with her free leg, slamming her foot wildly into his nose and mouth over and over until he finally let go. Then she scrambled away, her foot wet and numb, crawling until she could once more rise and hobble into the darkness.

Silent Hall loomed ahead. "Help!" she cried. "Psander, help! Hunter!"

"I'm right here," he panted, appearing behind her out of the night. "Keep going. I'll be right behind you."

The gate was open before her. She ran, as best she could. By the time she reached it, she could hear the thudding of boots behind her as the enemy closed in. Then she was inside, and Hunter was leaping through the gate behind her. It shut with a slam.

There was light in the courtyard up ahead. Phaedra turned back, searching the near darkness for Hunter. He had not risen to his feet yet, and that worried her.

She found him still on the floor, his back heaving. "Hunter!" she cried, falling to her knees beside him. "Are you all right?"

He did not answer her. His whole body was shaking. Phaedra groped in the dark, trying to find an injury. "Where are you hurt?" she asked.

He shook his head, still face down on the ground. There were footsteps behind her.

"Phaedra? Hunter? Are you there?"

"We're both here," Phaedra answered. "We made it. But something's wrong with Hunter!"

Criton rushed over to them, and helped Hunter to his

feet. "I'm all right," Hunter protested, finally speaking. "I'm not hurt."

"Let's get you into the light," Criton said, "and we can decide then."

They stumbled out of the darkness together, into the light of the courtyard. There, Phaedra could finally see what was wrong with Hunter. He had a nasty cut stretching from his cheek to his ear, dripping blood down his jaw – but it was his puffy, bloodshot eyes that told Phaedra what she needed to know. She caught her breath, softly. He had been crying.

"Ouch," said Narky, inspecting Hunter's gash. "That was a close one. He almost went in through your eye."

"I'm fine," Hunter insisted, turning away. "It'll heal."

The tower door opened, and Psander hurried out to meet them. "You are here," she said. "Why have you come back?"

"We found Salemis," Criton told her. "We need your help."

"*You* need *my* help?" Psander asked incredulously. "Have you seen the army outside my door? Magor may pierce my wards at any moment, boy. He hasn't found me yet, but He's *looking*. Have you brought me anything to help with *that* problem?"

"Yes," said Narky. "That's what we need your help with."

Phaedra presented Goodweather's acorn. "We brought you a seed from the fairy world, from the plant monster that world is made of."

"The Yarek," Criton added. "Salemis said that if we infuse it with a God's power–"

"Who is this Salemis?" asked Psander, interrupting him. "The name sounds familiar."

It took until dawn for them to explain the situation properly, and to tell her all that they had seen and learned. Psander's eyes widened when she heard of their plan to cause a breach in the mesh. "Escape from the Gods forever," she mused.

"It's horrible there," Phaedra warned her. "We think they

killed all the wizards of Gateway."

"They know you come to them soon," Bandu added. "They try to eat you."

"But," said Narky, "it's less of a sure thing than dying here."

Psander nodded. "Most anything is."

"So," said Criton, "do you think you can do it? Find some way to put a God's power in the seed?"

"There has to be a way," Psander answered, sounding more desperate than confidant. Now that day had dawned, Phaedra could see how skinny the wizard had become, and notice the dark shadows under her eyes that did not retreat in the light of day.

Psander reached for the acorn. "Here, give me that. Go sleep upstairs, and leave me to my library. My wards will warn me if the Ardismen attack."

Phaedra obeyed, while Narky glanced about the quiet courtyard. "Hey," he said, "what happened to all the villagers?"

"They are indoors," Psander answered him, with a dismissive wave of her hand. "They do not awake at dawn anymore. We have eaten all the roosters, for one thing."

"And for another?" Narky asked, seeing through her evasion.

"And for another… they have all been ill."

"Ill?"

She nodded. "Yes. The blueglow mushrooms you gave me haven't agreed with them."

Phaedra gasped. Her mind immediately went back to the farmer ants, and to the pile of corpses where the mushrooms had grown.

"What you do to them?" Bandu demanded. "You kill them?"

"No, of course I haven't killed them," the wizard answered. "I told you, they've just all grown sick. I used the mushrooms and the calardium that you brought me to make charms for each of them to wear. They ought to be harmless, those charms. All they do is siphon off the unused magical potential each person possesses so that I can use it to defend us. I've had to tap it out to keep Magor from breaking through my wards, but as I say, it ought to be harmless."

"It ought to be," said Narky. "It just isn't."

Psander shrugged unhappily. "Right."

They stared at her, but she only turned and opened the tower door again. "Go to sleep," she said. "Or visit them, if you like. I don't care. Just don't disturb me while I'm in the library."

They did not visit the poor farmers in their houses, much to Phaedra's shame. Instead, they stumbled up the stairs to their rooms and fell instantly asleep. When Phaedra awoke, light was pouring in through her window. It seemed to be midday, which confused her. Had she slept for only a few hours, or for over a day?

The hall was quiet. Even Criton and Bandu's room was completely silent, which gave her pause. She tapped gently on their door, and then finally opened it. There was no one inside. Narky's room was empty too. Only Hunter was still in bed, and he awoke when she opened his door. He rose quickly, embarrassed despite having slept fully clothed.

"I'm sorry," she said. "Do you know where the others are?"

He blinked at her. No, of course he didn't know.

"What happened last night?" she asked him. "By the gate?"

Hunter's face took on a troubled look. "We almost didn't make it," he said. "I thought I might have to leave you out there."

"But you didn't," she said. "You stayed."

"I stayed," he repeated. "And we almost didn't make it."

"So it was relief, then."

He shook his head noncommittally. "Call it what you will," he said.

She stood there for a time, looking at him. He was so noble, so serious. She couldn't remember having ever seen him smile. It was strange: his brother Kataras always had a smile on his face. Hunter really wasn't like his brother at all.

"I don't hear Goodweather," he said, rising. "Where did you say they went?"

She followed him downstairs to the dining hall, where they found the others portioning out a single bowlful of oat gruel. The quiet grating of the spoon against the bowl seemed to mock the grand enormity of the room.

"This is all we found to make," Narky told them. "I hope Psander has another store of food somewhere. There aren't any animals – we checked already."

"We should visit the sick," Phaedra said. "They might need help."

Narky looked horrified at the suggestion, but the others agreed readily enough. They finished their meager breakfast and went out into the courtyard where the displaced village lay. The first thing that struck Phaedra, now that she was not running for her life, was the stench. The air was thick with the smell of so much rotting offal, and flies buzzed through the air with unmolested zeal. The trash heap that attracted them was hidden from sight by a pair of houses, but its size and location were unmistakable.

Only two villagers could be seen outside, even late as it was. They were both standing by the well, haggard and bent. When she approached, Phaedra saw that they were not nearly as old as she had assumed. The woman was probably twenty, the man not much older than that. They were pulling on the chain together, too weak for either to raise the bucket on his or her own. Their continental faces were pale and drawn, and both were losing their hair: patches of baldness dotted their heads. The silver chains hung around their necks like stones.

"Do you need help?" Hunter asked redundantly.

As if in response, the man's fingers slipped and the bucket

went plunging downward again, nearly taking the woman with it. She let go at the last moment and placed her hands on the well's edge, reeling. Hunter caught her by the arm to steady her. "Thh," she muttered.

Criton stepped forward and pulled up the bucket with ease. He poured the water into the two clay vessels by his feet, then dropped the bucket down again and lifted the vessels.

"Where are these going?" he asked.

They spent the rest of the day tending to the villagers. At first, only Hunter was brave enough to touch the sick townsfolk with his hands, but soon they were all helping however they could. There did turn out to be more food than Narky had found for breakfast, but it was more of the same, and had to be rationed out carefully. This much, at least, was easy. The villagers hardly ate a thing.

Phaedra asked once about old Garan, the woman who had first spoken to her of Psander and the Gallant Ones. The man she had asked shook his head weakly.

"Dead," he mumbled. "Weeks ago."

Phaedra was not sure why this shocked her so, but it did. She kept thinking of the old woman, and of her belief that nothing good could come of joining the wizard in 'his' castle. She had said that it was too dangerous, trusting in wizards. How right she had been.

The villagers could barely get out of bed to eat, and the sickest ones had mysterious lesions all over their necks and chests. They had opened spontaneously over the last few days, the strong ones said. Still, it was hard to miss the fact that the lesions all seemed to be radiating outward from those calardium pendants. The sight horrified Phaedra, and followed her even when she closed her eyes. Few besides Garan had died so far, but she doubted it would stay that way for long.

The siege went on. The Ardismen did not approach the walls again, content so far to starve the inhabitants out.

Hunter and Narky climbed up to the parapets the next morning and reported that the earth around the walls was black and scorched. Apparently, Psander's wards were good for more than hiding.

On the third day, the wizard finally emerged from her library. Evening was falling, and the islanders had just finished their portions of oat porridge with one of the sick families in their house. They were on their way back to the tower when Psander appeared at the door and ushered them inside. She looked as though she hadn't slept since they had last seen her.

"I found a solution," she told them, her eyes wide and manic. "But you're not going to like it."

Phaedra's stomach growled. "Tell us," said Criton.

"Two Gods will have to suffice," the wizard said. "From what I can tell, Eramia has already blessed the seed, so that leaves just one."

"Well," said Narky, "out with it."

Psander ignored his impatience. She spoke in cold, measured tones that seemed meant to compensate for her wild appearance. "I'm going to need you to get me something," she said. "I need tears from a man cursed by the Gods. Cursed personally, mind you, and the tears must be fresh, so you'll have to bring me the man himself. Alive. The good news is, I know where you can find him."

"Where?" Hunter asked.

"On Tarphae," the wizard said.

57

Criton

"Are you insane?" Narky shouted at her. "We can't go there! We can't even get out of *here*, and if we could, Tarphae's the last place we can go!"

"Whichever God sent the plague could still be looking for us," Phaedra protested. "We've talked about this already. If the plague was sent just to punish the king, it was still obviously meant to leave him alone among his dead subjects. It doesn't matter how long we've been away. If we go back, the plague will find us too."

Psander looked unimpressed. "So you say," she said. "But you also say you have spoken with Eramia, and that means that She is watching you. Not right now, perhaps, but She will find you again once you step out the door. Everything you have told me indicates that the Love Goddess wants nothing more than to release the Dragons' Prisoner back into our world, which means that She has every reason to protect you from the other Gods while you journey to Tarphae and back."

"How about the sea voyage?" asked Narky. "We've managed to anger Mayar since the last time you saw us."

Psander sighed in exasperation. "It's the only option," she said. "We'll just have to hope that Eramia's protection is enough, or that God Most High takes a hand in your protection too. As for Bestillos and his army, it's true that She can't shield you from them, and that means that we can't let them see you leave this place. Luckily, I've become something of an expert in making things hard to see."

With that, she swept away from them. "Where are you going?" Narky asked.

Psander did not even turn her head. "To prepare," she said. "Sleep now. You'll need it."

She left them standing in the hall, looking at each other with wonder and fear and more than a little curiosity. Criton could barely fathom the idea that they would be going back to Tarphae. Tarphae, the island of his birth and his oppression. The island where his mother had died.

Bandu balanced Goodweather against her hip and took his hand. She knew what he was thinking about. Phaedra looked over at them and smiled. Then she said, "Bandu, we'd better get you some proper clothes before we go. That dress won't make it to Atuna before it falls apart."

"Where are you going to get more, though?" Narky asked. "From the villagers?"

"Some are dead," Bandu stated. "They don't need."

"We're not going to steal from the dead!" Phaedra cried, shocked. "Psander's thin, but she's also a little taller than you. We can ask her for a spare dress, and I'll alter it."

Bandu looked surprised, but then she shrugged. "You want to ask her now?"

Phaedra nodded, and Bandu squeezed Criton's hand. "I come back," she said. "You can hold Goodweather?"

Criton held out his arms. "Of course."

He took the infant from her and she followed Phaedra up the steps to Psander's library. Goodweather remained beautifully asleep, her little breaths barely ruffling his shirt even as her chest fairly heaved with them. Such a tiny little thing, he thought. Bandu had found her some strips of cloth the day before, which Phaedra had shown them how to use as a swaddle. He was glad she knew about these things.

They slept uneasily that night. Criton still had not recovered from their nocturnal travels, and Goodweather woke frequently, demanding to be fed and changed. There were barely any clean swaddling clothes left by daytime.

Late the next morning, after Criton had washed the dirty clothes but before they had dried, Psander arrived carrying a small box. The islanders gathered quickly and Psander took off the lid, revealing a number of irregular candles.

"I don't have the power for anything permanent," she apologized. "Maybe if Magor were not searching for me... well, these will do. I made one, two, three, four... I made twelve of them. You should only need eleven. Hold them while you walk, and so long as they burn, no man will see you."

"Even Bestillos?" Criton asked. "He has the Wizard Sight, you know."

"I do know," Psander said. "But you have it too. Tell me, how close do you have to get to my home before you finally see it?"

"Close," he admitted.

"Keep Bestillos at the same distance, and you should have no trouble evading capture."

Psander gave out two candles to each of them, and then gave the two that remained to Phaedra.

"Use only one candle on your way out," she said, "so that you will have one for the return journey. These last two are for your king, though he should only need one."

"What about our daughter?" asked Criton.

Psander blinked. "She's very small," she said, slow and patronizing. "As long as one of you is holding her, she shouldn't need her own candle."

Hunter jerked his head toward the door. "Let's go then."

They walked over to the gatehouse together, Psander carrying along a wooden torch. Criton was about to take it from her when Bandu said, "Wait. Where is Goodweather's seed?"

Psander stiffened. "It will remain in my library until you come back," she said. "I will need to study it for longer if we are to be successful. It would only weigh you down on your journey."

"Don't worry," said Phaedra, coming to the wizard's defense. "Psander is right. It'll be easier if we don't have to carry it around. We were planning to use it here anyway."

Narky frowned. "And if Magor tears this place down before we get back? It would be good to have some fallback, wouldn't it?"

"That's a risk you'll have to take," the wizard said with finality. "The seed stays here."

She didn't trust them, Criton realized. They had never failed her once, and yet Psander, the woman who had fooled the Gallant Ones into serving her, and whose fortress had devoured an entire village, did not trust *them*. The thought infuriated him.

Still, what could he do? The wizard thrust the torch into his hands and walked back toward the tower door.

"Come back with your king," she called over her shoulder, as she closed the door behind her. "You do not have long."

"Well," said Narky, "I guess that settles that. Let's get on with it."

Criton blew gently on the torch and a flame sprang up on its end. At the gate itself, they stopped and lit their candles. When that was done, Criton placed the torch in a sconce, opened the gate and stepped out into the daylight.

The Ardisian guards stood before him, staring straight through him without any recognition. The army bustled noisily behind them. Men and horses were carrying cut logs into camp from the forest, to be sawed and carved and hammered by their comrades into something new. Ladders. Criton looked to the others to see if they saw what he saw, but they had vanished. He was standing alone.

"Bandu?" he whispered. "Are you still here?"

"Yes," her voice came back, from only a few feet ahead. "We go now. Candles don't burn long."

"Try to go due east," said Hunter's voice. "We'll regroup when the army's no longer in sight."

Criton nodded, then realized that they could not see him. He sighed, and, shielding the candle flame with his hand, strode for the enemy ranks.

Luckily, the Ardismen were far louder in the day than during the night. Criton slipped between tents, wagons and workers without so much as a single one of them noticing him. He dodged a pair of soldiers as they nearly walked into him, then turned and hopped to one side as a horse trampled by. Even so, his progress was swift. Soon he was halfway through the camp, and his candle had barely burned down by a quarter. He silently congratulated Psander for her excellent work. This was going quite well, so far.

He stopped at the sound of Bestillos' voice. He spun around to find the priest standing not far to his left, talking to Charos of the Gallant Ones.

"We've caught them now," the priest said. Then he turned and looked directly at Criton.

Criton froze under his gaze, and his throat seemed to swell shut. Psander's magic hadn't worked after all – the red priest was too powerful even for her.

"Hey you!" Bestillos called to him. "Yes you, fool. Come here."

There was so much power in his voice that Criton began to obey. Yet he had only taken a single, unwilling step when a voice behind him suddenly said, "I'm sorry, Your Holiness. How may I serve you?"

Understanding came to him slowly, and Criton only barely leapt aside in time to avoid colliding with the young man who had been standing behind him. He was so close that he felt the man's shirt sleeve brush against his arm as he walked by. Criton's throat reopened. Bestillos hadn't seen him after all!

His nerve left him, and he fled. He ran, leaping over obstacles and dodging between soldiers as he sped through the camp. His candle nearly went out as he ran, but he lifted it to his mouth and kept it alive with his own flame. The hot wax dripped down onto the scales of his hand. The whole thing would melt before he got out of here!

He forced himself to slow down, but it was too late. In his hurry he had already melted the candle to a tiny nub, and he hadn't even left the camp yet. He considered simply running or flying onward, trying to escape despite his visibility, but that would be disastrous. It would spark a chase and a search that could only end up with the others, at least, being captured. He thought too about disguising himself as an Ardisman, but here in the camp, *someone* was bound to notice his sudden appearance out of thin air. It was no good. Criton lit his second candle.

As soon as the camp was behind him and he was alone in the woods, he brightened his skin and blew out the flame. His claws transformed into hands as he stuffed the half-length nub in his pocket. All he could do now was keep walking eastward, and hope that his friends would eventually find him.

He stopped to rest after a while, sitting down on a fallen tree. The others were likely somewhere behind him, assuming that only he had been reckless enough to run.

It took only half an hour before Hunter came tromping through the woods to meet him. After that, Criton climbed a tree and spotted Narky and Phaedra, who had found each other on their own. But wait as they would, Bandu did not come.

"She'll find us," Hunter reassured him. "Nobody can track like she can."

Criton nodded, but he was troubled. He wanted to tell them about his encounter with Bestillos, but the words wouldn't come.

After two hours of waiting, Criton began to suspect that

Bandu was ahead of them rather than behind. "Either way," Narky said, "we haven't got forever. Let's go."

They made camp in the woods that night, taking watches. Though the night was warm, Criton sat by the fire and shivered. With every rustling leaf or snapping twig, he thought he heard Bandu approaching. Or had Bestillos somehow captured her? No, it couldn't be. She would come. Any minute, he would hear Goodweather's cries and know that everything was all right.

When she arrived the next morning, Criton was so relieved he wept. Bandu embraced him until he pulled away to wipe his eyes and really look at her. She looked strong and healthy and covered with dirt. Being alone in the woods with their tiny daughter had apparently done her no harm at all. He asked her where she had been, but didn't understand her garbled answer. He hardly cared, though. She and Goodweather were safe. That was all that mattered.

The journey to Atuna went by in a blur. They had no money but ate whatever they could find, be it a handful of mustard greens or a stray lamb from some inattentive shepherd's flock. Only when they finally reached the city did they realize that having no money meant that they could board no boat, for Tarphae or for anywhere else. They stood helplessly watching merchantmen and fishing boats come and go, wishing they had thought to ask Psander for money before they left. Then, without saying a word, Hunter strode away from them toward the docks.

"Hey!" called Narky, "Where are you going?"

"To claim my inheritance," Hunter said.

They followed behind him, wondering what he was talking about, until finally he stopped and pointed. "There," he said. "That's the one."

Criton followed his finger and saw, moored to the farthest dock, a familiar fishing boat bobbing on the tide. Hunter set off toward it with long, confident strides, and they all hurried across the planks after him. When they arrived they found a man inside, mending a net with a needle and thread. The man was perhaps twenty, with the olive complexion of Atunaeans and a dark scraggly beard.

"This is my boat," Hunter told him, ignoring his stares. "I will be needing it today, to go to Tarphae. You can take us there, if you like, or you can get off."

"This ain't your boat," the man answered, looking simultaneously confused and intimidated. There were five of them, after all. "I bought it myself," he added.

"The man who sold it to you did not own it," Hunter told him. "The boat is mine."

"I don't know anything about that," the fisherman said. "All I know is, I paid good money for it, and I'm not just going to give it to you for nothing."

"Where is the fisherman who sold it to you?" Phaedra asked. "If you take us to him, I'm sure we can sort this out. He'll have to give you your money back."

"I don't need to take you anywhere," the fisherman retorted. "I bought the–"

Hunter drew his sword with such speed and violence that the fisherman fell over backward in terror. Hunter leapt into the boat after him.

"Get out," he said. "Show us the way. We'll all go together."

The house he led them to was large, with an extensive vegetable garden visible through a tall fence. A servant answered their knocks.

"We're here to see your master," Hunter said.

When the old fisherman saw them, his face froze. He was sitting in a padded chair with a crutch resting at its side. He had lost a leg since they last saw him, and from the horrified way he stared at Bandu and the way his eyes fell to waist height as he glanced nervously past them, Criton had no trouble guessing how. Infection. It had killed Four-foot, and it had nearly killed him.

"What do you want?" he demanded. "Where's the wolf?"

"You kill him," Bandu said, her eyes flashing.

The cripple gulped, and his eyes widened. "Why are you here?" he asked, with dread in his voice.

"This is a nice house," Narky remarked, glancing about the room with his one good eye. "Not half bad for a cripple."

"My father bought your boat," Hunter spat, "and you turned around and sold it again."

"You didn't claim it!" the old fisherman cried. "Your father was dead, and then you all just disappeared. My nephews died in Karsanye thanks to you, and I can't sail anymore, not alone. What was I supposed to do?"

"Lend it," suggested Narky. "Or rent it. That's really not our problem, is it? Our problem is that we need a boat, we *own* a boat, and you went and sold it to this guy."

The old fisherman's eyes finally found the younger one's. "Well, what do you want me to do?" he asked.

"Give him his money," said Hunter. "We're taking the boat back to Tarphae."

"I haven't got it all on hand," the cripple objected.

"Give him what you can," said Criton. "We won't be in Tarphae long. When we come back, he can have the boat again. The least you can do is rent it for us."

"What if you don't come back?" the younger fisherman demanded. "Where will that leave me?"

"Here," said Hunter. "Alive. If that's not good enough for you, you'll have to come with us and make sure we don't sink."

Goodweather awoke and began to cry.

"I'm not going to that island of ghosts," the fisherman said.

"All right," Hunter said, with a shrug. "Then you can either make do with the money he *can* give you, or you can call him a thief and punish him accordingly. Again, that's not our problem. I suppose I can bequeath the boat to him as soon as we come back from Tarphae, and then you can consider the sale honorable. But until then, it remains my property and mine alone."

With that, he turned and swept from the room with Criton and the others in his wake. The two fishermen, stunned, simply watched them go.

"Oh my," said Phaedra, when they were back outside. "Hunter, that was… amazing. I don't know how you had the nerve to do it."

Hunter clearly did not know what to do with such praise. He said nothing, nor did he slow his pace until they had reached the docks again and were able to climb aboard their new property. Old property? Ah well, it didn't really matter, did it?

Their voyage to Tarphae was a little too calm for Criton's liking. Though none of them were sailors, they had no trouble reaching their homeland over the strangely peaceful ocean waters. The tides and currents seemed eager to welcome them home, tugging them gently into the harbor of Karsanye. Goodweather fell asleep again from the rocking of the boat, and by the time Hunter jumped out to tie them to the dock, even Bandu seemed only half awake.

The empty docks groaned as they stepped off the boat. Hunter groaned too, a soft groan that could barely be heard above the lapping of the waves. Phaedra caught his hand and clutched it tightly. It was harder for them, Criton thought. To these two, even this harbor felt like part of home.

They proceeded up the planks toward dry land, and Criton saw Hunter turn back for a moment. "What is it?" asked Phaedra.

"Our boat's the only one," he said, a little shakily. "All the ships are gone."

"Scavengers," said Narky. "They might be too afraid to step onto the island, but a ship's something else."

"Not too afraid," said Bandu, pointing with her free hand. "Only dead."

Criton followed her finger and jumped a little when he saw the corpse on the edge of the dock. A pile of rope had mostly obscured the body from his view, but the stench as he approached was unmistakable. The man had been rotting away here for at least a couple of months.

"The plague?" Criton asked.

"Maybe," said Phaedra. "Either way, it was definitely a God that killed him. Look, the seagulls haven't even touched his body."

Criton nodded quickly and turned away. Gulls or no gulls, it was still a nauseating sight.

They reached the end of the planks and stood there hesitating, afraid now to step onto the dry land.

"Karassa protect us," Hunter more or less pleaded. "Eramia too. And God Most High."

But it was Bandu who first stepped off the dock, with Goodweather still cradled in her arms. "We are alive," she stated. "We go now."

Criton wanted to scream at Bandu for the way she'd endangered Goodweather, but he held his tongue. Soon they would pass the customs houses and reach the city. His clawed hands shook in fright and anticipation.

A man stepped out of the customs house, reaching out to them. Criton let out a weak cry and stopped in his tracks. The man turned to him and disappeared for an instant, winking in and out of sight as if he were somehow too flat to see head on. His face was blurry and indistinct, but his hollow eyes had a longing in them that Criton could not ignore.

"What's the matter?" asked Phaedra. She and the others had turned around when they heard his cry. Could they not see the figure?

"There's a..." Criton began, and stopped. The man's pleading eyes were fixed on him.

"Go away," Bandu hissed. The man took a single step back and disappeared.

Narky looked around, frightened and confused. "What?" he said.

"Ghost," Criton finally managed to answer.

They were everywhere in the city. Apparitions met them at every turn, coming out of houses or simply appearing out of nowhere on the dusty streets. Some of them pointed angrily at the living islanders, their silent shouts causing the air around their mouths to ripple. And yet apparently only Criton and Bandu could see them.

"What do they look like?" asked Narky. "Can they see us?"

"They definitely see us," said Criton. "And they're angry."

"Why?"

A whole crowd of them was gathering now, staring and pointing. Criton shuddered. "I think they blame us," he said.

They fled from the crowd of angry spirits and went to Karassa's temple, where the bones of the dead lay all about the altar.

"The king's not here, is he?" asked Narky. "You don't see his ghost, I mean? I know we think he's alive, but I just want to make sure."

"What does the king look like?" Criton asked him, surveying the few half-seen figures that wandered about the area.

Narky frowned. "I don't know. Like a king, I guess."

Hunter sighed. "The king is about ten years older than my father," he said. "He's tall, and his gut is bigger than my father's. At least, it used to be. He's been living here alone for a year. I wonder if I'll even recognize him."

"That shouldn't be too hard, as long as he's still alive," Narky pointed out. "Just find a man who isn't dead, and it'll be him."

That wasn't nearly as easy as it sounded. The king wasn't anywhere to be found, in his palace or his unkept gardens, or anywhere else they could think of. They wandered through the city streets until the sun began to dip perilously close to the horizon, and still the king was nowhere to be found.

"We're going to have to stay the night," Phaedra said, her voice strained.

"We're not going to my house," Criton said hurriedly. "*He* might be there."

"We should sleep somewhere without ghosts," Narky suggested. "What if they attack us while we sleep? There must be some place here where nobody was around to die."

"I don't think they're tied to the place where they died," Criton told him. "They're all sort of wandering around."

Bandu pointed behind them. "That one follows us," she said.

She was right. When Criton turned, the apparition from the docks was standing in the street behind them, its soulful eyes still pleading. The sight made Criton shudder.

"How long has he been there?" he asked Bandu.

The girl shrugged. "A long time," she said. She handed Goodweather over to him and stretched her back. "Wait here. I go talk."

Criton clutched Goodweather to his chest, watching his wife approach the ghost. She came within an arm's length of it before she stopped and said something, too quietly for him to hear. The ghost pointed past her at the group, its blurred mouth moving silently.

"What's going on?" Phaedra asked.

"Wait," said Criton.

Bandu nodded at the spirit and held out her hands to it. "Bandu!" Criton cried. "Don't!"

He ran toward her, but he was too late. The spirit took her by the hands, and its ephemeral body melded with hers and vanished. She turned to him just as he reached her, and held up her hand.

"Please do not stop me," she said, her voice low and male and completely foreign to her body. "I am here for Hunter."

Criton stopped in his tracks. Goodweather awoke,

clutching at his shirt, but for once she did not cry. Bandu brushed past him and walked toward the others. He followed helplessly.

The others had started toward him, and their faces were pictures of alarm. "What happened?" Narky asked.

"Bandu..." Criton moaned.

"I am not Bandu," Bandu said, in that other voice. She stopped walking and looked at Hunter appraisingly. "You've changed," she said.

Hunter's eyes widened. "Father?"

"Yes," said Bandu. "I was hoping you'd come back."

"What happened here?" Hunter asked, his voice cracking. "What happened to you? The plague..."

Issuing from Bandu's lips, Lord Tavener's voice was warm. "What happened," he said, "is that I saved my son."

58
Hunter

Hunter couldn't help it. His eyes filled with tears, and he wept like a child.

"You've changed, Hunter," his father repeated.

Hunter looked down at his callused feet, ashamed of his tears. "I lost my shoes," he croaked. "And I lost my shield, and my armor. I lost everything you gave me, and it was like… it was like I lost pieces of you."

Bandu's face smiled sympathetically, and Father's voice said, "But you knew you'd lose me one day, Hunter. You wanted to be the king's champion, and you never would have been, so long as your brother and I lived."

Hunter shook his head. "I didn't want you to die," he said. "I wanted you to see me and be, and be…" He couldn't continue.

"I know," said Father. "I know."

Hunter chuckled ruefully. "The life I wanted was stupid," he said, "and I have nothing to replace it with."

Bandu put a hand on his shoulder. "You are still young," said Father. "There will be time. The important thing is that you have the opportunity to live and grow, and find your way. I'm proud of how you've grown already. I'm proud of you."

Hunter looked down into Bandu's eyes, grateful and

confused. "What for?" he asked.

"Look at you!" Father exclaimed. "You're not the same boy you were back then. That boy was single-minded and stubborn, and his armor never left his back. Honor was everything to him, and people were nothing.

"When I left you at the docks, you were surrounded by strangers. Now you're surrounded by friends. This girl was willing to lend me her body just so that I could speak with you. What do I care if you've lost your shoes or your shield? I would have liked to give you friends instead of all those things, but I didn't know how. I'm glad you've made the exchange yourself."

Hunter couldn't help it then: he broke down. Bandu embraced him, but he pulled away after only a few seconds. It was too strange, feeling her breasts press against him when he ought to have been hugging his own father.

He dried his eyes on his sleeve and looked around, as if for the first time. Phaedra was gazing at him with warmth and admiration. Narky made an effort to smile, though such a genuine expression didn't look quite natural on his face. Criton stood holding the baby to his chest, his concern for Bandu carving wrinkles in his brow. Hunter turned back to Bandu. He nodded, and smiled in relief.

She beamed back at him, tears welling in her eyes too. "You were always your mother's child," Father said. "Perhaps that's why I cherished you more than Kataras. He resented it, poor boy, but what could I do? Ah well, that's all over now.

"You should leave this place," he added, his smile fading from Bandu's lips. "I've given you everything I can. There is nothing for you here."

"We're here for the king," Hunter told him. "We need to bring him somewhere."

Bandu's eyebrows shot up. "You're rescuing Kestan?" Father said. "I hope you succeed. If he leaves, we may finally be able to rest."

"Do you know where he is?" Phaedra asked. "We've looked everywhere."

"He fled the city some time ago," Hunter's father told her. "Those who blamed him followed. I didn't."

Bandu glanced at Criton, then back to Hunter. "I have taken too much advantage of this young lady's generosity. I should return her body to her."

"Wait," Hunter pleaded, but Bandu closed her eyes and his father's spirit left her. He would never come back, Hunter knew. He was gone now.

Bandu blinked a few times and rubbed her eyes. "Are you all right?" Criton asked, rushing forward.

She nodded. "I'm tired," she said.

They slept that night in Hunter's old house, surrounded by Lord Tavener's desolate estate. The linens were all moth-eaten by now, but the hide rugs were as soft as ever. No other ghosts approached them here, though Hunter stayed up for a while, hoping. Surrounded by childhood memories, it took him a long time to fall asleep.

Phaedra too stayed up late, staring at the ceiling. "I used to imagine sleeping in this house," she said quietly.

Hunter said nothing. She had liked Kataras, he knew. Everyone had liked Kataras. Until Father's ghost had spoken to him, he had never thought to pity his brother. Now he felt bad for the bruises he had inflicted during their sparring matches, and for avoiding Kataras after his brother had refused to fight him anymore. He had truly understood nothing back then.

They lay a while in silence, and then Hunter asked, "Phaedra? What's the underworld like?"

Phaedra boosted herself up on an elbow. "What do you mean?"

"Well," said Hunter, "you've read a lot about the Gods, and I was wondering, what's hell like? Does any God rule there? What do the dead *do?*"

"Not much, I think," Phaedra said cautiously. "And

there's no God of the Underworld that I know of. Followers of the Sun God in Atuna believe that the underworld is a cold, wet place where the dead lie in uncomfortable sleep, but that if you're cremated you'll join Atun in the heavens instead. A Mayaran philosopher I've read suggested that those who drown or are buried at sea become absorbed by the Sea God Himself."

"Do people stay themselves when they die on land?"

Phaedra sighed. "No one really knows," she said kindly.

"Oh," said Hunter. He rolled over. "Good night."

"Good night," Phaedra whispered.

They awoke just after dawn. They raided the garden and the larder for any foodstuffs that had survived a year's neglect, and ate a breakfast of cucumbers, dates, and the highest quality Laarna olive oil. The luxury of this last item did not escape them: the world would never again taste Laarna's olives.

They left the city after breakfast and went once more in search of the king. Grasses were growing in the middle of the roads, and yet the country felt much less deserted than the city had. At least here it felt more natural to go an hour without seeing anyone.

They found King Kestan on the southern crags, less than a mile from Karsanye. They were able to spot him from some distance, climbing along the jagged cliffs that overlooked the sea. Hunter would not have recognized him had he not known he was looking at the king. Kestan the Third was skeletal now, and his beard was long and bedraggled. He was not wearing the royal garments that Hunter remembered – at least, not unless the tattered muddy rags that he now wore had once been a deep, rich blue. Teetering there on the cliffs above them, he looked to Hunter as if he might blow into the ocean at any moment.

"He's surrounded by ghosts," Criton said. "How do we get him down from there?"

The king was looking out to sea, and had not noticed them yet.

"I don't know," said Phaedra. "Who knows what kind of an influence they're having on him? What will he think when he sees us? We don't want to alarm him."

Narky lifted his eyebrows. "Alarm him? He hasn't seen anyone alive in, what, a year now? I'm pretty sure he'll be alarmed."

"So what do we do?" Phaedra asked, looking sidelong at Hunter.

"We climb," he said.

Bandu nodded and reached out to Criton. "Give me Goodweather," she commanded. "Then you go."

Up they went, scrambling over the rocks toward their king. Yet even as Hunter climbed, his mind filled with doubts. What were they doing here, really? Were they here to rescue King Kestan, as Father had believed? No. They were here because Psander had sent them. They were here because Criton wanted to free his ancestor and awaken his people's ancient God.

Bandu had agreed with Criton because she loved him, and Narky had agreed because he was afraid of the Gods and wanted one on his side. And those weren't bad reasons, really. But what would become of the world when the dragon returned? Would God Most High be kinder to humanity than His rivals were? Hunter wanted to believe that He would, but he couldn't know, and that worried him. He couldn't help but feel that they were really acting out of selfishness.

The king turned just as they were nearing him. When he saw them, his eyes widened with fear. "Keep away from me!" he cried. "Keep away!"

"We're here to help!" Phaedra called from the rear.

"No!" shouted the ragged king. He turned from them and began leaping frantically from rock to rock, trying to escape.

They hurried after him. Partway there, Criton slipped and skinned his knees on a boulder. "Forget this," Hunter heard him say. In a moment, he had leapt off the rocks and was flying toward the king. Hunter watched him with envy, but did not stop his climb.

"Stand back!" the king cried, backing away toward the cliff's edge. "Keep away! She will punish us!"

"Your Majesty," called Hunter. "Stop."

The king looked over the precipice, and then back at them. He fell to his knees on the bare rocks. "She will punish us," he whimpered, over and over.

Criton reached him then. He stood beside the crouched figure and put a hand on his shoulder, just in case he decided to leap off the cliff after all. "It's all right," he said. "We'll get you out of here."

By the time Hunter and Narky arrived, the king no longer seemed in danger of jumping. Phaedra remained stranded halfway down the hillside, her progress hindered by her ankle. "Help him down from there!" she yelled to them.

"Go away," begged the king. "Save yourselves."

"We're here to save *you,*" Hunter told him.

The king chuckled and looked up at him. "I know you," he said.

Hunter nodded. "I'm Lord Tavener's son, Hunter."

Kestan blinked. "No, it doesn't matter," he said angrily to himself. "It can't make any difference. She has no power here, not against Karassa."

"What are you talking about?" said Criton. "Who has no power here?"

"Let's talk about this when we're a little farther from a deadly high cliff," Narky suggested. "Come on down with us."

The king shook his head, and Criton said, "Don't listen to them."

"What?" said Hunter.

"Not you," said Criton, "the ghosts."

King Kestan looked startled. "You see them too?"

"Let's go," Narky said. "I'm getting nervous up here."

He reached down a hand to help the king to his feet. The

king stared at his hand fearfully.

"Take it," said Hunter. "We're here to help."

With the utmost hesitance, King Kestan reached slowly for Narky's hand. Narky, impatient as ever, grabbed the king's hand and pulled him to his feet.

The ground shook.

Hunter nearly lost his footing in the initial motion, but the second tremor threw him to the stones, and it was only his luck that he fell toward Phaedra and not toward the water. The king was less lucky. He tipped over backward and disappeared over the cliff, while Narky nearly followed him. The one-eyed boy stumbled and fell onto his stomach, with one arm hanging over the cliff face.

"Narky!" Hunter shouted, but he could not even hear himself above the roaring earth. He could not spot Criton either, though that didn't worry him as much. Criton, after all, could fly.

He crawled toward Narky over the jiggling stones, his heart pounding. Narky was struggling to get up, with no success. "Are you all right?" Hunter shouted at him.

"Hold on!" Narky yelled back, but every attempt to rise seemed to push him farther over the precipice. With an effort, Hunter managed to reach him and grab hold of Narky's legs. The next moment his head was thrown face first against a rock.

Dazed but conscious, Hunter wrapped his arms around Narky's legs and held on with all his might. The whole world seemed to be shaking. Narky was still screaming, "Help me!" but Hunter could do no more. Then he saw Criton swoop down past the edge of the rocks, and he realized that Narky was not talking to him.

"You have to climb up," Criton shouted.

"I can't!" a voice answered. The king! Now Hunter understood why Narky had looked as though he was struggling to stand: he must have held onto the king's hand even as he went over the cliff, and had been struggling to hold on without slipping over the edge himself.

Hunter felt a tug, and Narky groaned. With Criton's help, the king was climbing up his arm toward safe ground. Even though the ground convulsed beneath them, the king made steady progress. First his hands and then his head came into sight, until finally he was able to crawl past Narky onto the lower rocks.

There was a great cracking sound from below, so loud that Hunter could feel it in his bones. "Get away from the edge!" he cried, jumping up and helping Narky to his feet. "GO!"

They ran as best they could, leaping down toward Bandu and Phaedra with reckless speed. With a deafening rumble, the cliff behind them collapsed into the sea.

"The boat!" screamed Phaedra. "We have to get to the boat!"

They fled for Karsanye, frequently falling to the ground only to jump right up and run even harder. Fissures opened in the ground as they ran, and Hunter had to catch Phaedra once before she fell in. His hand found her hair instead of her arm, and the girl cried out. He tried to apologize once he had pulled her back to safety, but he was too out of breath. They ran on.

When they finally reached Karsanye, the city was barely even recognizable. Walls had collapsed; trees had fallen; whole buildings had been swallowed by the earth. The king's grand palace could not even be seen above the wreckage. Hunter suspected that it had been leveled.

When they reached the seaport, half the docks had splintered apart or torn away from the island in chunks, floating off toward the mainland like so many inelegant rafts. Thankfully, the boat was still there.

Overpowered by the quake, the tide seemed to have reversed itself. Water was rushing away from the shore in frantic waves, rippling out into the ocean and dragging along what planks remained in its path. The islanders ran across the undulating dock toward their boat, while Criton flew overhead with Goodweather in his arms. He arrived first, but could do little good there: he couldn't even put the baby down, because the boat was half full of water.

Phaedra's legs were failing her, and she and Hunter were the last to reach the boat. The others were already bailing out seawater by the time Hunter helped her in. "Let that sail down!" he shouted at her, and then turned and cut them off from their moorings with one clean stroke of his sword.

Their voyage was slapdash and desperate. The hull kept filling with water, and they quickly gave up on navigating in order to concentrate their efforts on staying afloat. Hunter barely looked up from his work until the keel hit bottom and he was nearly thrown overboard. They had reached shore… somewhere.

They splashed through the shallows as quickly as they could, never forgetting the grudge Mayar held against them. Only when they were nearly a mile from the shore did they finally fall to the ground and rest their aching muscles.

The king seemed completely dazed. "We escaped Her," he said, disbelief in every syllable. "We escaped!"

Phaedra rose slowly to a sitting position. "That was Karassa," she said, "wasn't it? We thought some other God had defeated Her, but She was the one who cursed the island all along, wasn't She?"

The king nodded. "She found out about the sacrifice, and She punished me. But everyone! All those people! I never dreamed She would take such offense."

"Offense at what?" asked Narky. "What sacrifice?"

King Kestan bowed his head. "I sacrificed a calf to Eramia on the morning of Karassa's festival."

"To Eramia?" cried Hunter, surprised. "Why?"

"Eramia came to me in a dream the night before and promised me that my people would be raised up above all others, to lead the world with strength and Godliness. I couldn't delay sacrificing to Her with a message like *that.*"

The islanders looked at each other. "Another prophecy," Hunter said.

"And another one about us," Phaedra added. "You're right, though: you had to make that sacrifice. To receive a prophecy of good fortune without repaying it with a sacrifice would be inexcusable."

King Kestan shook his head. "If I had known…"

"Karassa is a cruel Goddess," Phaedra said sadly.

Bandu snorted. "*Eramia* is a cruel Goddess. All Gods are cruel."

"Bandu!" Phaedra cried. "Eramia is on our side!"

Bandu rolled her eyes. "Gods are not on people sides, Phaedra. Gods are only on Gods' side. You think Eramia doesn't know that Karassa kills everyone after king's sacrifice? Eramia *wants* everyone to die."

"That doesn't make any sense, Bandu," Criton insisted. "Why should Eramia hate the people of Tarphae? She favors us!"

Bandu stared at him disbelievingly. "She doesn't hate Tarphae," she said. "She only doesn't care. Gods never care. She wants us to help Salemis. If island is still home to us, we never are helping him."

"But how could She have known about us?" Criton asked. He was beginning to sound desperate.

"Ravennis knew," Narky pointed out, "and He was watching us too. Is it possible He and Eramia were allies?"

"It's possible," Phaedra said uncertainly. "Eramia is Elkinar's younger sister, at least according to that book I read in Anardis. The Second Cycle, remember? It didn't mention Ravennis at all, which doesn't help much, but it may mean that He's a younger God. At least there doesn't seem to be any ancient enmity there."

"Great," said Narky. "So Eramia and Ravennis have been planning for us to release Salemis and awaken God Most High all along. Ravennis got us all to leave Tarphae while Eramia goaded Karassa into smiting the island so that we'd never go back. Bandu's right: these Gods don't care about us. They're ruthless."

"Quiet!" the king cried. "Don't say such things! Is it not enough for you to have escaped the plague? Must my people be twice-cursed?"

"I'm sorry," Narky said more quietly. "In any case, now we know that this has all been planned. We were meant to find Salemis all along. So much for us just being clever."

"Men have free will," Phaedra insisted. "Ravennis and Eramia could have been planning this for all of eternity, but it's still up to us to actually do it. We could still choose to do otherwise if we wanted to."

"Right," said Narky. "We could leave Salemis to rot, leave Psander to die, lose Eramia's protection, and be struck down by Her or by Magor or Mayar or even God Most High Himself. It sure doesn't *feel* like we're making a choice, or like we ever did. It's felt like we've been slaves more or less ever since we met Psander. Well, now we know it's been a good while longer than that."

"Hunter," Phaedra pleaded, "help me here."

"Me?" Hunter didn't know what to say. He was embarrassed to speak in front of Phaedra and Narky, whose thoughts on the matter were strong and precise. He had always thought about Karassa and the other Gods as being sort of like parents who tried to control their children's fates but were never quite pleased with the result. Would they even get credit if they succeeded?

"Now we know why the elves call us godserfs," he said.

They journeyed on in near silence. Propriety meant nothing to them now, and they foraged and stole whatever food they could find on their way. After a few days of traveling, they came upon a horribly familiar sight: the great swath of trampled earth and refuse left by an army on the march. This army was moving northwest away from the sea, along Atel's roads. It had probably come from Parakas, Hunter thought with some dread. Magor's army was already surrounding Silent Hall, and now His brother Mayar was coming to His aid. Were Atel and His roads complicit? The Traveler God was also the Messenger God, after all.

The islanders didn't even bother discussing it. They simply turned to follow the path of destruction. They all knew where it would lead.

Criton went ahead as a scout, returning frequently to apprise them of their position. Finally one day, he reported that the armies were in sight up ahead. They were preparing a joint assault.

The candles came out. Criton had used up their only spare, but there were still enough for each of them to hold one.

"If we can," said Hunter, "let's stay together this time. We can't afford to waste time getting us all in the door."

They lit their candles and pressed on together, navigating by the sound of each others' tread and sometimes brushing lightly against each other. When they reached the edge of the camp, Hunter's heart sank. Past the thousands of men preparing themselves for battle, Silent Hall stood ominous and still. The fortress was visible.

They wound their way through the camp, avoiding the clustering soldiers as best they could. Hunter prayed to Eramia and to God Most High that they were not too late, and that they would reach Silent Hall safely. For once, the Gods seemed to hear his prayers.

When they reached the gate the armies were already mustering behind them, ready to charge at any minute. Hunter's candle had burnt down almost to a nub when he pounded on the gate, shouting for Psander to let them in.

Her head appeared in a window above. "You have him?" she asked anxiously.

"Yes," said Narky. "Let us in!"

Psander disappeared for a moment, but the gate did not open. She soon reappeared above them, carrying Goodweather's seed.

"All is prepared," she said. "From what I can tell, the seed ought to grow once you plant and water it, and after that it should tear its hole in the mesh fairly quickly."

"Good," said Phaedra, "but you have to let us in!"

Psander shook her head. "The only way to get my hall into the other world is to plant the seed under the cornerstone, on the outside. Here, you'll need this."

She threw down the seed, and a shovel. They landed together with a thud and a clang that seemed to ring across the battlefield. Then the hot wax dripped through Hunter's fingers, and his candle burned out.

59
The Islanders

The soldiers were pointing at them and shouting. Hundreds of eyes turned toward them as one by one the islanders came into view. Phaedra blinked, adjusting to her new reality. She had dreamt of following Psander's path, of becoming the new "last" academic wizard. If God Most High supported her, no other God could smite her for studying the old ways, or for teaching whoever else wanted to learn. She had thought to breathe life into academic wizardry. Now she was being sacrificed to it.

She picked up the seed and turned around to look at the army. Ardisian spears and Parakese crossbows were already arrayed for the assault on Silent Hall. Phaedra suddenly realized that this would be her last view: the armies of Mayar and Magor, glistening and triumphant.

Psander's timing was off. She had gambled with their lives, and lost. Phaedra sighed. At least it was over.

Only Hunter seemed to disagree.

Hunter stepped out toward the enemy, sword raised to the heavens as if in triumph. "Send me your champion!" he shouted, his voice ringing in his own ears. "A man of Tarphae is worth twenty continental men! Send me your champion, and I will slay him!"

The bowmen hesitated, and Hunter repeated his call for single combat. He would not be refused, he knew; not if the Ardismen or Parakese had any pride whatsoever. They would send him a champion, and he would fight as he had been meant to fight.

Of course, it hardly mattered whether he won or lost: as soon as the single combat ended the battle would begin, and the twin armies would make short work of him and his friends. But time spent on single combat was time the others could use to dig a hole for Goodweather's seed. Perhaps when he died, he could die victorious.

Behind him, the others came to life and began moving toward the fortress' cornerstone. "Don't run," Hunter heard Phaedra say. "If you run, they'll shoot."

Ahead, the ranks shivered and parted to let a man through.

"I accept your challenge, boy," cried the High Priest of Magor.

All hope of triumph faded.

Bandu turned to Criton, thrusting their daughter into his hands. "Take Goodweather," she demanded. "Keep her safe."

She turned away. "Come with us," she said to the dazed king. "We need your help."

Criton remained at the gate, holding Goodweather to his chest. The tiny girl opened her eyes and looked silently up at him. Criton's heart ached. She knew nothing, nothing at all. She didn't understand death, and didn't know enough to be afraid for her life. All she knew was him.

Criton held his daughter tight and leapt into the air.

Below, Bestillos stopped in his tracks. He pointed his spear at Criton. "Down," he hissed, his voice somehow ringing in Criton's ears as if he was speaking straight into them.

Criton's magic left him instantly, and he plummeted

toward the ground. His stomach lurched. He held Goodweather close with one arm and tried to catch himself on the stone wall beside him, but it did little to break his fall. His legs crumpled under him and he fell forward, twisting his body to keep Goodweather out of harm's way. He landed on his side in the end, and his head hit the ground. The last thing he heard was Goodweather crying.

Bandu heard the cry and turned to see Criton fall. She gasped and made to stand up, but Phaedra caught her by the hem of her skirt. "We have to keep going," she said. "They won't survive unless we finish."

Tears came to Bandu's eyes, but she did not leave. Phaedra was right. They finished digging, and Bandu raised the acorn to the king. "It needs your tears," she told him.

The man stared at her blankly. "My tears?" he asked. "I have no tears, child. You rescued me from my prison, but there is no future for me. I realize that. We will die here, and why shouldn't we? This place is as good as any other. You have done me a great service. I thought I should die surrounded by the ghosts of those who suffered for my mistake, with only Karassa's anger above my head. But now, you've let me see a world bigger than my sorrows. I will not die alone."

"Your Majesty," Phaedra pleaded, "we don't have to die here! If you water this seed with your tears, it will–"

"I have no tears," the king repeated, a vague smile on his lips.

Phaedra and Narky began talking at the same time, trying to convince him, but Bandu knew better. The king did not understand, and never would. She lifted the acorn higher and smashed it down onto his foot.

The king yelped and hopped up and down, but Bandu didn't stop there. She hit his other foot until he fell to his backside, and once his face was in reach, caught him by his beard. She twisted her hand, pulling him toward her and bringing him to eye level with Goodweather's seed. The acorn's surface grew wet and shiny. It seemed that the king had some tears left in him after all.

Bandu released him and stuffed the acorn into the hole they had dug. *Grow!* she thought desperately.

Narky dropped his shovel. Phaedra was impotently apologizing for Bandu's actions as he turned back toward the gate, mumbling that he would check on Criton. When he lifted his eyes, Hunter and Bestillos were circling each other while the soldiers of Ardis and Parakas cheered the priest on. Narky walked toward Criton as quickly as he dared, watching his friend fight. Hunter was fast, very fast. He was also outmatched. Even at his advanced age, Bestillos was faster and stronger. Soon Hunter had given up on counterattacks altogether and was simply parrying and retreating, parrying and retreating. Narky tried to see things positively, the way Criton might have, but it was impossible. Anyone could see Hunter was losing – he seemed keenly aware of it himself.

Narky reached Criton and knelt by his body. He was still alive. Baby Goodweather was also alive, and screaming so loudly that a nasty part of him wished she had been knocked unconscious instead of her father. As Narky watched, Criton's eyes fluttered and opened.

"I can't move," he groaned.

"Don't try," Narky told him. "We can't do any good anyway. Bandu and Phaedra are planting the seed, and Hunter's getting himself killed in single combat with the red priest. All we can do is wait, and hope the girls finish what they're doing before the red priest does."

Criton only seemed to be half listening. The baby continued to wail. "Is that Goodweather?" Criton asked.

"Yes," said Narky.

Criton smiled. "It's all right, little one."

"Listen," said Narky, "do you feel any pain?"

"All over," Criton answered, "but my legs are the worst."

"Oh," said Narky, relieved. He had been thinking of Prince Tana. "Good."

He was about to stand up when he noticed something on the ground, a small black object. He picked it up, and found that it was a candle nub.

There were cheers from behind him. Bestillos was pressing his assault. Hunter backed away from him, his parries growing slower and weaker. It would not be long now.

"Criton," said Narky, kneeling down again, "I need your fire."

He held the candle nub over Criton's mouth. Criton nearly melted it entirely, and his breath set fire to Narky's sleeve. Narky transferred the candle to his other hand and frantically waved his arm about, but the flames didn't die until he threw himself to the ground and lay down on top of his burning arm, smothering the flame. He didn't waste time inspecting his burn, but got up and hurried toward the soldiers watching the fight. They had exactly what he needed.

As he reached the ranks, the fight behind him grew louder and more intense. He didn't have long. He chose a sturdy-looking man who stood with his crossbow held out in front of him. The knife at his belt was unprotected. Narky snatched it from the belt, and while the man raised his crossbow out of the way and looked down in confusion, Narky thrust the knife deep into his armpit.

The soldier screamed, dropping his crossbow. Narky caught it before it hit the ground. In a moment he was dancing away from the dying man, slipping between the many men who ran past him to see what had happened.

When he was clear of the crowd, Narky fell to one knee. He could already feel the heat from his candle as the wick burned down toward his hand. He hastily stuck it on the crossbow and turned back toward the fighters.

The fight was over. Hunter's sword had broken, and Bestillos was standing over him with the barbed spear inches above his chest. "You die with honor, child," Bestillos said, loud enough so that the crowd could hear. "I haven't faced an opponent like you in a very long time."

Narky aimed at the priest's back and loosed the bolt.

Phaedra stared down at the inert seed, her heart filling with panic. "Why isn't it growing?" she nearly shrieked. "It's supposed to be growing!"

"It is young," Bandu said quietly. "Does not know this place, this dirt. It is afraid."

"For the love of all that's holy!" Phaedra cried. "Can you reassure it?"

"I try," Bandu answered. She leaned over and began to hum, hesitantly at first but with growing confidence. "Don't be afraid," Bandu sang, somewhat tunelessly. "The dirt is good here. Grow!"

Still nothing happened. Phaedra suggested that Bandu try speaking to it in elvish rhyme and meter, but Bandu waved her away impatiently and kept to her song. Phaedra was reduced to watching and hoping.

The king sat with his back to the fortress wall, staring wordlessly at Bandu. Phaedra had expected him to react angrily to Bandu's abuse, to beat her or scream at her or otherwise fight back. Instead, he had retreated to this spot the minute she had released him. And from that vantage point, he simply watched.

Bandu's chant grew louder, and Phaedra looked back to the seed to see that its shell was beginning to crack. From behind her, she heard cheers. Was it all over? Had Hunter been killed?

As Bandu sang, roots burst from the acorn and planted themselves in the soil. After that, the growth happened too quickly for Phaedra to fathom. Bandu leapt backward as a gigantic tree trunk shot up from the place where the seed had been. Dirt and stones fell all around them as Silent Hall rose toward the clouds. There was a horrible rending sound, as if Phaedra's own head were somehow being torn in two. There were screams from behind her, with hundreds and then thousands of voices joining in.

High above, a massive dragon dove toward the battlefield.

60
Narky

The candle blew out as the bolt left his crossbow and buried itself deep in the priest's back, between his shoulder blades. Bestillos reeled and fell face forward to the ground. Narky dropped the crossbow and scrambled toward Hunter before any enterprising soldier could cut *him* down from behind. Nobody tried. There was a deafening roar and Silent Hall shot toward the heavens, borne by the Yarek's massive branches. Hunter's broken sword lay forgotten on the ground as the two of them stared upwards, watching Psander's fortress disappear atop the primordial tree. Then a winged figure appeared in the sky, flying down toward them.

The fire that came from Salemis' jaws made Criton's flames look like a dying ember. The armies of Ardis and Parakas screamed as their camp became an inferno, vaporizing men and tents alike. Those who were not killed in the first breath of flame scattered in all directions. Salemis caught some in a second breath before climbing back toward the heavens, his scales shining like a second sun. Narky did not see him pierce the clouds: he had to double up coughing from the smoke that rose off the battlefield behind him.

He stayed on the ground, waiting for the smoke to clear. His eyes watered. When he opened them, he found that he was staring straight at Bestillos' corpse. The priest of Magor's eyes were open wide as if in shock, and it took Narky a moment to remember that he hadn't even seen Salemis appear. He had died still believing in his side's victory.

Hunter knelt beside Narky and tried to tell him something, but Narky could not hear him. His ears were still ringing, and the Yarek was making a sort of enlarged creaking sound as its roots burrowed into the ground and new limbs burst out of its trunk, already halfway to the clouds. When the sound died down somewhat, Narky asked Hunter to repeat himself.

"You cheated," Hunter shouted. "You shot him in the back."

Narky nodded. He was a murderer; he had known it since the beginning. The hand that had killed Ketch knew no honor. He had hoped, once, that repentance might transform him into someone he was not, but such was not the way of the world. Narky would always take unfair advantage where he could. He would always be willing to cheat.

Hunter interrupted his thoughts. "Thank you," he said, as the world around them shook. "I never would have done what you did, and I would have lost a friend. I owe you my life."

"Don't worry about it," Narky said. "I probably owe you mine several times over."

They found Phaedra and Bandu kneeling over Criton. Bandu had Goodweather safely in her arms, and Criton was crying out in pain while Phaedra tested his legs. "You'll be all right," she said reassuringly. "I think they're only sprained."

"Where's the king?" Narky asked.

"I don't know," Phaedra said. "I haven't seen him since the Yarek started growing. I don't know if he's still alive. But he didn't really want to live. You heard him, right? He already considered himself rescued."

Narky nodded, but she kept her gaze on him. She knew, he realized with a sudden sinking feeling. *Let he who was murderer rescue the damned.* She might not know Ketch's name, or any of the details, but she knew.

Yet she said nothing. Did she somehow forgive him, even without knowing the details? Perhaps she felt that the prophecy absolved him – that the Gods had chosen him as the murderer long before it had happened, and had manipulated him into doing the deed. Or perhaps not. Wishing it worked that way didn't make it so.

Phaedra finally turned away from him, and Narky wandered off to find the king. The battlefield was still smoldering to his left, and Goodweather's trunk was growing to his right. He looked up at the heavens, wondering if he would find the dragon there. There was no sign of Salemis.

Everything is changing, Narky thought. Smoke and live wood rose up to the sky together, and clouds of gray ash billowed around the Yarek's new foothold in the world. Narky wiped stinging, smoky tears from his good eye. He did not know what tomorrow would look like. He hoped it was better than today.

Acknowledgments

There are so many people I would like to thank for their help in bringing this book into the world. Firstly, to my wife, my siblings, and our friends David Chapman and Kate Costello for helping me plot out the outline before we even knew it was an outline. Thanks to Shauna Gordon-McKeon and Molly LeBlanc for pointing out gender imbalances and other social assumptions in the first few chapters, and thereby being responsible for making Psander a woman. Thanks also to Sam Ross, to my sister-in-law Becca, and to my parents (and to Dave and my wife and siblings again) for helping me read through the whole thing out loud to catch my mistakes, and to Laurel Amberdine for being an excellent (and very fast) gamma reader.

Thank you also to Jon D Levenson, whose book *Creation and the Persistence of Evil* served as inspiration for the theology of my world. And thanks to Christopher Luna for recommending it!

Enormous thanks go to my agent, Evan Gregory, for finding this book a loving home, and to the talented and amazingly supportive folks at Angry Robot for being that home. I'm truly honored to be working with you all.

Lastly, thanks to you! Yes, you, the reader, for giving my book a try and even making it to the acknowledgments page. I hope you enjoyed it!

FLEX
FERRETT STEINMETZ
THE FLUX
FERRETT STEINMETZ
FIX
FERRETT STEINMETZ

STEAL THE SKY
MEGAN E. O'KEEFE
SUSAN MURRAY
THE WATERBORNE BLADE
SUSAN MURRAY
EXILE

THE FLOATING CITY
CRAIG CORMICK
ANDY REMIC
THE DRAGON ENGINE
ANDY REMIC
TWILIGHT OF THE DRAGONS